# YEAR OF THE
# SNAKE
## 1989

*For Lydia
with immense
gratitude
for your care
and suggestions.
Love,
Sue*

*June 2015*

# YEAR OF THE
# SNAKE
## 1989

*Sue Lile Inman*

## SUE LILE INMAN

## FpS

GREENVILLE, S.C.
2015

Requests for permission should be addressed to:

Fiction Addiction Publishing Services
1175 Woods Crossing Rd., #5
Greenville, S.C. 29607
864-675-0540
www.fiction-addiction.com

Author photograph © Sam M. Inman IV
Cover photograph by Leigh Stuckey
Cover design and book design by Vally Sharpe

ISBN-13: 978-1-934216-23-1

Library of Congress Control Number: 2015940848

Printed in the United States of America.

*For*
## Sam

*and the many fine women and men*
*in the Presbyterian ministry*
*whom we have admired*
*over the years*

# 1

# David Archer

On the trip down from Virginia, David drove. Nell refused to speak. The three days they kept watch over their daughter Jody had sapped their energy. ICU, then a semi-private room, then dismissal. But not back to the boarding school. Her doctor and the school officials recommended a psychiatric facility outside D.C., ideally suited for Jody. "The best available anywhere for cases like hers," they'd said.

David fumed. *She's a case?*

He and Nell had been stunned and desperate. In what seemed double time, they agreed to place her there and she was admitted. Jody's pale, almost blue, face and tangled curls lingered in his mind, her glazed eyes accusing them, as they said good-bye. He could hardly bear to leave her. Taking her home had not been an option.

David cleared his throat. "Why did she tell the doctor she wanted us to leave?" David took his eyes off the road to see if Nell would respond. His wife's face stayed turned away from him, shielded by her dark hair.

The pressure in his chest matched the ominous clouds gathered over the mountains as their car descended the steep drop of Highway 25 from North Carolina toward Goodwin, South Carolina. Even on a day threatened by storm, the beauty of the hills never failed to lift him out of his own concerns with their varied shades of winter browns, evergreens, myriad blues from hazy to deep blue-violet. Of all the entrances into Goodwin, David preferred this way—down through the mountains and past the lush Freestone University campus—although it meant he had to enter the city past worn-out, deserted buildings, cheap motels, a pawn shop, vacant lots overgrown with weeds amidst broken concrete slabs, seedy businesses, all reminders that this once had been a thriving textile town.

He recalled seven years ago how Nell reacted the first time they made the trip. The final interviews before Harmony Presbyterian Church called him to be Senior Pastor. "This has got to be the ugliest town I've ever seen," she'd said. "Let's hope you don't end up here."

They did. And he'd been generally satisfied, until recently. The town and the church felt like home to him. He wished Nell had been happier. He wished Nell were a happier person. Period.

On the other side of Goodwin near the interstate, shining glass and metal high tech factories from France, Japan, and Germany proclaimed the New South. Shopping malls, coffeehouses, discount stores and cinemas were gradually replacing rolling lawns of mansions once owned by textile executives. Peach orchards and pastures had given way to suburbs, hospitals, office complexes, branch libraries. Nonetheless, David learned soon after he and his family moved to Goodwin that the conservative Old South resided right below the surface, deeply embedded like red clay, within many of its people—including some in his own progressive congregation.

Harmony church nestled in an older part of Goodwin among large and small houses intermixed, the neighborhoods softened by age and gigantic oaks, tulip poplars, magnolias. David drove on in silence while Nell slept. He yearned to talk out what had happened to Jody. How lucky they'd been that her roommate had come back early from class and found her. In time. Thank God. Nell kept her face turned away.

He needed to decide whether to preach the next day what he'd planned before the emergency call on Tuesday. David liked to make his sermons adhere to what was going on in his inner life and that of the congregation, but Jody's situation had hit him hard. He needed time and space to absorb the news, begin to understand how and why precious Jody would do such a thing. He knew she'd become discontent at boarding school, but she'd chosen to go off for her senior year. No one had pushed her into it. He'd wanted her to stay in Goodwin, but had resisted saying so, hoping she'd decide on her own to be at home with her sisters, mother, and father for the last year of high school.

Maybe Nell would help him think out what had happened. "Where did she get tranquilizers? Could she have been slipped some drugs?" He glanced at Nell. "Or maybe she has an eating disorder we didn't know about."

Nell moved but kept her eyes closed.

"None of it makes sense to me," he said, "for Jody. She's always stepped to her own beat. So strong and independent. If sometimes moody." Jody was more a loner than Millie or Lyn. Depression? He pushed away the thought. He pushed away the picture of his brother, Drew, his mother. He glanced at Nell.

Nell straightened up and stared ahead at the road. "I do hope Jody hasn't inherited your family's mental illness." She didn't look at David.

David shivered. He didn't say, *What about your own?*

He steered the station wagon into their driveway. The young weeping cherry tree bent over, its bare, slender limbs whirling as the wind picked up. Dead leaves blew across the yard. Rain began to fall. He pulled into the carport and turned off the motor. He waited, hoping Nell would say something more, maybe help relieve the heavy weight they both carried.

Instead, Nell tied a plastic rain kerchief over her hair and dashed into the house. David unloaded their luggage and carried in the bags, piece by piece.

On Sunday David determined to preach the sermon he'd prepared earlier, before grief over Jody took up residence in his chest. His silent prayer upon entering the sanctuary was that God's strength and grace would see him through. The congregation knew something had happened to his daughter off at boarding school, so he spoke briefly about it, thanking the people for their prayers and concern. "Jody's under a physician's care. Nell and I have been assured that she's in good hands. After the hospital stay, she was transferred to a special community outside of Washington, D.C., that combines therapy with a continuation of academic courses once she is well enough." David felt he expended more energy in his remarks about Jody than he had on the sermon. Striking the right note between information and protection of Jody's privacy was important. He looked down at his younger daughters. Millie, almost fifteen, and Lyn, eleven, sat in the pew with Emily and Ted Parks and their sons. Lyn had her head down, drawing on a notepad. Millie kept her focus on him, a puzzled frown creasing her brow.

Nell spent Sunday morning at her estate jewelry business as she had since launching it two years ago. Even this Sunday. He forced his mind away from Nell, away from Jody, away from Millie and Lyn. He sipped water from the glass Mildred O'Bryan made sure was ready in the pulpit each Sunday and looked out at Emily and Ted, his good friends separately and together, and their teen-aged boys, Tom and Tim, who were passing Life Savers to the girls. Julian Denyar, church treasurer, sat across the center aisle with arms crossed, eyes closed, in his usual fashion. He would soon be asleep, as would the two judges Knapp and Barksdale, farther back across the center aisle from one another.

Natalie and Preston Ames sat close to the front on the outside aisle in their usual place. He counted on their support and friendship. Natalie sent a sympathetic smile his way and nodded her head. Like Jody, their son was away at prep school. Beside Natalie, Preston's mother, Charlotte Ames, held her regal head in total attention.

Deborah Baker, the young associate pastor, led the morning prayer. Smooth and polished as a radio announcer, yet with a tinge of irony in her tone. As the liturgist, she did a passable job of leading worship. He felt guilty for the irritation the timbre of her voice set off in him. She'd been with the church less than a year, and certainly she'd jumped in with energy and what the committee had called creativity in the youth programs and mission activities. Her charm and beauty already were attracting more young people.

Before he began his sermon, he prayed that the Lord would speak through the scriptures to all their minds and hearts and that they might grow together into the people of God giving of themselves for His kingdom. Silently he prayed to put aside his own concerns so that he might be used as a conduit of God's spirit. He called the sermon "God's Anachronisms":

"The Greeks had several words for time—*chronos*—from which we get our words chronicle and chronology. It is sequential, minute by minute passage of ordinary time. *Kairos:* the ripeness of time. In the fullness of time, Jesus came into the world." He expounded on the text for a while and then elaborated. "I am struck with how certain people of every generation seem not to belong to any specific age or time. They live beyond a particular era. They are not of the Sixties, or the Watergate era, or the Lost Generation or the Silent Generation. Today they are not of the Yuppie or Me Generation. Where do these people belong in time? They are anachronisms, just as they would have been if they'd arrived at Nero's gate, wearing a Brooks Brothers suit and carrying a Gucci briefcase. They are in this world we know, yet they do not belong to it. Who are these people? They, my friends, are messengers of God. They arrive in *kairos* time as witnesses to God's timeless truths. They are light bearers. They embody the Good News. After their lives in *chronos* time, they belong to the ages."

David paused and looked out at the upturned faces in the congregation. Faces revealing to him more than they would ever tell their neighbors in the pews, some with deep sorrow, some with guilt or fear. David stopped. He put aside his prepared text. He had to be honest.

"We can all rock along in our usual way in Ordinary Time, more or less convinced that we understand ourselves and our lives at least enough to get by. We go along believing we understand the people in our own families, at least enough to get by—until suddenly something happens. And we are jerked awake. As I have been this week."

Julian Denyar sits up and wipes his glasses. The judges stir and look at each other. Emily Parks's lovely features intensify. David continues, "Alarm. Pain. Fear. Suddenly we're swept out of ordinary *chronos* time into *kairos*." He hesitates, smiles briefly. "And the messenger who wakes us up may bring us alarming, painful news. I had planned simply to name God's messengers like Peter who gained power and courage on the Day of Pentecost to preach the good news of Christ. And Martin Luther who nailed up his protests against the corruption of the church in his day, or Martin Luther King, Jr. leading marches across the South.

"But now after the past week with my daughter Jody, another veil has been pulled from my eyes. I see how another kind of message can and does break into ordinary time to wake us up. Sometimes we wake up to how helpless we are to do anything meaningful for those we love and care for. Sometimes we wake up to how blind and deaf we've been to someone close and dear who may be in pain and feeling desperate. And so it has been for me. We can wake up to how much we need each other in our families and in this community of faith."

He urges the congregation to look and really see those with whom they live, to become more sensitive to them. And to think of the people they consider God's messengers of love and light. "Remember the words from Paul, 'Awake, O Sleeper, from the dead, and Christ will give you light.'" He ends with a challenge: "May all of us join the great company of those who are Christ's anachronisms, those who listen for God's word to move into action in the ripeness of time, ignoring the whims and pressures of current fads. To be light and life-bearers to the Glory of God. And to those of us who are startled awake by distressing news, may we be guided by God's love shown by the people in our lives into wisdom and right action. This is no ordinary time. We all need to wake up."

When he sits down, he's grateful for the clerical robe that covers his shirt, soaked from the sweat that preaching extracted.

After lunch and driving Millie and Lyn to the Children's Theatre for play practice, David settled on the bench in the garden to read and relax, the golden retriever Calvin at his feet. The January afternoon was unusually warm and the sun felt good. The back door slammed and Nell whirled out across the deck and into the side yard. He sighed and read one more paragraph before she reached him.

"So here you are." She pulled the black iron chair over and faced him. "So tell me. Why is it all right for a doctor's wife to start her own business, but every man, woman, and child in the church is horrified that the *minister's* wife has her own business."

David put down his book. "For Heaven's sake, what brought this on?"

"Oh, Mildred O'Bryan, naturally. In her high voice all laced with syrup and Bless-Your-Hearts. She went on and on about my responsibilities to be in church supporting you. Her hero. She's undoubtedly in love with you—sounds like idolatry to me." Nell glared at him, then regarded her nails.

"First of all, not everyone feels the way Mildred does. But your business does take up time on weekends. Namely, Sundays. A few session members have said to me that they think you should be in church, sitting with the girls in our family pew."

"So now you're passing it off on session members. Confess. This is what you believe, too. I should be right there with our family, looking up adoringly as you preach Sunday after Sunday. I tried that, remember. Now Sundays are some of our most profitable days."

David wished mightily for a cigarette. "What do you know about running a business anyway? You do indeed know how to buy things. That you have mastered. No wonder you sell estate jewelry—you own more than you or the girls could ever use or wear." He opened another tiny square of peppermint gum.

"David, that's not fair. First, you encourage me to find work I enjoy. Then when I do, you and your precious congregation can't tolerate it." Nell stood up, moved over to the flowerbed where a few crocuses speared upward from the hard ground. She began pulling weeds around the camellia bushes with her back to David. Then she turned around.

"I wish you could see," she said, her voice cracking, "my business is an accomplishment. I've put in countless hours, studying with experts. Antique jewelry is my profession." She dropped the stray grass in a pile at her feet. "I've been told I have a good eye, and I'm working to develop it."

"Nell, you chose your vocation when you married me."

"What? Being a minister's wife? My life's work? You've got to admit—it's not just men who need meaningful work. Women do too."

"Being a minister's wife is meaningful—or could be. Nell, I needed you there today. After the episode with Jody, it was hard. And the children are anxious." His throat closed up. He coughed. "What about telling Flora that you can go to the markets on Saturdays only and during the week? Or you could work one Sunday a month. And she could go the other Sundays. Isn't that what partners are for, to share the workload? Heavens, even Mildred O'Bryan misses church once in a while."

"There you go, trying to control how I do my business." She looked at the dirt under her nails and on her hands. She wiped her hair out of her face, leaving a streak.

David went to her, brushed the hair back. He tried to embrace her, but she stiffened. "Now, Nell, let's calm down and try to figure out what to do."

"Don't you tell me to calm down." She struck out across the yard, across the deck, and slammed the back door.

David opened his book but stared out into the garden. He needed Nell to be there for him. If only she could see. They needed each other. Jody filled his mind. Jody lying in the hospital bed with tubes attached, her eyes frantic, crazed. She seemed to beg him to understand her. Oh how he wanted to help her, to heal her. How he'd wanted to bring her home and protect her. After the doctor proposed Winslow Farms for her care, he and Nell had argued. He for bundling her up and bringing her home. Nell had regained her self-containment and had stated, "No. We have to step back and let the professionals—impersonal as they are—take care of Jody. We, you especially, have too much personal stake in her health. You cannot *make* her well. You can't do anything. And neither can I." He supposed she was correct.

He closed his eyes. He hated feeling helpless. How could he have been so blind? Whatever could have driven Jody to such an extreme? No wonder Nell was angry. More so than usual. She needed to be in control as much as he did. Yet when they arrived and saw Jody, Nell had lost it—crying and yelling. No, No, No. He was angry, too. With their precious daughter. How could Jody want to destroy her life? What kind of example did that give her younger sisters? He was angry. With himself. For his blindness. His preoccupation. He pressed his fingers against his eyes until they ached, and he saw red, then purple, then black.

# 2

# Nell Archer

⁂

Nell drove to the warehouse near the river, where she and Flora kept their display cases. She intended to catch up on accounts and write the dealer in Philadelphia to bid on a sapphire and diamond cluster pin she'd seen at market. At her big roll-top desk, she leafed through the stack of papers. No focus. Just fuzz, as if her mind were clogged with cotton balls. A pulse beat in her throat. She would not succumb. She refused. Tears were not an option. She had to banish Jody from her mind.

She walked to the industrial window. The cactus plants struck bizarre poses of bulbous stems, leaves, and prickly thorns as if they were space aliens who had taken up residence against the dusty panes. Flora had brought them in a year ago, announcing cactus thrived on "benign neglect" and had promptly forgotten them. Nell grew fond of the weird succulents. This Monday, she felt a particular kinship. *Like me,* she thought, *you hold it all in.*

She felt the turtle pin at her lapel and unfastened the safety latch. Aunt Gaynell, her father's sister, had bestowed the elegant turtle on Nell when she turned twenty-four. Aunt Gaynell had confessed that her father warned: "Nell will break your heart. She shredded mine." Nell was grateful her aunt had ignored him. An heirloom from Nell's great-grandmother, an eighteen-carat gold turtle with ruby eyes in its inquiring head, stretched up to sense the world. Nell stroked the little turtle, feeling the engraved pattern and small diamonds on its arched carapace. That gift had lifted her out of random wandering and set her on the path to antique jewelry. At the time she had no idea she'd go into the business. She simply had to investigate every estate sale and antique shop, asking questions. She'd spent too long flattened and half-dead after finishing college, working one dreary job after another. A sudden urge to learn had surprised her. The smallest quiver of energy had shaken her awake. She and David didn't meet until the next year. He would never understand how acquiring a few treasured pieces had saved her life. She had to make the business a financial success. Now more than ever.

What could save their daughter? Nell abhorred the idea that Jody might be afflicted with the same terrible malaise that had affected her, and her mother, too. Nell shivered. The pregnancy and all the distress of the Florence Crittenton Home, giving up her baby son. The trauma of her father's rebuke. Until she was twenty, Nell had been his beloved "One and Only." His "O & O" as he'd called her. It only took one mistake and she was out—One and Out. Surely, all that had caused her depression, not something inherited. If Jody's mental condition was genetic, it came from David's side. There had been plenty in that family. Bitterness tasted metallic in her mouth. She reached for a lemon drop.

The thick door creaked open and then banged closed. Flora entered carrying a large cardboard box. Flora Townsend stood nearly as tall as Nell, five feet, nine. Her features drew attention even in a crowd of dealers. Amazingly large, deep blue eyes seemed to bug out slightly as if Flora could peer around corners. Nell had heard that bulging eyes indicated a thyroid condition, but she wasn't sure that was backed by science. Flora's prominent nose balanced the wide lips which were kept permanently coated with bright red lipstick. People often mistook them for sisters, if not twins. Flora favored long, flowing scarves wrapped around her shoulders chosen to match the outfit beneath, or to offer bold contrast. Nell herself favored a more understated appearance. Flora's dramatic presence served their business well, attracting clients who would then linger and peruse their jewelry. Often buy.

Loose strands of Flora's blonde hair hung over her face. She blew at it ineffectively. "Here's the order from Phillie. I bought several pieces after you left."

"Not the sapphire and diamond cluster, I suppose."

"I saw how you drooled for it. So, yes, I bid and got it." She began unpacking the box. "There's more padding than product. As usual." She reached down and pulled out a square velvet box. "Here, partner. The least I could do."

Nell wondered if she could tell Flora that she had no capital now to invest in such an expensive piece. Not after making the enormous first month's payment to Winslow Farms. Her hands shook as she opened the small box.

"It is gorgeous." She lifted the spray of diamonds and sapphires to the light. "Flora, maybe you should keep it to sell. Right now, I—"

"Nell, there's no hurry to pay me. We'll sort it out later." She busied herself unpacking other acquisitions. A garish multi-colored necklace with matching bracelets and earrings—iridescent glass beads interspersed with agate and turquoise. Nell wondered how Flora found the set the least bit attractive or likely to sell. A long box of pearls in graduated sizes, one strand a deep gray. A ring of one white pearl, one dark gray with five small diamonds between, set in yellow gold.

Before Nell could ask if she might sell the black and white pearl ring, Flora held it out to her. "How about this one? Think Dr. Levitts might go for that? He's after what he called a 'promise ring" for his OR nurse."

"I'd like that ring for the anniversary gift Mr. Cartwell asked me to find. Anyway, an OR nurse wouldn't have much occasion to wear a ring, would she?" She couldn't help thinking Flora was dangling the ring in front of her. Almost smirking. As if to say, *I know you can't afford this, but I knew you'd want it.*

"That's something Dr. Levitts and his nurse will have to deal with. Not my problem." Flora quickly placed the ring into a velvet ring box and tucked it in her handbag. And put the other pieces in the lockbox beside her work table.

Nell decided to ignore her and went back to the desk and her papers. In a few minutes, she turned toward Flora. "Take a look at this pin." She opened the small safe in the deep drawer of her desk and removed a drawstring bag. Unwrapping the tissue, she lifted a brooch the size and shape of an ivy leaf, made of ivory, onyx with yellow gold prongs holding emeralds and diamonds in an asymmetrical design. Flora gazed with obvious longing, just as Nell hoped she would. "What would you think of trading this for the pearl ring and the spray you brought me?"

"One, not both." Flora bit her lower lip as she did when she bargained with other dealers. Her dark blue eyes bulged with intensity.

Nell slipped her pin back into the little bag. "This pin is inscribed on the back, with the French designer's name. It's worth twice the ring and spray brooch." Inside, Nell's throat closed up, her breathing grew shallow. She touched her turtle pin and waited, exhaling quietly. *This is my partner. Why is Flora trying to one-up me?* She could feel her shields go up. *Was it the financial pressure of Winslow Farms that was giving Flora a smug attitude? And making me so defensive?*

"Think about it, Flora. In the meantime, back it goes into the safe. By the way, whatever happened to our equal partnership? Something in your attitude makes me feel like a poor relation."

"No, no. Please, Nell. That's ridiculous." Flora threw the wrappings into the box and headed to the door. "You don't need to be paranoid. We're in this together. I'll see you in the morning at the show."

"Right. You'll be on time?" Nell added as the door clanged shut, "For a change."

꙳

Ever since Christmas, Lyn had badgered Nell to teach her to cook. This Tuesday, she'd finally agreed to let her help with supper. Nell did not consider herself much of a cook and very often would stop by Fresh Market to pick up a prepared entree to heat up and serve. Food wasn't as important to her as it was to the rest of the family. Especially Lyn. If they weren't careful Lyn would never lose her so-called baby fat. David loved to cook pancakes or waffles for the children and hear their whoops of enthusiasm for all his creative additives—pecans or chocolate chips or some gooey fruit concoction with way too much sugar.

Nell stopped by the store to gather the ingredients for seafood stew. That would be a good January dinner. She had agreed they would make the cornbread Lyn liked.

Waiting for the butcher to wrap the scallops, shrimp, and white fish, she considered how David reacted when she'd accused him of purposely trying to make them all fat. He'd looked totally blank. All innocence. A blind eye. No wonder something drastic had happened to Jody. He hadn't paid enough attention. His sacred calling siphoned off too much of his energy that should be directed to his own family. When the butcher handed her the packages, she glared at him. Suddenly realizing her anger had flared out to the poor man, she paused and thanked him.

She needed saffron threads and dried orange zest from the spices. Way too expensive, but what the heck. She picked up three bottles of clam juice and the tomatoes. Lyn might take to the stew and begin cooking it herself. Plain corn meal for the cornbread and a fresh can of baking powder. Milk and eggs. They'd fix apple and walnut salad. She hadn't used the slow cooker for months. She hoped it still worked.

On the way home, she thought about how cooking had been done in her family growing up. The cook, Minnie Lee, favored frying chicken in the big black iron skillet. She saved bacon grease in an aluminum container in the refrigerator and would pour off the leftovers after breakfast, to keep a generous supply for frying. Minnie Lee let her eat the tiny hot morsels left after she removed the coated, fried chicken pieces to drain on the paper by the stove. Nell liked to follow Minnie Lee around as she worked, but she wasn't allowed to help. In fact Minnie called her "Miss Underfoot." Nell remembered how she'd claimed the kitchen for herself one morning when Minnie was off duty to cook a special dish for her father. Nell had learned to make cinnamon rolls in Home Ec, so while everyone stayed in bed on Sunday morning, Nell tried to recreate the rolls from scratch. Only she must have forgotten something important, like baking powder, because the rolls remained small and flat and hard as they cooked.

The next day Minnie had howled with laughter when she looked in the trash. "I bet Dr. Forche near about broke his teeth on them rolls." Even though her father had talked about how good the cinnamon smelled and thanked her for cooking for him, her mother had put one roll to her mouth and then returned it with a plunk to her plate. Nell was mortified. It was a long time before she tried cooking again. She wanted Lyn to have a better experience.

When she got home with the groceries, Lyn met her at the door, practically bouncing. "Mom, you're actually home in time for us to cook. Let me help you put these away. Millie's upstairs working on a research paper. Dad called and said he'd be home by 6:30. He was going by the hospital to see somebody-or-other."

"Slow down, baby girl. I know you're excited, but let me change out of these clothes. You can get out the recipe for seafood stew and assemble the ingredients."

Nell headed for the stairs and turned back. "Remember to wash your hands. I'll be right down." She could hear Lyn singing as she rummaged around the cabinets. She changed into her comfy pants with the stretched elastic waist and a large loose-fitting African print top. Dropped her heels on the rack and put on her Daniel Green slippers. If she had to cook, she might as well be comfortable.

"Mom, I've turned on the slow cooker," called Lyn. "Should it be on high or low?"

"We'd better put it on high, for now." Nell was impressed that Lyn had lined up the clam juice, cans of tomatoes, the spring green onions on the counter, and put all the packages of fish in the sink. "Did you wash your hands really well?"

"Yes'm." Lyn tied an apron on over her frayed jeans and tee shirt. Nell smiled at Lyn's effort to match her own apron, to save a tee shirt.

"Okay. First I want you to chop these onions. In little circles like this. All the way into the dark green parts." Nell got her started, and then dumped the tomatoes into the crock pot, added the clam juice. "Tell me how school's going. Learn anything today?"

"Oh, it's okay, I guess. Mrs. Arnold sure does expect a lot. And she moved me away from Missy. Which wasn't fair." Lyn chopped with increased vigor. "Will these make me cry?"

"Not as much as the big yellow or white onions do. You were talking too much again, weren't you?" Lyn nodded.

Nell directed Lyn to scrape the cut up onions into the pot, and then to add the orange peel and saffron. Lyn used a big wooden spoon to stir. She moved close to Nell. "Mom, thanks for doing this with me. It's fun." Lyn stirred and stirred, humming.

"Now, we'll let all this simmer a while before adding the seafood. You can help me rinse off all the fish and pat it dry. We'll cut it into medium-sized hunks and add them with the shrimp and scallops after a while." They stood next to each other at the sink, Lyn looking up at her from time to time. Nell lifted a strand of Lyn's brown hair from her face and tucked it behind her ear. "You're growing up, young lady. We need to go shopping soon for a new outfit."

"Mom, do you think I'm fat? This guy in class teases me. Calls me Pudge. I hate his guts."

"Some guys are jerks. Especially to girls they don't know how to talk to otherwise." She put her arm around her shoulder. "Ignore him. You're fine. Your body will find its mature shape as you grow taller. Relax."

She moved to the baking counter. She didn't say Lyn was probably going to be built like Aunt Gaynell, with her short, stocky figure. "It's time to start the cornbread."

"My favorite." Lyn got out the mixing bowl, the black skillet. "Mom, what's wrong with Jody? Why did she do that awful thing?"

"I wish I could tell you." Exactly why she'd dreaded quiet time with Lyn. Miss Curiosity had to ask questions. To which she had no real answers. "Your father and I are hopeful that her time at Winslow Farms will restore her to health."

"Dad calls up there practically every day." Lyn measured out the cornmeal and dumped it in the mixing bowl. "So far he doesn't know much either. Do you think Jody is crazy? Like, insane?"

"No. Not insane. But she does require medicine for clinical depression. Evidently it takes a while to see how well a particular antidepressant works, and what the side effects might be. How well she can tolerate it all." She measured the baking powder and handed it to Lyn to put in with the salt and stir. "I don't want to talk about Jody right now. All I know is that we have to have patience."

"Yeah, Dad says the therapist keeps saying that. He's driving her crazy, calling so much." Lyn laughed. "Crazy. Get it?" She poured in the milk. "Can I crack the egg?"

"Yes. Just be careful."

As Lyn rapped the side of the bowl with the egg, suddenly it smashed and egg goo ran down the side and onto her hand. She jerked and bumped the bowl. The bowl of cornmeal, egg and milk tumbled to the floor. "Oh, no," she cried out.

Nell snapped. "Now look what you've done!"

"Oh, Mama, I'm sorry. Please don't be mad." Lyn ran to the sink for paper towels and began wiping.

"That won't do at all." Nell brushed up the mess into the dustpan. "Now, you can wet the paper towels and clean it up. We'll have to start over. I hope we have enough ingredients." She hated mess. It would be a chore later to clean the broom and pan too. She washed her hands, her back to Lyn. "I should have known not to let you do that. You can be so boisterous."

When she turned back, Lyn, in tears, was untying her apron. "Mama, I'm so sorry."

She left the kitchen and ran upstairs. Nell heard Lyn's door slam.

As she mixed up a new batch of cornbread, Nell chastised herself. No wonder she left so much childcare to David. She was horrible at it. She couldn't help it. Children triggered some old fire inside she thought she'd put out long ago. Now she'd ruined a perfectly good afternoon, a time she'd hoped would build a good memory for Lyn. She'd have to figure out a way to make amends. Fortunately, Lyn usually bounced back quickly— almost as forgiving as their dog Calvin—when her worthless mother lost her temper.

# 3

# David

Two weeks later on his day off, David sat in his Honda with NPR playing something classical and watched two large black crows circling over the field next to the hospital parking lot. A field altered from a meadow into a construction site. More buildings for the medical complex. Red mud piled up in irregular hills, with the residue of dirty snow in the crevices. Bulldozers and other earth movers stood frozen in place, waiting out the winter where they'd been abandoned.

David lay his head back and thought about Jody and the non-information from her therapist, someone by the name of Amy who sounded nice enough but never told him anything substantive. He and Nell could not afford such an expensive private hospital. Yet when the doctors in Virginia suggested Winslow Farms, and described it, David had immediately agreed that would be just the right facility for Jody. But now he woke up in the middle of the night, calculating the cost. He figured that before Jody was declared ready to come home, the total might exceed six figures. Their health insurance didn't cover such treatment. The cost could easily be enough to pay for several college educations. What could he do?

In fifteen minutes he needed to be at the hospital to check on a parishioner he hardly knew, but the man had requested a pastoral visit before heart surgery. Then in the afternoon he had to meet Julian Denyar, his perpetually agitated treasurer, "to go over some items." David's day off was of no significance to Julian, a man in his late seventies, who routinely bragged about never taking a vacation from his accounting business.

David closed his eyes and let the early morning come to mind. After finally getting back to sleep, he'd dreamed something disturbing he couldn't quite remember yet couldn't shake off. He gave up and took Calvin out for a long walk. His golden retriever was a great companion, especially when David couldn't talk to anyone else. They set out toward downtown instead of his usual neighborhood route. At six o'clock on a January morning, it was cold and dark, so David wore his white warm-ups and heavy sweat shirt with a hood. The massive oaks rose around them in the silent dark like ancient giant guardians. Now and then a car would pass by, but mostly the street toward the park and downtown was deserted. "Calvin, old boy, there's nothing like a walk in the cold winter dawn to beat personal demons away," he'd said, and Calvin had answered with his wide smile and lolling tongue. That was the moment his new associate, Deborah, rounded the hill by the Goodwin Vietnam Memorial, speed-walking toward them. She wore dark tights and a long-sleeved pink tee shirt that clung to her ultra-lean body, her athletic bra underneath doing little to conceal her voluptuous breasts bobbing toward him. She stopped. He backed up.

"Reverend Doctor, how goes it?" she said. Her thick auburn curls were more or less confined in a ponytail with fuzzy pink earmuffs snuggled like small rabbits on either side of her head. Her shirt cut low revealed cleavage and the cold had tightened her nipples so obviously, he couldn't help gawking like a fourteen-year-old. He muttered that he had nothing to complain about. She touched the small gold cross around her neck and gazed up at him with her dark eyes, black as obsidian. David wondered yet again where the pastor nominating committee had found this wild child. Thin as could be, yet buxom. He recalled how Nell compared her figure to a Barbie doll. Charming and lively, yes. Nevertheless, he found her unsettling. He determined to give her the benefit of the doubt.

"David," Deborah announced, speed-talking, "I'm taking the senior highs to protest the protesters at the abortion clinic during spring break. Regardless." She made the pronouncement, jogging in place. To avoid ogling her chest, he looked off into the bare limbs of the oak trees, the sky beginning to lighten up. She probably thought he was avoiding the issue, not her.

Feeling like an overly cautious prude, he told her that the parents—or at least some of them—would not allow their children to protest, and besides, it would have to be approved first by the session. He'd tried to sound strong and definite.

She'd immediately laughed and said, "Don't be such a wimp, David." She touched the end of her nose with one long finger and sniffed. "We need to take a stand, at least as strong as those self-righteous pro-lifers." Then she went sailing off, her wild auburn curls flying out behind her.

David looked at his watch now, and walked from the parking lot into the hospital. He'd call Julian Denyar and postpone their meeting. He needed at least a fraction of his day off in the worst way.

He met Max Shumacher right before he was to be wheeled to surgery. Mr. Shumacher grabbed his hand with his thin, white heavily-veined hand with amazing strength and begged for a prayer. A large nurse stood beside the bed and offered to leave the curtained area. She looked familiar. "I'll be back in a few minutes, Dr. Archer." Her voice brought back where he'd seen her.

"Miss Vines, weren't you doing private nursing for the Smithsons last year? How are you? The Smithsons certainly relied on you a long time. You offered such strength and steadiness just when they needed it most."

"Thank you for those kind words." She ducked her head as if embarrassed to be praised and quietly left the area. Max Shumacher hadn't let go of his hand, so now David turned to him and sat in the metal chair. He prayed for God's all-embracing, healing presence to surround Max with his love and grace. He prayed for the surgeon and all the people in the operating room. As usual, sweat dampened his shirt. He walked beside Max as the nurse wheeled him to the OR. From the gurney, Max said, "My sons are on the way. Please tell them I love them. I forgive them."

David wondered if Max forgave them for not arriving in time to see him off into the OR, or if he referred to deeper past offenses.

He found a public telephone and called Julian to postpone their meeting. Then he entered the waiting room and found the two brothers, probably a dozen years apart, waiting out their father's surgery. Probably half-brothers. The younger, Michael, the son of Mr. Shumacher's second wife, was holding forth. David introduced himself and said he was glad to see them supporting their father today. The young man nodded at him, and continued his train of thought.

"One way I like to procrastinate is talking to people, like you," Michael said and included David in his remark. "One thing I really enjoy is talking to great hordes of people. In college, as vice-president of the student body, I feel like a god. People say I ought to be a stand-up comic. Just stand up there and be an exaggerated version of myself. When people are afraid to stand up even in the classroom, I tell them, 'Why do you care what those people think? Would you lend that person a hundred dollars? Do you trust him? No. So why care what they think?'"

The older brother inserts, "Yes. That's the idea—find out what you get a kick out of doing. You said that you like solving problems and talking out your ideas with people."

"Right now I'm taking economics and philosophy and actually like them both. There's been a lot of change in me from the time I was eighteen. Now I'm twenty-two and feel way different. I spent a year making really bad decisions. I've found out the hard way that I need a moderating personality around me to say—stay in school. Instead of letting yourself be bored, do something. Pursue some kind of hobby."

"Will you go to grad school?"

"No. I really don't care much for school. Even now, just to keep from being bored, I'll write someone's paper for them. No big deal. If you need a C paper, I can deliver that easy. Or an A. You name it, just let me do it. For a price, of course.

"What about you, James? Did you flounder around during your early twenties?"

The elder brother barked out a laugh. "You might say that. Mostly, I wanted to save the world, and I believed I could. Then I met a girl and everything derailed."

He glanced at David for the first time. He nodded at him and added, "Did you also have a tough time in your twenties, Dr. Archer?"

David paused. Sometimes it was hard in the ministry to maintain privacy. "Well, a good portion of my twenties, I spent in England in pursuit of a doctorate. An elaborate form of procrastination, you might say, since I wasn't sure what to do with my life. How exactly I should try to save the world, as you put it."

"So you decided to become a Presbyterian minister and gave up on saving the world, hmm?" James said. He barked another laugh.

"You could say that. There's nothing like the nitty gritty of everyday life to sift out idealistic claims." He thought about his time in Oxford and Daisy's face came to him with such clarity, he flinched. If she hadn't died in the bicycle accident, his plans, his future, might have been vastly different. His life had derailed in a different sense. "Now I just attempt to meet the demands of each day as they appear. Without expectation. You know, tend the garden where I find myself."

Michael moved his chair closer. "May I ask you something, sir?"

David braced himself. "Of course."

"Do you think it's possible for the individual to make any difference in the world today?" Michael scratched his head. "I'm not a cynic. By nature. Just discouraged, I guess." He stood and began pacing. He gestured at the TV, silent but showing one of the daytime soaps between commercials. "We're inundated with trivia and too much sensory stimulation. A load of crap. Crapola in the morning, crapola in the evening, crapola all night long."

He'd probably answer his own question soon enough. David waited.

James rose with a groan. "I'm going for some breakfast. May I bring you guys anything? Coffee? Cinnamon bun?"

Michael ordered coffee with lots of cream and a bun. David said, "Black coffee would be great." James left. David waited.

Michael sat again facing him, his back to the TV. "I worked in one political campaign after freshman year. The man seemed to be an honest Abe, you know. Then I heard rumors. You know, same ole, same ole—he'd cheated people out of their savings in some kind of investment scheme. Totally legit, but way too risky for simple folk like the ones he conned." Michael paced some more. "I left, disgusted."

"Did you ever find out if the rumors were true?"

"No. Didn't bother. He looked pretty swarmy to me by then. I started looking for something else." He moved closer to David and peered at him. "I'll ask again—do you think one individual can make any difference in the world?"

Myriad pictures flashed into David's mind. His old hero, Dr. Albert Schweitzer and his work in the hospital in Africa. Viktor Frankl and *Man's Search for Meaning*. Any number of other writers who had brought insight and wisdom to him over the years, one book at a time. Michael might not be a reader, but surely he'd had at least one teacher like he'd had in college and seminary that affected his life and thought. And central to David's life in ministry—Jesus Christ. And the ministers who had brought Jesus to David, including his own father.

As David pondered how to answer the restless young man, he turned his pen over, feeling its smooth glistening blue metal surface, absently noting the gold trim top, the subtle whorl pattern in the enamel. He looked up at Michael and saw him waiting with his eyebrows furrowed, his lower lip held captive on one side by his teeth.

David reached in his pocket for one of the index cards he carried and wrote the names that had come to mind. He stood and handed the card to Michael.

"You might want to add your own names to my list. Perhaps a teacher or coach that influenced you. Your philosophy professor, maybe, or your father. Or scientists whose discoveries have changed how we deal with disease. So, yes, I do believe one individual can and does make a difference. It helps, too, when the individual is a part of a team or group trying to bring about constructive change. When you encourage your classmates to speak up in class, you're having an influence."

Michael glanced at the card and put it in his shirt pocket. "I guess. It all seems hopeless sometimes."

James walked in with the coffees and cinnamon bun. "Everyone seems to be in line down there in the cafeteria. Have you heard anything from Dad's surgeon?"

"No, nothing yet." Michael took the coffee and bun. "Thanks. The preacher and I have been talking. He says one person can make a difference in the world. What do you think, Jazz?"

"What? Here, Dr. Archer, your black coffee." James sat on the edge of the low table in front of David and Michael.

David thanked him and said, "Making a difference can be for good or ill. And influences are sometimes not known to the person wielding the influence. It can be a small, almost unconscious stirring that can sway someone's convictions and actions. A gift you might forget all about until someone reminds you."

James looked from one to the other. "Deep, man. One thing I've learned that might be apropos is that we're all connected. In ways we little understand. Like, when you, Michael, write someone else's paper, you're not doing that guy a favor. He's likely to go out later, expecting to con someone else into doing his work in a factory or accounting firm. He'll be looking for shortcuts the rest of his life."

"Get off my case, Jazz. You sound like Dad. The super-critical judge of all things less than perfect." Michael gobbled the cinnamon bun in three big bites, swallowed down his coffee and rose from his seat. "See you later. Let me know if the old man makes it through." He turned to David and shook his hand. "Thanks for the names. Good to know."

David suddenly remembered Mr. Shumacher's request. "Oh, I almost forgot. Your father asked me to tell both of you that he loves you and that he forgives you."

"Well, hot damn," Michael said. "How about...do I forgive *him*?" He pushed open the door and walked out.

James said, "Please excuse my hot-headed brother. He and Dad have a running feud about everything. The prodigal son, you know. And I, the self-righteous elder brother, who feels taken for granted. Oh, well. I'm used to the role."

"I imagine you've been cast as the principal caregiver more times than not."

David saw James's face redden slightly, his temple vein pulsing. "You may have some forgiving to do too."

"You're right, Dr. Archer. But I'm not there yet."

They drank their coffee and waited in silence with the TV flickering relentless images.

When the door swooshed open, they looked up expecting the surgeon. In walked Deborah Baker, her hand out to James, who immediately got to his feet. She wore a navy blue suit with matching heels. Very neat and professional. She introduced herself before David could say anything. Then she nodded to David. "Reverend Doc, it's your day off. I'm here to relieve you and will gladly sit with James. I've spoken to Michael, down the hall just now."

James blushed and said, "Oh, please pardon me, Dr. Archer. I had no idea we were imposing on you. I'm so sorry."

"There's absolutely no reason for you to apologize." He rose and shook James's hand. The heat rose in David's head and neck. He forced himself not to glare at Deborah.

"So, David, you might just as well go. We'll be fine. I'll fill you in on the results later." Talking fast as usual, she spoke in a sweet lilting voice. "James and I know each other from a whole other world—although he may not remember." She moved closer to James. "It'll be fun for us to catch up as we wait." She pulled out her nose spray, turned her head slightly and inhaled. "Sorry. Dust allergies."

David wondered where they'd known each other. He tried to catch her eye, but she wouldn't look at him. She grabbed a hunk of her thick curly hair, twisted it, her eyes on James, and said, "Bye, bye, David. See you back at the salt mine."

James held her gaze and said, "Of course, my dear, I could never forget you." Then he turned. "And thanks, Dr. Archer, for coming this morning for Dad."

Dismissed and displaced. Not a good feeling. He did have a few hours left before he needed to be home. He'd go to the office and call Jody's therapist.

Back in his study at home, David reflected on the conversation with the two brothers at the hospital, and James's reference to the Prodigal Son. He'd read somewhere that every book written by a man retold the parable in some form. How often everyone takes turns being one or another of the characters—the father, the wayward son, the elder brother. His brother, Drew, came to mind. What a natural athlete—whether he played baseball, basketball, tennis, pingpong—he could excel with disgustingly little practice. Eye-hand coordination and what Eastern wisdom called "effortless effort." As the older brother, David expected to beat Drew, but found it increasingly hard as Drew matured. By high school, Drew made whatever team was in season, and ended up lettering in both baseball and basketball. David did well to make the fifth man on the tennis team.

As usual when he thought of Drew, ambivalent feelings surfaced—anger still that Drew took his own life, leaving him and their parents shredded. Resentment that Drew had been so gifted, especially when

David wallowed in meagerness and self-pity. But also deep tenderness and love for the brother he'd taken care of so many times and cheered on when he played on the court or at second base. A picture came to mind of a summer day at their grandfather's farm when he was ten and Drew seven.

They chase each other through the old pasture. Drew runs through tall grass and weeds, trips and tangles up in old barbed wire. His leg and his new jeans are caught. In a panic, he screams and sobs. David manages to pull apart the old wire. Drew cries, "Free me. Free me." David pulls harder and widens the wire, but the jeans tear. David cautions him to hold still. "Don't move a muscle until I say so."

Just as David separates the barbed wire, Drew jerks his leg out. The part of the old fencing closest to David springs like a coiled copperhead and rips into David's face. Blood gushes out. "Run, Drew. Run and get help." Blinded by the blood, he calls out, "I'm coming, but there's too much blood for me to go fast." The last he remembers is Drew running up the path toward Grandfather's chicken coops.

Then on the trip to the town hospital, his head in his mother's lap, David hears, "Mary Frances, you're so calm." Grandfather's voice from the driver's seat. His mother holding a cold, wet towel around his face, tight. A hard pulsing. He doesn't open his eyes. The smells, acrid and metallic. The taste of copper like sucking pennies.

Now David ran his index finger along the slight ridge of scar. A thin seam running from the corner of his right eye diagonally down his cheek to his chin. It had been years since he'd thought about the incident, how both he and his brother were given tetanus shots, how his Gram had fussed at Grandfather, "I told you you should have pulled up that old barbed wire fence years ago. Now look what's happened. He's disfigured."

It shook them both. Marked them too. Drew had wept for his new jeans, all ripped up. If he felt guilty for pulling his leg free before David gave him the go-ahead, he never admitted it. David didn't regret freeing his little brother, but he remembered that while the stitches healed, he became shy. He wouldn't go out to play. That must have been the summer he read so many books. *Call of the Wild, Lad: A Dog, Black Beauty, The Adventures of Huckleberry Finn*. All of Dumas. Lots more.

Later he liked to make Face jokes. Losing face. Saving face. Pull yourself together. At Halloween, he used to paint big black stitches and add Frankenstein touches. Inside, he still felt shy. And he never forgot how he got the scar.

# 4

## David

Early in the morning, before his staff arrived, David walked into the sanctuary. He didn't turn on the lights but made his way in the hushed cool darkness, his footsteps meeting the stone floor with solid, confident sounds, much more confident than he felt. He liked the glow the chunks of jewel-colored glass in the windows made on the floor, the walnut pews, comforting and mellow in red, yellow, turquoise, orange, blue reflections. Sitting in the pew beside the great "I AM" window, he looked at the symbols of Christ's ministry from the gospel of John. The butterfly for resurrection, the stately lamb for sacrifice, grapes and bread, the bread of life. Then he studied the open door with the Greek letters for Christ within it, and prayed wordlessly for that truth to enter his heart.

As he contemplated Christ at the open door, a memory of Jody at six years old seized him. When he'd asked her about the scripture verse she'd learned in Sunday school, she had peered up at him through her mass of blonde curls and said earnestly, "Jesus knocks at the door and if I open it, he'll come in and eat supper with me." The memory wrapped around his chest. Where had that lovely hopeful child gone? He leaned his head on the cool pew in front of him and prayed hard for her return to health, for himself and what he could do to help her, his sense of failure to protect her, for Nell and the anger she'd wrapped around herself for protection. And the terrible cost for Jody's care. He laid it all before the Lord.

He lifted his head. The walnut cross, suspended high above the communion table at the front of the nave, never failed to please him with its elegant modern design. The silver orb at its center reminded him that God's grace penetrated the world and transcended it, redeeming all with a mighty love. He let that message quieten his heart.

David felt enormous gratitude for the minister who had fought to bring the Harmony congregation into contemporary life and possessed the vision and persuasive powers necessary for the new sanctuary to embody that vision and relevance. He wished he could have met the man to thank him.

He stood, his inner turmoil subsiding, and went to his office, put on the coffee. He'd have two hours to work on Sunday's sermon. Judith knew not to put any calls through until after ten.


David sat at his desk and watched Julian Denyar. Denyar's graying black hair had receded on either side of a center clump, exposing his temple arteries. One pulsed noticeably as he warmed to his subject.

"Now don't get me wrong, David. I'm not trying to preach to you, but when are you going to stop being so passive?"

Passive? What was on the man's mind this time? Now the man did his version of foaming at the mouth. A little bubble of spit formed at the corner of his uneven lips, wetting his mustache. David suppressed a smile and glanced at the clock on his desk. His treasurer hadn't mentioned money and he'd already been there five minutes.

"She's bad news. Bad for what the church stands for. You've got to do something about the Reverend Ms. Baker. Or I will. Passivity among our leaders drives me to distraction. Look at what happens in Washington when our duly elected officials refuse to take action to cut back the deficit, wasting our hard-earned tax dollars on welfare—no-good, lazy people, especially unwed mothers having baby after baby, most of them retarded. Every one of them feels entitled generation after generation. And another thing—the way we support abortions as a method of birth control. It's murder and we condone it. Even here in Harmony church.

"Which brings me to my subject. Did you see them on TV? At six and again at eleven? Last night. Channel Four showed the Reverend Deborah Baker—your associate, David—and two of our elders, Natalie Ames and Emily Parks. Everyone knows that Natalie is a radical feminist, and an artist, for Heaven's sake. What do you expect from an artist, anyway? But Ted's wife, Emily? What, may I ask, were they doing at that medical clinic? Then, damn it—pardon my French—but that woman's libber Natalie Ames speaks up on the microphone about a counter protest to the anti-abortionists. For choice. I admit they didn't mention our church by name, but in a town this size, you know everyone knows where the Reverend Deborah Baker hangs her hat. What are you going to do about her? I ask you?" Julian smoothed his mustache and pressed the center at the indentation above his upper lip.

David considered answering him, but what was the point? Julian Denyar's face and neck were quite red. And he had more to say. "I demand action. And I am not alone. Deborah is a troublemaker. I'll speak to the rest of the personnel committee. We must review her activities."

David pushed his hair back. He focused on the star-shaped pock mark on Denyar's left jaw. He counted three other pock marks, two by his temple, one near his mustache. Julian must have had a difficult time as an adolescent, with terrible acne. He attempted to see Julian Denyar as he might have been in younger years, before attitudes solidified.

Julian coughed, a thick, ugly cough. David stood, poured him a glass of water from the crystal pitcher he kept on the credenza. He took his time when he gave him the water, and let his hand rest for a moment on Denyar's shoulder.

"Thanks, Preacher." Julian drank the water down like a shot of whiskey. "I know you do the best you can. But it looks to me like women and liberals and the gay-lesbian coalition are taking over our sacred institutions." He smoothed his mustache and did something to his mouth that resembled a smile, or the beginning of one. The redness in his face faded.

David remained standing. Julian set the glass on the end table, picked up his hat and raincoat. He shook hands.

David said, "I'll look into the situation, before the committee meets. Come back, Julian, or call me any time."

David rang Emily's office at Freestone University. No answer. He didn't know her teaching schedule, so left a message with the English department secretary for her to call him at the church. Then he called Natalie and left a message on her machine.

"Nat, it's David at the church. Please call me ASAP. It's 11:00. Meet me at Dix at 1:00 for lunch and get Emily." He'd have to miss Rotary.

He buzzed Deborah. No answer. He called his assistant. "Judith, do you know where Deborah is this morning?" She told him she'd gone to Dr. Ames's office for a scratched cornea, and expected to be back for the youth council meeting after school.

He thanked Judith and asked her to leave a note that he needed to speak with Deborah. He explained that he'd be at a lunch meeting and then to the hospital.

David watched the rain outside. The giant oaks and maples across the street stood in black outline against the gray sky; dead leaves rushed by near the curb. So Deborah Baker decided not to wait for permission to protest the protesters at the abortion clinic. He leaned his forehead against the cool window, breathed in deeply, and let out the hot air absorbed this morning.

Before he got back into his sermon study, he thought about Jody. What might she be doing at Winslow Farms on this cold rainy winter day? If he wrote her a letter, would she read it? Surely a letter would give her enough space to breathe freely. And why in the world had she refused to see them after they'd gotten her settled in her new place?

He had done the best he could with her, and so had Nell. Admittedly, he'd never quite understood her sudden mood changes, but God knew he'd tried. At age five, Jody would throw tantrums like a two year old for no discernible reason. Mind storms—that's what they were. They gradually disappeared and he'd believed she'd outgrown them. Now he wondered if she'd turned all those violent feelings inward against herself. How Nell felt about Jody's mood swings, he couldn't say. She changed the subject when he brought it up.

He called Winslow Farms and left a message for the therapist. While he waited for a call back, he penned a letter on plain paper, not church stationery.

> *Dear Jody,*
>
> *The main reason for this letter is simply to remind you that I love you. I have loved you from the first moment I held you in my arms at the hospital on the day of your birth when the doctor walked briskly down the hall with you resting along his arm, your head in his ample hand. Rather like a football. He, of course, was perfectly relaxed while I stood nervous and anxious and afraid I wouldn't know how to hold you.*
>
> *Your red scrunched-up face and tiny fists made me laugh out loud. You stopped flailing and I could swear you regarded me with an expression that I've seen on your face more than a few times—as if to say, "What's so funny? Don't you get it? Life is hard. I should know—I've just been through a hell of a journey to get here." Then you nestled against my chest, granting me new status: father.*
>
> *And your way has not been easy. As our first born child, you have carried the high expectations parents inevitably put upon their oldest. And you have lived up to those high expectations you have put upon yourself, making top grades through school, achieving recognition in gymnastics and later ballet, winning trophies that still line the shelf in your room. You have shown*

*by example how your younger sisters might achieve excellence in accomplishments. Not only do I love you but I admire you.*

*What I do not understand is this recent episode that landed you in the hospital. Your parents are in a state of bewilderment and terror that we might lose you. What have we done that you would not let us see you before we returned home? Whatever it might be, I ask for your forgiveness. Please know that I will do whatever I can to help you toward wholeness and happiness.*

*Love,*
*Dad*

*P.S. You may not know this, but my mother, your grandmother Oma, also suffered from periods of depression, so I guess I might be partially to blame for passing on a tendency toward dark moods.*

# 5

## David

꽃

The rain poured in torrents. David shook out his umbrella, propped it in a corner of the restaurant's foyer. Emily Parks and Natalie Ames waved to him from a booth near the back. The place was noisy with piped-in music and people at the bar out-talking one another. Sensory bombardment, the opposite of sensory deprivation, or was it? He might develop something about numbing the senses by too much of everything, like the young Michael Schumacher called it—*crapola*. One of the modern death-dealers. A definite sermon possibility.

He slid into the booth opposite. "Been waiting long?"

"We got here right before the deluge. Early, to snag a table." Natalie, the tall Nordic blonde, took the lead as usual. Emily, small, thin, brunette, quick as a mosquito to bite into whatever attracted her curiosity, today looked pale and rather subdued.

"I see we're in non-smoking. Have you quit, Nat?"

"You've got to be kidding. But I have learned to restrain myself from time to time." She glanced at Emily who was reading the menu. "Okay, let's order, then find out what's on your mind, David."

Natalie ordered chicken fajitas for all three of them, but Emily stopped her. "Not today. I'll have some chicken noodle soup. Maybe some hot tea, too."

David looked closer. "Emily, are you okay?" Emily and Natalie exchanged looks.

"A little under the weather is all. I'm sorry. But I felt you called us with some urgency. What's up?" Emily's hands were busy folding the napkin into smaller and smaller triangles.

"You haven't guessed? I hear you two and Deborah were on the news at six and eleven. There have been repercussions."

"That's just too bad," Natalie said and sipped her Coke. "It's important to take a stand once in a great while. In fact, you urge us every week to put our faith into action."

"Touché. You got me there. Nice to know someone's listening. Unfortunately, since Deborah Baker has only been with us a few months, she hasn't established herself yet. Now she's being blamed for instigating radical political action."

Natalie jutted out her strong jaw and looked sideways at Emily. "It wasn't her idea. It was mine. She just came along for support. Right, Emily?"

Emily sighed. "You could say that. She heard us talking Sunday about going over to the clinic, and she jumped right on it, said she'd come too."

"Well, if we have to, would you both meet with the personnel committee to explain that to them? Julian Denyar is hot. He's gunning for her. I'll try to head them off, but you know how he is."

Natalie said, "Julian would give his dying breath to maintain the Status Quo. He hasn't figured out the status never stays quo, no matter what." She rolled her fajita up into a tight bundle and took a big bite. Emily assured David they'd both go to the committee if they were needed.

"Besides," Natalie said, "we were not on a church mission. The church's name was never mentioned. We were acting as individuals, weren't we, Emily?"

"That we were." Emily sipped her tea slowly, lifting her vivid blue eyes to meet his. David studied his friends. He trusted both of them and their husbands. He wondered what Ted and Preston thought about the TV appearance, and about Deborah. There was a lot Emily and Natalie weren't telling him. Yet. He'd have to wait and in the meantime act as a buffer for them and for Deborah, if he could.

As if she read his mind, Emily told him that Ted said more forward-thinking people should stand up for the right of women to choose. He explained to the newspaper reporter who called after the TV spot all about Roe v. Wade, as if the guy had never heard of the case. Natalie chimed in with Preston's endorsement of their action, admittedly after the fact. As soon as she saw the TV cameras, Natalie knew she'd better call Preston and tell him what happened. He was surprised, she said, but fully supportive.

"Good," David said. "We may need them, too." Again he saw Natalie glance at Emily with a look of concern. They wanted the subject dropped. He went on. "My hope is that I can get Deborah to meet with Julian without involving the personnel relations committee at all. I'll let you know if you're needed." He rubbed his temples with both hands. "So don't worry."

He felt Emily's eyes on him. "Don't worry, okay?" David said. Her pale face gained color fast, and she bent to sip her tea. He speared a piece of chicken with pepper and onion and ate without the bread.

Natalie wiped her mouth and asked if he'd heard from Jody. He told them that Jody had not called yet, but the Winslow Farms director kept him and Nell informed of her progress. And he admitted making a pest of himself calling Jody's therapist. He hoped his anguish didn't show. "This whole thing must be awfully hard for you," Natalie said. "Especially not hearing directly."

Emily nibbled at the saltine beside her soup, then reached across the table and put her small hand on his. "David, we are your friends and we're so sorry about Jody."

She hesitated and then said, "She's going to make it through this bad patch. I know it."

Emily moved her hand to brush back her hair. Her voice that had been weak and trembly during lunch gained clarity and steadiness. "When she used to baby sit with Tim, I saw her strength. She seemed to understand what worked with him when no one else could. That year I taught the senior highs, and she was in the tenth grade, we used to take walks around the neighborhood. We had some good talks." Emily stopped and shook her head. "I'm sorry. I cannot begin to understand what you must be feeling. Or what was happening to Jody up at Saint Margaret's school. I just want you to know that I have faith in her capacity for health." She reached in her handbag and grabbed a tissue and dabbed her eyes. She laughed. "So why am I crying?"

Natalie gathered her bag and rain coat and picked up the check. "It's time to go and get you home, Emily, to rest up for your classes tomorrow."

"Who are you? My mother?" Emily scooted out of the booth.

David thanked them both for coming and added, "Thank you for all you said about Jody. If I let myself I could unload on both of you all my hurt and frustration, but that will have to wait for another time."

They left the restaurant as the rain dwindled to a fine mist.

# 6

# David

⁂

David could barely drag himself out of bed. His head ached from the back of his neck up to behind his eyes. He let the shower run down his back with the pulser on, hoping to loosen the tension. Vestiges of a dream caught at his mind. He'd been driving a large convertible with Emily Parks and Jody in the back seat playing cards. Nell made him stop the car and she got out. Jody took over the wheel and he didn't know where Emily was any longer. Jody drove them straight over a cliff. He woke before they hit bottom, his heart pounding. He rubbed his body hard with the towel to dislodge the dream.

When he stepped out of the shower, Nell was seated in front of the mirror, her face coated with a gloppy blue mask. She'd applied a lilac-scented foam to her legs. David watched for a minute the smooth paths she made with the razor. She's always had nice legs, he thought, long, shapely with slender feet that turned out like a dancer's. Slender ankles he'd like to kiss. Her hair was hidden by a towel wrapped like a turban. He leaned over and kissed the nape of her neck.

"What?" she said. "What's wrong?"

"Nothing. I just think you look cute—all blue paste and long legs."

"You don't have to be sarcastic."

He turned his back and dressed quickly. So much for affection. "What's on your schedule for the day?"

"Nothing that should bother or concern you."

"Nell, you don't have to be defensive. I thought we'd agreed we'd let each other know what we're doing, so if need be—"

"I'm not defensive. You just want to control what I'm doing."

"Forget it." He wished for a cigarette. Peppermint gum this early made him sick to contemplate. He looked in the mirror to tie his tie, feeling older than his fifty-three years, and discouraged. Dark circles under his eyes and the headache reinforced his mood, but he tried again. "Nell, what if we went out to breakfast this morning, after the girls leave for school? We could go to The Mug. I don't have a meeting until 10:30."

"What's wrong, David?" She wiped her legs clean and stood up.

"It would give us a little time to talk about Jody and about what we might do next."

"No, thank you." She moved closer to the mirror and her pink robe opened, exposing her belly, almost as big as when she was pregnant years ago. She quickly closed it, tight, as if shutting a door. She splashed her face with warm water and wiped off her mask, dried off before she said anything else. "As a matter of fact, I plan to be at the mall the minute it opens. They're having a January sale. Millie and Lyn both could use new outfits and I need new shoes."

David groaned. Their credit cards were carrying heavy debt already. Why did she keep doing this? Anything to deflect from the miasma with Jody.

"There you go. Trying to hem me in—all with a groan and a sigh."

"That's not it, Nell. When can we discuss Jody without Millie and Lyn around?"

"What good will that do? All talking does is make me feel more hopeless." She pulled on her pantyhose with efficiency. "And, I, for one, don't do hopeless well."

"Have it your way. I'll go wake the girls." He felt jagged needles in the air between them that he had to keep dodging. He rubbed the base of his skull, but nothing relieved the ache.

When he opened the door to the girls' bedroom, Millie was standing up on her twin bed with her camera aimed at Lyn, who was twisted in an odd position, like a rag doll dropped from a balcony, her mouth open, her long dark lashes resting on pudgy cheeks. Millie motioned him to keep quiet, winked, and snapped her photo. The flash brought Lyn to the surface.

"What?" Lyn tried to focus.

Millie jumped down and dropped her camera in the book bag hanging on the bedpost. At fifteen, Millie shared her grandmother's lean figure, straight brown hair and amused green eyes. Pictures of Mary Frances as a young woman always brought comments about how strikingly alike his mother and middle daughter looked.

"Hey, Dad," Millie said. "I'm working on a new series—A Gotcha Series."

David smiled and kissed the top of her head. "Good morning to you too."

He bent to kiss Lyn. "It's time, Baby." Her face felt warm. Although she was ten, she still retained a younger child's stockiness. Lyn appeared to outsiders as the relaxed baby of the family, but he'd long ago recognized her tenacity when a subject grabbed her curiosity. She, like Millie, picked up quickly on other people's feelings, expressed or unexpressed. He used to call her his little Teapot Short and Stout until he saw that it hurt her feelings.

"Five minutes more, Daddy, please." Lyn turned over and buried her head.

Millie went down the hall to the bathroom.

"Breakfast in twenty minutes, girls." He was relieved neither mentioned Jody.

After the carpools picked up the girls, David headed out on a walk with Calvin.

He dreaded the meeting he'd set up between Julian Denyar and Deborah Baker. He imagined the fireworks. Still he hoped that they could work out a way to clear up the issue without calling the entire personnel committee. He'd been amazed that Deborah readily agreed to talk with Julian. He'd heard her make snide remarks about his puritanical views. Julian had simply said, "Well, I guess that makes sense, Preacher, for me to try to talk some sense into her pretty young head."

Julian arrived fifteen minutes early as was his custom. David found him in the office behind the work station where Judith folded bulletins for Sunday service. Other people might be said to "chat up" another person, but not Denyar. Rather he pontificated on one or more of his favorite subjects. When David walked in, Judith looked up with relief on her broad face.

"Good morning, Preacher," Julian said. "I was just explaining to Judith here how our troops are dealing with Panama. Stability in Panama is of crucial interest to America. I'm proud of our president for sending in more troops last year. A goodly measure of force. Keep Noriega in line." Julian straightened into his own upright military stance, picked up his coat and hat from the chair by the door. "Judith, I enjoyed conversing with you this morning." She nodded and kept on folding bulletins.

David shook hands with him. "Glad to see you looking so fit, Julian, and I appreciate your taking the time to talk with Deborah."

"Time is something I enjoy giving to Harmony church. Maybe I can talk some sense into Deborah Baker. Set her straight." He smoothed his mustache and pressed on his upper lip.

David led him to the conference room. "She should be here any minute."

The conference room seemed to invoke serious deliberation with its walnut paneling and large custom-made walnut table surrounded by matching heavy arm chairs on wheels for easy maneuverability. Portraits of the former pastors lined the walls. This room could be intimidating, but David knew that it would take more than a row of dignified clergymen to affect Deborah or dampen Julian's intention.

Deborah burst into the room, her auburn hair flaring out from the gray headband intended to hold it in check. Her gray tailored suit and high-necked white blouse and sedate gray pumps sent the clear message that she knew what Julian Denyar expected from the associate minister— professionalism and modesty. David almost laughed. He hadn't seen her in such a sedate outfit since her first Sunday on the job.

"Thank you both for meeting this morning," David said. "I'll leave you to talk out what Julian has on his mind. I feel sure you two will be able to come to an understanding."

"Thank you, Preacher," Julian said. "I'll drop by your office when we finish." He took her outstretched hand in a gentlemanly clasp as if he were about to kiss her hand—not shake it.

As David stepped out of the conference room, he saw Deborah lift her large black eyes demurely to Julian, her hand still in his, her full lips in a slight smile, not exactly mocking, more self-mocking. Her voice possessed a breathless, girlish quality as she thanked him for asking to meet with her.


Back in his office David stared out his window, wondering if he should have arranged for Deborah and Julian to meet alone. Should he have stayed? He hoped and prayed their meeting would go all right and the full committee would not have to be called. He reprimanded himself for feeling so antsy and sat down to plan the next session meeting.

Close to noon Julian knocked at his hall door. Flushed and smiling, Julian Denyar walked in, his coat over his arm. "David, you may not know this about that young associate of ours, but Deborah Baker is actually a teachable young woman."

"Sit, sit. Tell me all about your meeting." David tried to keep the amazement off his face. He gestured to the sofa, but Denyar chose a straight chair, so David sat opposite him in another chair, carefully not behind his desk. He wanted to put them on an equal plane. He needed to hear everything.

"Let me sum it up first. There is no need to call the full committee." Denyar's chest expanded with pride.

"Really? I'm relieved to hear you accomplished so much. May I ask how?"

"First, I laid out how I and others in the congregation see certain important issues. Namely, abortion and the gay life style. And, Preacher, she listened. Wide-eyed, as if she'd never heard anyone explain these moral issues from a basic Christian perspective. And she said as much. Never had she heard them explained so clearly." Julian stretched his arms behind his head, elbows out on either side.

David nodded and waited. Julian had more to say.

"One funny thing. We both have these terrible deep coughs. At one point early on, I started coughing, and, Bless Pat, she did too. Anyway, we both were hacking away into our respective handkerchiefs. She used her nasal spray with such discretion. She's a lady, by the way, and carries a linen hankie, just like my beloved Esther used to do." He chuckled, gazing up at the ceiling. "After these God-awful coughs, we started laughing. When she caught her breath, she said, 'We're just alike, aren't we?' Then Deborah told me how she'd barely escaped a terrible house fire as a child of eight that wiped out her whole family, but she survived. Only thing was her lungs have been affected for life. And terrible allergies, too. Poor thing. I never knew that." He took out his handkerchief and wiped his eyes and around his mustache and mouth.

"And we even talked about you. She's a very compassionate person, David, and so worried that your daughter's situation may have put you off your game. She and I are both wise in the ways of the world—that's how she expressed it. She feels concerned about you. And she asked my help, too, with a worthwhile mission project she wants to start. At the Space for Hope." Denyar pulled himself up into his full military stance. "I'm ready to put our resources behind her project." He took his coat and reached out to shake David's hand. "Thank you, Preacher. I think we've built a significant bridge today. Miss Deborah and I are going to be on the same side from now on. You'll see."

David shook hands and told him to come see him any time. After Denyar left, David thought over all he'd said. He rubbed his forehead and the back of his neck. He failed to share Denyar's elation. So Deborah had relinquished her stance on the social issues without a fight. Too easily. On issues she'd sounded so strong on not two days ago. His headache felt like a precursor of trouble to come, although different from what he'd envisioned earlier.

# 7

## Millie Archer

After the youth meeting, Millie Archer stayed to clean up craft supplies and leftover refreshments with Deborah Baker. Millie felt flattered that Deborah asked her to talk. She'd said, "I could use your opinion about some things, Millie." The first personal words Deborah had ever said to her. Most of the time Deborah sought out the seniors or juniors, and Millie, just in the ninth grade, was new to Youth Fellowship. She might be the preacher's kid, but she felt like an outsider. Most of the youth group went to Westside, while Millie attended Goodwin Academy.

As they swept up the dropped tissue papers and construction bits, Millie watched Deborah's graceful movements, the way her auburn hair caught the light as she moved.

"Your hair is gorgeous, Deborah."

Deborah held the dustpan poised over the waste basket, then dumped out the debris. "My hair used to be mousy like yours, Millie. But I decided I could take control—with a little help from a box. And I did."

Mousy. She hadn't known her hair looked so bad. Deborah didn't seem to notice her words hurt. "You know, whatever nature provides. That's me."

"God's will or something?" Deborah laughed. "How old are you?"

"Fourteen. Almost fifteen."

"That's about the age I was when I took control and chose the color that suited me. You can too, you know." They finished their clean-up and picked up their coats. Deborah put her arm around Millie's shoulders and pulled her close. "If you want me to help you choose the right product, I'll be glad to."

"My parents would freak out. But thanks." Millie kicked the leaves in the driveway of the education building. She thought about her father and mother, each on their separate paths, both preoccupied. She looked at Deborah, so self-assured, such perfect creamy skin and dark long lashes, dark almost black eyes. "On the other hand, Dad's so upset about my sister, he probably wouldn't notice. And Mom dyes her hair, or her hair stylist does, so she really can't say much, can she?"

Deborah squeezed her shoulder and turned to face her. "There's something else I'd like to say." She stirred the loose grit on the driveway with the toe of her sneaker. "Because of troubles when I was young, which I won't bore you with, I sometimes need help." She talked fast, but seemed to force herself to slow down. "Sometimes I feel like I have no grounding, that I'm floating around like a feather on the breeze." She held Millie's gaze with those shining dark eyes. Millie felt her face grow hot. Deborah was asking for her help. She, Millicent Archer, the lowly ninth-grade outsider, preacher's kid, had been singled out. The beautiful youth minister wanted her help.

"It's as if I need an anchor. You may be young, but I sense you have great inner strength. You could help me determine how to take a strong stand for what is right and good. Can I count on you to do that?"

Millie could hardly say anything. What did she mean? She wanted to say she'd do anything for her. She managed to nod and stammer, "Yes, of course."

Deborah gave her a brief hug and waved to the blue Honda approaching in the driveway. Millie saw it was her dad. Deborah had already turned back to lock up. Millie called out, "Bye, Deborah. Thank you." A feeble response considering how exhilarated she felt. She leaped into the car, next to her dad.

"You're full of paprika. Good meeting?" David wheeled out of the church turn-around and headed toward home, barely glancing at her. He read her moods as if she threw off some special odor. No use keeping secrets from him.

"Yes, sir. And I worked afterward to clean up with Deborah. First time she's ever talked 'specially to me." Millie hoped she didn't sound too excited. She bit off the rough skin beside her index fingernail. The place stung and began to bleed. She sucked the spot and watched the street where two dogs pulled at a leash with a girl trying to control them. They passed Goodwin High. Millie's momentary elation seeped out. Monday she had to turn in two original poems to Mr. Zimmerman—and she hadn't begun to think about them—plus a test in biology to study for. She sighed.

"Did I detect a sudden cloud come up and cover your sunny mood?"

"Dad, I'm okay. Just a lot of school work."

"I find I'm sighing a lot myself recently. Mostly because of your sister."

"I know. Me, too." Maybe he'd tell her more about Jody since her little sister wasn't in earshot. Her parents were always trying to protect her, even though Millie knew Lyn was more daring and probably more unflappable than anyone else in the family. "Dad, what did the doctors say about Jody? Do you know anything new?"

"First of all, Dr. Brenner assured us that they're keeping close tabs on Jody. She has promised in therapy that she will not try again to take her own life. She made a contract with Dr. Brenner and they have her on medication now. It will take a while to determine if it's working. He stresses patience." Her dad looked at her with a pleading expression. "I don't know about you, but for me, it is hard to be patient about this."

"Me too, Dad." She bit another hangnail. "Dad, I don't know why, but part of me is angry with Jody. Furious, actually. How could she do such a thing? It hurt you and Mom and me and Lyn."

"Honey, I understand. Anger is part of my mixed-up emotions too. And fear."

"What made her do it?"

"I wish I knew. You can imagine all the things that have run through my mind.

"Something I may never have told you is that my mother, Mary Frances—and my only brother Drew—also suffered from bipolar disorder. Or melancholia as the ancients used to call it."

"So you think she inherited a mental illness?" A thread of fear worked its way through Millie's throat. What if she caught it too?

"That I don't know, but such ailments are not passed down like blue eyes. However, the tendency might be present given the right convergence of circumstances."

They entered the carport. David switched off the engine and they sat silent for a minute. "Darling, you know your mother refuses to talk about Jody right now. So if you want to discuss her, please come to me. I know I need to talk out this enormous anguish. I feel helpless. There's nothing substantial I can do to help her heal."

Twice today, someone she admired had confided in her. Millie lifted her chest and breathed in deeply. Somehow she felt more grown-up. She liked feeling needed and sought out. She leaned over and kissed her dad's cheek. It felt slightly whiskery. She could smell his aftershave and old coffee. "Thanks, Dad. I think I'll write Jody a letter. Do you think that would be okay?"

"Trust your intuition, Mill. You're usually right on the button, especially with your sisters."

*Dear Jody,*

*It's me—Millie. I miss you. So does Lyn. Of course, you've been off at boarding school all year and I haven't written you. Sorry. You may not have noticed or cared.*

*I have to write two poems for Mr. Z. You remember him. He was your favorite teacher I think. He's mine because he loves books and word games a lot. He gives me extra work and sometimes lets me grade papers. For one of the poems, I have to imitate a Shakespearean sonnet. Did you have to do that too? The other one is our choice although he wants us to find a modern poem we like. I found one I like a lot by Sylvia Plath, but it is too long—way too long—to imitate. "Tulips" is the name of it. The reason it spoke to me is that I pictured YOU in the hospital after you attempted the Unspeakable. Mr. Z says to talk about the I in a poem as the Speaker, not act like it is the poet herself. So I should say, the Speaker hates receiving the red tulips as a gift. They are an affront to her will to die. They call her back to life and those who love her. The tulips hook her and pull her toward the living when all she wants is stillness and white and quiet.*

*Jody, I want something or someone to hook you and tug you back to us. I may send you the poem, or maybe some real red tulips, or better still some pecan pie. Can you mail pie? I dunno, but think I'll try.*

*Please write me a note and tell me what you do on that farm.*

*I love you.*

*XXXOOO,*
*Millie*

*P.S. I may dye my hair. Don't tell Mom or Dad.*

# 8

# Preston

⌇

Two weeks later on a warm Saturday afternoon in February, Preston Ames headed out Highway 11 to Glen Springs. The evening ahead came loaded with a peculiar blend of bitter and sweet. A celebration that the property had sold for a fair price, so his mother would not be destitute, but sadness too. He and their friends had enjoyed many spring, summer, and fall gatherings on the lake and in the rambling house with many bedrooms and its long screened porch overlooking the lawn leading down to the water. They rarely used the property in winter, but here they were twice—once after his father's memorial service and now to say another farewell. He drove the ten miles out, letting his convertible swing around the curves in a rhythm that was second nature to him.

Preston wished Brett could have come, but he couldn't leave prep school again so soon after coming for his grandfather's funeral. Coy sent a beautiful winter wreath and a sweet note, but college classes demanded too much for her to leave. Both his children had learned to swim in the cold spring-fed lake. Both had taken up fishing because they knew he loved nothing better than to sit in his boat for hours with his rod and reel, whether he caught anything or not. Coy joked that she preferred fly fishing because at least you moved, took action, and tried to trick the fish with the clever flies she'd learned to tie. He missed both his children, wished they could have said good-bye to the lake. Jerking himself up from these thoughts, he drove into the turn-around and hopped out. He carried in the boxes of drinks and games Natalie had packed.

Natalie had already set up tables with pine boughs and candles on the porch.

She had U2 playing on the boom box. In the kitchen Charlotte was elbow deep in flour, rolling out her famous biscuits. Preston smelled his mother's fried chicken, the kind of fried chicken the lake house attendees counted on. His mouth watered for the dark crispy coating and juicy meat. No worries about cholesterol today. He greeted her with a peck on the cheek and went into the great room.

Natalie stood up from where she was laying wood in the big fireplace. She walked toward him with a wide smile on her face. His Tall Nordic Beauty, he liked to call her, and even after twenty-something years, she could make his heart jump into his throat. He was proud of her. The paintings of doors he'd teased her about, they'd become so obsessive—but now they were shown all over. In California, Texas, and up the east coast. And they sold. "Who'd want a painting of an old door in Tuscany, or a cabin door in Georgia?" he'd said. Obviously, some discerning collectors did and paid good money for them.

"I've got a small surprise for you later," she said. Then she kissed him full on the mouth, the kind of kiss that promised plenty more.

"All right, my love. Shall we send away these people, driving into our driveway?" He held her in a body hug a minute longer. Then she danced away to greet the Archers and the Parks.

Everyone came in bearing gifts. Ted and Emily Parks handed him a new recording of Wynton Marsalis. Tom and Tim carried a large planter between them of a bonzai tree for Charlotte. David, Millie, and Lyn carried boxes, one each for Natalie, Charlotte, and Preston. Inside were framed photographs of the families at the lake three years ago. Fred was in the group. So were Jody and Nell. Coy and Brett too.

"Y'all, this was totally unnecessary. But, hey, these are great gifts," Preston said. He didn't mention those who were missing, but their absence today hung in the air as the pictures made the rounds.

"Let's break out the wine and nibbles," Natalie said, ushering everyone to the great room. The kids settled at a table on the porch with the Monopoly game. Emily took bowls of popcorn and chips out to them with Cokes.

"I smell Charlotte's fried chicken," David said. "I remember how Maggie and Caesar used to work for your family. Maggie taught Charlotte to fry chicken, so Fred used to say."

"Not true," Charlotte yelled from the stove. "I learned from my grandmother. She and Maggie just happened to cook the same way."

"She says the secret is the black cast-iron skillet," Natalie said, "but I've tried that. There must be some other trick." She sat down on the stone hearth. "So I gave up and left that to my betters. Pres, go get your mother away from the hot stove. We need to talk."

It took a while, but Preston finally came in with Charlotte, wiping her hands on a dish towel. She looked flushed to him, but he chalked it up to her cooking. David jumped up from the wing chair in the center of the circle. "I've been saving this seat especially for you, my dear." Ted brought her a tall glass of ice water in one hand and sauvignon blanc in the other.

"Enough bowing and scraping," Charlotte said, nodding to each man in turn. "I know what you're up to. Your hearts are in the right place, but I don't need your pity."

"Mother, relax. We all love you and you are not a person to elicit pity."

Preston looked around and everyone chorused their agreement. "We do want to talk out what's happened and what we can do to find out where Dad's assets went."

"It takes a group to do that?" Charlotte fixed her son with eyebrow raised.

"How many Presbyterians does it take to screw in a lightbulb?"

"How many?" Emily answered, "A session committee to appoint an ad hoc committee to investigate and report back."

"Whatever," Ted said. "As your lawyer, and Fred's, I have to say, I don't have a clue what he did to lose his money. Two years ago, we went over all his assets, your joint assets, when you both updated your wills. Last year, everything seemed in order. I met with him and his stock broker." Ted took a quick drink from his wine and grabbed a handful of chips. His face a dark red.

Preston saw how uncomfortable this made Ted. A man who prided himself on control. Control through complete knowledge of the subject at hand. He was clearly at a loss.

Charlotte leaned to her right and patted Ted's arm. "Never mind, dear. I know you'll do your best for me." She looked at David on her left. "Now, David, what do you think?"

"Have you spoken to his broker since Fred died?" David looked to Ted for the answer.

But Charlotte answered, "Robert called me when he read the obituary. Nonplussed, I believe is the word. He said that a week or so before Fred died, he instructed him to sell the last of his big holdings, that he'd been selling off this and that for several months." Charlotte sat up even straighter with her chin raised higher. "Robert assumed I knew that Fred had been selling assets right and left. But, no." Her voice faded to almost a whisper. "I knew nothing of what he was doing. Not one blessed thing." She sipped her water, replaced the glass carefully, then dabbed her mouth with a cocktail napkin.

Preston said, "Dad died so suddenly. Whatever he was up to, he certainly never expected to die before he cleared up the trouble."

Natalie voiced what everyone was thinking. "The question is what *was* he up to?"

"How shall we find out?"

Emily looked first at Natalie, then at Charlotte. Preston watched her. She seemed at the moment to be a shy young girl who wanted to suggest something to a bunch of grown-ups but wasn't sure of the reception. He asked, "Emily, do you have an idea?"

She said, "I hesitate to mention this. Y'all will think this is really weird, especially you, Ted. But I had a strange dream the other night. Ted, don't roll your eyes. Charlotte, you were swinging on that double swing down by the lake, and Natalie was pushing you. You kept saying, 'Higher. Push me higher. I have to see over the hedge.' Then I could see over the hedge, and there was a man with a Sherlock Holmes hat on. I woke up. That's when the idea came. We should hire a private detective. We could all chip in."

"Good idea," Natalie said. "The art school had to hire a P.I. when some money disappeared a few years back. He did a good job, I think. His name was Irv Wolfe, with some nickname. Irv Wolfe. Let's hire him."

"Is this necessary?" Charlotte asked. "It sounds rather unseemly to me."

"Mother, hiring a private investigator could save us a lot of time." Preston knew they'd need Ted's approval or maybe someone he'd recommend. "A P.I. knows how to find things out a lot quicker than most of us. Of course, Ted, you might suggest someone else."

"Wolfe has a good reputation," Ted said, "and he would keep what he discovers for our ears only. He's discreet."

"So it's decided then," Charlotte said. "The committee has appointed an ad hoc committee and will report back. Ted, you will tend to this unpleasant business for us."

It was more a statement than a question. Preston smiled at Natalie. They'd heard that tone more than once. Charlotte stood, and all the men rose from their chairs.

"At ease, gentlemen. I'm going back to the kitchen and assemble supper if you ladies would like to help me. Preston, please see to the young people on the porch."

# 9

# David

The group gathered after the church session meeting at the Red Lobster. It had been ages since David had been to that den of buttery-fried delights. He'd called home and asked Nell to meet him there and to make sure she'd say yes, he spoke first to Millie to secure her as the official sitter though Lyn, at ten, hated for anyone to imply she needed baby-sitting. So Nell joined Preston and Natalie, and Ted and Emily, and they had all prevailed on Charlotte Ames to join them. Even the treasurer Julian Denyar met them in the restaurant parking lot. He turned red around the ears as if embarrassed to be going to a social function. Deborah Baker swung her electric blue convertible into the space next to Julian, hopped out, and linked her arm in his to walk into the restaurant, all the time talking confidentially in his ear. Julian's entire head glowed crimson by the time they reached the big table.

David was relieved that everything at the session meeting had gone smoothly. Contributions and pledges were on a par with last year, reports of the committees were routine. David ordered a big iced tea, the rainbow trout dinner, and listened to the banter between Natalie and Julian Denyar, one of her favorite targets. She loved to tease him about his conservative politics and sexism. And Julian in turn jabbed back with quotes from his favorites— William F. Buckley and *The National Review* or *The Public Interest.* David enjoyed watching them match wits. So far in a spirit of goodwill.

Emily straightened up and broke in as they all began to eat their dinners. "Okay, y'all, tell what was the worst job you ever had. Maybe a summer job."

"You brought it up, Emily. You tell first," Preston said.

Emily drank a sip of coffee, thinking. "Let's see. Probably the worst, in the sense of the most boring was before my freshman year in college. I typed license permits for owners of half-ton pick-up trucks in the basement of the state capitol in Little Rock. It had to be the hottest summer in Arkansas and the basement wasn't air conditioned. For lunch, the girl I worked with— Selma Plowman—and I would take our bag lunches outside, hunting shade and maybe a breeze. That summer to beat the boredom, I figured out a way to make the job of filing our work more efficient. The big woman who was a permanent state employee snapped at me, 'Don't you know if we do it your way, we'd all be outta' work in no time.' So much for efficiency. Bureaucracy. No, thank you. After the bus ride home every day, I was so hot that I'd soak in a cool tub before I could face supper or anything else."

Ted looked up from his platter of fried shrimp, winked at Natalie, and addressed his wife. "The anything else was probably one of your hot dates, right?"

"No comment." Emily laughed. "Now someone else has to say. Deborah, you're new to this crowd. What was your worst job?"

"Well, that's hard to say." Deborah cast her dark eyes on Preston with an amused expression. "There've been so many."

Everyone laughed. Natalie broke through with, "You mean in churches?"

"No, no. Not in churches. Before I ever went to seminary, way back when. Probably the worse was when I had to work for, well, I guess you could call him my foster father. I was probably just eleven or twelve, and my foster mother's boyfriend was a vet. That summer I had to wash a zillion nasty dogs, none of which could tolerate being sudsy. To this day, just the smell of wet dog and antiseptic shampoo makes me gag." She leaned over the table with her chest practically in the bowl of cocktail sauce. Then she straightened up tall and continued at a fast clip. "And the worst part. All that hard work did nothing to win over my foster father. He still hated my guts and had the gall to blame me for my foster mother's psychological problems. But that's another story."

She looked around at the audience, touching the end of her nose and smiling broadly. She flipped her hair back. "It's someone else's turn. David, how about your worst job?"

"That's easy. Right after my sophomore year at Davidson. It was one of the hottest summers on record in Arkansas. Much hotter than Emily's hot summer. My job was to paint—actually repaint gas meters around the county. Mostly I worked with a spray gun of silver paint and only used a brush on the parts near the face of the meter and in the crevices.

"One day I had to work on meters near the yard of the women's prison. The women gathered at the fence whistling and yelling at me. First, only two or three, then soon what must have been twenty or twenty-five. They got to hollering things like 'Hey, Silver Man, you can spray me.' And 'Hi, Ho, Silver Man, bring your spray gun over here.'"

Everyone laughed and he laughed along with them.

Nell looked at him. "You never told me that story." Her unsmiling face stopped conversation.

David's face grew hot. He smiled across at Preston and Natalie, but answered Nell. "I guess you never asked about my worst job." He added to himself, *or much of anything else. 'I* haven't thought about that in years. Come on, Nell, what about your worst job?"

"I'll pass. Growing up I never had a bad job. I worked for my father until . . . This is boring. Terribly loathsome, darling. I shall pass." Nell sat up straighter, more regal than ever. Closed off. To David, in a quiet aside, she said, "You know how it was for me, back then."

Soon everyone began talking in two's and three's, leaving him to deal with Nell.

He wondered what she was referring to. Whatever it was, she seemed to think he should have read her mind and not put her on the spot. A vague wisp of an idea tickled the edge of his mind. He couldn't quite bring it to consciousness.

Emily and Natalie were laughing and joking across the table. He wanted to say to Nell, in private of course, how much he wished they could have fun together. Play. She knew little about play. He wished again that she were a happier person.

Then a picture flashed into his mind of a time right before they married.

They were seated in her parents' solarium at a small game table, drinking iced tea with mint. Nell, with tears in her lovely gray-brown eyes, had explained to him that she was going to tell him something that had happened to her. She would tell him once and then never wanted him to mention it again or even refer to it. When she'd been twenty in her junior year at that exclusive women's college in Virginia, she had to drop out. Her mother had lied to the authorities that Nell was sick with mononucleosis. Nell had gone later to the Florence Crittenton Home and the next spring had given birth to a baby boy whom she gave up for adoption. Nell's beloved father had spurned her. From then on, their relationship had suffered a terrible breach.

David flushed with shame that he'd allowed something so crucial to slip from his memory. He reached for her hand, her nails manicured to perfection, bracelets on her wrists glittering in the restaurant lights. He smiled at her, hoping she would see understanding in his eyes, but she avoided looking directly at him.

Julian rose from his end of the table, lifted his glass. "Everyone, I want to say a word. Thank you. Basically, just thank you, for inviting me to be with you young people. I haven't had this much fun in many a year. Now, it's past my bedtime, so I must leave, but before I depart, I'd like to tell you about my worst job."

"By all means," Emily said. "Was your worst in the military?"

"Indeed not. That service, my dear, was close to glorious. At least at times. Hard but glorious to serve our country." Julian smoothed his mustache, pressing the center of his top lip. "I grew up in Atlanta. Buckhead. My father decided I should know more about how he'd grown up, you know, on a farm. So one summer—I must have been seventeen—he sent me to north Georgia where my Uncle Franklin worked—in a chicken factory. That summer I was a bleeder."

"What in the world?" Natalie asked. "That sounds gross."

"Well, I tell you, with the smells, I fast became a vegetarian, long before it was fashionable."

"Perhaps you can spare us the description of exactly what a bleeder did," Charlotte said.

"Only the pertinent details. Suffice it to say, after the chickens were hung upside-down and sent toward me along the conveyor belt, my job was to slice them open and drain out their innards. The first day I vomited twice before I could endure the dreadful process."

"Enough," Nell said. "Now, I'm going to be sick."

David stood. "I think we can all agree: Julian Denyar wins the competition for the most horrendous job." He led the applause.

"As I said, thank you, one and all, for a delightful evening." Denyar smoothed his mustache and looked around the group, lingering on Deborah's smiling face. "Do I get a trophy or something for the most repugnant summer job?"

"We'll see what we can do, when next we meet," Emily said and looked at Natalie who nodded slightly. "Perhaps a red lobster holding a gilded, gutted chicken."

"Constructed out of paper mache. A pinata," Natalie added. These two knew how to play. He wished they'd ask Nell to do something with them. Lunch or something.

# 10

# Millie

The two of them set up the game of Clue. Millie chose Miss Scarlet, her favorite character, and Lyn picked Ms Peacock. David and Nell had left Millie in charge while they were out for the evening. The girls had finished their homework before they could play, just as they'd promised. Lyn clicked on the TV.

*Family Ties* began as Millie dealt the cards. Millie watched Michael J. Fox smiling and looking deceptively innocent as he set off with his brief-case. She had to admit he was cute, although she thought the character he played—Alex P. Keaton—was too competitive and ambitious for his own good, to say nothing of being way too conservative. Lyn loved the young-est sister Jennifer, who could really put her brother in his place, also their parents. Lyn sat glued to the show.

"Come on, Lyn. You said you wanted to play. It's your turn." Millie tapped the board at the entrance to the kitchen. "Who killed the professor and where and with what weapon?"

"Millipede, I think this episode is going to be scary. I need Funny Bunny." Lyn jumped up to run to her room, bumping the board and spill-ing the weapons and men all over the place.

"Now, look what you did. Are you going to play or watch the show?" She stopped at the door. "Both." Lyn began putting the pieces back on the board, barely glancing at the Clue game. Her brown eyes, as big as a lemur's, were fixed on the television.

Then she ran out and back into the room with her blanket and Funny Bunny. She snuggled up to Millie. "What if there's a stranger outside watching us?"

"Sweetie, we're okay. Let's solve the mystery."

"Please, Millipede, would you please close the drapes? Just in case."

Millie pulled herself up off the carpet and pulled the drapes across the wide windows. It was like when Lyn saw a spider and made her stop whatever she was doing to come and kill it. Reading *Charlotte's Web* did nothing to help Lyn get over her fear of spiders. Was she cultivating a new fear?

Lyn hugged her Funny Bunny and leaned against Millie. Lyn smelled good, like her strawberry-scented shampoo. Millie played for both of them until the show was over. Now and then Lyn grunted a yes or no with all the guesses Millie proposed in either a high voice or a low one. But nothing distracted Lyn from the nightmares the young Jennifer was suffering on screen.

When the story resolved itself, Lyn let out a long deep sigh. Millie clicked off the TV. She was close to winning. She proposed, "I think Mr. Green did it in the library with the iron." She loved mysteries, but this game wasn't much fun when she had to play all the parts.

"Can I ask you something?" Lyn chewed on Funny Bunny's ear.

"Sure, Lyn-bug. What is it?" Millie waited, hoping her little sister's fear had abated. She smoothed her hair and twisted it into a long loop.

"You think Mom and Dad hate each other?" Lyn let out a sob.

"Oh, my goodness, no. Of course, they don't hate each other. Why would you think such a thing?" But even as she said that, she realized Lyn must had picked up on the atmosphere in the house since they came home from seeing about Jody. "Okay, it wasn't Mr. Green. Your turn, Lyn."

Lyn paid no attention to the game. She was busy reciting other clues. "Well, I heard them fight again. Not yelling exactly, but you know that hissing Mom does when she's mad, and that rumble like thunder that Dad does. They figured we were asleep." She stood up and Millie looked up from the game at her little sister.

"I've got another clue, a secret clue. But first you have to promise not to tell. Promise?"

"I promise. But first, take your turn."

"Cross your heart and hope to die?"

"Cross my heart. Tell me, Lyn, what's your secret clue?"

"It's something I found in Daddy's desk. Way back in the bottom drawer."

"How come you went into his private stuff?"

"'Cause I'm training to be a spy for the CIA."

Millie was used to Lyn's imagination. One reason she was so much fun, even if she was just a kid. Millie moved Lyn's Ms. Peacock down to the kitchen.

"You don't think I have anything real, but I do. It's a letter. I'll get it."

"While you're gone, I'm going to win the game." She marched Miss Scarlet back to the library. "It's Mrs. White in the library with the iron."

Lyn ran back in, waving a piece of stationery with their dad's writing on it. Millie stood with her under the floor lamp and read. A thrill moved through her even as she felt guilty for reading her father's letter. It was to their mother, written on Valentine's Day. Some weird valentine. Millie read it aloud:

*Dear Nell,*

*Today is Valentine's Day and though we have rarely celebrated with candy or gifts or flowers, I've been meaning to tell you that despite our recent unpleasantness, I want to thank you for letting me know how you feel.*

*I can count on your consistent resentment—sometimes at a simmer, sometimes at near volcanic eruption—but always present. I've begged you to come with me to therapy, and consistently you refuse. When I think back, I realize you've been unhappy for a long time. For years. I blame myself for not making you happy.*

*Now I want to ask you to consider a way to let go of the anger and resentment and—need I say—the needless jealousy, and give us both a fresh and new beginning.*

*You now have a business with Flora you enjoy, a business that takes you away on weekends from the church—that you know I resent—but it is an enterprise I can see feeds your spirit, and may actually be making some money.*

*But, Nell, we are growing further and further apart, and have been for several years. Ever since Jody's near suicide, we've not been the same. Either of us. Each of us has sought solace where our natures have taken us.*

*So, my suggestion is that we consider the way of separation and divorce. To that end, I've spoken to a lawyer—not a member of the church, lest there be gossip.*

*Because you cut me off every time I try to discuss this or the situation with Jody or any other serious matter with you, I'm writing this letter. Whether I will have the courage to show you the letter I don't know. Whether I can risk the possibility that the church might turn me out I do not know. A divorce is something, as a minister of the gospel, I never thought would be my lot. But the dear, beloved wife I married 23 years ago has disappeared from my life, and the woman inhabiting our home I believe despises me and all I stand for.*

*Will this get your attention? Will you consider this as a way out for both of us?*

*Your frustrated husband,*
*David*

Just as they finished reading the letter, their car crunched over the gravel driveway. "Run, Lyn-bug. Get that letter back where it belongs. Put it exactly as he had it. Quick!"

By the time David and Nell entered the den, both girls were concentrating on the Clue game. "Hi, Mom. Hi, Dad. We're finishing up our game," Millie said. "Lyn's been good. We got our homework done before we played."

"Thank you, Millie. Go straight on to bed now, both of you," Nell said.

"Tomorrow's an early day," David said. "It's our turn for carpool. We switched with the Parks." He leaned over, mussed Millie's hair and let Lyn climb onto his back for a piggyback ride upstairs. Nell kissed each of them good night, yawned, and headed to the bathroom. Millie felt funny in the pit of her stomach. How easy it was to keep a secret from her parents. And now she knew for sure they had secrets too. At least her dad did.

# 11

## Emily

⁓⟅⟆⟇⟈

Emily wiped her face with the small white towel the Y provided. Natalie put back her free weights on the rack and reached for her towel. They left their file folders on the front desk.

"See you girls tomorrow?"

"Yes, but Lucas, we're not girls." Natalie always said that to Lucas and he always laughed and replied, "Bye, girls."

Emily shivered in the cool February breeze against her damp shorts. She and Natalie had parked next to each other. Before she got in her truck, Natalie asked, "Em, how are you feeling? You know, since our rather publicized visit to the abortion clinic."

"I'm chilled. Hop in the car and let's talk a minute. If you're not in too much of a hurry." She gestured to the passenger seat of her Camry and Natalie joined her.

"Are you feeling okay now?"

Emily couldn't decide how much or how little to say. She'd trusted Natalie with so much already. In fact, she'd needed her support that day in January and as it turned out, Natalie's quick response and outspoken nature had saved her when the TV anchor had questioned them.

She looked in her bag for a tissue and wiped her face again. "I can't complain."

"Yes you can. Go ahead. Tell me."

"Well, it's sounds crazy. The cramping stopped two weeks ago and my system is more or less back to normal, I guess. The trouble is I keep having dreams about the baby. The baby who will never be."

"Do you regret it? Surely not."

"Not regret, exactly. Mostly, I couldn't risk having another child." She suppressed a sob and twisted the Kleenex around her finger. "Am I a horrible person?"

"You are sad, Emily, not horrible."

"It's not regret. More guilt and a weird kind of grief. In the latest dream, the baby's a boy. He's standing up in a crib in the middle of a meadow. Not crying. But he's looking for me. And I woke up before I could get across the field to pick him up. Yes, sadness, grieving, guilt. At my age, I was afraid to risk, you know, a handicapped child."

"Come here. You need a hug." Natalie put her arm around her shoulder and gave what amounted to a symbolic hug. "I know you. You'll be fine, Em. For one thing, you're so connected with your inner self. Maybe you can write some poems about the process. Or the dreams."

"Thanks, Nat. You're such a dear friend. I don't know what I would have done without you that day. Especially when Deborah appeared on the scene too."

"Speaking of, what do you think she's up to? She seems to have shifted her views totally to the opposite side."

"You're right. From what Tom and Tim have reported from Senior High Fellowship, Deborah is rallying the troops to do some kind of campaign for Pro-Life."

"Has the Session approved her campaign?"

"As far as I know, it hasn't been brought up. And I haven't missed any meetings."

"What do your boys think?"

"They're pretty laid back. Both of them think she's cool, but I doubt they'll do much. I keep wondering what David thinks and whether he's up to date on her plans."

"Why don't we ask him?"

"I could do that today. He's called a committee meeting on a Space for Hope project Deborah's proposing." Emily pondered what seemed to be spreading throughout Harmony Church. She felt that David needed his friends to protect him in some way. He was special to her. And to Natalie and Preston, to all their friends. She couldn't deny that something sinister had crept into the spirit of the congregation since the new associate pastor arrived. Like an ominous dark gray shadow spreading from a neglected corner to cover more and more of the light-filled church. It was something she sensed rather than thought out. She considered herself a visual thinker in that when others spoke in abstract terms, she would see images in colors and sometimes with smells and tastes accompanying them. She kept this oddity to herself. Sometimes Emily used such images in pieces of art, but Natalie was the real artist, the professional, and certainly the outspoken one. And she could be seeing out of proportion to reality.

"Would you like to go grab some coffee, Emily?"

Her question brought Emily out of her reverie. "No, I'd better go shower and prepare for the meeting."

Natalie opened the door and blew her a kiss. "See you tomorrow bright and early."

After her shower, Emily dressed quickly, left her short hair to air dry, ate a bowl of cereal, and drove to the church. She tried to ignore the strange feeling behind her eyes, a sensation close to dizziness, but not bad enough to stop, slow down, or change her plans. The only conciliation she made was to drive slower than usual to the church, barely making it on time. No opportunity to bring up anything with David.

Four committee members sat at the large conference table when she entered. Julian Denyar, in the chairman's seat, nodded solemnly at her.

Charlotte Ames, to his right, greeted her warmly and patted the place next to her, so Emily sat there. This position put her directly across from Deborah. Judge Knapp came in talking to David, who smiled at Emily in that direct open way of his, something she counted on. He spoke in turn to each person at the table.

Nancy Maddock, next to Deborah, got up from her seat to face David, grasped his hand. "Oh, David, I'm so glad you're here at this meeting," Nancy said. "Deborah and I were just saying how much we need your support for this project. You know, to show that the Senior Minister is behind this worthy mission. You know, to convince the Session to sponsor it."

Emily wondered if Nancy ever said anything without gushing. David gave Nancy the same open smile and acceptance, without saying that he was the one who called the meeting in the first place. Julian began the meeting with a prayer of thanksgiving for the day, the church, the country, the city, the gathering, and concluded with a request for guidance over their proceedings and decisions. Then he invited discussion on whether to act on Deborah's proposal to help a particular needy family she'd met at the Space for Hope.

Just then Emily heard clearly Deborah's thought piercing the air between them across the table, a thought aimed directly at her: *There's a murderer inside you.* Emily shook her head to clear it. How could Deborah think that? Unless she'd guessed that day at the clinic.

The discussion progressed with Deborah explaining the circumstances, the poor mother of twins and two other children, the father in jail for drugs, how Deborah and Harmony church could take them up and find housing. "But first let's just give them money for groceries. And I'll take the mother to the grocery store myself."

Nancy Maddock agreed, nodding like a dashboard ornament. As soon as Emily's eyes met hers, Nancy's thoughts rang in Emily's head: *I'm in love with her and soon you and everyone else here will be too. Don't be a bitch and hold out.*

Emily rubbed her eyes. She recalled how her mother once accused her of being psychic. Her tone had been angry and alarmed. Emily had shrugged it off as part of her mother's desire to protect her oldest child and keep her inconspicuous. But this was a first—actually hearing other people's thoughts as if they'd been spoken aloud. It made her dizzy. She must be losing what was left of her middle-aged mind.

She glanced at Charlotte beside her. Charlotte was thinking about her right bunion and the pain shooting through her foot. Emily shook her head. Definitely overly sensitive, just like her mother used to say. Her imagination was running away with her. The eighty-year-old emanated a warm presence like a large purring cat. Emily relaxed. She pulled out her notepad and pen.

Now Judge Whitney Knapp questioned the cost of doling out money to one specific family. "Usually, traditionally, Harmony church sponsors a program that helps a whole group of people. Not just give one poor family cash money."

"True," Julian said, "and that's our on-going After School Program in the Fit for Good gym. That wouldn't end. What Deborah's proposing, I believe, is that we allocate a moderate-sized fund she would manage that would allow her to furnish specific families in need with cash. This family now and others as similar situations arise, from time to time." His face flushed a deep magenta.

Emily recalled how surprised she and the others had been when Julian Denyar had joined them at the seafood restaurant, how Deborah had linked arms with him as they walked from their cars, how smitten he was by her charm. He'd actually enjoyed the evening. His usual stiff disdain dissolved before their eyes.

Charlotte stirred in her chair and spoke, looking around the table. "I'd like to know how much we have in the discretionary funds of Witness and Service. Do we have enough beyond our other missions to use for this family?"

Nancy Maddock shot her a stern look and replied, "Several thousand dollars as I understand it." Her thoughts sounded louder in Emily's head: *Plenty, you old crone, to do what we should do.* Emily rubbed her temples. The discussion went on. Emily doodled on her notepad, hoping to stop the thoughts from invading further. If she so much as looked at anyone at the table, she'd hear their hidden feelings. Whether it was actually happening she didn't know, but it was real enough in her mind.

Deborah told a story from her own childhood when she and her mother had lived in a tiny camper trailer for a year, moving from one state park to another, how they'd gone several weeks without any groceries to speak of. She dabbed her eyes with a small handkerchief, suddenly at the ready. Her eyeliner and mascara did not smear a bit even though her dark eyes glistened with tears. No raccoon eyes for her.

Deborah turned to Judge Knapp when she said, "Suffice it to say—as our esteemed judge might say—I know how it feels to suddenly have no money, no real place to live, and no fresh food to eat." She turned her head aside and used nasal spray she took from her purse.

The sympathy around the table was palpable.

David quietly spoke in favor of giving Deborah permission to use a limited amount of cash each month for particular families in need. As a pilot program. "We could consider it a discretionary fund such as the Deacon's Fund, the one entrusted to me for people in our own congregation who need emergency help from time to time."

Nancy patted Deborah's arm and made the motion to recommend to the Session that Witness and Service make available enough cash from its budget each month for Deborah Baker to use at her discretion to give immediate financial help to particular needy families she meets in the mission work at Fit for Good gym and the Space for Hope. Judge Knapp seconded the motion.

Emily ignored the qualms she felt in her gut and voted yes. The motion passed unanimously.

# 12

## David

⁓↑⊱

David went in to wake up Lyn for school, but she was already up and singing in the shower. He glanced around her messy room, the pile of stuffed animals and tousled sheets. A story she'd begun lay on her small desk, a basic table he'd built for her when she'd requested a desk like her older sisters'. David remembered how he'd slaved over building it from scraps of good cherry wood Preston had given him. Preston constructed authentic reproductions of Colonial Williamsburg with the perfectionism and precision he brought to his practice of ophthalmology. David might proclaim the gospel of Jesus of Nazareth, but he'd never be a skilled carpenter like his Master. He'd hammered his fingers more than the boards, and although he managed to complete the desk, sanded it to a smooth finish and applied a pleasing stain and sealer, the thing itself looked like what it was—the first awkward attempt of an untalented klutz. Yet Lyn loved using the table desk. He picked up her notebook paper and read the beginning of her story.

*Once upon a time three sisters lived in a faraway land in a small cottage on the edge of a big forest. They used to live in town with their mother and father, but alas!*

*When the plague devastated the country, their mother and father caught it and died.*

*Only the girls—Eliza, Eunice, and Erin—escaped. They found refuge in the forest, far from town, living on berries, nuts, and food their dog Sequoia brought to them while they slept.*

Lyn had underlined *devastated* and *refuge*. Spelling words for the week, no doubt. He thought about a story of three sisters, like so many fairytales. And their own family. He sighed. His lovely daughters, each with such promise. And now, Jody gone, hospitalized, and he had no idea when or if they'd ever be able to bring her home. If they did, she'd be changed, and the rest of the family as well. In fact they'd already been changed by her illness. Writing a story was probably one way his youngest was dealing with the loss of what had been normal. He wondered how she'd develop the story. Lyn sometimes had difficulty finishing her imaginative creations. Millie might be called on to help her bring it to completion.

David had more or less promised Millie she could go visit Jody at spring break, provided the doctors said she could have company. The trouble was, of course, that he had not told Nell he'd promised Millie anything. It would be hard, if not impossible, to convince his wife that Millie could handle the visit on her own. It could be her fifteenth birthday present.

He picked up Lyn's dirty clothes, dropped them down the chute, and went to the kitchen. He cracked six eggs and whipped them in the small stainless steel bowl, buttered the bread for the toast. Nell had put her cereal bowl in the sink before she left for work. If Nell complained that they didn't have the money for Millie to fly up to D.C., he thought he'd pop an artery. With all the recent purchases she'd made, it might be true, but making the trip was crucial to Millie.

After her track practice last week, David had walked with Millie as she cooled down. He'd arrived early so he could watch her run—her long lean body moving smoothly, brown hair streaming out behind, long legs like a gazelle's. As they strolled, Millie told him her bad dream. She trembled as she said how terrified the dream had made her. Something about Jody in a dark spooky place calling to her for help. "Dad, please, I've got to go see Jody," she'd said. "She needs me."

David felt the tug from Millie he always felt. He liked to give her what she asked, she so rarely asked for anything. He'd told her they'd work something out somehow. She counted on him to come through. Especially as a counter-force to Nell.

Now he had to work it out with Nell, who never seemed available to him. What had he not tried yet? As he stirred the eggs, he considered possible tactics. Maybe he'd go to Nell's booth at the Expo Center. He called upstairs to the girls that breakfast was ready and poured himself a cup of coffee. Yes, he'd go there with flowers. Woo her in front of her friends. Get her to leave for a quick lunch and they could talk. Flora would cover the booth for a while.

In line at the Fresh Market, he carried eighteen roses in the gorgeous shades of a sunset. Maybe this would do the trick. The man in the blue vest at the register took a look at the bundle. "Good choice." He scanned the roses, took the money, and looked up at David. "I don't know what you did, man, but good choice. Those roses ought to make up for just about anything bad you've done."

David grinned at the cashier. "Thanks. Hope so." As a minister, he had very few opportunities to be considered wicked. Most people, at least those who knew he was a man of the cloth, would separate themselves from him as if he didn't know anything of what regular human beings experienced. One aspect of being a preacher that irked him. He left the grocery feeling warm inside, as if he'd just reconnected with the human race, in particular the male of the species.

At the Expo Center, he searched the huge grounds for Nell's beige van. On the second go-around, he found it with her logo and bumper sticker—*The Old, the New, the Beautiful, and the Unusual.* He parked in the waiting zone near the closest entrance and went in to look for her booth. This was the first time he'd visited her at work. His heart pounded hard and fast. He reprimanded himself for being nervous.

The place was gigantic with a high ceiling supported by fretwork of steel and on the concrete floor were long tables of antiques, lamps, furniture, doodads, and what he considered tacky junk. After walking up and down long rows of merchants, he finally located glass cases of smaller goods. Dolls of every description, small beaded handbags, china dishes, miniature furniture for dollhouses, cigarette lighters, chess sets. At last, estate jewelry. Merchants beside long glassed-in counters, some in rocking chairs knitting and chatting. Others clustered in small groups around coffee. A few played chess or cards. David spotted Flora Hendrix, but not Nell.

"Well, hiya, Dah-veed," Flora sang out, patting her stiff frosted blonde hair. "Nell ought to be back in a sec. She and another dealer went to check out a shipment from a big estate in Rhode Island." She eyed the bundle of roses. "Well, well, well. Look what you brought, you big handsome romantic, you. Let me quickly procure a vase." She pronounced it *vauzz*. She reached under the counter and pulled out an ugly painted container and swiftly filled it from the water cooler across the aisle.

David felt awkward, like a teenager on his first prom date. "I thought maybe Nell could leave for a lunch break with me."

Flora studied her red fingernails. "Well sir, she and Stefan should be here soon, but they probably grabbed lunch on the way back. Sorry." She didn't look sorry at all. In fact, she looked secretly amused. David felt more embarrassed, out of his element. The place smelled like a musty attic with a layer of Flora's heavy cologne topping it off. He'd better leave.

"Tell her for me, please, that I came to see her." He heard how stiff and formal he sounded.

"Why, David, what are you doing here?" Nell called from behind him. "Slumming, perhaps?" Beside her stood a tall young man in tight jeans and a red flannel shirt, carrying a large box fastened with metal bands. Nell touched the man's arm possessively and gestured to the cases in the corner.

Flora rushed over with the vase of roses. "Look what someone special brought you, Nell." David smiled and watched as Nell glanced first at the young man, then pulled her eyes away and over to him.

David nodded, waited. Nell glanced at the roses. "These are lovely. Lovely. What's the occasion, David?"

"Aren't you going to introduce me to your friend?" He nodded and put out his hand to the young man. "David. David Archer, Nell's husband." He hoped not with too much emphasis.

The man put the box on the floor near the corner, wiped his hands on his jeans, and stretched out his hand. "Stefan Wallington. Nell's helped me get my business started. She's great." His grip was the kind that crippled arthritic fingers, yet did not fully engage the other person's hand. David had felt every handshake ever extended—after church in the vestibule, in the business he was in. He looked hard at Stefan. *Watch out*, he wanted to warn Nell, but she'd never listen.

He turned to Nell. "I thought maybe you might take a break for lunch and we could talk. How about it?"

Flora spoke up before Nell could say anything. "Go on. I'll mind the store. No one's coming in, anyway, at least until the seminar's over at 3:00. Go on with your sweetie." She smiled flirtatiously at David. "I would if I were you. A man bringing a dozen and a half beautiful roses in your favorite colors has to be obeyed."

"Okay, okay. I'll go, but look for that couple from Florida who came by yesterday. They swore they'd be back for the diamond and sapphire combo." Nell grabbed her handbag from the cabinet beside her, slung it over her shoulder, gave one more look at Stefan, and led the way out. David mouthed *Thank you* to Flora, who shrugged and nodded. So much for courtship of his wife, he thought as he left the cavernous expo center.

"I'd better take my car," Nell said as they walked through the parking lot.

"Why is that? I'm glad to bring you back, any time you say. I thought we'd just go over to City Range. That's close. Or the Phoenix. We haven't been there in ages."

"David, I don't know what you've got up your sleeve, but this is a business day for me, and anyway, I've eaten lunch, so I'll just have some tea while you eat." Nell walked straight to her van. David followed.

"All right, then. I'll ride with you." He was sick of her avoidance techniques.

"Have it your way." She flung herself into the driver's seat, slammed the door, turned the switch and revved the engine before he got his seat belt on.

"Are you selling much this week?" He'd ease into the subject. She always assumed he resented her business, so usually he didn't inquire. These days nothing he attempted worked well. A tension headache was beginning its relentless pressure at the base of his skull. It would soon work its way up and over his entire head, behind his eyes, his temples.

Nell ignored his question and switched on a cassette, and sped out of the lot onto the road leading to the by-pass. "Where do you want to eat lunch? I'm not going to decide. I've eaten, as I said."

"City Range will be fine. A booth will give us privacy." From the cassette, a crazy group was belting out a song about wild women and younger men. David listened to the words. Amazing. Amazing that his strict wife who supervised the girls' habits, music, TV shows, and even took careful note of what books they read in school, who their friends were, would possess, much less listen to such music. He stifled a laugh. A new, refreshing side of his wife. "Interesting song you're listening to. Where'd you get that? The girls?"

Nell gave him a scathing glance. "No. It was a gift. Like it?"

David stretched his arm out on the back of the seat. "It's raucous, raunchy, and I have to say—pretty funny. Have Millie and Lyn heard it?"

"Goodness, no. I'm not a fool, David." They pulled into the only parking spot available in front of the restaurant.

"As usual, a perfect parking place. You must be living right."

After the waitress brought him a chicken salad and water and Nell a sweet tea, Nell called her back and ordered a chocolate dessert with a look of defiance at David, as if he might reprimand her. That would be the last thing he'd do. He had to convince her to let Millie visit Jody.

"I believe you're enjoying your venture into the estate jewelry business, aren't you?" David took a bite of his salad and waited.

"Of course I am." She opened her Daytimer and checked something, then looked at David. "You didn't drag me away from market to ask that. What do you have on your mind that couldn't wait until tonight?"

"You're right. I do have something on my mind. Here's the thing." He swallowed some ice water. This was going to be difficult. "During spring break, Millie wants to go up to see Jody. By herself. She approached me about it, and I told her you and I would discuss it. Before you say anything, let me say that she believes Jody needs her, and the doctor said the last time we talked that she was about ready to see some family."

Nell glared at him with her Hate Look. A combination of jealousy, pure despising, and something that might be sheer terror underneath—her eyebrows in high arched position with wrinkles between deepened and her strong jaw set to match her intense glare. He remembered the first time he witnessed that look, and before he could have named it or believed the beautiful, statuesque woman he was engaged to was capable of hating. They were eating dinner with her parents in the solarium. Dr. Richard Forche, her formidable father, was entertaining them with a story of a surgery one of his residents had conducted. He referred to a distant cousin of Nell named Dane something. And said, "You remember him, Nell, the young attorney. He married a resident recently. She's a lovely and most capable surgeon. Reminds me a little of you, or how you used to be." That's when she gave her father The Hate Look. David thought at the time he hoped never to be on the receiving end. Over the course of twenty years, he'd been withered several times by the look.

After a beat or two, she spoke. "I smell a conspiracy. You and Millie are at it again, scheming to do something you know I will oppose. You two gang up, like kids on a playground."

"This is not a scheme. Remember I told her you and I would discuss it. Let's do that, Nell, please. Not just oppose each other out of hand. Let's see what might be the benefits, if any, for her to go. And what might be the drawbacks. Money, for one. I happen to believe we can afford her plane ticket, and she could stay in the guest quarters of Winslow Farms. What are some of the good things that could come of her making the trip?"

"You tell me. Doubtless, you've already made up your mind."

"Nell, please. Say something that might be good or bad about the trip."

"Well, I can't take any money from my account. It's all needed in the business right now. If you think you can afford it, then money's not the problem." She took out a tissue and dabbed the corners of her eyes. "What if Jody's situation upsets Millie? What if she can't handle seeing her adored big sister in a locked room, away from anything she might use to harm herself or others? Millie may like to act grown-up, but she's only fourteen. How can we allow her to travel by herself on an airplane?"

David reached across the table and took Nell's hand. "First of all, Jody's not confined in a padded locked room. She stays in a dorm room and has chores of some sort on the farm or the dining hall. She's in therapy, group and individual. Jody's condition isn't catching. She's not going to pass it to her sister. And Millie's made of sturdy stuff."

He gently rubbed Nell's hand along the index finger. Smooth and well-groomed as usual. He kept his eyes on her face, now in a more relaxed expression. "There's something intuitive about Millie that deserves our respect. She and Jody have a special bond, which, frankly I don't feel with Jody. I wish I did. You may, but I don't."

"But, David, what about the plane trip? She's never flown by herself, and she's only fourteen. Can you get free to go with her?"

David cleared his throat. Millie had her heart set on traveling alone. "Nell, she'll be fifteen by that time and anyway she'll be all right. For one thing, the airline assigns someone to look after minors traveling alone. And she won't have to change planes. It's a straight shot to D.C. The trip can be her birthday gift from us."

Nell removed her hand from his caress. "Millie's stronger than I am. That's probably something I resent. I admit it. But I worry about her. She's too sensitive." Nell suppressed a sob, coughed into her tissue instead. "I'm afraid. I'm afraid she'll be hurt down deep." She straightened in her seat. "I'm afraid I won't be able to help her at all." She glared at him, her eyebrows in battle position. "You. You, on the other hand, are more on Millie's wave length."

Was she relenting? Her steely armor might be softening. He thought of the metal artist he'd watched, mesmerized, when they visited Penland School of Crafts last year. The slight, gray-haired man who looked too old and thin to handle something so heavy and dangerous had bent the red hot steel with such quiet strength, almost gentleness, it had amazed him. The image of the sculptor returned to his mind at odd moments. Now he watched Nell's color deepen in her face and throat.

His therapist had reminded him often enough that his wife was one of those people who needed constant reassurance, but sometimes he balked. What kind of a gift was it if you felt maneuvered into giving it? Still the present cause warranted it. He smiled at her. "You do fine with all the girls, Nell, and each one presents her own challenge. Maybe, at the moment, Millie finds me acceptable, but you know how it is with a teenager. That could change in an instant." He called for the check as the waitress passed and turned back to Nell. "Let's give it a try. I believe she'll be a great advance scout for us. Jody will open up to her, where right now she won't give us the time of day."

Nell opened her bag, took out her compact and lipstick, reapplied the bright red with a practiced hand, snapped it closed, and said, "Okay. You make the arrangements. And you'll pay for it, right?"

"I'll do it, but, Nell, let's both tell her tonight. She needs to hear it from you. That'll mean a lot to her."

She gathered her things, gave a slight nod he took for agreement, and stood up.

Again the confident business woman. "I've got to get back. You've accomplished your mission."

David left the tip and followed her out. Dismissed. They didn't talk on the way back. He tried not to care so much. The headache he hadn't considered while they talked came roaring back full force.

# 13

## David

David moved fast to get out to the Freestone campus by 2:30 for Leadership Goodwin. Today instead of sitting in a meeting with a community leader speaking, they were to be led in group exercises. As part of trust building, they were paired up, one blindfolded, the other designated as the Alpha-leader and away they went through the Freestone University gardens—the twenty-some-odd participants, among them David Archer and Ted Parks. As luck would have it, David drew the role of Alpha and Ted was blindfolded. David laughed to himself over this—Ted loved control and he did too, but he practiced being receptive, circumspect. Some would say passive. "Alpha-leader is a bit redundant, don't you think?"

"I hate games," Ted said from behind the bandana, loudly, as if covering his eyes made his partner deaf. "Especially games like this."

"Somehow that doesn't surprise me, Ted." David laughed. "But at least you're not with a total stranger. You trust me already, right?"

"Well, sure. So why do we have to do the damn exercise?"

Ted was the kind of elder every Presbyterian minister needed and depended on—competent, committed, and unrelentingly self-confident. Today he was different. He looked awkward like that young moose he'd seen staggering behind the tall water shrubs in Maine. Belligerent yet shy, trying to hide from scrutiny. He touched Ted on the arm and he flinched. "It's all right, man. A blind man we used to pick up for church when I was a boy told me that it helped for him to hold my arm, instead of the other way around. So, Ted, take my arm and let's smell the garden together."

He did as he was told. David heard his deep intake of breath. Resignation, he thought.

"Okay, Ted, in about two steps we'll be on a fairly rough area with some broken flagstones, so just sense where you are by how I'm walking. I'll warn you of any bad spots."

Ted let out something that could be taken for assent. More like a cough. They did fine for about fifteen feet. David wanted to take in the scene around him—the roses in their early buds, the oaks with golden tassels—but he kept his eyes focused on Ted and where they were heading. An acrid odor emanated from Ted. *Fear.* David recalled an essay on bees and how they and larger animals could easily pick up the odor of fear from humans. This must be what was meant. Dogs certainly knew and so did cats. He knew for a fact that Ted disliked animals. No pets allowed, Emily had told him once. Emily, on the other hand, felt comfortable with all sorts of creatures, animal and human; no odd traits seemed to put her off. That was probably one reason he felt he could let down his guard with her. David liked thinking of Emily, but today he needed to focus on her husband.

There were still vestiges of winter in the gardens, and the recent surprise frost last week had left the lilac leaves drooping and woeful though he could see a few pale lavender blooms resisting the effects of the recent freeze. "Ted, we're at the end of the first section. How're you doing?" The day was cool with a slight breeze, but Ted was perspiring.

"Remind me, David, not to go blind. I can't stand not knowing where I'm going, what's ahead, who might be waiting to jump me. I've got to see around corners, anticipate everyone's next move. This is hell."

David laughed. "Practicing law has made you quite the defensive one, huh?"

Up ahead were the tall trimmed hedges of Freestone's famous maze—complicated and tricky to navigate even with 20/20 vision. Many a new freshman had suffered panic attacks, so Emily had told him. Now he and Ted had to walk through it.

"Ted, it's going to be a bit tougher up ahead. We have the famous Freshman Rat Trap, as the Freestone kids call the garden maze. Can you sense how tall the hedges are on either side?" He waited for Ted's response. When he didn't say anything, David went on. "Now I guess you'll have to trust me in more ways than one. Not only to keep you from falling, or ramming your shin on boulders or slogging through wet flower beds, but to get us through this maze without too many blind alleys. Pardon the pun." Ted's grip on his arm tightened. "I think I'll just do it without thinking too much. Use my intuition. How does that sound?"

Ted turned his covered face toward him. "Do what you think best."

"All right. Steady as we go. Tell you what, I'll talk about some things I've wanted to talk over with you as we make our way. That might take your mind off your blindness, and it surely will help me stay off worrying too much about getting us hopelessly lost."

"They'll come after us, won't they? If we stay out here too long."

"Talk about trust. Good old Ted, don't worry. we'll find our way, or they'll send a search party." He needed to talk out his misery with a friend, not just a therapist. He'd just blurt it out and hope Ted could give him a good listening ear, maybe forget his fear of no control while they walked. "Here's the thing. I'd like to talk over something with you. You and Emily seem to have a good close marriage. I'm having a difficult time, more than ever, with Nell. You know, it's hard for a minister to confess such—or any problem to anyone, especially a friend who's in his church, but there it is. Marital problems. In your preacher. I'm quite sure that Nell would pitch a fit if she knew I said a word. Not that she would admit we have problems. She's always on the defensive with me, ready for a fight about everything and nothing." He guided them around a strategically placed granite boulder and took the next bend. Voices came through the tall hedge to their right, so maybe this was the right path. "She will not discuss Jody. We're both torn up about her. I am for sure. I assume she is too, but all she wants to do is shop and fill her life with stuff. More and more I'm feeling anger and resentment and utter frustration with her." He decided not to mention the lunch conversation where they had come closer than they had in months to actually talking about Jody.

Ted stumbled but caught himself and stopped, turned toward him. "You know, David, I don't do divorce law, but I can recommend one or two. Not in Harmony Pres."

"Whoa, not so fast. Who said anything about divorce? I just want your wise counsel, as a man who seems to be managing his own marriage rather well."

Ted took a deep breath. "Thanks. But it's not always easy for me with Emily. She's been a great wife, a real helpmeet, in many ways, though she hates to entertain. But sometimes she'll say something or take a notion that I can't fathom. How does a woman's mind work anyway?"

David turned them gently away from the dead end they'd reached in the maze. "Let's try this way," he said, guiding Ted to the path off to the left at a crazy angle.

"What kind of notion? She always appears so level-headed."

"It's kind of a long story. And something I don't talk about." Ted took another deep intake of air. "Are we nearly out of this confounded trap? It smells like manure back here." David noticed he hadn't said shit. His usual discretion must have returned.

"We'll make it, eventually, I suppose. But with women, who knows?" Maybe Ted wasn't the friend to discuss this with. Ted seemed to want to tell him something troubling about Emily. If so, David would be in his usual role—the listener. Emily once had told him that women talk with each other about nearly everything. He thought of her and Natalie and knew they confided in each other, without reservation. He envied women for such close friendships. Did Nell have any close friends? She seemed to keep herself apart, not just from him, but from all others. Maybe not Flora.

He hoped so. She'd need friends if they should separate. And what about that young guy in the flannel shirt?

He was beginning to sweat too. "What about you and Emily? How do you maintain good communication?"

Ted stretched and loosened his grip on David. "Well, I've always believed that we should have time off by ourselves, away from the children. Fortunately, before my parents died, they took care of all three several times a year. Of course, Meredith is at college now, so it's just the boys. Now we ask a young male teacher to come when we go off for a weekend."

A crow flew up from the hedge ahead of them, his black wings iridescent in the sunlight. Ted walked with that proud stride David knew to be his usual lawyer walk. "So, a weekend away has been the secret? Of course, in my line of work, it'd have to be during the week. And I suppose she'd have to enjoy sex."

Ted laughed and puffed up a bit more. "That helps, yes." They were at another decision point with paths going to right or left or straight ahead. David hesitated, listening. He heard the waterfall from the lake's dam off to his right. Everything else seemed quiet, except some chittering sparrows in the closest hedge. Ted tightened his hold on David's arm. "We're lost."

"No, I don't think so. But we are at a decision point. What do you say? Left, right, or continue on the central path?"

"Is this question political or religious?"

"Could be either or both, I suppose."

Ted said, "Well, hell, preacher, you like to lead us down the middle or to the left. Not ever to the right."

"All that does is eliminate one way."

"When in doubt, what do you usually do?"

"Let's see. When I'm feeling cloudy in my thinking, with no clear direction, I tend to keep to the middle path. Under the illusion it's the safest way." The big bell began ringing. "I think that's our warning bell. We have ten more minutes." He hadn't gotten clarity about his relationship with Nell, nor had Ted told him what bothered him about Emily. It wasn't sex—Ted had more than implied Emily enjoyed sex. He wished Nell did. It had been a long time. Had she ever liked being with him?

He pulled himself up, loosened his shoulders and back. "All right. This time I'm not leading us down the wide middle way but up this narrow path to the left. Here we go, and Ted, we are going to walk fast up this trail. It's fairly smooth—no big rocks that I can see—but it bends quite a bit, so hold on and let's climb out of this conundrum."

They set off, without talking, just moving side by side on the path not much wider than the two of them. Four hairpin turns and they reached the finish. They walked under an arch of privet hedge entwined with thorny bare branches of climbing roses not yet in bud. A low gate made of twisted tree branches opened out to the lush green field near the lake. A pair of black swans glided by in the middle distance. A table set up with water, snacks, and the smiling faces of the leaders greeted them. At the signal from the chairman, David turned to Ted and removed his bandana blindfold.

Ted blinked and frowned in the sunlight. "Thank you, David." He gripped his hand. "Thank you for leading us through the damn maze. And for your trust." David studied his friend's face, now open and vulnerable. "That means more to me than you know," Ted said and coughed.

"Likewise, my friend." They shook hands and joined the others.

# 14

# David

Two weeks later on his day off, David sat on the gray and teal sofa, facing his therapist Madeleine Crispin. A small fountain gurgled on the bookshelf behind her. Madeleine was dressed in light purple and turquoise, a loose-fitting outfit of pants and top. Her feet rested on a padded footstool to help relieve her back. Silver gray hair framed her narrow face in a neat short style. After he talked about his anguish over his oldest daughter and his worry about Nell, Madeleine asked him to tell her about any recent dreams that he remembered.

"I usually don't remember my dreams, but this one woke me. I got up, went to the bathroom, and when I got back in bed, I went immediately back to sleep and dreamed the same thing again. We're in a brightly colored hot air balloon—me, Emily Parks, her best friend Natalie, and Preston, Natalie's husband. All good friends of mine. Nell is nowhere in the dream, except that, even dreaming, I'm worried about where she is and wondering if she's out shopping, how much she's spending. But in the balloon, Preston is pretending to be fishing over the side. Nat and Emily are singing U2's "With or Without You" and giggling like little girls. We sail over a beautiful landscape like a National Geographic special of a verdant South American country."

"You dream in color?"

"Yes, doesn't everyone?"

"No, but go on. How did you feel?"

"Exhilarated. And free. Though I couldn't catch my breath at first. But then the scene changed and I was trudging along a muddy path, stumbling over tree roots, big gnarled roots jutting out. It was the kind of mud that sucks at your boots, only I wasn't wearing boots. I was wearing my sandals in that awful mud. My good Birkenstocks. I was at Montreat, our church conference grounds, only different. Pitch dark on a muddy road. Lost and exhausted and soaked to the skin in the rain. I had to lug this big suitcase my mother had given me, she called a grip. I couldn't find the right inn where we were staying. Everything looked strange. Every door was the wrong one. A tornado was heading this way and I needed to find my family and warn them. The children were all young. That's when I woke up, soaking wet with sweat, my heart pounding."

"What do you make of the dream?"

"I thought that was your business to interpret such." He smiled at her, teasing. "What do you make of it?"

When she didn't say anything, he waited a minute and then tried to make light of it. "What do I make of it? Other than I shouldn't have eaten leftover chicken divan last night. I don't know." He paused. She waited.

"Well, the last part of the dream is pretty obvious, I guess. A perfect visual of how stuck and frustrated I feel. And I'm afraid my children are in danger." He paused again and waited for Madeleine to say something.

When she remained silent, he ventured another thought. "Also, it's a recurring dream. Not the mud, but it's one of what I call the lost-outside-a-building-where-I-can't-find-the-right-door dreams. And usually there's a time pressure, like this one with the tornado. I've never understood them, but they leave me upset and frustrated." He looked at his hands and realized he was wringing them.

"David, you're on the way. The subconscious mind can inform the conscious. I want you to go over both sections of the dream, all the details, and write down what occurs to you." Madeleine stood up, smoothed her skirt. "Look at how the dream applies to your life right now." She poured a cup of water and handed it to him. Then she sat and recorded something in her notebook. "Now I want to circle back to Jody. How does it serve you to call her therapist so often?"

"I'm not sure. It's related, I think, to how helpless I feel. I want her back to normal, you know. Healthy, and preferably back home in Goodwin. Why doesn't the therapist give me a clue how I can help? All she does— nearly every day—is to assure me they're taking good care of Jody, that Jody right now doesn't feel ready yet to talk to me or Nell, and that she'll let me know when the time is right. No comfort there."

"So again, how does calling her so often serve *your* needs?" She looked expectantly at him, searched his face with her penetrating eyes.

David suddenly felt that he might cry. Crazy. He rarely cried. Certainly not around other people. He turned his head toward the window, cleared his throat.

"Probably it does no good at all. But I have to call. It's not logical, but what if I skip several days? Something awful might happen to Jody."

"David, do you blame yourself for her attempting to take her life?"

"In the sense that my brother killed himself, yes. What if Jody has inherited the tendency that drove Drew to suicide?" Heat rose through his body. Anger surged. "I want to yell at Jody, 'You don't have to make that choice! Just because you have a faulty gene from my family, you do not have to do that. It's not fated. Or preordained.'" He rubbed his face with both hands. "I'm sorry. But sometimes I want to shake her back to her senses."

"When you said a minute ago that you want Jody 'back to normal' and 'back home' and just now 'back to her senses,' I hear you saying that you'd like time to roll back until everything is as it was before she left."

"If only that were possible."

"Right. You know as well as I that everyone moves along on his or her own path. One action sets up what happens next and so on. David, Jody is growing and changing in her own individual way. She may someday return to your home, but she will never *go back* to who she was before the suicide attempt."

"In other words, I should be open to her emerging as a new person. Certainly in my line of work, I should." He let out a long breath.

"That gives you something else to work on. Our time is up for today." She stood and shook his hand and regarded him with her kind eyes.

David suppressed his desire to have more time. Once every two weeks seemed to be the only time he could talk out his inner turmoil with anyone, especially someone not associated with the church. "Thank you, Madeleine. This certainly isn't easy."

"You're right. It's not an easy process."

David liked her voice. For such a small woman he'd have to describe as feisty, she possessed a full-bodied voice that soothed even when she spoke hard truths. Her voice wasn't deep like a man's, yet it gave him the impression of depth. He might be seeing her twice a month, just to be reassured by her quiet, deep voice.

In the parking lot, David sat in his Honda, closed his eyes and played back the session. He wished he could share with Madeleine or someone, the deadness of spirit that occupied so much of his mental landscape, as if a large part of him were slowly ossifying, transforming him into petrified wood. What could he do to be made new? One of the famous seven deadly sins—*acedia*—that's what plagued him. Sloth was the name traditionally given to it, but acedia expressed the condition more accurately. Not sloth or laziness. The pit of self pity was close to the quicksand of acedia. He tried to pray. No words came. Wordlessly, he appealed to God for mercy and help.

As he rested his eyes, the scene from the crucial time of Drew's suicide returned.

David had been in grad school in England and flew home for the funeral. He remembered how agitated he'd been, flipping through the airline magazines, pacing the narrow aisles, working crossword puzzles, gulping down water. How he dreaded seeing his parents. He knew in his heart of hearts that both his mother and father had adored Drew. They were proud of David, yes, pleased he'd planned to follow father and grandfather into the ministry. But they loved Drew with the kind of effortless love that did not have to be earned. As he, David, had habitually tried too hard to earn from both parents. And he, too, had loved Drew, had seen in him from the time they were boys that his little brother was the natural athlete. He'd taught Drew to bat and pitch and throw, to catch flies and retrieve grounders. He'd excelled. At basketball, the same thing. He'd taught Drew to dribble, pass, dodge and weave, pivot and shoot. He'd been as proud as a coach at the way Drew outplayed him.

David took out his wallet and looked at the last picture he had of the four of them together. Before he left for grad school, Drew had teased him that he'd come back with a British accent, hamming it up like a snooty butler or lord of the manor. They'd laughed and then had gone to the closest thing to a British pub Little Rock had to offer. The plane circled and landed at the airport in Norfolk, Virginia, a city foreign to him. His father had retired from the ministry here—this town was only a temporary residence.

His parents had stood side by side waiting for him at the gate. They had not seen him yet, so he caught their unguarded faces. It was as if each were encased in a plastic resin mold, totally separate from each other. Both had aged in just the year he'd been away. His mother, Mary Frances, seemed not stooped, but lopsided, one side of her body markedly lower than the other. His father, Claude, usually the soul of dignity and military uprightness curled in on himself, as if he might fold up at any moment into a fetal position. Their faces were ashen and incredibly weary.

When they saw him, they jerked themselves up, replacing the masks they used for the world. How do you comfort people whose favorite son has killed himself?

Not for the first time, David saw that he was the elder son from the Prodigal Son story, but also the prodigal who'd been absent when his younger brother needed him, when his parents needed him. By pursuing his own dream of education abroad, he'd let them down. Even back then,

David recognized that he couldn't have prevented Drew from doing himself in, yet he should have tried.

What had Madeleine said about each person's individual path? Drew—still an enigma—the why never fully answered and never would be. The old anger burning at his brother, his gifted beloved brother. Such a waste. And afterward, a terrible example of one irreparable choice that would go down as possibility from one generation to the next. He'd go home now and call Jody's therapist.

# 15

## Nell

~⟫~

Nell and Flora drove the van from the show in Nashville to a Cracker Barrel, the one closest to I-40, heading east. Flora was driving, but Nell couldn't keep from giving instructions. It would be dark when they left the restaurant.

"Park as close to the front door and the windows as you can."

"You paranoid or something?"

"Just careful. We've got our best of the best in there." Nell knew she worried more than Flora all the time, but she had so much more at stake now. What with the cost of Jody's care.

Flora circled the building twice. Nothing close available, so she parked in the back. "Oh well, don't worry. Our safe is safe. The place is swarming with people. Mostly families with kids."

Nell knew half her mind would remain with the van as they ate supper.

She ordered her favorites—pancakes, crisp bacon, soft scrambled eggs—the works.

"Breakfast again, Nell?"

"I need comfort food."

Flora ate steak, a loaded baked potato and green beans. "Me too. I suppose your handsome preacher husband is looking after the girls this weekend."

"Actually, only Lyn. We allowed Millie to fly up to D.C. and see Jody."

"Really? She must be doing better."

"Maybe. Anyway, the powers that be seemed to encourage a visit from her sister." Nell peppered her eggs and tasted them, added salt.

"Not parents yet?"

"No, not yet. David's good with care taking. Better than I am, actually."

"Really? That's good, I guess. It allows you to get away without worrying about your children."

"Right. Not about *them* anyway." Nell swirled the syrup over the pancakes, watched the butter make a pattern like small yellow islands in a brown swamp. She preferred hot syrup that melted the butter, but you couldn't have everything.

"Nell, would you say that David is pious? Does he pray all the time or something? I can tell you don't like something about him. Like my Edgar—I detest the way he lounges on the couch watching those incessant football games, alternating with stupid sitcoms. Or he's out back in what he calls his "auto studio," building or repairing a car. Screw him, I say. So, what about David?"

"He spends a lot of time up in his Crow's Nest or Eagle's Eerie or whatever he calls the office room in the attic. With the door closed. Studying, reading, writing sermons, praying? For all I know, he could be up there jerking off."

"You're so wicked."

They looked at each other and burst out laughing. The waitress returned.

"Pie for anyone?"

"No, no pie. Just coffee, please," Flora said.

They drank their coffee for a few minutes in silence.

"What do you think he fantasizes about?" Flora asked.

"You mean besides getting me to give up jewelry shows on weekends. He wants me to sit beside the girls in church, preferably in a pew up front, looking up adoringly as he expounds on some boring subject. You know, Flora, I thought he'd end up after seminary teaching in some prestigious university. Never mind. That was a long time ago. I'm just glad to have this business with you."

"Escape?"

"You bet. Escape from suffocating expectations." Nell drank her coffee, grateful to be away from home.

"I for one like to escape from Edgar's fantasies. He likes role playing—you know—all the cliches. Nurse. BoPeep. Lady cop, complete with handcuffs. You name it."

"Too much info, Flora." Nell's mind floated to the way David watched Emily. She knew he'd shifted his focus from her to the petite, brunette wife of his friend Ted. How disgusting was that? She caught the waitress's eye.

"On second thought, I'd like a piece of pecan pie. And more coffee. Two forks, please." Pecan pie might not satisfy the gnawing pain in her stomach, but it would taste like comfort.

As they shared the gooey sweet dessert, she told the story of how Millie had spent her allowance on a whole pecan pie from Strossner's Bakery and had them mail it to Jody. Nell laughed at herself for being so skeptical at how Jody would receive it. She'd loved it and called home for the first time since she'd been at Winslow Farms. "You might call it the $2000 gift pie. Jody's call may mean she's better—at least enough to let Millie be our emissary, as David calls her. So maybe she's saved us some money."

When they reached the van, Nell saw something was wrong. A light was on inside and she'd left it dark. She ran around to the rear. Scratch marks. "Oh, no. Flora, we've been hit. Quick! Check the safe.'

"Let's not overreact," Flora said as she opened the back.

They stood side by side, staring at the boxes strewn around, their covers off, and the blankets thrown in the corner. Flora reached under the mat and lifted the metal covering over the spare tire where they kept the safe. "It's gone, Nell."

"No. It can't be. Let me see." Nell felt around the trunk . "The best of the best. It has to be here." She couldn't believe the thieves had found the safe. Used metal cutters to get it loose from the chain lock. Took the whole thing. She leaned against the side of the van. "No. No. No."

"Back to the restaurant, Nell. We've got to call the police."

"I told you we should've parked in front. At least under the lights."

Flora looked around at her, but kept walking fast. Without a word of apology.

In what seemed to be hours, two policemen drove up and parked. Nell and Flora led them to the van. With flashlights flashing and notepads, pens recording what Nell and Flora said, the lead man said, "I suppose you have adequate insurance to cover the items."

Flora explained that estate jewelry couldn't be insured in their business. The frequent turnover of inventory made that impossible. The thin young guy beside the lead cop inspected the under side of the van.

"Just as I thought," he said. "Someone put a tracking device on your van. They simply followed you from the show. They may have been observing what you had and watched you pack up. As soon as you went in to eat, they broke in."

"We've seen something like this before, but haven't been able to pin it on anyone. So far." The older man yawned. "We'll contact you if and when."

"So what can we do? It's our business. They wiped us out." Nell could hear her voice turning shrill.

With a shrug and murmurs about trying to get to the bottom of the crime, the two cops drove away.

Nell and Flora decided to find a room rather than drive through the night. As Flora snored in the adjoining bed, Nell stared into the dark, her eyes drawn to the crack of light in the drapes. Finally, she got up and took her handbag into the bathroom. At least she had the cash and checks in the zipped section from the Thursday and Friday sales. She counted everything. How far would $3500 go? Especially, when they divided it in half.

She dug around until she found the folded envelope she carried everywhere. A sob and a deep sigh escaped, as if her body registered the hurt her mind kept denying. She remembered what a surprise the letter had been, just as her father predicted. Opening the folded letter, she read:

*Dear Nell,*

*You may faint when you see this note from me. It's been years since we had any contact, and I know you never expected to hear from me again. Your mother gave up trying to persuade me— your stubborn, prideful father—to reach out to you. The question of forgiveness had been raised any number of times by your mother until I put an end to it. STOP. No more references to our wayward daughter, I proudly declared. Yes, I always maintained you should have asked my forgiveness for the way you disappointed me by allowing yourself to become pregnant by that young man we'd all been enamored by. But your mother maintained that I should have asked forgiveness of you for my strong reaction when you confessed your indiscretion.*

*If you are reading this letter, I have passed from this life. When I was in Emory Hospital, I sent for my attorney and with your mother as a tearful witness along with Dr. Ogletree, my primary physician, I set up a trust fund for you.*

*I acknowledge that hardening my heart did nothing good. In fact the bitterness grew and twisted within me, while you went blithely on with your life. Missing out on walking you down the aisle at your wedding accomplished nothing, except to reinforce bitterness, this time between your mother and me.*

*When Dr. Ogletree gave me the terminal diagnosis, I finally came to my senses. Memories of your early years flooded in—walking hand in hand, talking to you about my business, watching you grow into such a fine young woman. Little O 'n O, my precious daughter,*

*I wish this money could make up for the chasm I allowed to develop between us. I know it cannot redeem the wasted years, but perhaps it can give you some measure of financial help along your way.*

*Your sorrowful and loving father*

Nell smoothed the letter and folded it back into the envelope. "Oh, Daddy, how I wish we could talk. Whatever am I to do? Jody's care is astronomical. Every blasted month. David's salary can't carry the expense. Our cards are maxed out, or nearly so. The fund you set up for me has afforded me this business, and now so much is gone. Gone, gone, gone." She pressed her eyes and tried to relax.

A knock at the door. "Nell, are you okay?" Flora's sleepy voice.

"I'll be out in a minute. Sorry to take so long." Sniffling and blowing her nose, she packed up her handbag, flushed the toilet, and slipped out and back to bed. The clock beside her bed said 2:30 a.m. They had a long drive ahead, come morning.

# PART TWO

# 16

# Millie

On Thursday of spring break, March 23, 1989, Millie Archer began the most exciting adventure of her fifteen years. Backpack over her left shoulder, she boarded the commuter plane and found her seat, 12-C, an aisle seat. An older guy in army fatigues sat by the window. Millie hoped it didn't show, the fluttery feeling in her chest where ribs meet breastbone. She shoved her backpack under the seat in front, remembered her book, pulled it out again. Soon after she got back from visiting Jody, her paper on *To Kill a Mockingbird* would be due and she had barely started it. She planned to read it on the plane to D.C. She felt the soldier's eyes on her.

"Do you like it?" he asked.

"Flying? I like it, yes, but this is my first trip solo. What about you?"

"I meant *To Kill a Mockingbird*. It was my favorite ages ago when I was your age.

And the movie's great. With Gregory Peck as Atticus Finch. You seen it?"

"No. I don't get why Harper Lee named the book with that title. So far there's nothing about birds of any kind."

"Maybe not. But you've got to admit there are plenty of strange birds in that small town." The soldier rubbed his graying crewcut hair. "You know, that guy nearby that never would come out."

"Boo Radley. My favorite is Scout. She's spunky and has a big vocabulary. And I love her daddy. He sorta reminds me of my own father."

"You're lucky to have a father you can admire. One reason I joined the Army. To get away from mine." He looked out the window and then back at Millie. "Course, back when I joined, I'd have been drafted anyway for 'Nam. Served there twice."

"You're still in the Army?"

"Yes m'am, it's my career. Heading back to Germany after leave. My mother's funeral. Everything in my old home town looked strange to me. A time warp, a different plane of existence, you know."

Millie studied his face. The skin under his eyes looked bruised from some deep tiredness. She glanced out the window beyond him. The sky was bright, perfectly clear. They were flying over fluffy pillows, comforters completely covering the earth. She felt a lot older than fifteen. The drone of the jet engines put her and the soldier and the others in an existence totally apart from normal life. "What do you do with the strange feelings you had in your hometown?"

"Nothing. What about you? Where are you off to? College hunting?"

"I wish. No, I'm on spring break, going to see my sister. She's—she's in a special school outside D.C. in Virginia. She's eighteen and may have to be there a while. Actually, it's a hospital. Or like a hospital, but it's a farm." She smiled at the soldier. "A different plane of existence, too, you might say."

"Right. It's great you're going to see her. Hope she'll be okay."

"Thanks. I'd better read my book. My paper's due right after I get back."

Millie wanted to tell someone about Jody, but she wasn't ready to discuss her with a stranger, even one who'd poured out his story. She thought of what she'd studied about Vietnam and wondered how he ever recovered from combat when you couldn't identify the enemy and where so many villagers, mothers and children, were slaughtered. He'd probably lost some of his best friends, too. She knew her dad would have known what to say to the soldier, but she didn't. And so would Deborah. She thought about how beautiful Deborah was and wondered again whether she should try dyeing her hair. Maybe platinum blonde. Certainly not stripes. She'd talk it over with Jody.

The rest of the way she read her book when she wasn't stewing over how she'd find the shuttle bus to Winslow Farms. The director had promised to have the bus waiting for her.

A flight attendant escorted her off the plane, as if she were seven years old.

Millie stood tall and straight and polite, but she thought, *You're so condescending.* While they waited for the bags, the soldier asked her if she needed any help. She said no and thanked him. Trembling inside, she waited for the bag. The soldier grabbed it off the carousel for her and retrieved his huge duffel bag. "Good luck," she called to him.

"You, too. I hope all goes well with your sister."

"Me, too." She headed to the buses lined up on the street.

The rain began as soon as she walked out to the street. Millie lugged the suitcase and her backpack toward the buses and looked at each one. A blue van with a white sign said *Winslow Farms.* She waved and tried to run, but her suitcase was too heavy to make much progress. The driver blinked his lights and pulled up to the curb, got out. He wore a cap and jacket of bright green with Winslow Farms written in dark blue. He was tall and skinny, maybe in his twenties.

"Are you Miss Archer?" The guy's large Adam's apple and bulbous nose and scrawny neck drew her attention. "Miss Millicent Archer? Are you Miss Archer?"

"Yes, sir. I'm sorry. I'm not used to being called Miss, I guess."

He lifted her bag easily into the back and motioned her to the middle seat behind him. He maneuvered the van into the traffic slowly to the next airline where he picked up an older man and woman. Millie assumed they must be parents of a patient.

The man nodded and spoke, "Howdy do, little missy."

She replied and turned to watch the rain. Too many Miss and Missy's to suit her.

By the time the van arrived at the town of Washington, Virginia, Millie knew they were nearly to the hospital farm. The trembling inside began as they drove down the main street. *What if Jody doesn't want to see me?* She reached inside her backpack and felt in the pocket for the tiny glass snail she'd brought for Jody. A gift Jody had given her two years ago when Millie was in seventh grade and scared when their mother and dad argued. Millie kept it on the table beside her bed and touched it right before she turned out the light. She touched it now and said to herself, "Slow and steady goes the snail." She began to breathe and relax.

The central building was a traditional white clapboard with dark green shutters and an entrance portico. Inside the wide hall, Millie waited beside her bag with the other people. Smells of supper cooking drifted into the hall. Soon double doors opened and a young man loped toward them and into the arms of his mother and father. Millie continued to wait, trying not to be nervous. She picked at her cuticles. The driver had disappeared into an office off the main hall. Should she go in there and ask for Jody?

Then the double doors opened again and a girl walked toward her— heavier, a lot heavier than Jody. But as she came closer, she saw. It *was* Jody. Millie ran toward her, then stopped. What if?

Jody said, "Millie. You're here."

Millie couldn't stand still. "Jody, Jody, Jody. I've missed you. I love you." Feeling like a seven year old, she hugged her big sister.

"Whoa, little Millipede. You're here. I can't believe it." She pulled away and held her with both hands on Millie's arms, studied her up and down, at arm's length. "Come with me." Jody grabbed the bag's handle and together they hauled it down the hall to her room. "What did you put in here? Your entire wardrobe and library? I bet you brought lots of books, right?"

"Yes, and some cassettes. You do have a player, don't you?"

"I don't, but I think we can find one to use."

They walked all the way to the end of the long hall. Millie noticed a lot of the doors had decorations—pennants of colleges or fake flowers or wreaths. Jody's had nothing. All the doors had a small window near the top, she guessed so the staff could check on the people inside.

"My humble abode," Jody announced as she opened the door.

"No key? No locks?"

"You're right. Supposedly there's an honor system here. I can latch the door at night from the inside. That's a good thing—with all the crazies around." She laughed and snorted. "I don't want to wake up and find some nut case at the foot of my bed." She shivered.

"Yeah, I would too. Lock up, that is." Millie inspected the maple twin bed with drawers underneath.

"Surprised it's not a padded cell?"

Millie shrugged. "I didn't know what to expect." She ran her hand across the desk and pictured studying there. From the window she saw a long path winding toward a barn in the distance, a field on one side and woods on the other. "Great view. It seems peaceful and relaxing."

"How like you to put a positive spin on this." Jody pulled the blinds closed.

"Too bright at this time of afternoon. If I were to open the window, you'd know for sure you're in the country. Too stinky for a city gal like me." She sat on the bed and gestured for Millie to use the one arm chair. "Anyway, this is home for me now."

"Until you come home to your real home, of course. We all miss you, but especially me. Lyn, too."

"Yeah. Probably not Mom or Dad. At least not much. I'm too much trouble, and they're always busy."

"How can you say that, or even think it, Jody? They're about nuts over what's happened to you. Daddy's worrying himself sick, trying to figure out how to help you."

Millie leaned toward Jody. She had to make her understand how what she did, or tried to do, scared all of them. Jody's face seemed to harden. Her silence told Millie to ease up. Right then wasn't the time to say more.

Millie hunted in the pocket of her backpack. "I brought you something." She held up the small clear glass snail in the palm of her hand. "The snail you gave me has helped me. Now it has come to live with you for a while. Remember what you told me when you gave it to me?"

Jody shook her head slightly. "No, 'fraid not."

Millie couldn't believe she'd forgotten. Jody's words had meant so much and taught her to relax when she was tense. She tilted her head until Jody's eyes met hers. Then she said, "Slow and steady goes the snail."

"Not terribly profound. But thanks. He's cute. Hope I don't break it."

"Every night for two years I've touched it and said the words." Her voice caught. "Profound or not. They've helped. You helped."

Jody hopped up. "Let me show you around the place. You'll be staying in the guest room, off the main lobby. It's private and has its own bath. They won't let guests stay in our rooms. Regulations from The General." She laughed and pulled down her sweater over her stomach and hips. "I'll introduce you. Her name is the Reverend Doctor Gena Flowers, but she's The General to us inmates."

"She's the director, I suppose. And a minister and a doctor?"

"You got that right. Let's walk the yard." Jody went to the mirror in the bathroom, inspected her teeth, smoothed her eyebrows, and brushed her hair. Millie had always loved watching her big sister put on her make-up, but now make-up seemed to be of no importance. Jody pulled lip balm from her pocket and applied some without looking in the mirror. "You need to use the bathroom before we go?"

Millie was about to pop. She hadn't asked because she wasn't sure what the regulations were for guests. She peed, washed up, and smoothed her hair. Mousy, just like Deborah had said. Jody's hair glistened with hints of red in the light blonde and possessed a natural wave on the sides and in back. Hers seemed lank and listless, no body, no sheen. She had to do something about her pitiful hair.

The March wind had picked up, blowing their jackets open and mussing their hair this way and that. Millie matched her stride with Jody's. The rain now was just a fine mist. They dodged puddles on the path in back of the dining hall.

Jody became a fast-talking, fast-walking tour guide. "To the right is the herb garden, then those raised squares over to the left will hold a big vegetable garden later. Right now they just grow broccoli, spinach, and the beginning of lettuce. She led the way under an arbor to the path toward the barn. Before they reached it, Jody said, "Hold your nose. We're close to the pig pens." Jody stood on the bottom rung of the rail fence, so Millie did too. Under some trees were lots of pigs lounging, resting their huge bodies on the incline of ground worn bare by their habits. "They have their routines like the rest of us. When it gets cold, they haul themselves up and stump into the enclosure over there. We have to hose down their house for them. Believe it or not, pigs like to be clean."

"Do you-all call out 'Whoo-Pig-Suey' like Dad's Razorbacks' call?"

"When we want to call them over, we do. I haven't done it, but I've heard some guys sound off. It's funny. Those big lugs are pretty smart. They've got it made—with all us inmates working for them."

Why did she keep calling the people here inmates? It seemed to be a lovely place to live and work. Millie didn't ask. It was part of Jody's attitude that she was trying to understand.

Jody led her toward the big barn. Music from the back section of the barn drifted their way. "Sounds like Shelly and Michael are tuning up for tonight's program."

Inside, Millie breathed in the warm smells of the hay and animal muskiness. And it was dry. Millie dropped the hood from her jacket. Horses sniggered from stalls down the right side. How exciting. She'd never been around horses, or any farm animals for that matter. She looked at Jody. Was she excited about all this? What an opportunity. Ignoring the animals, Jody headed straight toward the music. Notes from a horn of some kind along with a stringed instrument came from a room at the far end.

"Jody, have you ridden a horse here?" She hurried to catch up with Jody, who was knocking on the door. She slipped into the room, so Millie followed.

The girl played a guitar and the guy a sax. They played to the end of a section and stopped. "Hi, Josephine," the girl said. "Who's this?"

Jody introduced Millie as her sister visiting for the weekend from South Carolina, and she didn't call her *little* sister. And Shelly and Michael as sister and brother from Florida. "We're in the same group. Group therapy, that is."

Millie spoke to each by name. "I loved hearing your music float down to us as we came toward the barn. Are you rehearsing for something or just like to jam?"

They looked at each other and laughed. "Yes," they said in unison. Michael said, "The General asked us to play tonight after supper, during Sharing Time."

Jody jumped up. "Come on, Millie. We'd better let them get back to it." She grabbed Millie's hand and pulled her to the door. "See ya."

As they left the barn, Millie asked, "Why did we have to leave so quick? I wanted to hear them play."

"No reason. I just have to keep moving." Jody marched on ahead across the road to a yellow concrete building with windows in a row up under the overhanging roof.

"The Art Building. I spend a lot of free time here." Millie had no idea Jody cared a thing for art.

Four people worked at the long tables covered with white butcher paper, about as far from each other as they could be. No one stopped what they were doing, or even noticed them. A cassette played "Age of Aquarius" on a scratchy boom box. The walls were covered with paintings and drawings showing a wide range of ability. Millie moved to a large poster board painting of a vase full of huge red tulips done with thick tempera paint. Black jagged lines covered the background except for a tiny window up in one corner with blue sky showing. Jody walked up beside her.

"That one's mine." She faced Millie. "You remember when you wrote me about Sylvia Plath's poem 'Tulips'?"

"I do."

"Not great art, but at least it gave me a subject. Of course, no tulips were blooming so I had to try to remember how they're shaped." Jody moved to the back of the room. "Over here, we mess around with clay. The kind that hardens. We can put what we make in the kiln when the clay teacher is here." She whirled around. "Naturally, they don't trust us inmates with so much fire." She stalked to the shelves against the wall. "Those pieces at the top are mine. They're almost dry enough to fire."

Two small cylinder-shaped bowls, on the rim of one a cat arched its back and pointed its tail up. On the rim of the other a small elf perched with hands on hips.

"Those are great, Jody. I love the little elf, especially." Millie grabbed Jody's hands in hers. "You're good. You know that?"

Jody pulled her hands free. "Over here is what I'm working on now. Another painting, but this one's on canvas with acrylics."

Millie studied the painting. In the top third dark purple and black clouds hung over the roof of a house. A deep gash zigzagged down one wall. From the center to the right side of the canvas, the house was cut open to expose something that looked like a pantry with shelves of food, pots and pans. A little girl sat on the floor pouring liquid from a fat teapot into a cup. Across from her sat a long winding creature with lots of legs and a head. So far, the figures had been drawn in pencil and a light wash.

"Guess what I'm painting?"

"The pantry reminds me of the one we used to have. Is that going to be a snake? But a snake doesn't have legs." Millie laughed. "No, wait. I know. A millipede."

"Right. You and me and the little Teapot, Short and Stout."

Millie wondered what Jody was trying to express. She hoped that the millipede wouldn't be a monster.

"You remember how we used to play in that pantry?" Jody said. "The house was old and cramped and Mother hated it. You seemed oblivious and of course Lyn was so young when we first moved to Goodwin, she just wanted to be with us wherever we played. The more Mom and Dad argued, the more you and I played in the pantry and made tinier and tinier paper dolls."

"You said they were fairies and elves," Millie said. "I'd almost forgotten. But you know what? I've kept my little paper elf and his clothes in my cedar chest. I didn't know you even remembered playing with me. And I sure didn't realize Mom and Dad were fighting way back then."

"I think you put the elf's clothes in a matchbox, right?"

"Yep. Daddy smoked a lot back then. We had plenty of those little matchboxes."

"Has he started smoking again?"

"Not as far as I know. He chews gum or sucks on peppermints when he craves a cigarette." She thought about saying how worried she was about the stress he was under, but Jody might blame herself. *Well, why not? She should blame herself.*

"Come on, let's get you moved into the guest room before supper." Jody led the way back to the main building, walking fast. Millie ran to keep up.

At midnight, Millie lay in the guestroom bed, not sleeping. The streetlights outside along the circular driveway shone through the thin curtains. Shadows on the wall played with her imagination. She got up to make sure the door was locked, first peeping through the peephole. The hall beyond expanded like a fishbowl. Everything quiet. Tomorrow and Saturday would be her only other days with Jody. Would she confide in her the way she used to? When was the last time Jody told her any secrets? It must have been before she left for boarding school. Had something happened during Jody's junior year in high school that made her turn away?

Millie let pictures run through her mind of her big sister that year. It was hard to remember exactly because her own life took all her concentration. That would have been the year their mother went into the hospital for what must have been a month. No one ever told her or Lyn anything substantial of what had been wrong with their mom. If Jody knew, she never said. Dad had reassured her when she asked by saying that everything was all right now. She'd be fine.

One thing about their family she was coming to realize—it was extremely important for their surface life to be calm and placid as a lake without wind. She pictured Glen Springs Lake where they liked to go with the Ames and the Parks. Small ripples were tolerated, but it was crucial for all to go smoothly. Why was their mother in the hospital? What if something terrible had happened to Jody during her eleventh grade year? What if she felt it would have been unacceptable for her to disrupt the Family Norm? That must be it. She'd ask Jody in the morning. She closed her eyes and let memories of canoeing on the spring lake lull her to sleep.

At seven Millie woke up to sounds and smells drifting into the guest room from the dining room and kitchen. Bacon cooking, the inviting aroma of bread turning into toast, and coffee brewing. Jody hadn't said what time to meet her. Millie preferred to know exactly what was expected of her, how much time she had to get ready. She hated to be late for anything, so she showered and shampooed in less than ten minutes and dressed in her stonewashed jeans and favorite shirt. She was brushing her hair when Jody knocked.

"Good timing, Millipede. Let's eat." She studied her hair and lifted the wet strands. "Got an idea. What say we dye your hair today?"

"Well, maybe. I haven't decided yet. I wanted to talk it over with you."

They went through the line and got scrambled eggs, bacon, toast and sliced apples, Millie following Jody's lead. Four kids served, joking with Jody and inspecting Millie. She felt shy, like a new kid at school.

Michael and Shelly waved them over to their table. That made her feel a little better. "You all were great last night," Millie said. "I love music from the fifties and the folk songs from the sixties."

"Thanks, Millie," Shelley said. "It's nice to have a responsive audience."

"Yeah," Michael said in an undertone, "zombies around here just stare into space."

Millie looked around the room as she drank her milk. Even though people sat with others at the round tables, most were in their own separate worlds, with their eyes fixed on their plates or looking vaguely into the middle distance. Jody and the brother and sister at her table were more engaged with what was going on. Maybe they were healthier.

Just then a tall imposing woman with steel gray hair done up in a twist appeared in the doorway. "The General," Jody whispered. The woman in the doorway reminded Millie of someone from the nineteenth century. She wore a modern gray suit with a long hemline, and she held herself with a straight, stiff spine, long neck, and her backside protruded so much it might have held a bustle back in the day.

Jody stood and motioned for Millie to follow.

"Dr. Flowers, this is my sister I told you about. Millie, The Reverend Doctor Gena Flowers, Director of Winslow Farms." The General's hand felt smooth and surprisingly cool. She grasped Millie's other hand as well in an attempt perhaps to show warmth.

"It is a pleasure to have you visit us, my dear. I do hope you had a restful night's sleep." She nodded toward Jody. "I feel confident that Josephine has explained that you are quite welcome to attend classes with her, and, of course, all meals, and you might enjoy helping with her assigned chores. The individual and group therapy sessions, however, are off limits to visitors." The Director's tone possessed undeniable authority but did not seem unkind or harsh to Millie. Dr. Flowers gave a quick smile and nod and left them.

Jody led her outside to the chicken coop down the hill from the art building. "My only chore this morning is to feed the chickens and refresh their water." She pulled on a pair of old black boots over her sneakers, handed Millie a scoop and gestured toward a big keg. Inside Millie found corn and some other kind of grain. She scooped up a load and followed Jody into the chicken coop, wishing she had on boots too. The odor in the cage proclaimed that fertilizer was produced in abundance right there.

Jody sprayed water from the hose into pans for the chickens at different locations. The hens scattered, but came up to Millie, squawking and peeping and generally telling her to hurry. Millie poured the grain into several metal feeders and the hens ignored the girls. Most were white or speckled but three or four were fancier with curly dark iridescent feathers.

"You watch these stupid chickens long enough and you come to believe every kind of animal has a pecking order. At least now I understand where the expression comes from." Jody pointed to a large speckled hen at the central trough. "She's the big general out here. No question." Before Millie could say anything, Jody led the way out, shed her boots, and headed back to the main building.

Jody explained that they had fifteen minutes before philosophy class and to meet her in the classroom beyond the dining hall. "Bring your notebook. You might learn something. The teacher's pretty cool."

Millie brushed her teeth, grabbed her notebook and pen and dashed to the classroom.

Mr. Strayer perched on the desk with his legs crossed as if he'd been meditating before class. Jody introduced Millie and she shook his hand. A large hand with dark hair on his fingers and the back of his hand. She appreciated the way he shook her hand, as if she were an adult and an equal, not a mere girl. His head, also massive, was covered with wild black curls he hadn't bothered to tame. His features seemed oversized—huge black eyes with brows sticking out in all directions, large nose and lips. His light brown skin made her think he might be from the Middle East, or India, somewhere foreign. "Take a seat anywhere and prepare to be astounded."

"Just what I've always wanted in a philosophy class," she said before she thought. Where had that come from? She turned hot. No doubt she'd been impudent. She looked at her sister. Jody paid no attention, waved her to the next desk.

"As most of you know this is no ordinary philosophy class. It is what I call Pneumology or The Breath of New Life Class." Mr Strayer hopped up and wrote this on the board. "Every day we take up an aspect of life that most high schools and colleges never approach. Colleges nowadays are geared to teach a trade—like business or accounting or pre-something, usually pre-law or pre-medicine. What's happened to the noble study of liberal arts? In short, the art of thinking. The art of examining our lives and determining for ourselves what should be the purpose of our lives."

He stretched his large frame to his full height and lifted long arms, fingertips touching the acoustical tile of the ceiling. "Everyone, up! Up! Stand. Stretch to your full height. Arms up."

A lot of shuffling and scooting of desks followed; with giggles, muttered protests and jokes, everyone complied.

"Now breathe. Exhale. Now breathe in a deep cleansing breath. Exhale. Be seated."

Millie bubbled with laughter. Already the class was astounding.

"Now, class and visitor from South Carolina, today we are going to look into the troubled soul of a man of God who happened to write the most astonishing poems you will ever read." He pulled a book from a stack on his desk, flipped open to a well-used section. "Before we approach even one of his poems, let me ask you something. Have any of you ever felt such despair that you could not imagine ever getting out of the dark hole you were in? Have you?" He peered at the students one by one and waited.

Millie looked at Jody, alarmed. What if his question triggered some kind of episode in her sister? Jody's face remained implacable, unreadable.

"Have you? Have you felt such utter despair? Or if you prefer the medieval word for the Midnight Disease, have you known deep melancholy?"

Slowly one hand after another went up, around the room. Millie lifted her hand, then wondered if her periods of sadness qualified. Jody looked straight ahead, but nodded slightly, or so Millie thought.

"All right then. These poems by Gerard Manley Hopkins are for you and you and you and me." He passed out copies of three poems to everyone. "I shall read first his sonnet called 'Carrion Comfort.'" He read.

Millie sat mesmerized by the resonance of the teacher's baritone voice and the poet's strange combinations of words. She glanced at Jody, whose face was in rapt attention.

Mr. Strayer asked, "How many times does the poet use the word *me?*"

"Eight," the answer came from a guy in the back.

"What is the carrion comfort? First, what is carrion?"

"Road kill." This from Jody.

"Good. You might very well define it as such. Now what is he naming as road kill?"

"Despair." Again from Jody.

"A gruesome, desperate image, is it not? Notice also how he uses the word *not* five times in that first stanza. What effect does that have?" He waited.

A male voice again in the back corner spoke up. "The *nots* give short punchy notes like in music. Makes his determination against all odds come through insistently."

Millie turned to see that the guy was the sax player, Michael.

"Good for you," the teacher said. He turned to the others in the class. "You can tell a poet and a musician every time, can you not? The speaker is determined not to feast on his despair, the carrion or roadkill. Yet his despair is all he can see to eat there before him, right?

"Now, class, tell me whom the poet is addressing. Who is the *thou?*"

First silence. Then gradually hands went up. A girl by the windows said, "Like maybe God?"

"How does he depict God? A loving father? A meek lamb? No. God lays a 'lionlimb against' him and has 'darksome devouring eyes.' A ferocious image, is it not?"

Jody held up her hand. "Mr. Strayer, if we tried some of these rhymes in our own poems, you'd laugh us out of here. Like, "me frantic to avoid thee and flee." Too obvious. Too kitschy, or something, you'd say."

"Could be," he said. "But, his odd verses are his alone. Idiosyncratic indeed. But I'll tell you something. His peculiar music and his way of facing his own anguish have helped many a time in my own misery." He lifted himself up and again stretched his arms to the ceiling. "It may not change the circumstances. But his poetry can name what I'm feeling."

Millie studied her sister's profile. Elegant with perfect, narrow, arched brows, dark as her brown eyes, a perfect nose and complexion. Yet Jody held her face expressionless as if she might break if she showed any feeling whatsoever. What was she hiding? What was she so afraid of? Millie looked back at Mr. Strayer who was now writing on the board. The assignment was to read more Hopkins and choose one poem to explicate for the next class. Then he added, "I'd like for each of you to take one strong emotion or traumatic event in your life and write your own poem with your own music, no matter how peculiar or weird you might believe it to be. Anything goes."

Back in her room, Jody threw herself onto her bed and turned her face to the window, the blinds still closed. Millie sat in the lumpy armchair and picked at her cuticles. After a while, she asked, "Are you okay, Jody? Cellophane? Remember how I used to call you Cellophane? But you know what? You're anything but transparent. Still to me, Josephine sounds close to Cellophane."

Jody flipped over and faced her. "Shut up! Don't you dare call me that in front of my friends here!" Her face was deep red. She'd been crying.

"Jody. Don't worry. I won't. Are you all right?"

"Actually, no. Let's take a break. You go back to the guestroom, or somewhere. Go outside or something. I need to be alone."

"In other words, get lost! Okay. Okay. Opaque. Not Cellophane. You're opaque."

"What did you say?" She was facing the window shade again.

"Nothing." Millie slipped out of the room, closing the door quietly and ran down the hall to the guestroom. Jody's rejection lodged in her throat and chest like a bad cold. What should she do? Jody hated her. Should she go home? She couldn't until Sunday. She lay on her back with her eyes closed. Images from the class played through her mind. She liked the big man who stretched his huge arms to the ceiling and taught poetry with such passion. She loved poems too, although she didn't know much about writing them. Maybe she'd try the assignment. Soon she was asleep.

Repeated knocks on the door woke her. Millie opened the door to find Jody, Michael, and Shelly in their coats and boots. "Come on, Sleepyhead. We're heading to the art building for an Easter egg picnic," Shelly said. Jody looking pale, smiled an I'm-sorry smile but didn't say anything.

Millie hurried into her coat and again wished she had brought boots. Her Keds would have to do. The four entered the yellow building to find the place decorated with bunnies, chicks, and lots of Easter crepe paper doodads and balloons.

"They must think we're four years old," Jody said.

"No. Remember this is a party for the daycare kids from the homeless shelter this afternoon," Michael said. "Shelly and I have to play. But first let's eat."

Sandwiches, chips, and deviled eggs were spread on the art tables. Lemonade in cups and cupcakes were on the counter. Millie followed the three to a table in the clay area. Would Jody even speak to her? She ate and listened to the talk around her.

Jody wasn't talking. Michael and Shelly discussed what to play for the kids. "Itsy Bitsy Spider" and "I'm A Little Teapot" figured prominently. Millie smiled at Jody. Jody looked right through her, then away. Millie felt a pang in her chest and her throat tightened.

"Now, young people, it's time to go out and hide the eggs for the children," Dr. Flowers announced when they finished eating. "Please remember these are young children. We want them to find the eggs, so place them in plain sight, and not too high up, if you please."

"It's time for the inmates to file out into the fields," Jody said in an undertone.

Everyone picked up baskets of plastic colored eggs beside the door. Millie loved hiding eggs and for a few minutes forgot Jody's mood. There were about twenty people placing eggs in the grass, along the walls, and in the small bushes near the walkway. Jody's sneakers were soon soaked from the wet grass, but she didn't care.

When all the eggs were distributed, everyone brought the baskets back and lined them up for the children to use later. Back in the room, Millie walked around looking at the paintings again. She stood in front of Jody's painting of the girl in the pantry with the millipede and teapot. Funny, Jody hadn't depicted her or Lyn as people. What could that mean? She felt someone beside her. It was Jody.

"I'm sorry, Jody, for what I called you."

"Never mind."

"Can we talk after this party?"

"Well, I have group. Then maybe. Or we could dye your hair."

Jody lifted a strand of Millie's hair.

"Do you think it's mousy? Like Deborah does?"

"Well, it could use some highlights, I guess. But it's okay, the color. I'm used to you with brown hair, you know."

"I still don't know what I want to do. I'd love to impress Deborah. She's so cool and beautiful. Mostly, I don't think about my hair or what I have on once I get dressed and leave for school or whatever."

"No kidding. I never forget how I look. Actually I check every chance I get." She took Millie's hand. "Come on. The kids are here."

She and Jody found seats close to Michael and Shelly, who played songs for the children while they ate. One little girl jumped up and danced to the music. Jody opened her sketchbook and drew a little boy in a cowboy hat who sat alone absorbed in eating a heaping plateful of food. Then the hunt was on.

After a whirl of giggling children dashing around with baskets and lots of gooey cupcake crumbs and wilted crepe paper, the Winslow Farms residents cleaned up. Then Jody and Millie headed back to the dorm.

"While you're in your therapy group, I think I'll work on a poem your teacher assigned."

"Why bother? You won't be here for the next class. But hey, knock yourself out." Jody waved good-bye at Millie's door. "I'll come by here for you in an hour or so."

Millie couldn't shake the troubled feelings she had after being with Jody. She stretched out on the bed with her notebook and pen. She jotted whatever came to mind and drew doodles along the page. Inside, she felt empty, a terrible hunger. Outside she felt coated with something sour-smelling, bitter-tasting. She shivered and pulled the spread over her. Maybe she shouldn't try to write a poem. If it turned out to be about Jody, her sister might find it and hate her more. Mr. Strayer had said to write about something with strong emotion. Or something traumatic. Nothing traumatic had happened to her. To Jody in January, yes, but not to her directly. She wrote, "Nothing ever happens here." Then she thought about how much fun she and Jody used to have playing together. She'd been such a great big sister. What had she done to mess that up with Jody? Things were different now. She sat up and looked out the window. Two mockingbirds were leaping around each other in a kind of dance. She wrote, "Nothing stays the same." Stuck for any other words, she wrote rhyming words down the page. "Fear, we're, clear, dear, name, fame, blame."

Millie reached for the book she read every night even though it was called *As the Day Begins.* She found March 24 and read the devotional and the Bible verse and prayer. The book didn't always speak to her, but she stuck with reading it every day, almost like a superstition. Her daddy had given it to her with the words, "You might find this book helpful." He gave it to her soon after she'd asked him some questions that bothered her. He hadn't really answered her questions, but he hardly ever preached to his own children. Preaching must be for church only. He'd said something she didn't understand about "living the questions." He must love the Bible, he studied it all the time. She figured she'd read it for herself even if she didn't know what a lot of it meant. She read at night before sleep, and really liked the Psalms. They were sort of poems.

Outside the mockingbirds separated. One hopped across the drive-way. The other followed, then changed its mind and flew up to a tree near-by. Maybe she should read some in the book she'd brought along. She opened *To Kill a Mockingbird* where she'd marked and soon was following Scout, Jem, and Dill as they dared each other to approach the dreaded Radley house.

A knock, Dum-dum-dee-dum-dum. Jody stood at the door as if no bad mood had ever affected her. She walked over to the bed, her eyes fall-ing on the devotional book. "Are you still reading that baby book?" Her perfect eyebrows arched higher than ever, just like their mother's did when she disapproved.

Millie grabbed the book and held it to her chest. "So why shouldn't I? Daddy gave it to me." She put it on the bedside table with her Bible. "I had some questions. Still do." She laughed. "He's not big on giving answers, is he?"

"Don't you think that's incredible for a minister?"

"Did he give you books too?"

"Maybe. I guess. If he did, I didn't read them."

"You must not be as hungry as I am."

"No. We're hungry in different ways. You, little Millipede, for all that metaphysical stuff. Millicent Archer, spiritual goody-goody."

"That stings. What about you? Don't you want to know God? Understand what all this means?" She spread her arms to embrace the world, and all the puzzling complexities of the people she'd thought she knew. Especially Jody.

Jody shrugged. "I must take after Mom. You know, more materialistic."

"You don't collect things the way she does."

Jody looked down and spoke in such a quiet tone Millie almost missed her words. "Oh, I collect. I collect obsessions," she said and walked to the door. "We all have our habits, our rituals, I guess. Come on, I've got plans for you before supper."

"No, wait." Millie patted the bed beside her. "Jody, I have to ask you something. Why did you go off to school? I've missed you. Why did you?" Millie couldn't bring herself to ask about the Desperate Act.

Jody picked up Millie's Bible, thumbed through the pages. She didn't sit down. "I don't know." She set the Bible on the nightstand, walked to the mirror and fiddled with her hair. "Millie, you know, in our family you're the peacemaker. And Lyn, our chubby cherub, little sister. Lyn's the princess. But me?" She pulled at the long sleeves of her shirt and looked out the window, glanced at Millie, then back out the window. "Me? I'm the Outsider. 'What's wrong with Jody?' If I heard that once, I've heard it a thousand times. B.D. that's me."

"What are you talking about? B.D.?" Millie sat up straight. She wanted to hug her sister but didn't dare move. The spell would be broken. At last, Jody was talking to her.

"B.D. Big Disappointment. To Mom, I'm too clumsy, too careless, to ever be the gymnast or ballerina she envisioned. Too moody, and mostly too much trouble. To Dad—I just don't get what he's given his life to. Service to God? Ordained servant of word and sacrament, whatever does that mean? I don't get it. I don't believe a word of it. He suspects I'm an atheist and all that does is make him look at me with his big blue eyes filled with sadness. 'A man of sorrows, acquainted with grief,' that's Dad. Like his Jesus."

Jody stalked over to the wall mirror again and glared at her reflection. "See why I say I'm The Outsider? The B.D.?" She looked past her reflection and met Millie's eyes. "So I figured you're all better off without me."

Millie hopped off the bed and hugged Jody, who stood stiff, unyielding. "No, no. Jody, you have no idea. Everyone loves you. How can you think that?" She backed away from Jody. How could she convince her? She felt utterly deflated. There was nothing she could say to change Jody's perception. "Is that why you . . .?" The words for the Desperate Act stuck in her throat.

Jody turned away and headed for the door. "Enough of this. Let's go out. I have something for us to do." She tugged at her long sleeves and smoothed her already smooth hair. "Grab your coat. If you've got any spending money, bring it."

Millie ran to catch up with Jody and Shelly, who were trotting out the gateway to the main road. "Do you have to have permission to leave the farm?"

They stopped and waited. Jody said, "The General gave special dispensation because you, Millipede, are here. So the inmates can run free for an hour or two."

"On foot, we can't get far," Shelly added.

"So where are we going?" The two of them sure had a lot of energy for depressed people. She remembered how she and Jody used to race. They'd cross the busy street and then walk together to the city park. Millie always felt taller and older when Jody walked with her and told her about the boy she had a crush on or what her favorite teacher had said. When they'd reach the park, Jody would take off running. Millie determined to keep up, but after a lot of effort learned to find her own rhythm. She'd run and not worry about her big sister's faster pace. That's when Millie came to realize how much she liked looking around as she jogged, noting what birds were overhead in the tall oak trees, noting how people of every age walked their dogs, how dogs matched their owners in such funny, uncanny ways. Now she looked at the older girls, who were giggling like young kids. "What's so funny? Where are we going?"

"Don't worry about it. Ain't it great to be free?" Jody said, then broke into song with Shelly, "Boom, Boom! Ain't it great to be crazy. Happy, foolish, all day long. Boom, boom! Ain't it great to be crazy!" They interlocked arms with Millie in the middle. They skipped in unison and chanted, "Lions and tigers and bears oh my!" as if they were with Dorothy on the Yellow Brick Road, and made their way toward the shops along the main street of Little Washington. Abruptly, Jody stopped and pointed to the second side street toward a small shop. An art deco sign swung from an old hinge with the words Curly Q Beauty Salon, creaking back and forth in the cold breeze.

"Come on, Millipede. You've got an appointment. An hour or so in here—you'll be a new person." Jody must believe she needed to be completely over-hauled.

Millie stood still, waiting for Jody to look at her, listen to her, maybe even consider what she, Millie, might want or might not want. Jody kept moving, nodding her head, pulling on Millie's arm. "Here we go. Transformation Time."

"Hold it. Stop, Jody."

"What?"

"Don't I have a say in this? It's my hair, after all."

"You said you wanted to consult me about coloring it, so let's at least hear what Lucille recommends, okay? Right, Shelly?"

Shelly stood off to the side, as if to say this wasn't her fight. She nodded tentatively.

"Oh, all right. I'll hear what she has to say." Millie didn't like her hair. She could admit that. Straggly, straight, fine, parted in the center and tucked behind her ears, or swooped up with a banana clip. Sometimes two ponytails out to the sides. She knew she had no sense of style, but she'd always believed in staying natural. Anything else would have been pretentious.

She used to love her hair back when she had long braids. Her mother insisted she cut them before seventh grade. After the cutting, she didn't know how to deal with her limp brown hair. When she had braids, she felt distinctive and loved growing her hair as long as possible until she could sit on the ends. She loved shampooing her hair in the shower with lemony shampoo and then on warm days, sitting outside in the sun to dry it while she read *Girl of the Limberlost* or *Little Women*, both old books that had belonged to her grandmother, Mary Frances, her daddy's mother. She liked being old-fashioned, feeling like Jo March or chasing butterflies like the girl in the Limberlost.

"Come on, Millie. As our mother used to say to me, don't be obstinate," Jody said, pushing her firmly in the back as they reached the steps.

As if she read Millie's mind, Jody said, "Millie, you never have liked change, have you? I remember if I rearranged furniture in our dollhouse, you'd say, 'No, it has to stay put.'"

"I guess I just like the natural way. I want things to stay the same."

"Same as what? What about braces? I had to wear them for two years to straighten my crooked teeth. What about the time when Lyn was a baby and she had that operation on her leg. Nature's way? She would have been handicapped all her life without it."

"Okay, okay. I get it. You're right. I dread changing. Maybe I'm just scared."

They stood facing each other on the entrance stoop. A cold wind ruffled Jody's naturally curly light blonde hair, as if teasing out Millie's resistance. In the distance a train whistle let out its mournful call. A call of longing. She loved that sound. Reminded her of home. What would her parents say if she came home with different hair?

She shivered. Church bells rang out from the Episcopal church on the low hill above Main Street. Good Friday. Her dad would have preached at noon with other Presbyterian ministers on the Last Words of Christ on the Cross, an old tradition that her father said was going out of style. In fact this would be the last year for that long three-hour Good Friday service. She fingered the small gold and silver cross at her neck. Good Friday. Jesus on the cross and she was worried about her hair. She flushed with shame and guilt. What was there to be afraid of? It was just hair, and it would grow back. She shivered again.

"Okay. Come on, let's see what happens," she said.

After the cold outside, the air inside felt oppressive and hot, almost steamy. A pungent chemical odor with an overlay of strawberry-scented room deodorant—or maybe it was shampoo—assaulted Millie's nose. Music played from a boom box behind the counter, and the women inside called out to one another like old friends, old deaf friends, over the hair dryers. Lucille stepped around the counter from her station to greet them. She was not a tall woman, yet she held herself erect like a ballet dancer, her neck extended. Her hair was dark, teased, and smooth with bangs softly curled over her forehead. Her dark brown eyes were accented with mascara and eye-liner and perfectly shaped narrow eyebrows. She wore a flowered smock over her mini-skirt and white shoes a nurse might wear, although she looked like a woman more suited to spike heels. Lucille's wide red mouth and amused eyes made Millie feel exceedingly young.

"You must be Millicent. Sit right here and we'll see what you all might want to do today." Lucille's voice had warm tones, but Millie thought she must be assuming a Southern accent to make her more comfortable. *You all* never referred to one person.

She lifted Millie's hair and played with it back and forth, studying her face in the mirror. Jody and Shelly stepped up on either side and studied her too. They all three discussed possible colors—darker brown, brown with reddish highlights, auburn red all the way, blonde all the way, honey-blonde. Millie felt like a manikin, said nothing.

Lucille put some of Millie's hair over her forehead and nodded. The others agreed. Bangs were in order. Soft, curly bangs like Lucille. A perm? Yes, a body wave so she could take care of curling it later. Finally, after tilting their heads this way and that all the while playing with color samples and hair styles, one after the other said, "Millie, what'll it be?" Millie, the manikin, came alive and with a trembling voice said, "Okay, I think I want some soft curls. Only I don't have any curlers. And I don't want any extreme color, so I'll go with honey-blonde. What do you think, Jody? Shelly?"

"We'll buy some curlers and a good brush. You did bring your spending money, didn't you?" Jody said. Shelly added, "Good choice, Millie."

So Lucille began her work. Jody and Shelly read magazines, looking up every few minutes. Millie told herself to relax during her shampoo, inhaling the fresh smell of lemon and yielding herself to Lucille's sure hands scrubbing her head. She closed her eyes during much of the process.

After an hour and a half, Millie studied her new look, still a little shaky from taking what seemed a daring step. Jody and Shelly encouraged her. "Look at yourself. Aren't you gorgeous? You're going to break some hearts back home. Just watch and see."

Millie touched the little cross at her neck. "I just hope I don't break Mom and Dad's hearts. What will they think?"

"Stop worrying about them," Jody said. "They'll come around. Any way they know you're with me and what a bad influence I am."

Millie looked from the beauty shop mirror out the window, then back. She couldn't believe it. Her mousy, brown, straight hair had been transformed into loopy curls of blonde, in subtle darks and lights. The soft bangs across her wide forehead changed the shape of her face ever so slightly. She glanced at her sister who gave her a thumbs-up.

And then she looked at Shelly, who had risen from her chair and was pointing excitedly. "Snow! It's snowing! I'm from south Florida. I can't get enough of this stuff."

Lucille groaned. Her dark eyes grew darker. "A late March snow— just what we need."

Millie and Jody laughed. Millie remembered a terrific snow in March in South Carolina soon after they'd moved there, how everyone got caught off guard. Their dad was stuck at the church until a guy picked him up in his Jeep. Their mother was out of town, in Atlanta with her sick mom. The girls had days out of school. They drank lots of hot chocolate and went sledding. Millie smiled at the memory. Jody smiled back, as if she was remembering the same snow.

Millie looked back at her new image in the mirror. "Oh, no. After all your work, Lucille, I'll ruin it walking back."

Lucille opened a drawer at her station and whipped out a small packet. "Wear this over your hair. You'll be okay."

Millie opened the packet and unfolded a plastic rain bonnet. Lucille helped her place and tie it under her chin.

Jody was enjoying the sight. "What a dork! But hey, maybe it'll save your new look. Like all the blue hairs." Jody paid Lucille.

Millie asked about the curlers and brush. She bought some pink plastic rollers with spikes and holes and a brush like the one Lucille used, with natural bristles, and some Aquanet hairspray. They put on their coats and gloves. Again Millie wished she had boots like Jody and Shelly instead of her thin Keds. They thanked Lucille and headed out into the snow for the walk back to Winslow Farms.

Millie sniffed the air like a dog, so pleased to be out of the steamy, chemical atmosphere of the beauty shop. The snow was falling steadily in large gentle flakes. Already the bare oak trees and maples along the street were trimmed in white. A lone red cardinal struck a pose on a limb of a small dogwood. Jody's and Shelly's boots crunched through the growing pile along the street. Millie's sneakers squeaked along. Her feet grew colder and wetter until they felt numb. She stuck out her tongue to taste the snow.

By the time the girls got back to Winslow Farms, they were all wet and cold. Shelly's head was covered by a knit cap and Jody's with the hood of her coat. The plastic rain bonnet may have helped Millie the first few blocks, but by the time they entered the gates, she felt the plastic hugging her head like a collapsed tent on a rainy camping trip. "Let's run the rest of the way," she called and bounded through the slushy snow in the driveway. Inside they stamped the snow off their boots and shoes onto the absorbent mats by the door.

The Reverend Doctor Flowers stood at her office door, hands on hips. "So you found your way back home, I see. It took long enough. Were you waiting for the snow storm? You're late for supper and all three of you look like drowned rats. I suggest you go to your rooms and attempt to dry off, don clean warm clothes and meet me in the conference room." She stared at each one, while they nodded and mouthed "I'm sorry."

"Now go."

Jody and Shelly stifled giggles. Millie shivered. She waved to them and headed down the hall, glad for the hissing radiator in the guest room.

Millie had postponed calling home even though she knew they'd expected her to check in right after she got to Winslow Farms. Now it was Saturday, the day before she was to fly home. She dialed the operator and asked to make a collect call. The phone rang and rang. Finally, Lyn answered, breathless like she'd run in from outside.

"Will you accept a collect call from Millie Archer?" the operator asked in a crisp tone.

"What?" Lyn asked.

"Say yes, Lyn," Millie yelled. "Get Mom or Dad on the phone."

The operator repeated the question. Lyn dropped the receiver with a loud thunk.

"Dad, Dad. It's Millipede."

David picked up the extension. "Yes, we'll accept the charges. Darling girl, hello. How are you? How's Jody? We miss you terribly."

"Not me," Lyn chirped from the other phone. "I've taken over your entire room."

"Dad, I'm fine." She ignored Lyn. "We're both okay. Dad, I've— umm—I've learned a lot. Jody took me to class and I've met some of her friends. The teacher was so cool. Have you heard of the poet Gerard Manley Hopkins?"

"Yes, of course. You sound good. I hope this means Jody's better."

"Well, I don't know. Maybe. She's helped me make some changes with—"

"Ask her for me if your mother and I might visit her. We'll work it out whenever she's willing."

Millie pulled at her new honey blonde curls. He sounded almost pleading. Not good, she thought. He was putting her right in the middle. Jody called her the Peacemaker in the family. Maybe that's what happens to the peacemaker. You're caught smack-dab in the middle.

"Will you do that for me, Millie?"

"I'll try. But, Dad, I'm not sure. If the moment seems right, I'll ask. I'm trying not to push. She already thinks I came to spy."

"Darling girl, I trust you. Do what you think best. However, you know how helpless I feel. Please consider it. We're looking forward to seeing you tomorrow afternoon." He cleared his throat and coughed. "I tell you this will be a strange Easter morning without you here, Chickadee."

"I love you, too, Dad. Lyn-bug, you better clean up my side of the room by 3:05 tomorrow. Tell Mom I've changed my hair some."

"Happy Easter, Millipede," Lyn said. They clicked off.

Millie stood in the Winslow Farms telephone closet. The odor of spaghetti seeped under the glass door. She took a deep breath. She'd been gone from home just since Thursday, yet it felt longer. She could picture what everyone would be doing, but she saw it all now from a distance. Not as a stranger. A stranger wouldn't feel such an ache in her stomach.

The rest of Saturday morning, Millie followed Jody, helping with her assigned chores. First they made their way through the snowy, muddy path to the stable and groomed the horses, fed and watered them. Jody seemed to enjoy showing Millie how to brush them, how to lift each hoof and pick out debris. She showed her how to hold out an apple on the palm of her hand as a treat when they finished. Millie giggled when the big chestnut mare nuzzled her, begging more. They went from the barn to the art room to clean up for the next week. Shelly and Michael joined them. For a while all seemed to be going well. Millie relaxed.

Michael complimented her on her new blonde curly hair. "Makes your blue-green eyes sparkle more than ever," he said with a smile.

She felt herself blush. She looked over at Shelly and Jody. Shelly gave a thumbs up. Jody stared straight ahead. Millie said, "Thank you. I couldn't have done it without these two urging me on." She watched Jody's blank face.

"And the snow would have ruined it if they hadn't help me curl and dry it again."

"He gets it. You needed our help. We gave it. Your hair looks good. You look pretty." Jody stood up, walked to the storage closet, put her mop inside, closed the door with a decided bang. "I've got to go. Millie, I'll meet you at supper. You can have the rest of the day to yourself. I'm done." With that she walked out and away.

The brother and sister exchanged glances. "What happened?" Millie asked. "Did I do something wrong?"

Shelly said, "She does that sometimes."

"Yeah," Michael said. "It's as if a little alarm bell goes off inside her. It doesn't mean that anyone did anything to cause her reaction."

"At least, that's what we tell ourselves, or we might be taking the blame," Shelly added. "We're her friends here, you know." She didn't add, *her only friends*, but Millie heard that in the air.

Michael finished spreading the fresh butcher paper on the work tables. "Don't take it personally, dearie. That's what we tell ourselves. Shelly and I have to practice our music, so I hope you won't mind if we cut out too."

"No, no. Please, I have plenty of studying to do for next week. A book report to write." She looked out the window at the snow all around. "A snowman to build maybe." She could hear the false cheeriness in her voice. How could she not take it personally? Jody had hurt her. Was Jody jealous because Michael had given her a compliment? She waved good-bye to them and headed back to her room.

For a while, Millie stared out the window at the white landscape. She wished she had the little glass snail she'd given Jody. Jody obviously didn't want it or even remember giving it first to Millie. She said the mantra anyway, recalling how the snail's coiled surface felt to her fingers, cool and comforting as she used to follow the swirl upward to its peak, then back down: "Slow and steady goes the snail." That saying did sound dumb, not at all deep and meaningful as she'd thought it just because her big sister had said it to her. She stretched out on the bed and turned on her stomach. She flutter-kicked her legs. She'd rather do anything than go slow and steady. She'd like to run or swim flutter-kicking across the lake or fly straight up and away.

Had Jody always been that way? First warm and easy to be with, then suddenly hateful and cold and distant? If so, she hadn't noticed. Too busy with her own concerns, she guessed. Mother did say that Jody was moody plenty of times. Dad had used a word she had to look up: petulant. Could she do as Dad had asked and find out if Jody would let them visit? Why not? Might as well give it a go. How could it be any worse between them?

Millie went to the mirror and studied her new look. Not bad. Michael said she looked pretty. And she saw that he was right. She'd been regarded as a "brain" long enough at school. Maybe now she could be pretty and smart. But if she wanted to be smart, she'd better finish *Mockingbird*. She read and underlined in pencil some of the sections she thought she could use in her report, made a few notes in her notebook.

When she finished the book, she went back to the opening. She'd forgotten all about the beginning when the author referred to Jem's broken arm. Now she saw that Harper Lee had told a long story of how Scout's big brother broke his arm. That's the way some people wander all around when they tell a story, especially in the South. Or so they say, although in her Southern family, people didn't tell many stories. They held in stories, especially stories with secrets. She closed her eyes and thought about Jody. What secret story would explain her near-suicide? Millie fell asleep thinking about Jody's art.

She woke up from a dream about Jody. She grabbed her notebook and wrote it as a poem.

**My Sister as Alice**
I see my sister throw colored blocks
into a boiling pot. She stirs
until they melt—dates, years, my birthday, hers.
I call out, "Wait! When time's so fluid,
memory blurs to smudges
of color, no distinctions."
"That's the point," she says. "Watch this."
She pours the sludge
into a waiting mold to make a mug.
"Wait!" I call and catch her as she jumps.

Alice in her blue dress, white pinafore, white stockings, and Mary Jane's,
my sister's the handle: her hands grip the rim,
her skirt flares out, her feet touch the mug:
Timeless Alice forever holds the edge—
and I hold her, holding
this hot drink.

Millie felt pleased with her poem, almost a shaped poem. It didn't make much sense and hardly rhymed at all. Maybe she'd go back later and work on it. What did it mean? All she knew was that it appeared as images in her dream and somehow she'd caught her sister before she drowned and melted with the time-numbers. She'd like to show it to Mr. Strayer. Her sister could make art with paint and clay. She, Millicent Archer, would make art with words in lines.

It wasn't supper time yet, but Millie decided she'd see if Jody would talk to her. She stood outside Jody's door, praying that whatever was wrong between them would be healed. She remembered the feeling of urgency when she begged her dad to let her make the trip. "Jody needs me," she'd said. If her sister needed her, she had a funny way of showing it. Except helping her get her hair dyed—that might have made Jody feel like a big sister again. Millie couldn't hear anything behind the door.

Finally, she knocked their signal knock: dum-dum-dum-de-dum. Nothing. After a second try, she opened the door. "Jody? Jody?" No answer.

Millie slipped into the room. The bathroom door was open, so Jody wasn't there. She'd write a note and leave it on her desk. The middle desk drawer held index cards and pens. On the side was a small box that might hold a piece of jewelry beside a ledger book. She looked in the box and was surprised to see on the bed of cotton, a razor blade, the kind used to scrap off paint from the windows after painting the trim. That's weird, she thought. She put it back carefully and looked in the ledger book. Some kind of record with initials and dates. She thumbed through the pages. Her letters to Jody fell out. And two from their daddy. She stuffed the letters back into the book, hoping it didn't matter where they'd been. Millie's heart thumped hard. She felt like a spy for sure. Why would Jody keep a razor blade in a jewelry box? What were the initials for?

She got up and walked to the bed. Under the pillow was a plastic bag in which Jody had stored a towel and small wash cloth. Both were bloody. If she had heavy periods, she would clean up in the bathroom. Why keep a bloody towel under her pillow? She put the bag back and smoothed the pillow, but not before she heard Jody behind her.

"Snooping into my stuff, huh? You did come up here to spy on me. Just like I thought." Jody's face looked swollen and very red.

"No, Jody. You don't understand. I was going to write you a note. But I saw something strange." She couldn't go on.

Jody pushed her against the wall. "You want to see what I do? What my current obsession is? My way of coping with what I live with?"

Her face was so close, Millie could smell her sour breath, see black heads on her perfect nose. Jody pushed harder, pinning Millie's shoulders against the wall. Then she let go.

She rolled up her sleeves, exposing lots of cuts, as if she'd fought a wild cat and lost. Some were raw and still oozing blood. Others were dark and nearly healed.

"See why I always wear long sleeves?" Jody's mouth twisted in an unnatural way. "You're shocked. I can see that. Shut your mouth before you catch flies." Jody laughed. "As we used to say in happier days."

"Oh, Jody, no. You're cutting yourself? That's what that razor blade is for. That was the strange thing I found." Millie started to cry. "Why? Why are you hurting yourself?"

"Now you know. I'm what they call a cutter. Mom and Dad don't know and you better not tell them. Or anyone else." She handed Millie a tissue.

Millie dabbed her eyes but felt like someone had knocked the wind out of her. She tried to catch her breath, then blew her nose. She had to get through to her sister.

"Jody, please. Don't do that. I love you. Mom and Dad love you. Lyn-bug loves you. Your friends Shelly and Michael do too. Please, Jody, don't hurt yourself."

"I'm working on it. In my private therapy sessions. But see, at first a little cut relieved the pressure inside that threatened to explode. Or im-plode. Anyway, now it's like I have to cut. Not all the time, but it's like cutting focuses my pain. I can stand a little pain from a cut, so then I'm not so overwhelmed by the larger blacker dense storm of pain." Jody's face looked proud and clean as a porcelain goddess.

"Jody, I had no idea. I'm so sorry." Millie couldn't imagine such pain and wondered what caused Jody to suffer so much. Her tears started again.

"Stop that crying, Millipede, or you'll have me boo-hooing too." She reached for Millie and hugged her for the first time. A real hug. No stiffness. "I love you too. And I'm glad you came to see me." She held her

135

at arm's length. "It's a good thing you came, so we could do something about your hair."

The next day before Millie boarded the van to return to the airport in D.C., Jody walked with her arm-in-arm. Millie asked when she thought it would be all right for their mother and father to visit, that they wanted to very much. She braced for a rebuff, but instead Jody turned it over in her mind before saying anything.

"Tell you what, Millipede. Please tell them not to worry so much. I'll be leaving for college anyway next year. I could probably see them one at a time, for a short visit, but not before summer." Millie knew she was making it up as she went along, but at least it would be an answer she could take home with her.

"Another thing, Millie. Not a word about the other. Promise."

"I promise." Millie hugged her big sister and added, "I pray that your pain eases without you-know-what."

"That sounds just like you, my metaphysical sister."

They laughed. Millie climbed into the van. They blew kisses and waved to each other as the shuttle pulled away from Winslow Farms. She wondered if she'd be able to visit again. It hurt to leave, but Millie was ready to be home.

# 17

## David

Easter services were over. The magnificent music from choir and organ, trumpet, trombone, and timpani left a reverberating silence in its wake. David felt exhausted but content. Typical of Protestant churches all over America, Harmony Presbyterian had been crowded for both worship services. Ushers had lined the aisles with folding chairs to accommodate the overflow—the regulars and members who attended only once or twice a year.

Every Easter presented him with the challenge of preaching on the same subject of the resurrection of Jesus yet vary the approach enough so that people might possibly hear something new and fresh.

With Jody at Winslow Farms and Millie—the apple of his eye— away visiting her sister there, David had waked up early and spent more time than usual in silent prayer, holding up both the girls with urgency, pleading for God's healing and grace. He prayed too for Nell en route home from Nashville. He admitted to God how much he resented Nell's being away on Easter, then laughed and admitted that he needed her to be making money to pay for Jody's care.

With his daughters acutely on his mind all week, he'd planned his sermon using Mary Magdalene at the empty tomb and the appearance of Jesus in the garden, whom she mistook for the gardener. His theme: "He calls us from death to life." He said, "Whatever has deadened your spirit, or mine, He calls us to new life. Whether the death-dealer is chronic illness or grief over a loved one or hardness of heart from years of bitterness or hurt or loss of a job or hopelessness and despair, He calls us out of whatever dark place entombs. Into life. It is no accident that we celebrate Resurrection Day in the spring. Have you seen how daffodils can push up through the hardest ground, even through asphalt, and bloom in a blaze of golden glory? Just so, the tomb could not hold Jesus." He read John Donne's poem, "Death, Be Not Proud." He ended the sermon with the words, "Christ Jesus meets you and me, as he met Mary Magdalene in the garden—outside the tomb—and calls you and me by name, as he did Mary. He gives instructions to go and tell the others that He lives. He, the Risen Christ, meets us where we are right now."

The words from his sermon played through his mind that evening. He himself needed to believe what he preached, that he too could be brought into new life. Jody's near suicide had awakened him to the fact that she suffered, as his mother and brother had, from clinical depression. He felt deadened, almost paralyzed by fear for his beloved child, really all three children. Millie had returned safely. Nell was home, in her warm-ups and slippers.

The evening had turned unusually cold and overcast with spring storms moving through upstate South Carolina. David built a fire in the hearth and slowly began to feel warm. Warm with gratitude for Millie back home, for Lyn so tickled to have her big sister by her side on the floor playing Concentration, for Nell actually sitting quietly in the den with the family. Nell seemed almost happy and content, thumbing through a magazine. She wasn't on the phone or away with her business buying or selling. He wished he could stretch his arms around all of them. Instead, he went in the kitchen and concocted his famous waffles.

David smiled to remember how everyone reacted to Millie's new hairdo. They had all gone to the airport and watched the people at the gate coming out. A tall, slender young woman with blonde curly hair bounced through the crowd toward them smiling and waving. It took a minute for him to recognize Millie. Lyn ran to her immediately. "Millie, you look so shiny and curly," she said, grabbing her around the waist.

Millie hugged Lyn and swung her around, then turned to Nell, who gave her a quick kiss and asked, "What's happened to your hair?"

"Like it?" Millie asked but didn't wait for an answer, turned to him and buried herself in his embrace. "Darling girl, you look beautiful to me," he'd said. "And older."

"Mom?" Millie asked, breaking away and facing Nell. "What do you think?"

"You look—you look lovely, but different. Was this Jody's idea?"

"This was my decision, but she and a friend helped me. They got the appointment and went with me. Then it snowed, and I thought my hair was ruined forever."

While they'd waited for the baggage, she talked in a rush about how Jody and her friend had rolled her hair, dried it and restored her new look. She went on about Winslow Farm, how beautiful it was, and Jody's room, the animals, her chores, the art building, some kind of picnic/Easter egg hunt for day-care children. David watched Nell's whole body begin to relax as Millie spilled out her experiences.

In the kitchen now, David saw Millie's shoulders tense up and her face grow somber as she set the table for supper. "Are you all right, Millie?"

He waited. While he waited for her response, he warmed the syrup, poured milk for the girls, started coffee for him and Nell.

"Dad, it's complicated." Millie moved to the window. Without looking at him, she said, "I feel different. Not just my hair. The trip seemed longer than a weekend."

"Millie, darling girl, you were our advance scout. You've been in Jody's new world. That's bound to have had its effect on you." He stood beside her. "And on how you see everything here as well."

"Yeah, well. In some ways, I think I like Winslow Farms better than she does. The Funny Farm, that's what she calls it. And she talks about

139

herself and the other people there like they're inmates in prison." She leaned her head against his arm.

David put his arm around her. "That's Jody. She makes fun of her situation and the place as a defense. A way of protecting herself."

"I liked her friends—Shelly and Michael. They're sister and brother. And she has a fantastic teacher. I told you about the poetry."

"Yes. Yes, you did. Gerard Manley Hopkins, I believe. I think she's in a good place. From all you've said. Did you get a chance to ask—"

"Yes, but, Dad, you'll have to wait a while. She's not ready for more family."

"Not yet. Not yet. I know I should be more patient. But it's hard. At least she let you visit."

Millie let out a big sigh. "But that may not happen again."

There was something she wasn't telling him, but he could tell she wasn't going to elaborate. So he suggested they call the others to supper. He'd have to leave it at that.

All his women loved his waffles and ate a lot. "You're going to make us all fat, David." Nell looked at Lyn when she reached for a third helping. "You should learn to master something healthier, like oven-roasted vegetables." This was followed by a chorus of groans.

Later, David stretched full length under the cool sheet and light quilt until his feet touched the foot rail. Bed at last. "It's great to have Millie back home, isn't it? And such a good experience with Jody."

Nell gave no response.

How good it was to be horizontal under the "cool kindliness of clean sheets." He drifted off, thinking of the Rupert Brooke poem that had so fascinated him as a boy. He might tell Millie about how that one poem turned him on to poetry as something that could actually convey physical sensation.

Just then Nell rolled over to face him, wide awake. "David, I need to tell you something. You're always begging me to talk to you, so now I'm going to."

He sighed and turned toward her. He never begged. He caressed her arm. "Nell, I have to get up at 5:30 tomorrow. Dirk Pinyard's going into surgery and I promised the family I'd be there with them."

Nell pulled her arm away and covered it with the sheet. "David, you remember the guy at the trade show who helped me haul those crates from the Millerton estate? He's maybe ten or so years younger than I am." Her voice had taken on a dreamy quality, as if she were on the edge of sleep herself. Oh, yes, he remembered him.

"You don't need to get up so early," he said. "I'll stop at The Mug for some breakfast before I go to the hospital." He lay back on his pillow.

She laughed a low torch singer sort of laugh. "He's become, this guy, even though he's younger than I am, he's become a good friend." She giggled. "And, of course, he's Flora's friend, too." Nell stretched out on her back.

David hoped she was through talking and would hear him. "Yeah, well. Listen, please. You'll need to get the girls off tomorrow. Millie's got a ride with the Parks, but Lyn will need you to drive her. Her science project is in the special display case I built for her. It's in the garage on the work bench, so please remind her."

"The guy's name is Stefan Wallington. And I'll be going to the big market sale in Raleigh with him next week. And with Flora, of course. I thought I should mention it." Nell yawned and turned on her side away from him. "And another thing—Flora and I were robbed of most of our inventory, right outside Nashville. At the Cracker Barrel. Out of the van while we ate."

Did she say they'd been robbed? He'd ask her tomorrow. She must have been drifting into a dream. Had she heard a word he said? "Okay. Well. I don't know why they start science projects so early for the kids now. She had the idea, but I had to do most of the logistical work. So please don't let her go to school without it. You know how absent-minded she can be. It's half her grade in science." Nell's breathing grew deep and regular.

"Good night, Nell."

"Hmmm."

He could never sleep after they talked in bed. Now he'd be mulling over the young man Stefan. He recalled the guy's smirk, his ironic tone, the overly elaborate manners toward him as if he, David, only 53, were elderly. David sighed. He might as well get up and load the science project into Nell's car, not wait for them to forget it tomorrow.

He looked at the clock glowing green in the dark. It was already tomorrow.

David's appointment with his therapist followed his time at the hospital with the Pinyards. He'd offered a prayer before Dirk was wheeled into surgery and then listened to Heddy Pinyard complain about how inconsiderate their adult children had become in the past few years. If Dirk were to die during the triple bypass, they'd be mildly irritated that their plans had been disrupted. They had tickets to the Masters, after all. He ought to cut them off without a cent. After an hour and a half, when Heddy was escorted to Recovery to be with her husband, David had said his good-byes.

Outside the hospital, he felt like shaking off her whining voice the way dogs shake off water. He breathed in the spring air—pollen and all—with relief.

Madeleine Crispin's office gave an entirely different atmosphere, one that brought David into a world separate from the quotidian—the fragrance of sandalwood from a russet candle on the window ledge, the small fountain gurgling, soft variable light reflected from the triangular stained glass at the top window. He felt tight in his shoulders and neck. In her quiet, soothing voice, Madeleine led him in their routine muscle and breathing exercises. He rotated his shoulders and lifted and lowered each one ten times. Then he followed her lead with what she called "the centering breath" by breathing in through one nostril, pressing the other closed, holding for a beat or two, then releasing and breathing in through the other side. Repeating this slow breathing right and left several times helped him become centered and relaxed. He told her he now used the exercise before he entered the pulpit every Sunday and thought he didn't sweat quite as much under his clerical robe.

"Good," she said. "Now, David, I have a question for you. Usually you spend our time together telling me about your concern over Jody, Millie, and Lyn or your growing resentment toward your wife, or sometimes the rumbling within your church. Today, I want you to answer this question. What do you, Claude David Archer, want?"

"I want Jody to be well. I want her to be in a good relationship with each of us in the family."

Before he could say more, Madeleine said, "David, what do you want for *you*? For *your* life? Didn't we agree on your last visit—you cannot save any life but your own. You said that to me and I agreed. So, what do you want?"

"Well, I'd be a lot happier if Nell were happier. I'd like for her to—"

"Wait. Stop. Not what you wish Nell would do or be. What do you want? Take a minute and let all your present situation and problems subside. Let a picture form." She waited.

David breathed in the fragrant atmosphere. He glanced at the clock. He was using up his hour doing nothing. He closed his eyes and thought, this is a safe place. "I see a curving path in the mountains. Tall, green trees are on either side, shadowing the path with dappled light and dark patterns. I'm walking at my own pace, neither fast nor slow."

"How do you feel there?"

"Unburdened. Relieved. Free, or almost free."

"Are you alone?"

"Yes. But I'm—"

"You're what?"

"I'm anticipating something or someone. I'm on the way to meet—"

"You're on the way to meet—?"

"Emily. Emily Parks. That's who." He shivered involuntarily. "Now I've said it."

"What do you want, David?"

"I want. I want a different life." He opened his eyes and held his gaze on Madeleine's steady eyes. "Madeleine, I feel basically numb, wooden. Almost paralyzed to do anything to change the way the church is going. I feel in a way too deadened to allow myself to want anything. Usually, I just want to get through the day, or the week, keeping faith with what I've promised. I haven't allowed myself to feel what I'm actually feeling deep inside."

"Okay, David, what are you feeling deep inside?"

"A kind of fear. And I think the fear is that life is slithering away, before I can do anything worthwhile. Nothing like I dreamed. To make my life count for something. It sounds adolescent, but I thought being a minister would make a difference in the world. Now I feel burned out. I'm more than resentful toward Nell. I feel betrayed by her. We signed on to this vocation together. Or at least I believed we did. Now she hates me. She wants to get away from my vocation, as a minister. Actually, I think she wants to get away from me."

"What about you, David? You, not Nell. You are not wooden, except on the surface. I sense great passion under your pleasant facade. No matter where it leads you—you're onto something important here. And don't forget what you pictured as you walked the mountain path. Emily. Why Emily? You might explore that too in your notebook."

"Forget I said anything about Emily. She's—she's an impossibility. She's married. I'm married. I'm a minister of the gospel. There are boundaries that I won't cross and neither will she. So, forget I mentioned her."

"We won't talk about her unless you choose to, but she did appear in your meditative walk. And once or twice before in dreams you've described."

David felt restless. The clock clearly showed his time was up. He stood. Madeleine remained seated for a moment as if she refused to release the Emily-thread. He thought but didn't say that Emily listened to him. He felt more alive when she was around. He waited until Madeleine closed the notebook and stood. Then he thanked her and said he'd explore his anger and fear in his journal.

In the car, he leaned his head on the steering wheel. How could he ever make progress? He never managed to talk out all that went through him during their sessions. And even if he did, how would that help him find his way again to new life? Dante's opening of *The Divine Comedy* flashed into his mind: "Mid-way in my life, I find myself in a dark wood, my path lost."

It would be better to what? Return to his usual way of coping—just put his deadened spirit out of mind and do the next job waiting for him? Too much on his back burner. He had to ask Nell what she said about being robbed. Surely he imagined it. She must have been drifting to sleep, dreaming.

David drove home and whistled for Calvin. Exercise was in order whether he felt like it or not. Calvin greeted him with his eager wide smile, lolling tongue, waving tail. They set out for the park down the wide McDaniel Avenue. Cherry trees were in full bloom, a few petals like party confetti flittered down, dotting the sidewalk. Oak trees sported their gold-green tassels. Of course, Robert Frost had it right, "Nothing gold can stay." But how glorious while it lasted. He summoned gratitude from under the emotional debris that cluttered his despairing heart.

# 18

## Charlotte

The six women gathered at church on Wednesday evening after supper and sat in the comfortable upholstered chairs grouped in a circle. Although they varied in age and appearance to some degree, they were all in that stage of life where no tactful person would hazard a guess as to their ages. Only two allowed gray hair to show. One lady had been totally white-haired since her early thirties—her full page boy was stunning and gave her youthful face distinctive beauty. Another had decided to let her dyed auburn hair grow out, so the middle part widened in whiteness every week the women met as the winter moved into spring. One with big coiffed jet-black hair draped a huge rug across her ample lap where she bent over tiny flowers in a tedious pattern of intricate embroidery. The youngest in the group with a long blonde braid down her back frowned in concentration as she cast on stitches to begin a multi-colored scarf or sweater. Natalie had suggested that Charlotte might enjoy the group. It would take her mind off worrying that she might lose her house.

Jerry Ann, the obvious leader of the group, welcomed them and pushed in two more chairs. Although Harmony church was not enormous, Charlotte hardly knew most of these women. No doubt, one of the new groups formed in the past year. Jerry Ann's hair possessed that natural wave that Charlotte imagined allowed her to wear the same basic short do nearly all her life. The soft gray and brown curls capped her head neatly and accented her large brown eyes, magnified by glasses. She briefly introduced Charlotte and Natalie all around. Charlotte promptly forgot the names. She saw that the women were already in the midst of a conversation. She pulled out the scarf she'd started knitting before Fred died and attempted to recall the pattern. She listened to the talk swirling around her and felt as she used to feel when she sat on the pier and let the cool lake water swish around her feet. Natalie was right; this could be relaxing.

"I heard he filed divorce papers. It shocked her. She had no inkling."

"No kidding."

"No kidding. He'd taken up with a girl, a nurse I think, that worked in the same big medical practice."

"No," the youngest woman said. "She's a doctor too. A resident. Not a nurse."

"What's Annie going to do?"

"Don't worry about her. She's got the best divorce attorney in Goodwin. And her job with Pepsi keeps her plenty busy."

"Yeah, she's flying off here and there all the time."

"It's all so clichéd, you know?" Jerry Ann was smocking a dress for a child, probably her granddaughter. "The guy's a rat. How could he do that to such a beautiful, smart girl?"

"Weren't they together before the wedding?"

"Yes, but his parents are divorced and he's never been much of a church person."

"But still, there are plenty of non-church children with divorced parents who don't act that way." The hook-rug lady spoke with obvious disdain. "I went to their wedding—so lovely. And he's so handsome. What was he thinking?"

"Obviously, he wasn't."

"Yeah, he couldn't keep it zipped."

"What else is new?" The women chuckled.

"Anyone have any good news?" Jerry Ann looked from one to another.

Charlotte looked up. The young blonde met her eyes, smiled and said, "I know something good. Deborah Baker is awesome. She came to our house the other day. Asked me to be an advisor for the young people. And she was super great with my dad. Didn't stare at his amputated legs or anything. Made him laugh. Joked around with him, kinda flirting."

Jerry Ann said to Charlotte, "Man oh man, you can see why people have a problem turning her down. That Deborah's a keeper, if you ask me." She gestured to the young blonde.

"Valerie, you'll do a fine job as an advisor. Speaking of Deborah, I heard her say that she was worried David might be losing his focus, what with Jody's serious psychological problems. Plus the cost to keep her in that place. You know it must cost a fortune. Per month. She wondered how they are able to pay for Jody's care."

The lady with the white hair said, "Good question. We pay him well, but not that much."

Natalie spoke up for the first time. "Well, Nell deals in very expensive jewelry. Backed at first by an inheritance, I think."

"Yes, that's what she's done with it—plowed it into estate jewelry," the white-haired woman said. "Ned bought me a piece that Nell and Flora acquired at auction. Sothesby's, no less."

"Wow. Sell a couple like that and you could pay for a half a year at the Ritz Carlton."

"Maybe, but—" Jerry Ann said.

"But what?"

"Deborah told me that David reported in staff meeting that Nell and Flora were robbed Easter weekend. Right out of their van. While they ate supper."

"Oh, dear. In a way, they have to start over."

"That's what she gets for not being in church. Not even on Easter Sunday." The woman with the growing path of white hair said, looking around for approval.

"Oh, that's cruel." Everyone laughed.

"I'm just saying—what does that say about David? That she's never here?"

"One thing—he can't control his own wife."

"Hold on. Since when do you think a man should control his wife? What's happened to you, Jerry Ann? All that feminism down the drain?" Natalie said.

"Deborah has helped me see that we've got to take the Bible more seriously. It's in Paul's letters, you know."

"I can't believe you. There are some things you have to rack up as archaic customs of a by-gone era," the lady with jet-black hair said, looking up from her rug. "As my great aunt used to say, 'Paul is important, but he wasn't divine.'"

"Amen to that," Natalie said.

"Still, it does make you wonder. If what Deborah said is true, David and Nell are having financial troubles. No telling what he might have to do to pay those expensive bills." Jerry Ann spoke with authority.

She was used to being listened to, the one in control. Charlotte wondered if Jerry Ann exerted such control in her marriage, missing the irony in her words. She sighed and counted the stitches again in her pattern. David and Nell weren't the only ones with financial problems. She knitted and purled with growing determination to take action to dig herself out of her own hole.

# 19

## David

⁂

In the church office, David Archer checked his messages and looked through the stack of mail that came in Monday. Judith sat at her desk typing and chewing gum. It was either gum or the stash of carrots she nibbled for her ongoing battle with weight. He asked her where Deborah was this morning.

"Oh, she called that she'd be in around 10:30. She said she was helping a family pack up and catch a bus to some relatives in North Carolina."

"So she's at the Space for Hope?"

Judith put her pencil to her lips and glanced at David, then at the clock on the wall to his right. "Either there or the cheap motel the homeless family was staying in."

"The director of the Space for Hope should know, right?"

Judith nodded, still poking the pencil at her front teeth. She's thinking something she's not telling, David thought. He put his blazer back on. "If she comes in, keep her here. In this office. With you. Do not let her pass Go."

"What?"

His Monopoly reference was lost on Judith. He wondered if she ever played games. "Keep her here, please. With you." He attempted a confident smile.

"But what shall I say? The Reverend Deborah Baker never holds still a minute. She might come behind the counter here." Judith shuddered at the notion. "Or she'll bug the financial secretary like she did last week. About the books. She stood behind Maria and demanded to see who's giving what."

"Deborah did that? Last week you say? What did Maria do?"

"Oh, she gave her what she wanted. She told me later she assumed you okayed her request. Did you, sir?"

"I most certainly did not." He took in a deep breath. His throat tightened. He made his voice grow quiet. "Judith, from now on, I want you to let me know about anything you feel instinctively is a bit, shall we say, peculiar, in what Deborah is doing, or asking. Can you do that for me, Judith? It would really help."

"Yes, sir. I can do that."

"If she comes in before I return, get her to help you stuff envelopes with youth publicity, or something. Okay?"

"Yes, sir." Judith scratched under her stiff brown hair with the pencil. Her brunette helmet kept every strand in its designated place and barely moved as the pencil did its work. She resumed her rhythmic typing.

David drove toward the west side of town and made most of the lights, but close to the high school, traffic was backed up. Instead of turning, he swerved into the other lane and took a side street over to Pendleton, all the time with an eye out for patrol cars. In the driveway of the Space for Hope, he honked at a man pushing a grocery cart packed to the brim with his meager belongings. David stopped himself. *What could be so imperative that I had to honk at a poor homeless man?* He took a deep breath.

The woman in the office said that Deborah should be at the bus station by now. David thanked her and headed to the station.

151

He parked on the street and walked under the domed shelter where city buses and Greyhound buses came and went, billowing heavy exhaust fumes. David saw Deborah talking to two men. They were laughing. Deborah touched the arm of the taller man, who turned and walked into the waiting room. Soon he emerged with a pregnant woman and two toddlers. David waited until the family and the other man boarded the Greyhound. Only then did he approach his associate minister.

"Deborah. Hi."

She whirled around, startled, quickly recovered. "David, what are you doing here? Checking up on me, huh?"

"We do need to talk, you and I. Shall we go back to the church? Or would you rather talk over a cup of coffee somewhere?"

"Let's grab a cup of joe. Ride with me, Reverend-Doctor. I'm parked on the street."

"We'll probably need both our cars afterward, so I'll drive mine. Meet you at Coffee Underground in five minutes." He hoped she wouldn't elude him and would actually be at the cafe. If they were to talk frankly, they'd need a booth away from other patrons.

Over two mugs of coffee—his black, hers with two scoops of sugar and a load of cream, they sat opposite each other in a back booth. He'd have to speak up and find out what was going on in that puzzling mind of hers. Before he could say anything, she took the initiative and got them off on the wrong foot.

"Just like lovers meeting secretly in broad daylight," she said with a wink and a flick of her outrageous red hair. She managed to disconcert him with little or no effort.

"Deborah, please be serious for a few minutes. I need for you to catch me up on what you've been doing with the young people. Somehow the weekly staff meetings have yielded nothing concrete to inform me of your work. Nothing specific, that is." How officious he sounded. Perspiration dampened his shirt. He took off his blazer and draped it across the chair back, conscious she watched his every move.

"Surely, you don't believe I'm not working enough, David." She cocked her big black eyes up at him, the long lashes batting in mock flirtation. She lifted her inevitable nasal spray from her pocket and sniffed deeply. "Sorry. Allergies."

"You know that I know you're working hard. Just fill me in on some of your programs and plans. There have been some questions raised."

"I certainly hope so. No doubt people in the congregation are catching the spirit of my work."

David should have been used to her teasing by now. She'd been his associate for seven months, but this particular day he felt more annoyance than usual. As if a rash were about to break out on his arms and legs. He rubbed his arms and waited. He sipped his hot drink, strong and bitter, suitable for what he had to do. He waited, watching as she doctored her coffee with more cream, stirred. She touched the tip of her nose with her index finger.

Almost purring she leaned toward him. "What questions have been raised?" She licked the tip of her right index finger. Her nails were shiny with white paint on each tip.

"Nothing very specific. But I got the impression that you're busy generating a new program. A movement of some kind. Enlighten me."

Deborah flashed a smile, then turned serious. Still she seemed to be mocking him and her own seriousness. She said, "The last time I had the opportunity to preach, the response was—well, flattering—to say the least." She put down her mug and touched David's free hand. "Not to take anything away from you, of course."

David pulled his hand away. "Well, that kind of reception is all to the good. Congratulations." Again he waited.

She shifted in her seat, crossed her legs. "With the senior highs, I brought up issues I felt they should consider. First with study, then with direct action." She lifted her chin and brushed her hair back. "So it's under the usual youth planning already approved by the Session. No need to make a big deal. In school, the kids had been studying the Civil Rights

Movement and the anti-war protests of the sixties and seventies, so that's probably why they thought to name it The Movement."

"So, is this the subject for the next Youth Sunday worship service?"

"You could say that. Although we haven't discussed it yet. Mostly, they're ready to put their faith into action, I'm pleased to report."

"What position are you advocating, Deborah?"

"How about missionary?"

"What?"

"Never mind." She looked around the coffee shop. "We could come here after one of our protests. I think they'd like this rathskeller ambience."

"What exactly are you advocating?"

"The one advocated by holy scriptures, of course, Reverend-doc." She gave him the wide-eyed mock-innocent expression in her obsidian eyes, her full lips in a pout.

"Meaning what? You know as well as I do that the Bible can be used to prove any position you wish to take. So what issues are you talking about?"

"Oh, how about homosexuality and anti-abortion, for example?"

"Nothing about abortion is directly addressed by the Bible." He heard his own sharp tone. "And certainly with modern scientific knowledge, we have to consider 1989 issues in the light of what we've learned of genetics and not take the scriptures literally. Anyway, even our most conservative brethren do not accept all the archaic Hebrew laws, and you know it."

"David, we may just have to disagree." She reached across the table and patted his hand.

He pulled away. "What about your counter protest at the abortion clinic? As I recall, you joined Natalie and Emily to face down the pro-lifers. In January, you were for choice. What happened?"

"Since then, I've seen the light, as our conservative brethren say." Her dark eyes glistened. "You set up the meeting, with our treasurer, Julian Denyar. Remember? He helped me understand. And I mean to preach action. In the name of the Lord, of course."

Deborah rose from her seat, smoothed her suit skirt, brushing away invisible crumbs. "About gays—they're spreading the plague of AIDs even into the South. It's not just in Africa and San Francisco. I have to go—to be about our Father's business, so to speak." She sashayed out and waved impishly from the door of the Coffee Underground.

David scratched his itchy arms. He laughed at the truth his body told him. Deborah got under his skin. She spoke so fast, yet continued to be elusive. Something about her provoked his own allergic reaction. Now he'd more or less confronted her. He still knew no concrete plans she'd made. What was he to do to counter an extreme position? Her viewpoint could have a terrible polarizing effect on the congregation.

After Deborah left the cafe, David refilled his cup and opened his notebook. Energy surged through him. In a strange way he almost resented, Deborah had revved his rusty engine, a motor he'd allowed to idle far too long, under church routines. David took a deep breath and scribbled in his notebook:

*What should I preach? What's most important to me? How day-to-day in the first century, Jesus moved among people and broke down barriers. A quiet revolution. How he built bridges between people estranged from one another. His regard and respect for women, the marginalized and outcasts. Remember Gandhi, MLK, Jr., their non-violent resistance, the stories that he knew well of the Civil Rights struggle, the story of my own father's strong stand in Little Rock for school integration. Courage, that I need.*

*Jesus championed people on the margins. Even now in 1989, racial barriers and prejudice still exist, sometimes hidden. Women are discounted. Gays marginalized. Many have to hide true identity to succeed. To survive.*

Yes. A series on the New Creation. Calling us to become "repairers of the breach," a part of Christ's New Creation. That's what I'll do.

Outside, a stiff breeze caught and blew open his jacket. He looked up at the midday sky, cool for spring. Yes, he'd begin the series on Pentecost. He might not be on fire with the Holy Spirit, but what few embers remained inside him, all but extinguished, had flared to life. For that, he thanked God. And, begrudgingly, Deborah Baker for waking him up.

After everyone in the household was asleep, David searched the captain's chest in the attic for the diary his father kept during the fifties. He'd never read it, but maybe he could gain some insight, some courage for what was ahead. His mother must have saved everything she deemed special. Under his childhood books and papers from his time at Davidson, he uncovered a cracked leather binder zipped closed. Inside were old *Time* and *Newsweek* magazines and clipped articles from *The Saturday Evening Post*. Under the 1957-1959 articles about the integration struggle in Little Rock, the diary nestled, preserved by his mother in plastic wrap, and sealed with tape. Discouraging casual reading. It'd been too much trouble until now.

Inside the cedar-colored leather journal was his father's distinctive script—*Claude David Archer*. David admired his father and his grandfather greatly, both ministers. From his toddler days onward, he'd felt the burden of carrying their name. His grandfather had been called *C.D.*, his father *Claude*, and David slipped easily into *David*, never using Claude. He followed their vocation, but he'd never live up to their high standards.

He'd been fascinated and horrified by the violence that had erupted in Little Rock, and had written home asking for any and all the news clippings. His father, a courageous man, had long advocated improving the lot of the black folks who lived only a few blocks away from his small church in an older white neighborhood. A transitional neighborhood, but no one called it that back then. The boundaries in the fifties were rigid for both races. David had considered Little Rock a moderate city. That is, until nine Negro boys and girls attempted to integrate the large white high school, his alma mater. Hatred erupted. Distorted faces of white teen-agers and adults screaming at the Little Rock Nine became national and international news.

The facts were hazy in his mind, but he remembered his mother would write him at Davidson and then the next year when he was on his Rhodes in England, describing the disruptions, the yelling mobs, the governor's calling up the National Guard to prevent the nine Negro students from entering Little Rock Central High School. Her letters told about the long conversations Claude and his best minister friend, Dunbar Ogden, held in their den debating what actions Christians should take. When President Eisenhower sent in paratroopers to enforce the supreme law of the land, David had rejoiced. In 1958, one young man of the nine graduated. Yet Governor Orville Faubus, in a way, had the last word. He closed the public high schools. Then everything seemed to unravel.

With the tape off, the diary was closed by a leather tongue that slipped through a matching loop. Just holding the book and smelling the musky odor brought back his father's study at home, the pine paneling, pipe tobacco smoke, the studio couch. Every evening before bed, his dignified father would gather the family in a circle. They would clasp hands and he would pronounce a benediction. David had not continued the tradition with his family. After Drew's death, David determined to make his own future family life different.

He'd loved his kid brother and believed he'd achieve a far more successful career than he. Drew had been brilliant. David couldn't read the journal this night. Grief seemed right under the surface. Jody flashed into his mind. Surely, her psychotherapy would help her pull through the desperation and depression that had driven his brother to suicide. He prayed for his daughter in what had become a mantra, "Please, God, save Jody. Heal her, I pray." David wiped his face and closed the chest. He took the journal downstairs to read in the morning.

At Harmony church the next day, David closed the door to his study, supposedly to work on his sermon. Instead, he opened his father's diary and began reading the confident, angular script. Claude Archer's hand-writing was so familiar, David felt he was sitting at their old breakfast table listening to him read aloud. Claude ranted, *Faubus is a self-serving ideologue, catering to racists.*

157

David wished for his father's guidance. He wished he could borrow his father's courage for the battle he saw ahead. How could he save the church he'd worked so hard to build into a progressive congregation, one devoted to a positive, inclusive approach? For all her youthful attractiveness and the zeal she inspired, he suspected Deborah Baker did not actually care much which side of the issues she supported. She wanted to stir up trouble. Trouble for him. Trouble for the church. Unity did not serve her purpose, whatever that might be.

Immediately he corrected himself. That was judgmental and unkind. He should respect her right to have her own interpretation of the faith they shared.

He read his father's words about going to Dunbar Ogden's home to discuss walking with the nine children into the high school. As he read the section, he noticed the script became cramped and hesitant. On the next page, in tiny writing, his father had written, *I admit it, I'm afraid. In fact, terrified of what the cost might be, if I were to escort the children, as one of only two white ministers. Our black brothers of the cloth, of course, are urging us on. I know what is right and just. I also know my church. What shall I do?*

David closed the journal. He shut his eyes and laid his head on the desk. His father, Mr. Intrepid, afraid? A side of Claude Archer he'd never seen.

The phone rang. Judith said that Emily Parks was on the line with "a quick question."

"Yes, Emily. How are you today?"

"David, I'm fine. Sorry to disturb you, but I'd like to send a note and a small care package to Jody. Could you give me her address?"

Her voice sounded like a gift. He gave her the address, then asked if she could come by the church. He told her briefly about his father's journal and the clippings from the attic. "Weren't you affected when the Little Rock high schools were closed? I'd like to talk with you about what you remember."

"Yes. What an odd year. I haven't thought about it for a long time." She said she'd pick up sandwiches and they could talk over lunch.

They took their picnic to the Columbarium beside the church, away from phones and interruptions. Emily headed to an iron bench under the cherry trees. Fallen petals covered the bench, which she brushed off with a sweep of her free hand. Sun and shadows played over her short dark hair and light skin. She wore a cotton dress with bold red and black geometric shapes on a white background. David felt good just looking at her. A lot better than being alone, enveloped by his father's words. Disturbing words.

"We're surrounded by saints of the church out here, but they're not likely to bother us," he said. He glanced at the brass plaques with names of members whose ashes were encased in the brick walls. "Thank you for bringing lunch. And for being willing to talk."

Emily handed him a chicken salad sandwich and lemonade. "Are you doing research on the Little Rock crisis? How did you come to dig out your father's journal?"

"I'm not sure why. But now that I've read it, I guess I need to talk about what I found with someone who can understand." He placed the diary beside him on the bench. Would it make what his father did more believable, more real, if he read it aloud to Emily?

"David, you seem, I don't know, unsettled by something." She bit into her sandwich, her vivid blue eyes on his face.

"Unsettled. Yes. I'm unsettled, in more ways than one." He took a drink of the lemonade. "Let me ask you what you remember from that time?"

"Since you mentioned it on the phone, different memories like snapshots popped into my mind. Like the basement of a neighborhood church where my class had to meet the year the schools were closed. Parents took turns teaching. One friend was shipped to Memphis for school. My mother was always on the phone protesting, demanding action to reopen the schools. The basement smelled sour. That year to my mind has a sour smell." The concerned expression on her face softened and she smiled. "Of course, your dad preached some strong sermons during that time." She picked a piece of chicken that dropped and placed it in her mouth.

"Plenty of people in the church were ready to tar and feather him. So my parents told me later. He took early retirement, didn't he?"

"Yes, he did. But I never understood why until I read the diary. You know, I was at grad school. I guess I didn't inquire pointedly enough." He opened the leather book. "If you're willing to hear this, it might help me to read my father's words aloud."

"Of course, David. I'd be honored."

He read to her how Claude was terrified and yet knew the right and just thing to do. Then he turned several pages to the day the Little Rock Nine were escorted to the high school and the crowds screamed and the Arkansas National Guard refused to let the students enter. He read:

*We held hands in a circle at Mrs. Daisy Bates's house and prayed together.*

*Mr. and Mrs. Bates, the Negro ministers, Dunbar, and I with the students and their parents. Then it was time to go. Two of the black clergy spoke to Dr. Ogden, as they called him. "Are you going to walk with us? It's time to decide." I couldn't hear his answer. Then they spoke to me, addressing me as Dr. Archer. "Are you with us? Will you walk with us?"*

*Now I confess to you who may read this journal after my death. We shook hands and I said to these fine men of God, "All night I have wrestled with this decision. You know I am with you in spirit, but I cannot walk with you." And then I left the house, got in my car and drove to the church as if it were a regular work day. I knew, or thought I did, that if I walked with them, my church would turn me out. Like the rich, young ruler, I went away, sorrowing.*

"Weeks go by and he doesn't write anything. The last entry is simply, *I tendered my resignation and announced my retirement today.*" David worked to control his voice. "Emily, I can't begin to tell you how this revelation affects me. All these years. I was led to believe by both my mother and father that he had indeed walked with the Little Rock Nine into the opposition, that he had faced the angry mob and the National Guard with courage alongside his friend Dunbar Ogden."

He saw tears in Emily's eyes and tried to lighten the mood. "I did wonder once or twice why his picture was never in the papers. I thought it just a mistake that the news media mentioned only one white minister."

They ate in silence. Birds resumed singing in the cherry trees. David studied Emily, her friendship utterly essential to him, but he couldn't speak of that.

She balled up the sandwich papers and placed them in the paper sack. "So, David, what are you thinking right now about this discovery?"

"What am I thinking? I'm thinking rather cynically that when you're faced with a hard choice of standing up to injustice and wrongdoing, or turning away as a coward, that either way, you pay the price. Regardless." He banged his fist into his left hand. "My father, my whole family, paid a dear price. He should have walked. Everyone reacted to him, and to my brother, as if Claude Archer had summoned his courage and escorted those students. He was called Nigger Lover, Fellow Traveler, Pinko Liberal, just like they called his good friend. The guys at the mechanics shop where Drew worked persecuted him. I consider my brother a casualty of the integration struggle."

David stood. "Let's walk some. I can't sit still."

Emily dropped the picnic leavings in the trash and they left the Columbarium. He adjusted his usual long stride to match her shorter steps, and began to relax. They walked down the sidewalk of the back street, leading into the neighborhood. Emily skipped to keep up, so he slowed down again.

"What does Nell say about all this?" Emily asked.

"Nothing. I haven't shared any of it with her." He stopped at the corner and took off his blazer, loosened his tie. "You know how she is about her business. That's where her focus is. Takes her mind off Jody, and all."

Emily switched her handbag to the other arm. "It's getting hot out here, but walking feels good. David, I may not have told you this before, but when your father was our minister, I adored him so much. I made my mother and father and brother move up front from our pew in the back, so I could sit right under his nose."

"How did you feel when he left the church?"

Emily laughed. "I organized the other kids and we draped the big Sunday school assembly room with black crepe paper and found dark, almost black, tulips for the table. We threw a fun party. Basically, a wake." She looked up into his face. "Of course, we had no idea what had been going on behind closed doors. All I knew was that I loved him and he was going away."

"So that year you lost your school and your minister."

"That's right. I'm surprised my parents let me put that party together, since the church had pressured him to leave. But on some level, they knew how important he was to me."

They passed the elementary school. Children, white and black, were playing kick ball and jumping rope double-dutch, their calls back and forth like background music. When David and Emily turned back to the church, Mrs. Morris waved to them from her porch. They waved back. "Wonder what she'll say about our walking together?" Emily asked.

"I've found most people in the church assume the best, not the worst. However, there is something I hope you'll keep an eye on, and let me know what you think."

"What's that?"

"Deborah Baker has initiated something with the youth called The Movement."

"Not terribly original, is it?"

"I'm concerned that her intention may bring about a split." He walked Emily to her car. "Along political lines. Anyway, something insidious and reactionary is afoot. Now I'm sounding paranoid. Please, just keep your eyes open."

"Don't worry, David. I doubt there'll be anything as dramatic as the Movement we've been talking about. Or the cost as great."

"I hope you're right."

She started her car and lowered the window. "Thank you for sharing the journal."

He watched her car until it turned the corner.

# 20

# Millie

M illie looked around at the crowd gathered by the snack bar. She
could see that Deborah Baker was seated on one of the stools, facing the group. Her red hair shining out from among the boys standing
around. Two girls giggled and gestured her over. Becca and Laney. Two of
the most popular girls in her class. Such a relief to be included.

"What's up?" She saw Becca's new braces filled her mouth big time.

"Nothing much. Deborah's telling us about the time she nearly
drowned off the coast of Florida when she was fourteen and some big
black dude swam out and pulled her in. Not even a life guard. Just someone who saw she was in trouble."

The boy in front of Millie stuck his hands in his rear pockets and
backed up. She dodged and stood closer to the counter. Deborah hopped
off the stool and the crowd parted for her to pass. "Come on, you guys.
Let's set up for the meeting. Make a circle with the chairs. If we have to,
we can use two concentric circles and stagger them so everyone can see
the center."

Millie dragged two at a time to the circle, watching the way Laney
and Becca scooted their chairs, chasing Ace Murphy and Rivers Carlton.

Ace and Rivers, both rising juniors, couldn't have been more different. Ace was a hairy monster, a good-looking hairy monster. Always had what her mother called a five o'clock shadow. Swarthy and bulky, but not fat.

Rivers Carlton, tall and lean, looked like he could model for a tuxedo ad with his clean lines and high cheek bones. He wore a plain faded tee shirt and jeans and old sneakers. Still Millie thought he was the best of the bunch. Not that he'd ever notice her. Especially with Laney and Becca flirting with the two of them.

Laney was smart and wore the world's most fashionable clothes. Her hair was big and bouncy and blonde. Her figure perfect. The total package down right intimidating. Becca was maybe five-two with straight, shiny black hair and bangs. She always exuded self-confidence despite an awkward gait with one leg slightly longer than the other. She told Millie once that she'd had polio when her family lived as missionaries in Congo. Millie wanted to know her better. She loved to watch her talk with her tiny hands gesturing this way and that.

Deborah moved to the center of the circle and gradually the twenty or so young people filled in the inner circle of chairs first and then the outer. Millie sat beside Becca with Laney on Becca's other side. The boys sat directly behind them. "So we can harass you properly," Rivers said. Millie turned and grinned at him. He nodded. Jim Dunwoody jumped onto the chair beside Rivers.

"Hey, Dimwitty, how you?" That voice was Ace Murphy, no doubt, but Millie kept facing forward.

Deborah never raised her voice to quiet the troops. She merely waited, then raised her hand. Soon others raised theirs and settled down. She began speaking fast with a fierce earnestness. "You've seen the importance of standing up on these issues. You all did a fine job at Youth Sunday last week, bringing these issues to the congregation. As we've discussed abortion and the gay lifestyle, I think you all—every one of you—" She turned slowly to look into the faces of every teen there. "Each one of you has seen the rending effects on our society of tolerating behavior that is counter to the values that we as Soldiers of Christ hold dear. Now—today—I challenge you to do what you can to persuade any gay teen-ager you happen to know to give up the life and go into treatment. You may have to use forceful persuasion."

Ace Murphy snorted and muttered, "I can do that." Dunwoody added, "Me too. Count me in." They scraped their chairs, as if to jump into action. Millie saw them glare across the room at Macon Collier who sat on the front row away from the other boys. Ace and Dunwoody obviously believed he was gay, whether true or not. Macon kept his head down, his eyes on the floor.

Macon had recently moved to South Carolina from somewhere in the Midwest with his mother. Millie had seen him in history class, figured he was in ninth grade too. She hated it when people jumped to conclusions about others without any knowledge. Besides what difference did it make if Macon was gay. He had feelings, too.

"And on the subject of protesting abortion in our city," Deborah continued. "I will be going to the clinic on Laurens Road a week from Monday afternoon—if any of you would like to join me. We can make placards using these photographs. You can all help make the posters tonight." She held up a stack of pictures. Then handed them to the inner circle to pass around.

Millie studied the pictures showing an aborted fetus. Graphic and gruesome. She saw the curved body, outsized head and tiny feet. Terrible and gory. She quickly passed them on. The girls groaned and said, "Yuck." Most of the boys on the back row passed the photos on without really looking.

Deborah collected them and waited. People grew quiet. She said, "I want you to think about how you, yourself, each one of you, can answer the call. When you're in your bed tonight, ponder in your heart what action you, as a Soldier of Christ, can do to further our Movement. This is a two-front war. You may be called to protest taking the life of a embryo, a baby on the way to becoming a full human being. Or you may want to answer another way, by speaking out on the homosexual lifestyle that's growing in our community. Or you may become active on both fronts when the opportunity to act arises."

Millie was struck with how intensely Deborah spoke, yet her voice was so soft that you had to strain to catch all her words. Deborah coughed her troubling cough, then used her nasal spray. They all seemed to hold their collective breath. Later, Millie sipped her Coke and watched the guys as they crowded around Deborah. She caught part of what Ace and Rivers were saying at the edge of the circle.

Rivers must have confronted Ace. Ace came toward Rivers jabbing his chest with his index finger, "You know it'll be just the thing. Make a strong statement." In a husky voice, "Make her proud of us." She couldn't catch what Rivers said back as he walked away. Then Ace grabbed Dunwoody and they headed out the door to the parking lot.

Millie and the other girls lettered posters in large block letters, using wide markers. Deborah glued on some of the pictures. All the time she worked, Millie wondered if she could actually protest against abortion when the time came. She didn't know how she felt about the issue. Mostly rushed. She felt rushed to make a decision and hadn't really studied the pros and cons. Nor had she discussed any of the campaign with her father. Somehow she sensed he'd get all prickly. They never had talked about sex and it must fall under that category, where he'd give her a book to read and let her form her own opinion. Like the book he handed her when she was in the sixth grade—*Facts of Life and Love for Teenagers.* Definitely outdated and pretty lame.

Of course, she didn't expect her mother to broach the subject of sex or anything else that might be messy. Certainly abortion would be. Her mother might fly into a rage concluding that she Millie needed one. Anyway, she couldn't bring up the subject with her and risk distrust and suspicion. She didn't even have a boyfriend, but her mother wouldn't believe that.

"You're awfully quiet." Rivers leaned down and into her face.

Millie jumped. "Whoa. You startled me. Now I've messed up."

"Never mind. Now we improvise." He took her black marker and filled in the faux pas with a flourish around the letter T of *Think before you act*. He picked up a red marker and trimmed the words and underlined with a flourish. Together they found a picture of a young woman with her hand on her stomach.

"I didn't know you were an artist." Her face was hot.

"You assume I'm a dumb jock, I suppose." He was smiling down at her from his lofty height. She guessed Rivers must be well over six-two, even taller than her father. Before she could answer him, Deborah called a halt to the work and said the meeting was over. Laney and Becca called her to ride home with them. She waved good-bye to Rivers. Though she felt ambivalent about the issue, she knew one thing. That had been fun and exciting. To have Rivers' attention, even for a little while.

# 21

## Emily

⁑

The four women spent a weekend in May at Dale Weller's cabin up near Cedar Mountain—Dale, Natalie, Emily, and Madeleine. Usually they met for lunch once or twice a month, when they could get free from work and family. A weekend away proved more difficult to pull off, and on the occasions when they managed it, they would spend at least the first hour telling each other how their husbands and children had reacted and how they guessed they'd have to pay for the time away, with the conclusion that whatever they had to pay was worth it, to be away from the usual routine and to be together.

The exception was Madeleine who had no children or husband and seemed to balance her therapy practice to suit her own rhythms, with little stress. At least none she mentioned to the group. Emily found herself envious of Madeleine, who seemed, from the perspective of friend, to lead an unencumbered life.

Emily needed to discuss the growing tension between her and Ted. Still her old conditioning kicked in the minute she thought of saying anything. She could almost hear her mother's voice: *It's fine to listen to others, but keep your home and husband sacred. Private.* She could see Charlie

May in the kitchen rocking chair with the phone to her ear, murmuring encouraging words between long pauses as one friend or another confided in her. Emily did her share of listening to friends and cherished the trust they showed her. Most recently, David. A warm feeling filled her, thinking of him.

Madeleine's work required that she keep quiet about who came to her for counseling. She'd never said a word to divulge to the group that she saw their pastor as his therapist. Emily knew only because David had told her. And Emily never said anything to Madeleine about him. Although there were times she would have liked to consult her professionally too, she'd held back, afraid that would change their friendship.

All the other friends belonged to Harmony church. Madeleine made it clear when they began meeting as a group that religion played no part in her life. "If anything, I'm a deist. You know, like Thomas Jefferson." Everyone accepted her and valued what she brought to them.

She set up her small loom and proceeded to send the shuttle back and forth while everyone else was still unpacking. Dale had asked that they all bring a craft or art project to work on while they talked. Emily enjoyed Dale's skill at multi-tasking. Dale was Emily's tallest friend, even taller than her best friend Natalie. Dale wore her hair long in loose curls. Thin as a willow, Dale's color was yellow, buttery and rich as a lovely calla lily. She'd married her high school boyfriend, Whit Weller, a six-five athlete who ran a successful business just outside Goodwin. Dale managed to work part-time for Whit, keeping his books, help at their son's school, and serve on City Council.

Today, Dale worked on a collage. She'd cut up her photographs of mountain streams and vistas into strips to reassemble. She worked on the dinner table, while the others sat around the fireplace. Natalie had taken a break from her large paintings and was weaving a basket from some vines she'd cut and soaked before she arrived at the cabin. They'd both done some prep before they left. Emily had just thrown in her colored markers, pencils, sketchbook, and water colors, along with her journal.

She laughed to think about all she wished she could do in one week-end away. Blink, blink—like the witch in that TV series. Blink, blink—the housework would be done. Emily suffered from curiosity and too many interests. Writing children's books, drawing and painting but without the talent Nat the professional artist possessed, reading poetry and compos-ing poems that might last longer than next week. Yet she spent most of her time grading comp papers from her freshmen, prepping for class, and tending to her family. Blink, blink—finish seven masterpieces all in a weekend. A weird kind of hubris.

As if Dale had been eavesdropping on Emily's thoughts, she called them to order like the chair at a committee meeting. "We are gathered here to discuss a particular person's dilemma, whether she knows it or not. Namely, Emily Garland Parks. We want to hear from you about your search for direction and focus, if that's not putting too fine a point on your hopeless meandering."

"Hold the bus. What's going on? A conspiracy?" Emily felt ganged up on. And by her friends. Had she been complaining that much?

"Not exactly," Dale said. "Maybe something of an intervention." She looked over at Madeleine and Emily's eyes followed her.

Madeleine didn't look like a therapist today. She wore no make-up and went braless under her oversized tee shirt and long peasant skirt. She glanced up from her loom and frowned. "Emily, you're among your dearest friends. Relax. We're not judging you."

"It sounds like you are. Judging me." She looked from one to the other. What did Natalie know about this? She had given no indication that she would be in the hot seat.

Natalie met her eyes. "Okay. I think we simply want you to express what you most want to do."

"You mean what I want to be when I grow up?" Emily laughed, as if she hadn't bothered them about this a dozen times before. "You remember the children's game, 'Mother, May I?' You ask permission from the person who's It to take baby steps or giant steps and add 'Mother, May I?' All the time trying to disguise your voice so the Mother with her back turned can't tell exactly where you are or who you are before she gives permission."

Natalie cursed under her breath over the rough vines cutting into her fingers. "Are you waiting for permission from your mother, Emily?" She asked and sucked the side of her scraped and bloody finger.

"You could say that. But what I thought I meant was that mostly I take a baby step here and there, then fall back. Something always stops me before I really get going—either in painting or writing. I can't blame Ted or the children, but sometimes I do." Emily fingered her untouched sketchbook and colored markers. "It's something inside me. The Mother May I with her royal back turned may allow baby steps only. A poem now and then. Beginnings of paintings or a story, but nothing ever finished."

Dale moved into the den and sat on the hearth facing Emily. "Maybe you have not decided what you want most to do. I'll be frank: it's not a matter of permission. You're just hiding behind all that to avoid choosing. If you don't choose, you can continue to live under the illusion that you can choose all or any of these avenues. Any one of which, by the way, would take a lifetime to master." Dale stood up. "I'm sorry."

Emily blushed. "Got that off your chest, uh Dale?" She was aware that the others had nodded that they agreed as Dale unloaded. She looked from one to the other. "You're right. When I'm between projects—and those are usually assigned to me by other people—or when a semester is over and I've turned in the grades, that's when I'm flooded with ideas for creating something."

She squirmed inside thinking about their attention. She felt exposed. Usually she took the role of listening and commiserating with someone else's problems. "Here's an example of what I do to myself. I brought three books to read, my water colors, colored markers, pencils, and notes for four or five stories. All to do here during this weekend with you guys when mostly we'll be talking."

"You do have a major tendency to overwhelm yourself, Emily," Madeleine said, all the while continuing her rhythmic moving of the shuttle in and out and pushing the weaving firmly into the woven. "Why do you think that is?"

Emily ran her hands over her journal. What popped into her mind was that if she refused to be overwhelmed, she'd probably float away from her ordinary life, and not come back. She couldn't say that.

Natalie held up her basket, all finished. "Not perfect, but look, it's finished."

Emily laughed. "I get it. Small goal, limited in scale and scope. I envy you, but not your bloody hand."

Natalie smiled at her and said, "We women have to become domestic anarchists."

"What does that mean, anyway? I've heard you say that before, but frankly, I don't get it."

"Of course you don't. Who rules the Home? If we're not anarchists, at least we've got to be aware of where the control is, who's in charge. Right?"

"What does domestic control have to do with my indecision?"

"Nothing, maybe. Your indecision, though, may actually be a diversion from what's going on that's more painful than not deciding what art form to put your energy into."

From the weaver's loom, Madeleine said, "Now we may be getting somewhere."

"You mean, like a girl with an eating disorder who uses her obsession to focus her discomfort away from a deeper pain?" Emily felt a little shock of recognition, like an iced drink making her teeth ache. "Definitely something to think about. Still I could use some help with deciding. Do I paint? Write? Give it all up and clean house?"

"Horrors. Not housework," Dale said. She scooted the small needlepoint stool from beside the hearth to right in front of Emily and sat facing her. "You know, the word *decide* comes from the same root word as homicide, suicide, genocide. I think you're afraid of cutting off, killing off, some of your precious options."

Emily looked from one to other of her friends. "Is it always a choice between love and work?"

"Did anyone say that?" Dale peered into her face. "Choosing one project at a time is what we're talking about. Not the grand fallacy we women keep falling into. Just decide to write one simple children's story all the way from start to finish. Or one poem."

Natalie spoke up. "To do that you would be killing off—for the time being—all the other might-be stories, paintings, marbling, quilting, weavings, that you conjure up in your wild daydreaming." She reached over and took Emily's hand. "You can do that, you know."

Emily could feel her eyes filling. "Y'all make me cry. Just taking the time to care about my same old block."

Madeleine looked up from her weaving. "Just the thing for you to do during this retreat. A writer's block. Create that for us."

"Good idea," Emily said. "I can see it now. All four sides. No, a block would have eight sides."

"Great. More options," Natalie said. They laughed.

Madeleine stood up. "Oh, my aching back. Let's fix lunch."

"And, please," Emily added, "let's talk about something, or someone else."

The afternoon rain showers began, first with deep bass rumbles of thunder in the distance, then a slow plunking rhythm on the metal roof, soon a steady pounding with lighter notes splashing from the eaves to the ground. The women sat around the pine table and enjoyed the spread: sliced tomatoes, mozzarella and basil leaves drizzled with olive oil, biscuits with butter and honey, and a lamb stew Dale had made at home and heated up. Wine glasses with their favorite Bordeaux. Emily's gaze lingered on each woman. With each bite and sip of wine she felt more grateful that each would set aside her own concerns long enough to dwell on hers.

Yet she hadn't told them what most knotted up her stomach. Her turbulent feelings toward Ted and their financial predicament. Just as she'd tighten her belt, he'd find a new something to buy. Her growing resentment

174

edging toward rage when they had agreed to restrict their spending and suddenly he tells her he's bought a washer and dryer for Meredith and Joel "to help them out." She loved their daughter and could not hold that against him and he knew it. Or he whisks her off to San Francisco when he has to be there for a legal meeting. She loved their adventures to luxury hotels in interesting cities. These surprises had long been their way of escaping too much domestic folderol. Yet they were fast running out of money and would probably have to take out a second mortgage. Now she made herself focus on the yummy hot biscuit, slathering it with butter and honey.

Emily let the talk at the table swim around her. Dale told a story of brown bats that lived in the eaves of the porch and flew off at twilight every evening in summer and fall. She wondered where they went for the winter.

Natalie suggested they went to the closest cave. More likely a warm barn on a nearby farm, Madeleine said, and Emily agreed. "If I were a bat, that's where I'd go for winter."

Then Emily told the story of keeping a little brown bat in a tall birdcage in her bedroom during her junior year in high school as a biology project. She wished the story had a happy ending, but she confessed that he made it till she turned in her study. The bat had grown smaller and smaller, no longer stretching his black rubbery wings or taking the live meal worm she fed him with a tweezer. "He dwindled away. I think he was depressed. I'd planned to let him go free after I turned in the paper, but he died before I could do it."

"Your parents let you keep a live bat in your room? Hadn't they heard of rabies in bats?" Madeleine was horrified.

"Yes, I suppose they knew the risks, but when the mother of a friend called to say the little bat was on their stairway and would I like it and I said yes, my mother shrugged and let me keep it, in fact found the birdcage for him."

She probably could have gleaned enough knowledge from research and let him go soon as he stopped responding, but she'd been oblivious and ever hopeful that he'd perk up. Emily and two friends shared the project and they all made an A. They'd named the bat ELI for Emily, Lily, and Isabel.

"Who, may I ask, did most of the work on that biology project?" Natalie asked, with that strident tone Emily called her schoolmarm voice.

"Now that you mention it, probably me. But we had a good time. And frankly, we were all so glad to have the high school open again, everything seemed good. Except poor Eli's demise."

"What do you mean the high school opened?" Dale asked.

"Remember the integration trouble in Little Rock back in the late fifties? Our segregationist governor closed all the high schools to get around federal law. But a group of women, including my mother, gathered together and put the pressure on until finally Governor Faubus had to yield. And we got our schools back."

"Hurrah for the women. Let's toast those fine mothers." Madeleine lifted her wine glass and they joined her.

"Yeah, that's the kind of domestic anarchy you can believe in," Natalie said and stood up.

They gathered their plates and took them to the kitchen. Dale assumed the role of dishwasher. Natalie put music on the tape player and swayed around the den to U2's "Still Haven't Found What I'm Looking For." Emily sang the words softly and got out her colored markers, drew a circle on her sketch pad using a cardboard coaster. She let her mind go and simply drew with the turquoise marker, then the yellow, orange, red, and dark green. A mandala began to take shape, as if to music. This was a practice that never failed to take Emily out of herself.

Dale finished the dishes, rubbed lotion on her hands and sat down across from Emily. "You don't need to create a block," she said. "Just keep doing those circle things."

Natalie turned off the music and drew up her chair. "Listen, y'all, I'm wondering about Deborah Baker. Madeleine, I know you're not interested in church. Sorry to bring up something you may not care for. But I'd like to ask what Deborah might have told any of you about her early life."

"Don't mind me. I'd like to hear what you've heard." Madeleine went back to her weaving. "I may have heard a story or two myself."

Emily drew another circle and changed her colors to orange, red, and black. She'd wait to hear the stories before she said anything about Deborah. David's conversation was never far from her thoughts.

Natalie glanced around the group. "Deborah must have had a terrible childhood, and I wondered about it. She took me aside one Sunday when I was cleaning up after communion. She stood in the kitchen and watched me wash the serving trays and began talking about running away from her father's abuse when she turned fourteen. She said she lived for a time with a woman named Ruby and helped her do house cleaning until she made enough to go to a small college in Georgia. She'd earned her GED by that time, too."

"Interesting," Dale said. "Not long ago, she called and asked me to be on a committee for youth suppers. She said she knew about handicaps, referring no doubt to the fact that Jacob has Down syndrome. So I asked about her family growing up." Dale went back to gluing her collage. "She said something about her brother with cystic fibrosis who died when they lived in South Dakota. She said it had been a hard year. Her father had moved the family when she turned fifteen and she'd caught double pneumonia that winter. Now she has a chronic condition that makes her cough a lot and be short of breath. Some technical name I didn't catch. Her parents decided they'd better live in a warmer climate, so that's when they moved to Florida." Dale didn't add a comment. Instead she went to the kitchen and poured coffee into mugs.

Natalie sipped her coffee and walked to the sofa where Emily was coloring her mandalas. "May I try that out?"

"Of course." Emily was pleased that Natalie, the professional artist, would want to try something Emily liked to play with. She handed her a pad and markers. "Here, use this coaster for your circle." Natalie began drawing her circle.

"Okay, group," Dale said. "I'll ask the obvious question. Can both these stories be true?"

"Wait," Emily said. "Before you examine those stories, let me tell you what Tim reported after a youth meeting. At the time, I didn't pay much attention. But after hearing these other accounts, it sounds much more fascinating."

"Like what?" Natalie asked.

"Deborah told the young people that her father died when she was ten, so she and her mother had to live in a rusted-out camper trailer until her mother got a job in a textile mill. Tim said he guessed she wanted the group to understand more about poor people."

Dale walked with her coffee mug and stood right in front of Madeleine, silently daring her to speak up. Madeleine wore a slight smile on her thin lips and kept the shuttle dipping and rising among the long strands.

Dale leaned in toward the therapist. "You're terribly quiet. Help us out here. What are we dealing with in our young associate minister?"

"Are you asking for a professional opinion? Anything I might say would be a wild guess since I've never met the woman." She paused in her work. "She does have all of you mighty curious."

They waited. Soon they realized that Madeleine was not going to give them a label to plaster on Deborah.

"I'm curious what she might tell me," Emily said. "Think I'll make a point of seeing her next week and ask about her background. Also I'm curious how she got into seminary from whatever happened in her childhood."

"Deborah—whatever her history—now has the congregation in a stew. She's rallying the troops on some kind of military sounding campaign," Natalie said, her face red. She brushed her hand through her hair.

"How so?" Dale admitted she and her family hadn't been to Harmony church in about a month.

"The Sunday it was her turn to preach, she gave a fiery sermon calling for action on the issues of the day—as she called the flap over homosexuals and abortion and the like. At our church. Can you imagine?" Natalie dropped the markers and began pacing. "She used lots of war imagery and had some people all but saluting and marching in lockstep out of the sanctuary. I thought I'd puke."

"We must have been away, too. I'm sure I'd remember that sermon," Emily said. "And the young people on Youth Sunday did that skit on the bravery of standing up for what they believed and mentioned marching at the abortion clinic." She caught Natalie's eyes. "The odd thing is a few months ago, she acted in support of the opposite side. On the abortion issue, she was pro-choice. Remember when she went with Natalie and me to the clinic protesting the protesters, and then we ended up on the News at Eleven?" Emily would never forget that day.

"Curious indeed," Dale said. She stretched. "Let's walk. The rain's stopped. It ought to be cooler. I have walking sticks for everyone."

The afternoon sun brought out dazzling sparkles on rhododendrons and the dripping maple leaves. Emily breathed in the fresh damp air. The woods on either side of the gravel driveway emitted the loamy smell of wet leaves and old logs covered with moss. The stream hidden below sang loudly of the hard rain. Emily wished suddenly that she was alone up on the hillside, staying at the cabin by herself. She craved solitude. She watched Dale striding along ahead of her down to the asphalt highway, her long thin legs confident, graceful, and tan. If she asked her, Dale would no doubt schedule a few days for her. Maybe she could get away from the tension with Ted after she finished the semester.

Natalie skipped along and caught up to her. "Emily, a penny for your thoughts. You look quite pensive, I'd say, Me-Lassie." The woeful imitation of a Scots-Irish-Brit accent made her laugh.

"Pensive, uh? Well, if sad, guilty, mixed-up can be called pensive, then yes, that's me." Emily kicked a rock along with the side of her foot like a miniature soccer ball.

"Did the mention of the abortion clinic trigger these feelings?"

"Maybe. Actually, who that baby might have been comes to me quite a lot. In dreams, mostly." She hit the rock with her walking stick into the ditch along the highway. She knew they should be walking single-file but she was grateful for Natalie beside her.

"Intellectually, I know I did what had to be done, but emotionally, I'm still grieving."

Natalie put her arm around Emily's shoulder. "You know I'm with you all the way."

"Thank you. You're the only one who knows, so let's keep it that way."

"Of course."

They caught up with Dale and Madeleine, and the four crossed the highway to a dirt road lined with tall poplars. A few cows grazed in the field to the left, and above, a hawk floated in a lazy spiral higher and higher. The sky behind the dark bird had taken on a wistful shade of yellow.

"Quick, Emily. Now what are you thinking?" Natalie was also looking at the sky.

"That's easy. I'd like to do my next mandala with exactly that yellow sky and hawk. What about you? What were you thinking?"

"My mind had gone back to what we were talking about at the cabin. Deborah Baker. I feel a low boiling resentment toward Deborah. Partly personal reaction, I admit, but beyond that, she's playing some kind of power game and may ruin our church in the process. Harmony—Ha!"

Dale joined them. "So what can we do to stop her?"

"One thing I've thought about," Emily said, "is volunteering to help with either the youth programs or her project at the Space for Hope." She hadn't realized she wanted to do that until she heard herself say it. "We could at least learn more about her."

"Would you like company?" Dale said, surprising them both since she hadn't done anything much in the church for a while. Not after her son Jacob had reached the age where he needed to be transported to the special school every day. Dale worked there as an assistant.

"Count me in, too," Natalie said.

The three agreed to call the church office on Monday and sign up for the Space for Hope. Then they'd assess whether to do anything with the young people's new Movement.

Madeleine had jogged ahead of them and now sat waiting, seated on a huge boulder beside the road. "You three look formidable. I wouldn't want to be in Deborah's shoes if and when you join forces."

"We'll see," Natalie said. "At least maybe we can find out what's going on."

The four entered the small chapel called Faith. Small pine branches and assorted leaves had blown into the open-air sanctuary. The pews were damp but Emily sat for a minute while the others stood at the back.

"I could use more," she said.

"More what?" Natalie asked.

"Faith. More faith." She didn't elaborate, but the trouble with Ted, their money woes, her sense of guilt clouded her mind. Tears filled her throat threatening to drown her. Words entered her mind with clarity: *This kind can be driven out only by prayer and fasting.* Emily hoped that wasn't some kind of divine message. She wasn't much good at prayer and abysmal at fasting.

Her little brown bat in the birdcage came to mind. How she'd allowed him to dwindle away while she used him as a science project, yet lost sight of what he was meant to be and do.

If he'd been allowed to soar away in the twilight like the free bats that lived in the eaves of the cabin, he would have caught insects and fulfilled his nature. If only she'd kept him for one week instead of postponing his freedom until the semester ended. She recalled how she studied his frightful face, sharp teeth, big leathery ears, bright black eyes, soft furry body. She would talk to him at night and now and then hear him squeak. Until he fell silent and gave up biting the meal worms. Her timing had been off — when to take hold of what she needed, and when to let go of what no longer served a good purpose. Decisive early action could have saved him. She pondered what decisive action might help the situation with Ted and her. Then Natalie called to her that they were heading back up the hill.

# 22

# Emily

꼭

Emily and Natalie met Dale outside the Space for Hope, so they could walk in together. Dale wore a tailored light gray linen suit with a slender silver belt, gray pumps.

"Dale, you're styling, girlfriend," Natalie called out. Emily and Nat walked to the entry way in their casual summer slacks and sandals.

"Too dressed up, I know," Dale said. "I had to make a presentation to United Way. We're hoping to keep their support for next year. It's a biggie."

"What do we do here?" Emily asked, suddenly feeling shy.

They had to weave their way through the entry lined with out-of-work men of various ages, sizes, and shapes—all cast in a grayish-brown light like figures of wood, carved and weathered—some in clusters, several leaning, two stooping. Every one giving her and her friends the once over. Natalie said a general hello. Emily nodded and attempted a smile. Dale marched by, her eyes straight ahead.

Inside the office door, a woman spoke to them from behind a glass wall with an opening like a ticket-seller at a movie. "You lookin' to help Miss Deb this morning?"

"Yes, ma'am. Where do we go?" Emily asked.

"I'll take you." She disappeared and reappeared from a door at the end of the large reception room.

Emily looked around. Mothers with young children, two older women, and a slim girl of school age sat in the folding chairs, waiting for service.

The receptionist introduced herself as Alisha and led them to the gymnasium. Voices bounced around like basketballs. Teen-aged boys ran and yelled, dribbling and shooting. Deborah Baker waved from a knot of girls in the bleachers and walked toward Emily and her friends. She gave them each appraising looks, up and down, making Emily think she disapproved the blue cotton slacks she wore. She silently dismissed her and Natalie, but lingered on Dale. Smiling, she took Dale by the arm. "We're about to go into the craft room. You'll be a big help." Natalie and Emily fell in line behind Deborah and Dale and the five girls and walked to a room behind the gym.

"These fine Christian women are here to help you make some things today," Deborah said. Emily, Natalie, and Dale looked at each other. "Fine Christian women," Natalie mouthed. They laughed.

The young women slouched in their chairs. One, the only white girl, flung her long thick brown, pink, and purple hair over her head, creating a curtain to shut out any efforts to reach her. The others snorted and laughed. Emily and Natalie pulled up chairs to the table. Dale took the chair next to the Curtain of Hair.

Deborah spread out magazines, glue bottles, and scissors. Then she gave white plastic buckets, one to each teen-ager. "Go through the magazines and choose pictures that speak to you. We're going to cover the buckets. You'll be making collages."

Soon they began to follow her lead, ripping pictures, gluing, and joking among themselves. Alexia and Melanie started chanting school cheers as they cut out animals from old National Geographic. Natalie sat beside them.

"These will make good trash baskets," Deborah said. "I still have one

I made in a group when I was your age. Still use it." She looked around at each girl. "It can be for you or you may want to make it for someone special as a gift."

The girl beside Emily smiled shyly at her. Her name was Bobbisheena. Emily asked her about herself, and she answered in a raspy smoker's voice. "I wanna make mine for my big brother." Bobbisheena's hair was plaited in neat, complicated corn rows, her brown skin and dark almond-shaped eyes glowed with earnestness. Emily figured she was the youngest here.

"Tell me about him."

"He's in for armed robbery. It was just his regular luck, you might say. He just happened to be in that all-night store the Vietnamese man runs over on Nickel Street."

"What happened?"

"These dudes came in waving they guns. Monty tried to sneak out, but they got out with cigs and cash and Monty got nabbed." She sighed and smoothed a picture of a golden retriever with a loving touch as if the dog were her brother. "Like I said, his regular luck—always in the wrong place at the wrong time."

"What about you? What do you like to do?"

"Nothing to tell really. With Monty in lock-up, now Gramma's on my case all the fuckin' time." She touched her braids and smoothed her eyebrows, fixing her eyes on Emily. "Would you help me find some good pictures? He wants to serve our country, like our uncle. You know, fly jets, or something."

"What else does he like? What might remind him of you?"

"Maybe some birds. He call me his chickadee. That's some kind of bird, I think."

"It is, and it's a very lovely small bird." They thumbed through old National Geographic and People and house magazines. Bobbisheena found a jet and Emily found a tiny picture of birds at a feeder. One was a chickadee. She felt triumphant. "This can be like your signature, after you finish all the bigger pictures."

They bent over their work. Emily caught Bobbisheena's scent, a mixture of sharp rosemary and a faint floral fragrance. She glanced up at the others. Deborah was no longer in the room.

The cheerleaders were giggling. Alexia pulled out two magazines from her bookbag and showed Melanie. They put their heads together, turning the pages and giggling more. Alexia showed something to Natalie, who shrugged and said, "Why not?"

Emily said, "What?"

Natalie said, "*High Times* and *Rolling Stone* ought to have plenty of material for trash baskets, right?"

Dale and the Curtain of Hair were making a collage of buildings, a multi-layered cityscape. "How about sharing, Alex?" the Curtain asked.

Alexia tore the magazine in two and passed half over to them. "Here, Tesha, have at it."

Emily held out her hand. Alexia took *Rolling Stone* from Melanie and tore it in half. "Lil 'Sheen, this here's for you." Bobbisheena took the magazine and Emily thanked Alexia.

Soon they were all laughing and tearing out Rock groups and words like "Pot" and "Crack" and "Meth." Bobbisheena found a large photo of a jet plane and a man in an Air Force uniform.

"You're doing a great job of finding what will please your brother. I need to step out for a minute. Be right back." Bobbisheena said okay without looking up.

Emily slipped out of the craft room and started looking for Deborah. At the end of the long hall, Deborah was talking to a tall guy, maybe one of the basketball players. He leaned down to talk to her. Emily could see Deborah's slender back and full skirt, her wild red hair flashing under the fluorescent light as she gestured. Emily couldn't tell from that distance what they were doing or discussing. The gestures ceased and Deborah brought something out of her pocket and must have given it to the man. He left by the back door, and Deborah headed to the Ladies' Room without glancing around or seeing Emily.

Emily waited a minute and then followed her in. She heard Deborah in a stall at the end. Emily entered the next one over and listened. Sniffing noises and little sighs escaped from the next stall. Was she crying? After a series of such sounds, she flushed the toilet and went out. Emily saw a smattering of white powder on the floor and on a whim took a note card from her purse and pushed some of the white substance onto the card with a bit of toilet paper. Then she had the problem of getting it safely into her handbag without losing any.

When would she learn sequencing? Ted would have readied an envelope before scraping up the powder. She placed the note card carefully on the toilet paper dispenser and dug around in her handbag for an old envelope. Finally, she found an unanswered letter and took it out. She folded the card and placed it into the envelope, folding down the opening. Then she heard someone entering the restroom, so she flushed the toilet and went to wash her hands.

"There you are," Deborah said. "Bobbisheena said you left a while back."

"Sorry. I'm ready now." She hoped her face didn't show her suspicions. She washed her hands and they walked down the hall back to the girls.

On the way, Deborah stopped at the water fountain, bent her mouth to the arc of water, and then faced Emily. "Just so you're clear about something. Let me remind you that soon after I arrived at Harmony Church, you and Natalie and I went to the abortion clinic. I know for a fact that Natalie covered for you by pretending we were there to protest the protesters. I went along with her at the time." As she opened the door to the craft room, Deborah hissed into Emily's ear, "Of course, that was before I saw the light on the issue." Aloud as they entered, she said, "Just so you know."

Emily felt trembly inside not only in her stomach, but in her legs and arms. She didn't trust her voice, so she smiled at Bobbisheena, who was eager to show her the trash can.

Natalie looked over at her. "You all right?" she mouthed. Emily shook her head slightly.

Deborah spoke brightly to the group, congratulating them all on their fabulous trashcan art. If she noticed the references to drugs in the collages, she made no mention. She opened a cabinet and brought out large paper grocery bags to put them in. "Everyone, let's thank these fine Christian ladies for their help today."

Everyone laughed and the girls clapped. Dale, Natalie, and Emily hugged their partners and said their good-byes. Bobbisheena whispered to Emily, "Please come back." Emily promised she'd try.

# 23

## Charlotte

Charlotte covered her good dress with a smock and went upstairs to check on Houston and his work crew. He had his back turned, running the big saw he'd set up in what had been Hannah's room years ago. Two helpers were installing insulation in the new wall between apartments across the wide hall. Charlotte waved to them and walked around to face Houston. Not a good idea to startle a man with a power saw.

When he finished the long board he was cutting, Houston turned off the power and the noise. "How you, Mrs. Ames? Come up to witness the progress?"

"Yes, I did, Houston. I imagine this project's taking time away from your landscape business, isn't it?"

"Don't you worry none about that. I have some men cutting grass for me. My regulars, don't you know. Anyway, your house takes top spot with me these days." He wiped his face. "I want to show you something me and the guys found behind a loose brick in the mantle downstairs." He dug through his pockets and handed her a small envelope, smudged with red mud. A name was inscribed in faded sepia ink.

She needed to study the handwriting to decipher to whom it had been addressed. The florid script indicated the writer prided himself or herself on fine penmanship. She'd tend to it later. "Thank you, Houston. I'll let you know if you've found a hidden treasure. Right now I need for you to give me some idea when you'll be finished. Not that I'm rushing you or anything. It's just that my granddaughter will be married around Christmas. We'll need all the reconstruction to be complete well ahead of the wedding."

Houston grinned in that way he had of tilting his head as if he'd just heard a priceless joke and aimed to share it. His white teeth gleamed. "Well, Mrs. Ames, I reckon it to be about ten to twelve weeks more. You know, I'm willing to work some nights if the hammering won't bother you unduly. Me and Fawn are looking to move in soon as it's finished. You know I want it done too."

"Of course, Houston. I know you'll do your best."

She stopped part-way downstairs and opened the door to the sleeping porch. The old white iron bed stood against the back windows. Light sheer curtains hung over the windows all around the side and back. The room smelled musty and dusty. What should have been white had taken on the dull beige of neglect. In her mind's eye she could see Hannah and Preston jumping on the bed like a trampoline, and sitting across from each other playing Monopoly on a rainy day. She sighed. One day soon she'd have to give it a thorough cleaning.

In her bedroom she took off her smock and shoes dusty from sawdust and changed to her sensible gray pumps. The dirty envelope fell on the floor. She brushed off the dirt and placed it in the drawer of her nightstand, promising herself to study it later.

She remembered her mission. She had work to do. She had time to go over to the church and begin with a few pointed questions and then prepare for her student.

Her Lincoln Continental spent most of its time in the garage, especially since now she no longer had a license. Not after the fiasco at the highway patrol. When Natalie had discovered that she had an out-of-date driver's license—five years after the date on the front, she'd insisted on taking her to the DMV to get it renewed. They stood in line so long Charlotte thought she might faint. When they got up to the gum-chewing woman at the front, the woman looked her up and down as if she were riffraff and said she'd have to take the eye test and then the written test again. The eye test had gone okay, but the clerk refused to let Charlotte have Natalie in the test room to help her with the computer gadgets. Charlotte wanted to protest that pushing buttons on a computer hardly qualified as a *written* test. She'd ended up relinquishing her license.

Usually Margaret Templeton picked her up for church, but she wouldn't call her friend today. It wasn't a regular church day. She'd just drive over to the church herself. What independence she did possess she would not relinquish.

Preston had backed the Lincoln into the garage, for which she was thankful. All she had to do was go forward into the alley behind the garage. The faithful Lincoln started right up despite the fact she hadn't driven it since she lost her license.

Cinders covering the alley pinged against the car as Charlotte spun out of the garage and down toward the street. She must have pressed the accelerator too hard. She braked and stopped to catch her breath. Fred used to tell her to take ten deep breaths to relax before driving. Bless his heart. He'd understood her anxiety. So she inhaled deeply and exhaled slowly, and for good measure said a quick prayer for safety.

When she reached North Main, she saw two police cars on a side street. They seemed to be occupied with another car. She crept through the next stoplight, using the right lane. The car behind her followed way too close and finally passed her. The driver turned toward her and raised his middle finger. "Young man, there's no reason to be rude," Charlotte said aloud. "I have a perfectly sound reason for driving slowly." Her heart beat much faster than she allowed her car to go.

When she reached the Church Street bridge, she relaxed enough to turn on the radio. More commentary about the students killed in China. She recalled the photograph of the young Chinese man facing down a tank with a row of tanks following. An indelible emblem of bravery.

A car behind Charlotte blared on the horn. She'd been stopped at the light and the left-turn signal must have been green for a while. People were so impatient these days. Why did they have to be in such a hurry? Only three or four more stoplights and she'd be there. A police car followed her for a block and then went into the left lane. She smiled pleasantly at him at the next light. Her heart pounded and she gripped the wheel, hoping he'd go about his business. He sped on when the light changed.

When she turned into the church parking lot and parked close to the office, she bowed her head and thanked God that no cop had stopped her. Maybe driving without a license was not worth the anxiety she'd experienced. How in the world did criminals stand the worry that they might be caught at any moment? They must become accustomed to guilt and paranoia. With practice, she supposed, almost anything could be normalized.

The ladies in the office greeted her by name and inquired how she was feeling. She smoothed her dress and adjusted her attitude as best she could. She asked to see Deborah Baker. Judith said that Reverend Baker was out of the office, so Charlotte asked to see David. Judith called him.

It wasn't any time before David walked into the office from his study and greeted her warmly, taking both her hands. "To what do I owe the pleasure of seeing you today, Charlotte?"

"May I discuss something in your study?" Charlotte wasn't exactly sure how she'd approach the subject, but she'd promised her doctor she'd investigate the youth program.

David led her down the hall to his paneled office and directed her to sit on his sofa. She preferred the straight chair for her back. He sat beside her. "What do you have on that active mind of yours, Charlotte?"

Suddenly, Charlotte had the urge to confess her crime of driving without a license, but she resisted. David made her feel she could tell him anything and he'd understand. Most people in the congregation responded to him that way, so surely he'd know what her doctor had referred to as the movement. She quickly filled him in on what Dr. Van Pelt had told her and how concerned she'd been about what the so-called Movement might be and how it was affecting the young people, especially Dr. Van Pelt's own teen-aged children.

Charlotte studied her pastor's face as she told him. His blue eyes seemed to intensify. The scar that ran down the side of his face to his chin seemed to turn whiter as his face flushed.

"Well, I'll tell you what I know about the Movement. Our associate pastor has begun to gather interested members, especially the young people, into activities that would bring attention to certain issues."

"Like what?"

"She's become rather worked up on abortion and what she and others call the gay lifestyle."

"For them or against them? As I recall, she protested against the anti-abortion people at the clinic."

"She claims now that she believes that stance was wrong-headed."

"So Deborah Baker is rallying people to oppose the right of women to decide what is best for their bodies? What about homosexuality? Just calling something the gay lifestyle sounds like she's on the side of those who believe that sexual orientation is a choice, not biologically determined." Charlotte picked up a magazine on the end table and began fanning herself. "David, you sound so calm as you describe her stand. I for one do not feel so dispassionate."

David laughed. "Charlotte, I will confess to you. It is all I can do to maintain my composure. Frankly, I'm worried. Everyone, of course, can choose what to think about these issues. What concerns me is turning opinions like these into a crusade of some kind." He came around and sat on the edge of the sofa close to her chair. "And, confidentially, I'll say to you—and I'd appreciate if you keep this to yourself—I'm even more concerned that Deborah's campaign with The Movement may have a detrimental effect on our church family."

"Yes. I can see that. Like splitting us smack dab down the middle." She reached into her handbag and brought out her handkerchief. She dabbed at her mouth and nose. "David, what are we going to do? How can I help?"

"Right now all I suggest is that you stay alert and find out what you can. Perhaps from some of your flute students. Your friends over at the retirement center, like Margaret Templeton and Alice Sharp. What they might have heard. Anywhere."

"That I'll do. But what if she's already convinced too many people?" She dabbed her mouth again. "Listen, David. I have an idea. Since I'm on the Nominating Committee this year for the Session, maybe I can make sure the ones we nominate for elder are not under her influence." She hesitated. "If the others on the committee aren't already some of her people." She dropped her handkerchief in her bag. "You can count on me to try."

"Already she's managed to finagle some of her recruits to serve on that committee. I'll need you to counter their influence."

"How did she do that?"

"She got a couple of people on Session to suggest names of members who should be members of the committee. When you were elected, so were they."

"David, dear, I'll do whatever I am able. Rest assured, I do not want Harmony Church to lose its forward-thinking focus." She wished she could reassure him. He looked sad and worried.

Charlotte scooted her chair closer to David so their knees were almost touching. "David, you've been much on my mind—and not just about Deborah. And even before the crisis with Jody. I've noticed something awry. You seem . . . I don't know exactly how to put this. To be blunt, I want to ask you what's happened to the minister we brought here seven years ago? Have you forgotten or buried your passion for justice?" She watched his face. Was she too harsh?

David's face, except for the white scar, turned red. Even his ears. She might as well have slapped him.

"Thank you, Charlotte. You obviously have seen into what I've gone to some effort to conceal. Somehow I've allowed myself to become deadened to what used to give me life. Jody's crisis simply accelerated what's been with me for quite a while." He took her hand. She became conscious of how boney and discolored and veiny her hand was in his large tan hand. "Perhaps your words will go far to wake me up. Not that I know what to do about my numb spirit. Any suggestions?"

Charlotte released her hand and reached into her purse. "You know me. I happen to have today's horoscope for a Capricorn. Maybe it will help instruct you. *To find your way through the present conundrum, you must seek answers outside your comfort zone. A new path foreign to you will open soon.*"

"Thank you, Charlotte. Perhaps I'll seek out what you suggest. At least get out from under all the administrative clutter I've allowed to build up. Yes, maybe even find again my passion for justice, as you put it. Too long buried." He rose from his seat. "And going back to the business about Deborah, I know I can count on you." He reached down and pulled up one pants leg. "See, I'm wearing the black socks you gave me. Again, thank you." He gave her a hug and opened the door.

By the time Charlotte Ames had made her way again through downtown traffic and out to the tree-lined oldest part of Goodwin and home, she was utterly exhausted. She asked Houston if he would put her Lincoln into the garage, facing out toward the alley. He complied, and she went into her bedroom to lie down before her flute student was due.

# 24

# David

At three o'clock in the morning, David woke in a sweat. A vestige of a dream lingered, tantalizing him to return to the shadow world. Words from his dream floated through him: "Be not afraid. For freedom, He has set us free." Barking of a hound dog resounded from the hill across the way, with intermittent yaps from a smaller dog. *Country dogs,* he thought. Oh yes, he was in the old vacation house Ted and Emily used every season for a week. Time share. He liked the term and might use it as a sermon title. He stretched and made his way across the creaky slanted floor to the tiny bathroom under the stairs. His hosts were in the big master bedroom beside his room. He tried to be quiet so as not to wake them. They'd all stayed up well past midnight talking and sipping red wine. Ted enjoyed the fruit of the vine and fancied himself quite the connoisseur of Italian wines. David rarely had more than one glass at dinner. The two or three he drank last night had left him thirsty. He drank some from the bottled water on his night stand and flicked on the lamp, reached for his notebook and pen.

What a rare treat it was to be able to turn on the light without worrying about waking Nell. She was off with Flora on a buying trip and he had this delicious time away from her, away from church concerns, time to compose a sermon or two, and maybe himself. The girls were spending the two nights with friends. Emily and Ted planned to shop for antiques during the day, leaving him to much needed solitude.

He scribbled ideas in his haphazard fashion, as scripture, images, scenes from recent experiences popped into his mind. The dogs kept up their antiphonal barking, slowing a bit, then picking up the rhythm, as if rehearsing for a concert. He looked through his notebook. He smelled the familiar odor of its worn leather, a reminder of his father. Claude Archer had given David the notebook of favorite quotations when he retired from the ministry. "Maybe it will bring you wisdom, though not from me, Son," he'd said. "Still it may possess *baraka*—the gift of grace—the way old things can, as if they take on some wisdom from having been handled lovingly over many years through many crises." The heft that comes simply from lasting a long time. He remembered the weary look on his father's long, narrow face. At the time David had not asked what was making him so tired. He'd chalked it up to old age. Looking back, he realized his father hadn't been more than ten years older than David was now. Not old at all. He'd left the ministry before normal retirement age. Why hadn't he asked his father what made him quit? He had accepted the notebook without questioning him. Now he knew that his father's decision stemmed from the integration crisis and its terrible aftermath for his family.

Other Southerners complained about the endless stories told in their families, but not him. David's family seemed downright taciturn. For a man who used words well every week, his father had possessed a decidedly buttoned lip, clearly atypical. Perhaps more typical of his Scottish fore-bears, especially when it came to personal matters.

David thumbed through his notes. *Your dwelling place*, yes, he'd go with that. He'd counseled three alcoholics last week. One in his early twenties had been drinking since before ninth grade. That scared him, thinking about his own children. Working out of an addiction seemed almost impossible. He wrote, *"Dead to sin and alive to all that is good."* He recalled a book on his shelf back home, *Addiction and Grace*. He'd consult it again when he returned to Goodwin.

He jotted whatever flashed through his mind. His mother's urging him and his brother not to harbor grudges. She'd say, "Don't dwell on it. It's not worth your while." Wind picked up and whirred around the old frame house. This dwelling. This house he was in right this minute had stood on this windy hill above the small mountain town since 1923. The cracked siding, wrap-around porch with rocking chairs, the ill-fitting doors had given shelter to generations of people escaping summer heat before air conditioning. Layers and layers of white paint and layers and layers of living. Huge boxwoods anchored the tall house like stout, no-nonsense tribal women squatting beside the worn steps, protective, on guard.

He wrote, *You are where you live, where you dwell. Where your mind dwells, there your treasure is likely to be.* And from one of his favorite Psalms: the ancient 90th—*"Lord, thou hast been our dwelling place in all generations."*

He heard Ted's snores through the wall. Emily's face obliterated all other thoughts. Her listening face, the tight neat little features, her shiny black hair in the light and shadows of the trees. To be listened to with such quiet attention was a rare gift. What if they could enjoy each other without any barriers or restrictions? No. *Don't dwell on it.* Impossible. Covetous. Envious. Lustful. In five seconds, he could name any number of sins he was subject to. And yet—she could meet him in thought and spirit as if they'd known each other forever. *Watch it. Don't dwell on such an impossible off-limits relationship.* He'd have to be careful to keep their connection within acceptable bounds. He drank some from the bottle of water and closed his notebook, clicked off the light. He punched his pillow into a comfortable receptacle for his head. For once, he could sleep until he woke up, no alarm or calls.

⸙

The three friends walked down to the Wild Flour Bakery for sticky buns and coffee. The blue sky sported fast-moving clouds of varying shapes as if bragging about nature's palate and possibilities. The wind careened through the chestnut oaks and white pines lining the long driveway down to the road. Emily's dark hair beat around her face and her light jacket billowed out until she caught it to her and zipped up. David walked beside and slightly behind her with Ted on the other side taking long strides. Ted talked about the Presbytery's Committee he served on. David crunched acorns on the pavement the way he used to do as a kid. He'd rather not discuss church matters.

Emily, as if she guessed his thoughts, spoke up to Ted, "Dear, how about giving the subject a rest. I think David deserves a respite from church politics. What do you say?"

Ted looked back at the two of them, startled. "Oh, sure, uhh, okay. But I have one more thing to say." He stopped walking and waited for them to catch up. Ted always had one more thing to say. David smiled at Emily, who immediately pointed over across the street. "We like walking through this neighborhood. Some of these houses have been here for generations. Interesting Victorians. Look at the gingerbread on the one at the top of the hill."

To Emily, David said, "Bet it hasn't always been painted blue." Then he put his hand on Ted's shoulder. "Let's meet for lunch after we get back to town and talk out what the presbytery needs. Today, I want to absorb the mountain air and your good company and the sticky buns. Renew my weary spirit. How about that?"

Ted frowned, but nodded. "Okay, sure. After breakfast you might want to look at the garden shop next door. You and Nell have such gorgeous flowers."

The smell of warm yeast breads, cinnamon, and hot coffee met them the minute they opened the door. Jennie and Debby called out Good Morning and Emily introduced them to David. Just as they sat down, four guys with skin-tight outfits clopped in, their bicycle shoes announcing their ride up to Saluda from Goodwin. They carried matching helmets under their arms. David studied them and slowly registered that one was Preston. "Hey, Doc Pres, what you doing up here?"

Preston stepped over to their table. "Why, if it isn't Harmony Presbyterian Plottin' and Plannin' Group. It's my day off. What's your excuse?"

"Jenny's sticky buns, of course, and escape from internecine warfare." David invited him to join them, but Preston gestured toward the other bikers. "Better not this morning, but I have designs on you, Preacher. Coy's getting married at Christmas at Kiawah, and we want you to do the honors. Nat will call you soon."

"Sounds interesting, but you know that's my second busiest season. We'll talk about the date and see. Nell and the girls would never turn down a trip to the beach."

Ted and Emily drank their coffee, watching Preston walk across the restaurant to his group. Ted cleared his throat and spoke in a quiet voice, "I don't know whether you know it, but Preston is going through a mid-life crisis, or something. His practice seems great, but he's talking about quitting, and all is not going well with Natalie."

"Ted, please." Emily tried to get Ted to look at her, but he kept his eyes on the table at the end of the room. "What?" he asked.

"Don't talk about that. It's their business."

"I'm not gossiping, if that's what you mean. Only women do that, right?" He looked at David. David kept his face unresponsive. He didn't think it funny. Ted turned serious. "Don't get me wrong, David, I just think you ought to know. And Deborah Baker may have something to do with his present restlessness."

Emily straightened up, color rushing to her face. "What are you saying, Ted? This is news to me."

David leaned forward. "Oh, no. That's all we need. What with Deborah's campaign she's calling The Movement. She's got Julian Denyar on board and Myra, chair of personnel, to say nothing of all the youth, or most of them. Are you saying that he and Deborah are having an affair? Ted, don't be circumspect. I've got to know." He looked hard at Ted who seemed to be swelling up with the importance of his secret knowledge.

"Here's all I know. My secretary, Lottie Arnold, is the sister of Preston's nurse, Cris Harrington. Cris told Lottie who told me that not long ago, Deborah came in because her contacts had scratched her cornea again and she thought she had an infection or something. That was all innocent enough, but the odd thing was that she came back two days later and they spent an awfully long time in his examining room."

"So, what of it? What's so bad about that?" Emily sounded sharp and defensive.

Ted went right on without looking at Emily. "With the door closed. And no nurse present. Cris told Lottie that this was not at all his usual practice. In fact, he's always been a stickler for having one of his assistants in the room. But not that day. Finally, Cris knocked on the door because several other patients had been kept waiting a long time."

"So, then what happened?" Emily asked. David waited. Ted was holding off for effect. He'd never known Ted to enjoy this kind of story so much.

"Well, Lottie said that Cris told her, that after a minute or so Dr. Ames came to the door red-faced and angry, saying 'What is it? How dare you interrupt a delicate procedure?' but she said he sounded odd, not at all like normal. Those were her exact words." Ted took a sip of coffee and a big bite of his cinnamon bun.

David could feel Emily's eyes on him. He sipped his coffee, which had grown tepid. He wanted to pour it out and start over. "Tell you what, Ted. I'll be talking to Preston next week about his daughter's wedding. Maybe he'll have something else to share with me. Until then, I think we should give our friend the benefit of the doubt, don't you?" David got up, walked to the coffee urn and poured a fresh cup. He nodded to the bikers as he passed. He needed time to think. Deborah could indeed be making the situation worse. He'd never before had an associate pastor who came equipped with so much trouble-making personal gear. She'd been at Harmony less than a year and already her actions threatened to tear apart the fabric of the church.

When he sat down, he looked at Emily and Ted in turn. "Also, I'll have a heart-to-heart talk with Deborah and see if I can dig out the truth. Before the personnel committee meets on Thursday. Until then, let's keep all this under wraps, okay?"

"Fine with me. I hate this kind of gossip anyway," Emily said, glancing sideways at Ted. Ted nodded, reaching for another sticky bun. "Okay. Emily, I don't mean this as gossip. I think he needs to know what's being said."

The bikers clopped by their table on the way out. Preston stopped, shook hands with David and Ted, nodded to Emily. "Bye, you guys. I'll tell Nat that I ran into y'all."

"You do that, Doc. See you next week," David said.

"Bye, Preston. Happy pedaling," Ted said.

"Be careful, Preston," Emily added.

The three ate in silence. In a few minutes, Emily went to the counter and bought some nine-grain bread and a dozen oatmeal cookies. David watched her talking and laughing with the women who baked all the aromatic goodies. He wondered if it would ever be possible for men and women to be good friends without becoming sexual partners—or without being accused of it—in the culture where he and his friends belonged. Namely the church. Twenty-five years in the ministry. A calling he still affirmed, but a calling that was wearing him down. Like the smooth black stone he kept on his desk, shaped and smoothed into a pointed tool by some unknown hand many years ago.

Back at the house, David took his Bible out on the screened porch. Tiger swallowtails fluttered among lobelia blossoms and lantanas. The hills in the distance seemed muted by haze, their varied greens blurred.

He opened the Bible to Jeremiah, not exactly a cheery book. The more he read the prophets, the more he felt they were speaking right to America, his own people, to him personally, not simply the Israelites of old. He thumbed through the prophets—Amos, Isaiah, Micah. How often they called on God's people to show mercy to the poor, to practice love and justice and truth. A counter force to rampant greed, empty worship, power grabbing.

His mind flashed on Deborah Baker. Gradually, insidiously, the people in the church who were following her lead had taken on an air of superiority, as if they and she were the only Real Christians. No one else quite measured up.

He couldn't put his finger on how this was happening or exactly how to counteract the attitude. Still he knew that the sermons he'd been preaching on becoming the New Creation, his call to reach out to marginalized people nearby, had been well-received. He closed his eyes and prayed for wisdom.

Charlotte Ames's earnest face came to mind when she'd asked him, "What's happened to your passion for justice?" When he came to Goodwin seven years ago, did he possess such passion? What had fed that passion? In 1982 on up until two or three years ago, he'd delivered Meals on Wheels once a week and made sandwiches once a month at the neighborhood soup kitchen near the depot. His administrative duties increased as the church grew and managing his study time, sermon prep, and tending to the children filled his waking hours. Nell's work took her away a lot, but he couldn't blame her for his dropping those contacts with the poor. He wondered if he let the passion simply leak away from lack of attention. Now with his worry over Jody and his wariness about Deborah—he felt worn down.

He thought of all the people close to him that he'd asked to be on the lookout for Deborah's maneuvering. When he'd realized that his very asking people to be aware had probably made the problem worse, he'd stopped. He might be causing a split that existed only in his imagination. The game of chess came to mind. Yes, Deborah, a master chess player, was using the church people as her pawns, bishops, knights, and castles. Certainly not his natural modus operandi. He was no strategist. He recalled how his friend in ministry, Jonathan Savant, had accused him of being "absurdly unworldly." He prayed for guidance. And perhaps Charlotte was correct, he might need help "outside his usual comfort zone."

The phone in the hall rang. Once, twice, three times. He wasn't sure whether he should answer it, since Ted and Emily were part of a time-share group and usually they had rules about phone usage. Finally, he went in and answered.

Emily sounded frantic. "David, we need help. Something's wrong with Ted. Can you drive down to get us?"

"What, Emily? Is he sick? Having a heart attack? What?"

"He's been sort of bumping into things this morning, and now he's talking but not making sense. I asked him if we could call a doctor and he got belligerent. So I called you."

"Where are you?"

"We're at the Outback Hiking and Tackle Store. He's outside." Her voice choked.

"I'll be right there. Hold tight, Emily."

David pulled on his shoes without socks, grabbed his keys, wallet, and headed out to the Honda. He'd get closer to Goodwin and call one of the doctors in the congregation. Reese Cazort. He'd call Reese, his own internist.

By the time he reached the Parks, Emily was sitting on the asphalt parking pad beside her husband. Ted was lying in a strange position, one leg caught and bent under him. Two young guys who worked in the store had run out to see what was going on.

"I can't get him up," Emily said. Her hair was wet around her face from the effort to lift him. Ted moaned and mumbled something indecipherable. David motioned to the young guys. "One, two, three." The three of them lifted him and carried him as best they could to the car. Emily opened the back. "Man, that's one heavy dude," the skinny guy in the green tee said. Emily leaned over Ted. "Ted, dear, help the men out. See if you can climb in the back. David and I are taking you to town to the doctor."

"No! No doctor. Jes' let me lie down."

"Okay, dear. Just lie down right here in the back seat."

"Lady, can I call someone for you? An ambulance maybe?" said the big guy.

"I've heard it helps to give them aspirin. Do you want to try that? I may have them powdered ones in the shop." The skinny man wiped his face with a bandana.

David looked at Emily. "Do you want an ambulance?"

Emily shook her head. "No, I want to get him as fast as we can to Goodwin Hospital. Not this little town. Please, David, hurry."

David thanked the men and started the motor.

Emily jumped in the front seat, then got out and went to the back. "I'll sit back here with Ted." She lifted his head onto her lap.

"Fine. Let's go." David buckled up and started toward Goodwin. "Has anything like this happened before?"

"Not to my knowledge," said Emily. "But last night while we were all three talking, I noticed his face turned a deep red and stayed that way, and yours, by the way, looked decidedly yellow. Neither one could be healthy, right? Anyway, I chalked it up to all the wine we drank."

David drove fast through the watershed and down Highway 25, watchful for patrolmen. As soon as he got to Travelers Rest, he called the church office for Reese Cazort's number, called and got through a phalanx of assistants. Reese agreed to meet them at the ER in twenty minutes.

David and Emily sat in the curtained cubicle with Ted waiting for Dr. Cazort to return to them. Cazort and a neurologist were consulting off in an inner sanctum somewhere. The nurse had given Ted a sedative to quiet his thrashing. His wild muttering had ceased as well.

Emily's hand shook as she attempted to drink water David gave her. He took the glass and put it on the side table. Then he took both her small hands in his. They were icy cold. He studied her face, which looked tighter than ever.

"If Ted was red and I was yellow last night, you are white now, really, really white."

"David, I'm scared. Ted's always been strong, invincible, totally in control. He's only forty-nine. Maybe overweight, but strong as a draft horse." She hesitated, looked down at their hands clasped together. "Will you say a prayer for us, please, David?"

David bowed his head, silently asking for divine help in knowing what to say. Then he spoke quietly, "O God, our creator, redeemer, and sustainer, we need to feel the power of your loving, healing spirit today. We ask for your sustaining, upholding strength in our present distress and weakness. We ask for your healing of Ted, and give Emily and their children your comfort and strength for whatever is ahead. In the name of Jesus who lived among men and women, healing their afflictions, in the power of your holy name, we pray. Amen." David felt the sweat break out all over his chest and back, the way he did when he preached.

Emily's hands felt decidedly warmer. He lifted his eyes to hers. Her lovely blue eyes were wet with unshed tears. "Thank you," she said softly.

He let her hands go. "Do you want to call anyone?"

"Not until we know something. I don't want to alarm Tim and Tom or the sitter. They aren't expecting our regular call until suppertime. Maybe we'll know something by then."

"What can I do to help?" He looked out the curtained area. The nearest counter was empty, only wheelchairs parked, and the smell of antiseptic and an odor of unwashed flesh from the curtained cubicle next to them. Faint voices in the background. "What if I go back to Saluda and gather our things, pack you up and me too."

"Well, it's a cinch Ted and I won't be spending any more days or nights there for—I don't know when. Bringing our stuff back home would be great. David, it's a lot to ask. We've got groceries and supplies in the kitchen, both our bags and books. Plus, your suitcase and things. Are you sure?" She twisted the tissue she held. "And just strip the beds and gather the towels we used. The cleaning people will take care of all that when they come next week. Put them on the back porch near the washer. That will be a big help."

"It's the least I can do. Do you want me to go now, or wait till we hear something?"

She reached for her keys and dislodged the one for the Saluda house. "Maybe go now. That way, we'll have that part done. David, will he make it?"

"Ted, as you said, is as strong as a draft horse. I feel sure he'll pull through. Keep strong yourself. I'll be back as soon as I can."

Emptying the dresser drawers and repacking Ted's things and Emily's felt intimate and intrusive. Remorse for his covetous thoughts during the night gave his packing an urgency. Her scent, lemony with something like vanilla, emanated from her clothes. He tried not to rush, carefully folding and stacking shirts, jeans, underwear, socks and sneakers—his, large and musky, hers petite.

It was easy to see which side she slept on, which he used—by the bedside tables and what they held. Lotion, tissue box, and books she was reading—Wallace Stegner's *Crossing to Safety* and a slim volume that intrigued him, *The Miracle of Mindfulness* by someone with a strangely spelled name—Thich Nhat Hanh. All the *h*'s in unusual order. He thumbed through it and read the back. A Vietnamese Buddhist monk. Now that would be something outside his territory of knowledge for sure. He'd ask Emily if he could read it when she finished. Or buy a copy. Ted's side held a flashlight, a folder with legal papers, a paperback mystery.

In their bathroom, he gathered everything that looked temporary. Then he packed his clothes and books. The kitchen was last and wasn't as troublesome as she'd warned. He inspected the refrigerator and wiped it down. After he dropped the linens and towels by the washer, he checked around one more time, wistful and guilty that he'd had only one part of one day for his retreat. He recalled the Stegner novel of friendship of two couples. A touching story of four people who all loved one another, whose marriages were strong yet built on different dependencies. He wished his friendship with Ted and Emily included Nell as well. Nell made no bones about it—she resented Emily and had "never cottoned to Ted," as she put it. Maybe he had not tried hard enough to make it a foursome. He felt relief to be alone with the two friends, not worrying how Nell was taking everything. As he drove through the watershed back to the highway, he let the luscious greens soothe his soul.

# 25

## David

When David arrived at the nurses' station, men and women were scurrying here and there, all occupied, so he walked on to Ted's room. The sign on the door said, "No Visitors," but Emily expected him, and it was a pastoral call, after all.

The room was in semi-darkness with the wall-mounted TV screen flickering, casting weird light on the bed. Ted was lying supine, his head slightly elevated by two pillows. Emily rose from the vinyl chair beside the window. "Thank you for coming." With her back to Ted, she said softly, "David, would you mind sitting with him for a few minutes? I'd like to catch a breath of fresh air." Her slender body, usually so straight, slumped, her shoulders curving inward.

"By all means, that's why I'm here. To help you both any way I can." He went to her and she turned toward him. Her dear face showed the weariness of keeping watch. Lines between her thin eyebrows were deeply creased. Bloodshot eyes teared up as he looked at her. He had to hold still to keep from taking her in his arms. "Go. Get some air. Maybe a latte or something while you're out. I'm in no hurry."

"Thank you." She touched his arm as she passed by. Then she turned back to Ted. She touched his forehead and smoothed back his bushy straw-colored hair. "Ted, David's here. I'll be back soon." She kissed his cheek lightly, took her handbag from the hook, and glided out. She lifted her shoulders and straightened her back.

"Take your time. I'll be here."

From the hall, Emily turned back and smiled at him. Gratitude and wistfulness showed through her weariness. She mouthed *Thank you*, and was gone. The door closed with a quiet whoosh.

"David, would you raise the bed so I can sit up?" Ted spoke in a raspy voice, barely above a whisper. His speaking at all startled David, caught up as he was in his own thoughts at Emily's departure.

"Sure, Buddy." He pressed the button and soon Ted was sitting, more or less. His body sloped to one side and his head tilted to the right. David adjusted his head, remembering Emily had told him the stroke had impaired his right side—face, arm, leg, everything.

"David, I want to tell you something."

David leaned closer. "Sure, what's on your mind?"

"I've seen—" Ted strained to get out his words. "I've seen how you look at her. I've seen—" He coughed a deep cough, full of phlegm. David handed him a tissue, then put it in his left hand. Ted mumbled and dabbed at his mouth. "I've seen how she looks at you." Then he mumbled something David couldn't catch.

He gripped Ted's helpless right hand. "You know, my friend, you are going to get better. We are all counting on you to be strong. To come through this." He sat in the chair, still holding Ted's hand. "Maybe you should rest now."

"No." He tried to lift his head. His face flushed with the effort. "No. Listen. I know. Please. Take care of her." He eased back and closed his eyes.

"No. Ted, you're going to make it, friend."

David watched Ted's chest rising and falling, his mouth open. He placed Ted's hand on the blanket and sat back in the vinyl chair. Were his feelings that apparent? Ted, of course, was extra-sensitive about Emily. Still he'd have to shield his response to her. It was one thing to be honest with himself and hold to the parameters of what was possible. Quite another to allow other people to see his attraction to her. David walked to the window. The room looked down on a garden with a huge fountain in the center featuring a moving globe with water spilling over it into the surrounding pond. Crepe myrtle trees shedding their rosy blossoms sprinkled the tiny flowers over the grass and pond.

Emily returned with two coffees. She handed him one. "Black, right?"

He nodded and thanked her.

"Has he been asleep the whole time?"

"No. He talked a little. And coughed."

"The doctor wants him to cough. He also has him breathe hard into that contraption on the table. Exercises his muscles and lungs." She pulled over the straight chair close to the bed. "Sit in the big chair, David."

They sipped from the paper cups. "Has the neurologist told you what's ahead? What the treatment will be?"

"Dr. Chaseman explained the two kinds of strokes. Ted's stroke, they believe, was the one with hemorrhaging, not the kind caused by a clot." Emily kept her eyes on Ted. "Unfortunately, there's not a medicine for this kind. They had to stop the bleeding. That's why they did surgery so soon after he was admitted. Thanks to you, we got him to the hospital just in time, so Dr. Chaseman said. And Ted had been taking aspirin to thin his blood, so that had to stop, of course."

"He'll have some kind of physical therapy, right?"

"They'll start that soon." She sighed. "It's going to be a long haul. He may never be—as he was before."

"Let's hope he makes a full recovery." David stood. "Ted, I'll check on you again soon. Do what the doctors say, old buddy." Ted gave no response.

Emily walked him to the door. "Thank you for the little break."

"I can come back and stay the night if that would give you some rest."

"No. I've been spending the nights since he left ICU, but now he's resting well and doesn't want me or anyone to be with him at night." She reached for his arm.

He took her hand in both of his. "Please, call me any time. What about the boys? Do you need some help with them?"

"Natalie has pitched in. Once school starts, I may need you and Nell to help with carpool."

"Taking Tim to school and home will be easy enough. Emily, I'm at your beck and call."

# 26

## David

David had made the reservation a month ago at The Sanctuary on Kiawah Island, even though the beach was not his favorite place. He was a mountain man, having grown up inland with occasional trips to the Ozarks and once to the Colorado Rockies. But Nell loved the beach, so he'd made the reservations and braced himself with a scotch when he heard the price. They'd be on the west side of the East Wing which afforded a spectacular view of the ocean at sunset, as the unctuous man had crooned on the phone.

David hoped his therapist knew what she was talking about when she'd urged him to treat Nell to some romance and himself to a feast for his senses, long overdue.

Despite the definite fact that he was out of his element, he had to admit a certain amount of excitement. Maybe he could rekindle a bit of fire in their troubled relationship. Passion. Instead of the low boiling anger he felt emanating from Nell. Who was he fooling? It would be more like kindle, not rekindle. How long had it been since he and Nell had made love?

After he parked the Honda, he walked up to the spacious entrance. Everything in the hotel was grand. The murals of sea birds, reeds, and marshes stretched from floor to the second floor ceiling. A huge winding staircase enticed the imagination to picture actually living in this mansion and watching your beloved step gracefully down to meet you in a fetching gown. David looked back to the bellhop and smiled. "I guess you caught me gawking."

The young man wheeled the brass luggage carrier in front of him. He turned to David and gestured to the elevator. "It is an impressive place. This must be your first visit. Welcome to The Sanctuary."

On the way to the fourth floor, the bellhop confided to David that he had graduated from Freestone as an English major a year before and was earning money for graduate school. "Maybe seminary," he said.

David considered trying to dissuade him. Instead he tipped him generously and wished him good luck and God speed.

Nell was to join him at 5:30 after she finished some antique estate extravaganza in Charleston. Deborah Baker was to preach both services Sunday, and he'd told Judith not to call him unless there was a death. All other crises would have to wait. He took in the spacious room. It had indeed been a long time since he'd indulged his senses. He stretched and breathed deeply. The room smelled faintly of something citrus. He opened the balcony door and stepped out.

A brisk wind swept the smell of the sea to greet him. Three large pelicans glided by on air currents, their heavy wings and large beaks propelled them with utter unhurried confidence, as if to say to him that this was their domain and he might as well be a visitor from another planet.

Dark clouds hung heavy where the afternoon sun should have been. He went back into the room. Nell was supposed to show up in forty-five minutes. He'd had a hard time convincing her to come. He wished she'd been more enthusiastic.

He studied the king bed, so high, wide, and deep with all those confounded pillows and a downy comforter that threatened to suffocate him. The paintings on the wall were more beach scenes, real paintings, not cheap motel prints. He opened one of the bottles of water and took a long drink, and checked out the bathroom. Again, large, with a spacious glassed-in shower, large fluffy towels and plenty of them. A jacuzzi tub. Above the tub were shutters opening into the bedroom. Uh-oh. For Nell that would not be good. She preferred absolute privacy. He closed the shutters and fastened them. There was a separate toilet room. He sniffed the soaps and moisturizer. Good clean smell and something mysterious—the smell of luxury. The bathroom was twice the size of theirs at home, with fixtures that made him feel he'd dropped into the presidential suite.

In the shower, he scrubbed and lathered, letting the perfect shower spray do its magic. Finally, a shower made for a tall man. Hot and full out and then he switched to lukewarm and cool, and toweled off. He dressed carefully in the new black shirt and slacks and white tie. Only fifteen minutes until she was to arrive. He'd told her to meet in the room.

He laid out an outfit he'd bought for her, a simple black dinner dress that the saleslady had promised would be just right. He'd taken a dress from Nell's closet, one he'd seen her wear recently. She would look stunning, if it fit. He placed the necklace on top of the dress. Pearls and silver and some mysterious stone that matched her smoky gray eyes.

Suddenly, he felt spent, totally exhausted. He was no romantic suitor. His wife, utterly indifferent to him, when she wasn't outright hostile. He wished she were happier. He wished he could make her happy.

She would be here soon, he supposed. He lay on the bed in his socks and new clothes. He'd just rest for a few minutes.

The next thing he knew was Nell's voice, sharper, more annoyed than usual. "What is all this?"

David fought his way to the surface. He went to her and put his arms around her rigid body. "Now, Nell, relax. We're here to celebrate our anniversary."

"David, our anniversary was a month ago, in case you don't remember. As I recall, on that day you were occupied with two parishioners."

"Yes, they needed me. And anyway you were off on a buying trip."

"What about this dress? Where did you get it? You probably don't know my size." She held up the dress to her body. "It *is* pretty."

"Take your time, Nell. The bathroom is luxurious. I'm dressed, so I'll walk around and explore the hotel while you bathe." David tied his shoes. "Happy Anniversary, late. I hope you like the jewelry." He decided not to tell her that Flora had helped him pick out the necklace.

The next morning, David woke up early and lay in the luxurious king bed well away from his wife, who was snoring softly. He listened to the surf muffled by the heavy drapery over the French doors. He considered going out on the balcony, but knew that would disturb Nell. He needed to be quiet and reflect on the night's rather uncomfortable coupling.

The dinner in the Sanctuary restaurant had been as splendid as the price. When the staff discovered it was an anniversary celebration, they offered free champagne and chocolate truffles after their coffee and desserts. Nell managed a smile now and then, so David retained a modicum of hope that he could woo her away from her obsessive preoccupation with the jewelry business and all its associations, including the young man who had recently been so attentive. He'd lifted his glass and wished her business success and good relationships. For a fleeting moment, she'd smiled at him with the shy smile he remembered from their early days together. The candlelight on the table and Nell in the black dress brought back their first Christmas season together. They'd escaped her family after dinner and gone to a small restaurant off Peachtree Street. He couldn't take his eyes off her, and neither could their waiter. Later, he'd joked about the waiter falling in love with her, and she'd blushed, her face lighting up with that smile. That was the night he named her gray-eyed Athena, his goddess, and she'd called him Apollo. They slow-danced to the music of a jazz trio, who also seemed to appreciate her beauty. He'd been swept up in his love for her.

Music at The Sanctuary piped in overhead didn't invite dancing.

Gone were restaurants that provided a dance floor and live music. Maybe in a hip 1989 disco, but not here.

While they waited for the main course, he'd taken her hand at the table. She'd pulled her hand back, at first. Then, with a resigned sigh, she'd placed it in his. He felt a ping inside his chest as if, with her sigh, she'd stuck a needle into him. He kept his gaze on her face, and mentally sorted topics for what they could talk about that would avoid a mine field. Any talk about Jody was out. Nell consistently refused to broach the subject of Jody's illness. In fact, she would not acknowledge Jody was sick at all. "She's being self-indulgent, as usual. It's just more extreme and a lot more expensive this time. Who does she thinks she is, anyway? We all have problems." And on and on. He might have brought up the trouble at the church, but that bored Nell, so he couldn't use Nell as a sounding board at all. Emily or Natalie or Preston maybe, but not his own wife.

The truth of that sank into him. As he lay there, hearing Nell's deep breathing, her soft snores like the purring of a leopard, he knew he had to force himself to bring up their growing estrangement. Too many times he'd come close to speaking over the past few months, but lost his nerve. He had enough to deal with in the church, matters with Deborah growing worse. But he wouldn't think of that now. Only Nell. Their relationship, or lack thereof.

They used to play a game in the early days, before children. Even after all three daughters had arrived, they'd play—*If you had $50,000, what would you do with it?* Then with inflation, they upped it to $100,000. Now in 1989, they would probably go higher still. David could answer for her— she'd spend it on buying more antique jewelry to replace what had been stolen. He didn't bring up money. Only ambition and dreams. He'd asked her what she'd like to be doing in five years. In five years, he'd be 58, and she 54. He was careful not to mention age, another touchy subject.

Her answer somehow didn't surprise him. "Within five years, I would like to buy out Flora," she said, "and expand the estate jewelry business to include a contemporary line." She'd gazed out the dark window toward the moon. "I've met some designers who'd like me to represent them."

Nell hadn't bothered to ask him what he'd like to do in five years. She obviously didn't care and probably assumed it would be more of the same. This morning as the dawn light sent streaks across the bed, he let Emily's face come to mind. Her dark curls and intense blue eyes, her tiny figure and small, slender hands. He took in a deep breath and let it out slowly, allowing himself to entertain thoughts he'd been avoiding. He knew what he'd like in five years. He would like to be with Emily, not just as friends, but completely, as lovers.

He didn't wish his friend Ted dead. In his fantasy, Ted simply wasn't in the picture. With him so incapacitated from the stroke, Emily was more tied down than ever. David shook his head to clear his mind. Guilt laid claim to him: *Thou shalt not covet thy neighbor's wife.* Yet that was exactly the truth. He wanted Emily. Her listening and understanding, her quick wit and playfulness. Her gentleness and energy. Emily Garland Parks. He allowed himself to imagine her in this luxurious hotel. Her small body without the burden of clothing or responsibility. Emily, lying on his chest, stretching out her full length on his body. His penis responded. Then Nell moaned and turned over. Guilt threatened him again.

After the extravagant dinner, he and Nell had returned to their room. At first they'd circled one another like wary strangers, too polite. More like animals unsure of which was the Alpha. So David took the initiative, and embraced her. Then he gently unzipped the black dress, which had indeed fit her tall, curvy body perfectly. He called her his goddess with her strong arched back, red red lips, lovely bosom, firm buttocks, long legs. When she hadn't protested, or frowned, he began caressing her. All went well for a while.

Now looking back on their love-making, David admitted to himself, nothing would have happened if he had not pictured Emily toward the end. He wondered now if Nell had pictured that young man she worked with, Stefan what's-his-name. Yet, it had been good, and Nell had seemed totally content afterwards, curled against him. A sliver of hope awakened a spark inside him. Perhaps they could find their way back to each other.

David left a note in the bathroom beside her make-up, saying that he'd gone down to breakfast and she could join him when she woke up, but he hoped she'd sleep as long as she wished.

In the vast dining room, he was seated beside the windows looking out on a sweeping lawn perfect for croquet. Beyond, the ocean gleamed in spangles of morning light, promising a clear bright day ahead. The clouds and wind had totally dissipated. He and Nell would have the whole day to relax and talk. Walk the beach. Even make love again.

Ravenous. He was ravenous. He walked to the large buffet. David hated confrontation and the rancor that so often accompanied it. Such relief to think that maybe, just maybe they might enjoy each other again. Find a way to stay married. He took eggs benedict from a steamer. The beginning of a headache halted him between the steamer of grits and the platter of smoked salmon with all the accoutrements.

Before last night, he'd about given up on their marriage, yet now the sliver of hope made him dizzy. Or maybe it was his ambivalence.

"Excuse me, sir. Are you all right?" A waiter caught his elbow. "Let me take your plate to your table." The young man led the way, and then turned back to him. "I think your wife has joined you."

Nell wore the same suit she'd arrived in, a handsome royal blue with a cream-colored blouse, and heels that matched her suit.

David rubbed the back of his neck. "Good morning, Nell. You can order from the menu or go for the buffet, which looks great, by the way. That's what I'm doing."

"I can see that." She looked up at the waiter and gave him her I-can-be-gracious-to-the-servants smile accompanied by managerial instructions. "I shall order from the menu. A waffle with pecans, please, and bacon, crisp bacon. Thank you."

"Nell, they can make you a waffle up there at the buffet."

"No, I shall sit here and have a waffle from the menu, thank you."

"Of course, ma'am," the waiter said. He bowed slightly and left with a click of his heels. David felt a laugh about to erupt but suppressed it.

"You look lovely this morning, Nell. Very professional." He sipped his coffee and studied her impassive face. "But we're on vacation. What about changing after breakfast, so we can take a walk on the beach?"

Nell poured in some cream and sprinkled two packs of artificial sweetener into her coffee before she spoke to him. As she slowly stirred her coffee, she said, "No, I have to go back to Charleston this morning. A meeting with a dealer. It's important."

David felt tremendous heat growing in his body, gathering into a storm, completely obliterating his earlier queasiness. His head might burst if he didn't speak up. He kept his voice low, but he felt like yelling. "You're always leaving. Always working."

"You always have to be in control." She spoke coolly, indifferently. "You have no idea what it takes to run a business, especially having to virtually start over." She unfolded the napkin and smoothed it in her lap. "A Charleston dealer is going to take me on and pay a commission on what I sell of his inventory. I need this chance."

"Nell, please. We've paid a lot for this beautiful get-away. Let's enjoy it together." His voice sounded thick to his own ears. He wondered if Nell knew how upset she'd made him. Or even cared.

"This was your idea. To indulge in this luxury. Not mine."

The waiter brought her breakfast, poured them both more coffee, and quickly disappeared.

"Well, pardon me. I was just envisioning how we'd enjoy some time on the beach. Maybe stretch out on the balcony later and read or even, you know, make love again. Is that too much to ask?"

"David, I have to be in Charleston by ten."

"If you insist on going to Charleston, why don't you just stay there?"

"You should think about what you're saying, David."

"Nell, we might as well live on different continents. In some ways, we do. I'm tired. Exasperated. I could go on."

"Please, do go on."

He watched her face and waited. She poured syrup on the waffle in concentric circles without looking up.

"I want us to be together. What is it you want?"

Nell placed the bite in her mouth and seemed to chew in slow motion, watching him. Her gray eyes darkened and glistened.

He placed his hand on hers before she could reach her coffee cup. Her narrow eyebrows arched higher.

"Nell, what is it you want?"

"What do I want? Right now, I want to enjoy my waffle and coffee, without pressure. That's what I want."

David finished off his cooling eggs. He sipped the coffee, now tepid. The waiter returned and David asked for a fresh cup of hot coffee. Nell glared at him with her hate look until the waiter had brought the hot coffee and left.

She began eating her bacon in avid bites. She licked her fingers before wiping them on her napkin. David smiled.

"What's so funny?"

"You remind me of Lyn. Remember when she fell in love with bacon? Now she still can't get enough of the yummy greasy stuff."

"You do love to feed the girls fattening foods when you cook." A little jab there, but Nell relaxed her shoulders. Her eyes softened. David was leery of trusting that she might actually be opening up, her defenses down, at least somewhat.

"Nellie, it seems to me that just when we are getting close again, you close up. You surround yourself in an impenetrable carapace, and at the least provocation you hurl verbal spears at me. Accusing me of this and that."

Nell laughed. "David, wouldn't your friend Emily call that a mixed metaphor?" She took a long drink of water.

The mention of Emily's name caught him up. As usual, Nell's uncanny antennae worked overtime, but he had to push on. "Okay, okay.

221

I'll stop trying to describe what I've sensed for a long time, and just say what I've concluded. And here it is: either we commit to work on our marriage. Or we should separate." He took a drink of water. "In effect, we are separated."

"You've got it all figured out, do you? You should think long and hard about this. What would your precious congregation do?" Nell pressed the napkin to her lips, placed it carefully beside her plate, and scooted out her chair. She stood and reached for her handbag.

"Nell, don't you dare leave this table until we finish this discussion. Sit down."

"Keep your voice down. You don't have to yell at me."

"I'm not yelling, Nell. Sit down so we can finish."

"Well, aren't you the assertive one. All of a sudden." She obeyed him, sat and scooted in her chair. "But I do have to leave soon for the city."

"I'm just trying to say—Maybe we should make our lives match the reality of what is. The reality is that we are living separate existences."

"Nonsense. You always turn everything into a philosophical abstraction."

Nell drank the rest of her water and picked up her handbag. "Time is up. I must get to Charleston for my business meeting. You know, the jewelry business you so resent." She stood up, straightened her skirt. "Which, let me remind you, has paid for most of Jody's expensive care."

He stood facing her. "I agree on one point, Nell. Time is up. It is time for decisive action. You know, the kind of action you believe I cannot take. Watch me." He held her arm. "My question is simple. Will you move out, or shall I?"

Nell took a few steps, then turned half-way around. She jerked her arm free. "I shall return to our home on Sunday evening, and at that time, we'll see what we do from there." Nell walked toward the elevators, her high heels clicking decisively on the marble floor.

David returned to the table. The waiter stood beside his chair. "May I get anything further for you, sir?"

"Thank you, no. Just the bill." David wondered how many domestic disputes the wait staff had witnessed in this luxurious restaurant. He felt no headache, or queasiness, and the anger had long since drained out of him. He felt a clean kind of emptiness, as if he had purged a residual poison from his system. "On second thought, I believe I'd like a waffle and bacon from the buffet before I go."

"Very good, sir."

# PART THREE

# 27

# Emily

After the hymn, "We are living, we are dwelling in a grand and awful time," Deborah stepped to the pulpit and read selected scriptures where Jesus says he had come to bring not peace but a sword, and another that unless his followers hated his brother and mother and father, they could not be his disciples.

Deborah wore her black robe but left it unfastened, her red dress showing in the middle. Emily and Natalie looked at each other. Deborah had swept her auburn hair into something of a French twist, clipped in place with a silver bar, a few tendrils escaping on either side of her head.

Emily would like to be recording Deborah's sermon to give it to David when he and Nell returned from the beach. As Deborah got going, Emily wished it more than ever.

Deborah used her most impassioned tones, exhorting the congregation to fight the good fight. "As the hymn says, 'Up. It is Jehovah's battle.' We must set our sights on what the sovereign God is calling on his people to do at this time and in this place. We must summon courage to act on the issues of this day, the dire problems of our world. A sinful world, a world without God. That is the world we face in this last decade of the 20<sup>th</sup> century.

"Some in our midst call for peace at any price, but I call on you and you and you to join me in this God-given fight. Join the young people in our church as Soldiers for Christ, a Movement for Monumental Change.

"We must take a stand on the issues at hand. I call two such issues by name: homosexuality and abortion. And a strong third: those living in poverty while those of us with riches pay little or no attention. In these and other situations, where will you and you and you throw your weight and voice your stand?

"Read the gospels, read what Paul has said, read and truly listen to what Jesus Christ has said. Discipleship is costly.

"As for the poor, this very day I ask you to send a special cash offering to those in acute need. People I see every week at the Space for Hope. These, the least able to provide for their most basic needs. They will truly benefit. Just leave what cash you can spare in the offering plates today, over and above your usual pledges and contributions, and I will personally deliver your generous gifts. Let us stand up for the poor.

"And let us stand up and be counted against the gay lifestyle. The scourge of AIDS is the Lord's punishment on these unfortunate sinners. Not just in Africa and in California, but even in our beloved south. And let us stand up against the killing of innocent unborn babies. Abortion is an abomination.

"If our elected leaders in this church refuse to stand up, we should persuade them, or push them aside. We must rise and fight for our convictions.

"If you sense a fissure growing in the church, that is good. The division promised by the Lord, separating the sheep from the goats. Tolerance makes us tepid. Lukewarm Christians who turn aside from the battle in favor of pleasuring themselves and advancing self-will.

"I aim to turn up the heat under the complacency in our midst. Join The Movement. Like the prophets of old, I say: Question those in power. Not just in government, but those in power in the church. Follow me and we together can turn the world upside down. Look around you. Who is

227

in charge? Follow me. Follow me, says the Lord. Let the redeemed of the Lord say so."

Someone in the back called out, "Amen."

Emily jotted a note on the bulletin to Natalie: *What is she doing? Talking so fast, wired for reactionary action.* Natalie wrote back: *She's wired all right!*

The air in the sanctuary practically crackled with energy. Contagious fervor. Emily looked over across the aisle to where Julian Denyar sat with his grandson. He was smiling and nodding his head. Deborah had totally won him over. Emily recalled the night at the restaurant when Julian seemed under her spell, and since then advocated whatever she proposed in session meetings. David, however, continued to bear the brunt of Julian's criticism. Just a few months ago Julian had openly and sharply opposed Deborah. Now she could do no wrong.

Natalie wrote: *My guess — she knows which way the wind blows in this state. Her next move may be to urge people to carry guns to church.*

"O Lord, I hope not," Emily whispered.

After the service, they lined up with the others to shake Deborah's hand. Emily listened to comments as people spoke to Deborah: "You really socked it to us. More power to you." Emily and Natalie stood behind Judge Knapp and his wife, who each grabbed one of Deborah's hands. They exclaimed over the bravery of her preaching. "Of course, we must proceed with all deliberate care, Reverend Baker," the judge said.

Deborah looked up in her characteristic way, her dark eyes wide and inquiring as if to ask what the big man was thinking. Then she said, "Why, I believe in following what the scriptures say, don't you, Judge Knapp?"

Her robe fell open, revealing her red dress, a pearl necklace hanging low, leading his eyes to the shadow of cleavage.

Judge Knapp's eyes looked down, then moved back up to her face, his face quickly recovering. "Yes, yes, of course."

Emily wasn't sure what to say to Deborah. Before she could decide, Deborah seized her right hand and said, "Thank you for being here, Emily. Your careful attention means so much to me." She turned to Natalie, and looking back and forth, said, "I hope you'll both stand with me in the fight ahead."

"Well, we'll have to see exactly what you're talking about. I for one do not want to divide the church," Natalie said. "And you know how liberal I am on the very issues you named." She gave Deborah a hard look and pulled her hand away. Emily was relieved to be led away. They walked past a group of girls who were talking low with great intensity, gesturing toward Deborah. Emily couldn't hear what they said, but she picked up the adoring tone. They, too, were caught in Deborah's web. Natalie nodded at them.

"You were right, Emily, when you said that we'd better pay careful attention to what Deborah is up to."

They walked across the parking lot, speaking to other people until they reached their cars parked side by side.

"Trouble is I can't figure out her game," Emily added. Whatever psychic powers she might once have experienced now were blocked.

"Game. That's the right name for it. She's embarked on a dangerous game. No doubt she has a strategy."

"We'll have to keep our eyes open. I've got to get back to Ted. See you at the gym tomorrow." She felt sick at her stomach.

# 28

## David

David's appetite waned after Nell left. He managed to chew and swallow the waffle under the attentive waiter's eyes, and then headed to his room. What had he done? Would she still be there? Maybe she too had second thoughts. Although probably futile, he couldn't help but hope she'd be in the room, changing out of her business suit into warm-ups for a beach walk. He'd apologize and promise they'd work on the relationship together.

She was not in the room. Her suitcase and hanging bag were gone. Her room key lay on his pillow. No note.

Nell had taken him at his word. Besides, her obstinacy, which he'd always admired and named "tenacity of purpose" when she set herself a goal, was as adamantine as granite. He'd seen that stubbornness operate in relationships. The other party never knew what hit them. Nell got an idea about a person, felt wronged or neglected by a friend, and from then on saw him or her as the enemy, and stubbornly would not let go of that idea. She'd cut off any meaningful contact. No amount of regret or apology on the friend's part did any good to change her mind. Chop. Gone.

David put on his windbreaker, the cap labeled Harmony Bluejays, his shades even though the sky now was overcast, and headed to the beach.

He at least could use this time and place purchased so dearly. Most of Saturday, he walked and ran on the beach. He caught up on his reading. He mulled, took notes in his journal. He pondered.

Sunday morning, the sky, heavy with clouds, the horizon, ocean and beach itself conspired to reinforce his mood. Shades of gray from slate to pale concrete gray. He pulled up his collar and walked into the wind. The weather was more like November than Labor Day weekend. Somber as a nun, he recalled from some old poem. David stepped around the beach detritus washed up during the night. A horseshoe crab shell, yellow strands of some sea plant, broken sand dollars, a starfish dead but in perfect formation, and cola bottles dropped by careless humans.

Sanderlings pecked holes in erratic rhythms like percussionists in a miniature jazz band. Gulls glided overhead. Heavy-billed pelicans patrolled in threes. The heavy clouds above moved in their own rhythms. David increased his stride, and began a slow jog. He breathed in the cool air like answered prayer. One by one, the women in his life came to mind. Nell with her gray eyes solemnly assessing him. Jody the last time he saw her. The doctors and nurses had pumped her stomach and left her hooked up to IVs, her arms restrained in the bed. Her pleading eyes begged him to understand, to forgive her, to release her.

He could never let his first born child go. The fact remained—he had not known she'd been suffering so. Stunned by her action, he'd been blind and deaf to her need. He'd held her hand, caressed her forehead, smoothed the lovely curls around her face, all the time praying silently for her to live, to thrive even if she hadn't wanted to. Please, make her want to live, he prayed. Please, believe that you'll be glad some day you did not succeed in killing yourself. He swore silently that he would do all in his limited power, that the person she was in her very essence would be strengthened enough to defeat the enemy in her mind. Whatever it was that so taunted and shamed her. The exact nature of the enemy remained a mystery to him.

David bent and picked up a broken conch shell. With all his might he heaved it out to sea. The doctors still would not let him or Nell visit

Jody. Not yet, they kept saying. Millie had been their emissary Easter weekend, but that visit must not have gone as well as he first thought. Now he would sometimes find Millie disconsolate, closed off and weepy. She couldn't explain, or wouldn't. Jody's stability had shattered. And he couldn't understand why. He did feel confident that the decision to place her at Winslow Farms had been right. Despite the exorbitant expense, he trusted the doctors there and the program.

Millie's innate light-filled spirit comforted him. He could see the effort it cost her to emerge from sadness over her sister. He thought of Lyn's eagerness to learn, to write, to play the flute. He loved his younger daughters dearly, but he had to admit that Jody's illness had caused him to hold his heart somewhat in reserve. What if the same terrible fate hit each of them at age seventeen or eighteen?

And what of the gray-eyed Athena he'd wed twenty-five years ago? He admired Nell, respected her ambition to make her business a success. But she seemed to be systematically killing any love he used to feel. Her anger, constant antagonism, defeated him. Was she too grieving over Jody? Was she depressed? Why did she have to keep herself sealed off from him? Where did such terrible emptiness come from? What had he done to exacerbate her misery? He'd failed. Failed to make her happy.

David stopped running, aware that his heart hammered hard and fast and somewhat erratically. He wiped his face and head. Despite the cool breeze, he perspired. Three young guys on bikes passed him. He nodded a brief greeting. He'd return to the hotel slowly. Sunlight began to glow behind the clouds in the east. Maybe the weather would clear.

He picked up a piece of weathered driftwood twisted by years of tumbling in the ocean. It branched into a form like antlers and widened into what might be a head. Wiping away encrusted sand, he felt indentations that could serve as dark eyes and something of an animal mouth at the end. He rubbed his hand over the driftwood deer. What had been his part in Nell's discontent and anger? The onset of Jody's illness certainly brought things to a head. But the problems between them began long ago at the time of their courtship while he was in England. The way people present themselves to one another in letters is not the same as they are when they're actually together.

Right away at his first small church and teaching assignment in Arkansas, Nell had seemed startled and disconcerted by their surroundings. So alien to her former life as a debutante in Atlanta. The church had been in a blue-collar neighborhood with a sprinkling of rice farmers along with factory supervisors, a few educators, one banker. She taught herself to cook during those dreary five years, but that did little to make her happy. After Jody was born, Nell suffered terrible headaches and back pain. Her mother had hired a nurse to care for Jody. David remembered days when he'd come home exhausted from visiting the sick and working with committees and find Nell in bed, refusing to hold Jody. They'd both been ignorant and inexperienced. They knew nothing about postpartum depression. Had he accused her of hating their baby? God, he hoped not.

Tired as he might have been, he found himself bathing the baby, giving her the night-time bottle, and rocking her in the chair that had belonged to his mother. No doubt certain attitudes and habits got established. The nightly ritual with Jody comforted him. He'd welcomed the non-verbal connection between them. He thought about the baby's warm body against his chest, at first stiff with colicky misery, then gradually as he walked and sang to her, he would feel her body release its tension and slowly relax. Perhaps Nell felt judged by him after he took up so much of the baby care. Did she feel guilty? Did she assume he considered her a bad mother? Surely not.

Nell had been raised by an aristocratic mother and a wealthy vascular surgeon who possessed a strong entrepreneurial drive. No wonder she sought to become a successful businesswoman. And David's body had startled her. Maybe he'd wanted sex too often to suit her. After the three girls were born, she basically shut him out. By that time, her lack of enjoyment quelled most of his desire. A definite disappointment. Still, he felt no closer to figuring what he had done to make her perpetually angry at him. He kicked at the sand, stirring up the complacent gulls nearby.

His eyes sought the horizon, a fine silver line now. Rays from the sun behind the clouds above the sea created dramatic contrast of light and dark. Maybe he could ask her forgiveness for whatever unknown wrong he'd done her. He'd tried to talk with her. Her indifference quite literally turned him off. Had he listened to her? He spent his days listening to others, but he could try listening more to Nell. Maybe she'd tell him about the jewelry and the people at the shows and estate sales. Of course, she'd have to be willing, and now she might not be home when he got back to Goodwin. Or if home, she'd probably chop off contact with him.

The large hotel came into view. Two couples walked toward him, each man with a dog on a leash. One, a golden retriever, made him miss Calvin.

He stamped the sand out of the grooves in his sneakers and walked up from the boardwalk around the pool and into the back door of the Sanctuary.

"Hello, sir. Dr. David Archer?" A lady from the front desk came out to meet him. "Dr. Archer, you've had two calls. They sounded rather urgent that we find you."

"Thank you. Do you know who called?"

"No sir, but your room phone should have voice messages for you. If you have an emergency, we'll do everything in our power to help you. Please call on us."

David thanked them and sprinted to the elevator.


His heart was racing by the time he reached his room. An urgent call. His first thought was Jody. The care facility calling to report something dreadful. She'd killed herself. Or something with Millie or Lyn. What could be the trouble now? Nell. Did she make it to Charleston? He was sweating hard by the time he answered the flashing light to get the messages. Both were from Charlotte Ames.

He called her immediately. "Charlotte, dear, what's wrong? You sounded pretty upset."

"Sorry to disturb your weekend away, David, but I felt it imperative to reach you today."

"Charlotte, it's okay. What seems to be troubling you?"

"It's you. Your birthday is January 2nd, right?"

"Yes, but—"

"Your horoscope today for Capricorn specifically warns you to watch your back. I thought I'd better not wait for you to return to Goodwin to give you this most unusual message."

David sat down on the cushy bed and let out a long sigh. He and Preston had laughed about her harmless habit. Pres had reported that his sister Hannah was fed up with their mother's new weird practice. David felt that it must have been Charlotte's way of saying she was thinking about her loved ones, and had said so.

"Thank you, Charlotte. I'll try to watch my back, but you know as well as I that basically that's impossible. Let's just hope friends like you have my back."

"Listen, David. I wouldn't have called to report this if the horoscope were the only thing. You see, I have been keeping my well-tuned antennae up for some time now, and I suspect a conspiracy is afoot in the church. Our beloved Harmony Church that you and I and others have given our lives to build into a progressive, loving congregation—this church may be in for a difficult time. You should have heard the Reverend Deborah Baker this morning. David, she's out to split the church asunder. The message today was downright inflammatory. I just thought I'd better call." She trailed off as if losing her confidence about interrupting his respite.

"I appreciate your concern."

"I forgot to ask—how are you and Nell enjoying the beach?"

"Well, I just returned from a long walk, and believe me, it was just what the doctor ordered. Let's talk some more after I return, Charlotte." He hoped she wouldn't notice that he hadn't mentioned Nell. "And,

Charlotte, remember I'm counting on your influence on the Nominating Committee."

"Thank you, David. You always have a way of calming me down. But I'm still worried about the church and about you. Don't forget to watch your back, and I'll look out for you too." She hung up.

David wondered if she'd found out from Judith where he was staying. There seemed to be no place for a minister to hide, no way to escape. No wonder so many colleagues suffered burnout.

# 29

## Charlotte

Charlotte Ames decided this was the day to visit Ted Parks in the rehabilitation hospital, so she called Margaret Temple and Alice Sharp at the Presbyterian Village and suggested they go together. Alice had promised to help with a function at the home, but Margaret agreed to drive Charlotte. They stopped by Word of Mouth to pick up muffins. Charlotte loved the warm aromas filling the little cafe and the music playing from the speakers. "The Sound of Silence" immediately took up lodging in her head. She knew she'd be living with that song most of the day. If it weren't that tune, it would be another. Music furnished a good bit of her mental landscape.

Outside, the September air filled her with excited anticipation that fall inevitably offered—the beginning of the school year, memories of plaid dresses and new books. How she'd loved school. The Jews had it right. The year ought to begin in September, not January. She felt ready for the new as soon as autumn blew its crisp bright breath in her face. She wished she could offer Emily and Ted a measure of what she felt this day. Something hopeful. His future seemed mighty dim.

Charlotte watched Margaret Temple as she drove her old Buick out the bypass. Margaret certainly showed her age these days. Her shoulders sloped; her dowager's hump was more pronounced than ever. The flap under her chin must have doubled in the past year, and Margaret's once luxuriously thick, dark hair had decidedly thinned and faded. She still wore it scooped up with combs on either side of her head. The same basic style she'd used when they were both school girls at Eastside High eons ago. They'd known each other since the third grade, playing jacks, jumping rope, pretending to be World War I nurses. Later competing for grades and boyfriends. In each other's weddings and on and on. Always there for each other through all their years.

"You're mighty quiet today, Charlotte."

"Just thinking about old times, I guess. We've been through a lot together, haven't we?"

"That's the Lord's honest truth." She drove the Buick into the parking lot of Roger Hunting Hospital and parked near the building. She hung her Handicapped sign over the rearview.

When they reached Ted Parks' room, he wasn't there. A woman at the nurses' station said he was in physical therapy. "His wife just left his room. She may be in the cafeteria."

Charlotte walked fast with Margaret hobbling behind on her cane. Emily carried a tray with a small salad and iced tea. "Emily, dear," Charlotte called. "We've come to visit you and Ted. May we join you?"

"Of course." Emily led them to a table not far from the door. "Would you like something to eat or drink?"

They declined. She reported on Ted's progress, how his upper body strength had increased a bit, but his leg and arm on the affected side were non-functioning. Emily sighed when she said they were trying to remain optimistic.

"You've no doubt received pastoral visits from David, haven't you?" She thought Emily sharpened her gaze at the question as she assented. "Well, I'm concerned about what's happening at Harmony. With Deborah.

I want to rally his supporters before Deborah completely divides the church." Charlotte hoped she wasn't jumping too abruptly into her subject. No time to waste.

"Well, David's asked me to help lead an adult Sunday school class on the social and cultural issues of today," Emily said, "and how Christians can differ in their viewpoints. Deborah is the other leader." Emily's blue eyes teared up. "I said yes, and I'm doing it, but with Ted's condition and everything else, I admit it's hard to concentrate."

"Oh, my dear, I can see that. Especially considering how super-focused Deborah has become on the issues. And judgmental." Charlotte looked from Emily to Margaret, who seemed mildly disturbed by the conversation. Margaret stood and said she was going to the ladies' room.

While Margaret was away, Emily lowered her voice and leaned close to Charlotte. "I found something. Something mysterious. The time this summer when I went to the Space for Hope and worked with some teen girls and Deborah." She blushed and hesitated. "I don't really know what to do." Then she told Charlotte about the white powder that had fallen on the floor when Deborah had been in the adjoining stall of the bathroom. "I scooped it up with an index card and managed to put it in an envelope. But now what? How do I find out what it is exactly."

"You mean…is the white powder an illegal substance?"

"Exactly. I've hesitated to do anything. I don't want to imply that she's using or anything. For all I know it could be baby powder, or a headache remedy."

"I won't say a word." Charlotte could practically hear her heart thumping away. "Here's what we'll do. The private investigator I'm in touch with, you remember—Irving Wolfe. He can get it tested." She glanced up and nodded to Margaret approaching the table.

Emily inquired about the Presbyterian Village, how Margaret liked living there after spending so many years in her big family home. Margaret told the story of moving into her small apartment and treating her old house like her work. "For four months, I left every week day after breakfast and drove to the house to clear it, room by room, closet by closet. Like a job. I spent at least eight hours a day, some days ten."

"My, that's disciplined," Emily said. "How do you feel now?"

"Purged. Purified." Margaret sat up straighter. Her regal look of long ago returned. Her chin lifted and her neck grew longer.

"What in the world did you do with all the stuff? That's what defeats me," Charlotte said.

"Oh, the usual. Asked the children to take what they wanted, gave away their rejects, made some hard, hard choices about what few items and furniture I had room for in my new quarters."

Emily turned to Charlotte. "You're going through something of the same, aren't you? Squeezing your possessions into one-fourth your house. That must be a challenge too."

"Yes, indeed. Especially since neither Preston nor Hannah nor their children want my Victorian furniture. But besides my apartment, three others will be partially furnished. Houston and his helpers will put things where I direct them when the time comes."

"Are you close to finishing?" Emily asked.

"It's dragging along. I think before the end of October, it'll be finished. Anyway, I'm planning a party to which you all are invited."

Emily wiped her mouth and rose. "Let's go to the room. Ted ought to be back. He'll want to see both of you." She led them down the hall.

Charlotte thought Emily looked thin and sad. Maybe mentioning a party later in the fall depressed her. They found Ted in his hospital bed in more or less a sitting position, listing slightly to starboard.

"Ted, Charlotte Ames and Margaret Temple are here for a short visit." Emily brushed his bushy straw-colored hair back. He opened his eyes.

Charlotte moved closer. "Ted, how are you feeling? We've brought you some muffins—bran with nuts and carrots—from Word of Mouth." She heard herself rushing her words. Talking too loudly. Distressing to see him like that. She made herself stop.

Ted smiled with one side of his mouth. His large head turned slowly toward her.

He mumbled what she took to be his thanks. She looked at Emily who took the little bag from her. "I'm sure Ted will love them. Provided he can keep them away from his good-looking nurses," she said.

Margaret walked to his bedside. "Ted, I want you to know that you're on the prayer chain at the Village."

Again he smiled with the part of his mouth that moved. His light eyes looked blood-shot to Charlotte. She'd always been struck with how his eyes matched his hair with a touch of green added. Hazel or amber. Ted had been quite the hefty football star back in the day. Handsome and tall. Unfortunately he had gained even more weight since his stroke. His flaccid skin looked pasty.

"I hope the physical therapy is helping you," she ventured.

"I hope so too," he said, "but it leaves me…very tired." He closed his eyes.

Emily apologized and led them to the door. They said their good-byes. Margaret headed to the nurse's station. Emily caught Charlotte's arm. "Here, take this box. I put the substance in it. Been carrying it around in my handbag. Putting off doing anything. See what you can find out. Please."

"You've kept it since June?" Emily certainly hadn't rushed to judgment. Charlotte put the small box into her black bag. "I'll see what I can find out," she whispered. She hugged Emily. "You must take care of yourself, too, my dear."

As they approached Margaret, Charlotte said, "Emily, dear, your Pisces horoscope today said that you may want more from someone than the other person can give, but you should remember that you can reach out to others who care for you. That would be me and Margaret and your whole church family."

"Thank you, Charlotte. Call me." Emily waved to Margaret and blew a kiss to Charlotte.

Charlotte and Margaret entered the dining hall of the Presbyterian Village and joined Alice Sharp's table for lunch. The vegetable soup and cornbread offered comfort and the familiar. Charlotte told Alice about Ted and Emily, and asked what she did that took up her morning. Alice reminded her of a small bird. Perhaps a goldfinch. Always dressed in neat, colorful, stylish clothes. This day she wore a bright yellow blouse with a black skirt. If Alice became any thinner, she'd look more like a crumpled maple leaf. Her hair capped her small narrow head like a black cowl. Dyed jet black. She'd kept the same hairdo and color since high school.

"Oh, Deborah Baker had solicited my help in taking communion to Lillian Stelling. You know, poor old Lillian's bedridden now." Alice blushed with the obvious pleasure this mission had given her.

"So, how was the time with Deborah?" Charlotte didn't try to keep the sarcasm out of her tone.

"Oh, my, quite wonderful, I'd say. You know, she makes me feel that she really understands me. She said things like 'we have so much in common' and 'you're just like me.'" Alice's face grew even pinker. She told them how Deborah's gotten the young people fired up to speak out on difficult problems that Real Christians should act on. She added, "And she referred to the prophets of old and how they spoke out boldly in their time." She peered over her tea cup. "I think she does identify herself with the prophets," she chirped.

Charlotte stared at her friend. "So, what's she done? Called out your Inner Prophet?"

Margaret suggested that they go out to the courtyard for a walk. They excused themselves from the other residents at the table and walked outside to the benches.

The river birches bent in the wind, yellow leaves flying around like myriad butterflies. Charlotte shivered and drew her cardigan closer.

"We'd better prepare for some wind and rain. I've heard Hugo's heading toward the Carolina coast and on up the eastern seaboard," Margaret announced. Charlotte could tell Margaret had sensed her irritation with Alice and was doing her diplomatic best to deflect her reaction.

The three sat on the iron benches in the shade. Alice leaned toward them and spoke in a conspiratorial voice. "Last week Deborah visited all the residents here who are members of Harmony Church. Before long, she was recruiting me to join in a petition to presbytery to take action against the gay lifestyle, condemning anyone who shows undue hospitality to unrepentant homosexuals in our midst. And furthermore, the petition advocates stringent measures against those who call themselves Christian and yet support abortions."

"Margaret, did you know about this?"

"She visited with me about it."

"What did you say to her?" Why had Margaret not said a word about the petition?

"Basically, nothing. Except she'd have to get along without my signature." She looked into Charlotte's eyes, then glanced at Alice. "Deborah said she understood. Then she went on about David Archer and what a fine, gentle man he was and then added, 'but rather naive, don't you think?' I asked her in what way was he naive, and she smiled and said, 'Well, maybe he's just passive when he should be outspoken on important issues to be a stronger leader.'"

Charlotte felt like shouting and shaking her good friends to wake them up. Heat rose in her body. "How many other people is she saying such garbage to, I wonder."

"Charlotte, aren't you jumping to conclusions?" Alice chirped in her high, thin voice. "She seems brave to me."

"I hate to sound like a stickler for protocol, but I wonder how she thinks she can bring a petition before presbytery without first going through our Session. I'm on the Session and haven't missed a meeting. There's never been a mention of any blasted petition." She was thinking out loud, stopped herself, and turned to Alice. "By the way, did you sign the petition?"

Alice's glow faded. In her tiny voice she confessed that she had indeed signed it. Charlotte choked and coughed.

Margaret patted her back. "Are you all right?"

Charlotte pulled out her handkerchief from her bag and coughed again. "No, I'm not all right. I'm alarmed and disgusted. And now, dear friends, I must go and see what I can do to begin to rectify this situation. Deborah is dangerous. Make no mistake about it."

She rose from the bench. "Margaret, please take me home." She saw the growing concern on the faces of her friends. Margaret stood and Alice followed.

"Now, Charlotte," Margaret said, "I feel sure Deborah means no harm. She's simply following God's will as she understands it. In my view, such issues come and go. I remember when the church got bent out of shape over divorce. Now even clergy get divorced and we think nothing of it." She picked a yellow leaf off Charlotte's sweater. "In fact, I heard that David and Nell have separated and are headed that way."

"Where'd you hear that?"

Alice laughed. "How can you tell if they're separated? Nell's always gone on buying trips for her precious jewelry business, isn't she?"

Margaret pursed her lips and raised her imperious, capacious chin. "If you must know, and I suppose you must, Deborah told me. He announced it in staff meeting, she said."

"Poison. She's spreading poison." Charlotte thought she would burst. Her heart threatened to leap up her throat.

"If it is true, and I have no reason to believe she made it up, that's not poison. It's simply a sad fact." Margaret took Charlotte's arm and with her cane picked her way along the path to the door. Alice followed.

"I guess David will announce it to the Session and then the congregation. He can be counted on to be above board," Charlotte said. She wished he'd confided in her on this matter the way he had on his concern over Deborah's campaign. She turned to Margaret at the car. "Please tell me you didn't sign the petition, too."

"Now, Charlotte, relax. It doesn't matter. In my view, all these issues are all tempests in demitasse cups that eventually pass away." She sighed. "As everything does."

"Did you or did you not sign the petition?"

"I admit that Deborah can be charming. And she charmed me. Before she left that day, I did sign it. But it doesn't matter."

Charlotte looked from one friend to the other. How could she think it didn't matter? How could they both have been taken in by Deborah's shenanigans? "Thank you for lunch and for hauling me around. Mark my words: This tempest may destroy the teapot. And the demitasse cup. Look how Deborah Baker has already divided the three of us."

They didn't speak all the way to Charlotte's house.

# 30

## David

David regretted telling his staff that he and Nell were separating. As yet neither of them had moved out, although he'd taken up sleeping in his study. The Crow's Nest was cramped and hot, even in the fall with the windows open. A garret room not unlike the one he'd occupied at Oxford, except that one had been freezing cold.

He wondered if they could be legally separated when they were both under the same roof. Would that count toward a year of separation? Ordinarily, he would ask Ted, but he was in no shape to give legal advice. Besides he didn't do divorce law.

David paced his church office, straightened the New Testament commentaries on the shelf behind his desk, sat back down. He picked up the large smooth stone he used as a paper weight and put it to his forehead and the sides of his face. Cool and comforting. Cold comfort. A black stone carved sharp at one end to make a tool or weapon. He pictured an early Native American chiseling and buffing the stone.

Judith called to say Charlotte Ames was asking for him. "Put her on," he said.

Charlotte called to report that Deborah had told residents at the

Presbyterian Home he and Nell were separated and headed toward divorce. Charlotte sounded dismayed. He tried to convince her that he and Nell were still under the same roof, and he wasn't making general announcements about their marital status because he just wasn't sure what they would do.

Charlotte offered one of her apartments for him to live in. "Should you be the one to move out." Then she added, "They probably won't be ready for occupancy until the end of October. David, please be assured that you have a safe place to land."

He thanked her and said he'd consider her offer. If he moved across town, he'd have to rise mighty early to be at the house to get the girls off to school. And when Nell traveled in her business, which was a lot, he'd have to be at home to care for them. What a mess. No telling how Deborah would use the break-up of his marriage to cause further splintering of Harmony church.

"Who knows, we may try to stick it out."

"In that case, David, you must curb Deborah's zeal in spreading this unfortunate rumor." She cleared her throat and added, "By the way, your horoscope today contains a warning and a promise: *Brace yourself for turbulence with the flexibility of a willow tree and the patience of granite. A new season will bring new life.*"

"Sounds more like a fortune cookie, Charlotte, but your advice is always welcome." They hung up.

David worked on his sermon for a while. If Hurricane Hugo followed the path the meteorologists were predicting, South Carolina would be hit, and Hugo might be as large as a Category Four. He'd already turned in the scripture and topic for Sunday's bulletin, but he needed to change his emphasis from God's power to God's presence in the face of disaster. He began to scribble out his thoughts. He prayed. For guidance in preparing his words for Sunday even though he felt downcast, for courage to look unblinkingly at his personal dilemma and that of his beloved Harmony Church. And for his daughters, especially Jody. And then for Nell, for eyes to see her as God saw her, for ears to hear what he and she should do—for the greater good. For Deborah, that he might understand her and follow God's leading as he dealt with her.

The phone rang again. This time Judith said that Emily Parks needed help.

"Ted's insistent that he needs to be home," Emily said, without preliminaries. "The doctors have finally agreed that he can be moved. With certain conditions."

"He must be better if he's more stubborn. What conditions?"

"A hospital bed with the side rails. I have to hire a strong nurse to help him every day."

"Sounds reasonable. But expensive. There's no way you can or should lift him. What can I do?"

"We've rented a wheelchair already, but I need someone strong to help me get him home. Do you think you could be here in the morning? I hate to interfere with your work, but Ted wanted me to call you."

"Emily, you know I'm glad to meet you tomorrow. Just name the time."

"Is it true? That you and Nell have separated?"

"Actually, we're both still occupying the house. Anyway, she's in Raleigh this week, so we'll see after she returns." So Emily had heard, too.

"Are your children okay?"

"I think so. They're pretty quiet, as if they're watching and waiting to see what happens."

"How's Jody?"

"Jody. We haven't told Jody yet."

"You know that Ted and I are with you every step of the way. Whatever that turns out to be."

"What time tomorrow?"

"Nine, if that's not too early."

"Nine's good. Would you like for me to pick you up at home? That way we'll have only one car at the rehab hospital."

"Good idea. I hadn't thought that far. David, thank you more than I can say."

Her voice caught.

"Emily, are you all right?"

"I guess. It's all difficult. And about to be more so."

There was so much he wished he could say. He settled on saying he'd see her in the morning.

On Wednesday morning, David had little trouble maneuvering Ted into the car from the wheelchair, thanks to the fact that a nurse had taught him how to lift someone heavy. The wheelchair folded and fit neatly against the backseat. Emily sat in back. NPR reported Hugo's path. Governor Carroll Campbell announced evacuation plans for everyone living along the coast. Emily said that Tom would have to leave college and drive home. Hugo was aiming for Charleston.

As soon as Ted was settled in the front bedroom, Emily called Tom and left a message for him to pack up and leave for home immediately. David sat beside Ted. They listened to her urgency. When she went to the kitchen to make coffee for them, David asked Ted who the best divorce lawyer would be, the man he'd mentioned back in the winter. Ted motioned for his pad and pen. With great effort, he scrawled with his left hand, "*Benjamin Batson—in our firm.*"

"At this point, I'm thinking Nell and I might tough it out. But just in case. I have some questions for him anyway." David put the paper in his shirt pocket and stood as Emily entered the room.

As they drank their coffee, David asked Emily how the Sunday school class was going. Although she seemed preoccupied with thoughts of Tom and the approaching hurricane, she managed to answer that the discussions were lively and generally not hostile. "Except once or twice, like when I defended a woman's right to choose what was best for her in consultation with her doctor," she said. "Then Myra, Deborah's sergeant in arms, speaks up and says, 'Well, isn't that saying you believe in murdering the unborn?' And that caused several younger women in the group to come to my defense. Everyone began talking at once until I called for order."

"How did Deborah react during the discussion?"

"She pretty much sat back and smiled. Like a satisfied cat."

"Emily, I hope you're not sorry you agreed to co-lead the class."

"No, not really. Except I don't have as much time to prepare as I usually give classes like this." Emily glanced over at Ted. She rose from her chair and straightened Ted back to an upright position. "Would you like some more of your milkshake?"

Ted said yes and she went to the kitchen for his glass and straw.

As she handed Ted his glass, Emily said, "You were right, David. It is a good idea to air the different viewpoints on abortion and gays. There's nothing like bringing issues out into the light and fresh air." She laughed. "But there's still plenty of hot air a-blowing."

Hurricane Hugo struck the South Carolina coast in the middle of the night Thursday into the wee hours of Friday, September 21 and 22, 1989, as a Category Four hurricane with 137 mph winds. Six hundred miles wide, the storm wreaked havoc all the way to Charlotte, North Carolina. The news reports showed huge shrimp boats nestled against beach houses. Smaller boats landed on Charleston streets. Devastation everywhere, trees down and houses large and small destroyed. Tornadoes destroyed property in Charlotte. David heard that friends in Charlotte suffered tornado damage from downed oak trees, and completely lost their South Carolina beach house. The towns north of Charleston—Awendaw and McClellanville—were hit hard, so much so that McClellanville became known as Ground Zero.

Amazingly, most of the oldest houses along the Battery in Charleston withstood the hurricane with minimal damage. No doubt, the evacuation saved lives. Many people who had no transportation out of the city found refuge in Gaillard Auditorium. Despite the efforts, there were eighty-two deaths and twelve more in North Carolina.

David checked with Emily. Tom had arrived around 2:00 a.m. Thursday. The evacuation Wednesday had been slow and tedious, but orderly. Tom reported that before leaving, he'd taken his stereo into the interior bathroom, wrapped it in blankets and duct tape, then taped his bathroom door with duct tape. He stored his sea captain's chest and bicycle in his closet as best he could. He'd received a call from his roommate who said their apartment building looked like a sardine can—after the top had been peeled away. The building would probably be condemned and they'd have to find another place.

From the pulpit on Sunday, David preached on The Power of God. The subject, which he'd chosen days before Hugo even appeared on the weather maps, filled him with energy. "Where is God when disaster strikes?" he asked. "God is present here and now. God abides. God's infinite love surrounds his people. How many times in scripture do we read, 'Do not fear. Do not be afraid, for the Lord your God is with you.'" He recited Psalm 46 and then moved to his final point. "You and I ask where God is when disaster strikes. If we affirm that God is present with us whatever is going on, then the answer we can give the troubled world is that we can and must be God's eyes, hands, feet, bodies, minds. We are called to act in the midst of disaster. In the midst of *this* disaster. The power of God is within us. We are called to be Christ's agents of healing here and now. Therefore, I ask any of you who own trucks and chain saws to join me for a trip to help in the Charleston area this week. Anyone else who would like to help with clean up or could offer needed supplies for those who have lost their homes, please see me after worship."

After the benediction, he stood in the narthex as usual to shake hands and greet people. Soon twelve men offered to drive their trucks and bring tools and chain saws. Skip Milner was the first with his son Casey. Both contractors. David put them in charge of signing up other volunteers. Men, who had seemed barely resigned to sitting in church with their wives and children, came forward with eagerness. Judge Knapp introduced his nephew to David. "This is Carl. Temporarily out of work. He's good with his hands. Take him with you," he said in his no-argument-allowed courtroom voice. Natalie and Preston offered to sign up those who would gather needed household and medical supplies.

In the corner of his eye, he glimpsed Deborah Baker watching him as she stood with her back against the brick wall alone. He turned toward her, but she didn't change her expression or come toward him. Instead she headed away, toward the ladies' restroom. Whatever she might be thinking, he refused to let her spoil the elation that filled him. The devastation of Hugo had spurred him and his church to action. Simple, practical action beat abstract arguments. At least for the time being.

# 31

## Charlotte

Charlotte straightened up the stack of magazines and newspapers on the table next to her Queen Anne sofa and placed the unpaid bills in the central drawer of her desk. She'd never met a private investigator in person. She'd only seen such on an occasional TV show. So far all the contact with Irving Monk Wolfe had been on the phone. His voice possessed a down-home quality, his syntax decidedly faulty, yet he spoke with a reassuring tone of authority. Charlotte put a dab of cologne behind each ear, then sprayed the room with deodorizer. When the doorbell rang, she jumped. A bit shaky, she opened the door.

"Mrs. Ames? I'm Irv Wolfe, P.I." So there he stood, a slender man of medium height, wearing khaki trousers and a navy blazer, light blue shirt open at the collar, no tie, a gold chain above curls of chest hair. And a Braves baseball cap, which he whipped off as he entered the front hall.

His hair seemed uncontrollably wiry, springing forth in a black and gray corolla. His nose, long, large with wide nostrils, dominated his square face and was balanced somewhat by his thick black and gray eyebrows above perpetually amused brown eyes. What she called a country mouth—thin lips with a slightly sunken appearance as if he'd lost teeth or wore ill-fitting dentures. When she offered refreshments, he declined.

She insisted that he try the oatmeal cookies she'd made for him. "How about some coffee? It won't take but a minute to drip through." Charlotte led him to the small kitchen. "As you can tell, I'm in the process of renovating this old house. Four apartments, and this is one of them. It's small but plenty of room for me. Alone now."

"I guess I'll have a cup, if it's not too much trouble." He leaned against the counter. Under his arm he carried a zipped leather case. "Mrs. Ames, I want to sit down with you, go over some things I've found."

His voice sounded a warning that what he'd discovered might upset her.

"Mr. Wolfe, whatever you've found, I need to know. Nothing could be worse than having spent all these months wondering. Speculating. Not knowing." She carried the tray of coffee, cups, cream and sugar to the living room. "Will you bring along that platter of cookies and napkins, please sir?" He followed and placed the plate on the low table beside the tray. Charlotte directed him to sit on the sofa while she took the straight chair alongside.

"All right. Shall we begin?" She poured a cup and he doctored it with some cream, stirred, and placed the coffee cup on the end table.

Irv Wolfe opened his case and spread out the file on his lap. "First of all, let me say that to many, many people around Goodwin, Dr. Fred Ames lived and died a saint. Even as he depleted his bank account, the loan officer he dealt with over the years believed he would build up the balance any day. His banker kept extending his line of credit, never doubting." Irv shuffled through his calendar and notes. "Fact is, he dealt with several banks and they all trusted him. I interviewed people here and there. Pretty soon, I saw that I'd have to dig deeper and treat him the way I do ordinary people. Follow the trail no matter where it led." He cleared his throat and looked at her through his thick brows.

"Mr. Wolfe, please. What have you found out? Spill it before I go berserk."

"All right. Here it is. Your husband got into gambling. First, just a little bet on a football game at a local bar, here and there. Then he went with some guys—I talked to two of them and they confirmed it—to one of them video poker places. Before you could skin a cat, he was hooked. Mrs. Ames, I seen it before—perfectly good people, they get hooked. It's an addiction. Sure enough."

"But how? I mean, I don't understand. How could that have happened and I not know it?" Charlotte felt fluttery inside and out. Her hand shook. She placed her cup on the saucer, spilling a little. "How could he have lost all our savings and investments? Video poker, you say? That could hardly have taken everything."

"Well, ma'am. It's hard to say. But folks that get into gambling that way will fool themselves into truly believing they can control it. They think they can stop any time they want. Then after a while, they feel embarrassed. Especially the upstanding citizens of which your husband was one, for sure. It's kinda like a drug, you might say."

Charlotte studied Irv Wolfe. Could this be true? "What evidence have you amassed that would confirm what you say?" As horrified as she was, she had to learn the facts.

"As I said, these two guys were with him over a period of three years, give or take. They each separately swore that he loved the thrill of risk. They went with him to the horse races up in Kentucky. You know, the Derby. They said he put them all up in a nice motel. So, of course, I tracked that down."

Charlotte stared at Irv Wolfe longer than she meant to, unable to speak or move. She remembered when Fred made the trip to Kentucky. That was when she went to stay with Hannah after their daughter's hysterectomy. Now she felt petrified. Turned from flesh and blood into an ancient petrified tree.

Irv ate one of the cookies in two bites, wiped his mouth with the back of his hand. He spoke after a while. "This has shocked you, I know. Is there someone you'd like for me to call?"

She looked down at her arm stretched out from its sleeve, the skin puckered and wrinkled, blue veins on her hand snaking over bones and tendons. Flesh and blood, barely. "What? Call someone? No, no. It's just too much to absorb at once. I've been utterly blind and deaf to his troubles. Going about my usual life while he was sinking. Into what you call an addiction. Poor dear Fred. How could I have been so oblivious?" She stood and walked to the window, banged her fists on the window till the large pane rattled. "How could you do that, Fred?" She rested her forehead on the window, then turned back to Irving Wolfe. "I assume you also spoke with the stock broker."

"Yes'm. I sure did. With the permission you gave me, he let me see the statements for the past two years." He pulled out several pages from his leather case and spread them out on the coffee table. "As you can see right here, there was a jump along about last November. He sold all his holdings in GE, Coke, and John Deere. A considerable amount. Then withdrew the cash from his managed account in $9, 850 allotments over the next few weeks. By December he'd sold everything. Against the broker's explicit advice, so he said."

Charlotte looked at the reports, shuffling the pages. The figures blurred and she couldn't focus on the numbers. "I can't deal with reports like this. Always happens when I look at financial details. Only, I admit, right now it's worse." She regarded Irving Wolfe, whose brown eyes had taken on a decidedly sympathetic expression. "Fred knew how boring I found reports of this nature, so he spared me and took care of everything financial for us both."

"Well, at first he gambled in the market. He bought on margin, sold short, and tried out hedge funds and bet on futures of commodities. The broker said it was fun for them both. Then suddenly he lost interest and moved to what he called more tangible games. Tangible games, he called his new obsession, so the broker said."

"For an orthopedic surgeon, he made a terrible gambler." Charlotte let the bitterness show. Since January, she had resisted bitterness with the same intensity she fought halitosis. "I suppose he used the cash to pay for his losses." A deep sigh escaped her.

"Mrs. Ames, there's one more thing." He hesitated, swallowing the rest of his coffee.

"Mr. Wolfe. What else? Tell me."

"Okay. But it may strike you worse than the gambling." He cleared his throat. "I believe that he used more than $30,000 to pay off someone who threatened to reveal his gambling addiction. He was careful always taking out less than $10,000 at a time, so it didn't have to be reported."

"Mr. Wolfe, are you saying blackmail? Someone blackmailed Fred?"

"I believe so. Yes'm."

"Who?"

"Sorry. I'm not sure yet. But I'm working on it and will let you know as soon as I can." Irving Wolfe stacked up his papers and stuffed them back into his leather case, leaving his invoice on the coffee table. "This here's for what I've charged so far. Time and expenses, as you will see."

"Oh, great. I get to pay to hear terrible revelations. Fortunately, my son will help with the expense." Charlotte stood. "Thank you. Keep pursuing the trail wherever it leads. Frankly, your discoveries sound more and more like someone's been watching too much television."

"Yes'm. I know what you mean. However, it's been my experience that things people do in real life are so astounding no one would believe them if they happened on TV." He looked around the chair where he'd been sitting, as if to check if he'd forgotten anything.

"Oh, Mr. Wolfe, I almost forgot. I promised a friend that I'd ask you to help with a mysterious substance she found." She went to the bedroom for her handbag and brought back the small box Emily gave her. She handed it to Irv Wolfe and explained briefly how Emily had retrieved the white powder.

"Here's what I'll do," he said, looking into the envelope inside the box. "I can buy a field sobriety test and we'll see. However, I can tell you—no matter how it turns out, you won't be able to use it in court. To qualify, the test has to

257

be administered by law enforcement. When I started out as a deputy sheriff, I tested plenty."

Charlotte knew Emily had no notion of taking Deborah to court. She just wanted to know. "When do you think you could let me know about the test?"

"You'll know as soon as I do."


Irv Wolfe called Charlotte and Charlotte immediately called Emily. "Blue," she said. "The substance turned blue, Irv Wolfe told me." Before Emily could ask, Charlotte explained that blue denoted cocaine. "So the powder you picked up clearly shows that Deborah Baker dropped granules of cocaine. Only we can't prove it or accuse her in court. Still it's serious."

Emily thanked her and said she'd be back in touch.

"Surely you want to do something with this information, Emily. To stop what she's doing to Harmony Church. Right, Emily?"

"Please, let's not rush anything here. I have a good reason to hold on to this knowledge. So please, for now, let's keep this secret, just between us. Okay?"

"If you say so. Although I—"

"No, please. Tell no one. Yet."

"All right. Reluctantly, I'll keep it a secret."

# 32

# David

On Monday David wrote his sermon for the next week, so he'd be ready to leave with twelve men on Thursday at dawn. They planned to work through Saturday noon and be back in Goodwin that evening.

Nell returned from Raleigh on Monday late afternoon. The girls welcomed her so warmly, she almost relaxed the frozen attitude she'd adopted toward him ever since Labor Day weekend. He cooked supper, hoping her favorite foods would continue the thaw. Baked potatoes with shredded cheese, chopped chives, and bacon crumbles, grilled salmon fillets with Greek seasoning, and spinach salad. Lyn pitched in to help clean up afterwards while Millie led her mother upstairs to discuss what she should wear to the school spirit party.

When the girls closed the doors to their rooms for the night, David approached Nell in the den. She'd stretched out on the sofa, her heels kicked off onto the rug, her stocking-covered legs resting on a pillow. He pulled up a straight chair across from her. "We need to talk," he began, hoping she wouldn't squirm out of there before he had a chance.

She regarded him with cool detachment. "About?"

He explained that he and twelve men from the congregation were planning to drive trucks down to help with the Hurricane Hugo clean up in McClellanville. He'd be gone Thursday until Saturday evening. "So I need you to be here for the girls. If that suits your schedule. If not, we'll need to hire a sitter, someone who can chauffeur them." He waited. Her face had lost the flush and twinkle it possessed earlier. Now the fatigue emerged, giving her countenance a grayish cast.

"I'll be here all this week. Go ahead. You guys, have fun rescuing people with chain saws and crow bars."

"Great. We'll plan on that then." He started to get up, then sat back down.

"Nell, I think it's not a good idea for us to separate. With the girls the ages they are, and we haven't said any of this to Jody. No telling how she'd react." He shuffled his feet back and forth the way he did when he was a boy, afraid of what his parents would say about some misbehavior. "Obviously, I've had second thoughts." He searched her face for a kindred response. Finding none, he asked, "What do you think?"

"You mean feel? Other than hurt, insulted, jerked around, baffled, ignored, disgusted?" She drew her knees up, pulled the pillow out from under her and tossed it at him. "Oh, yes, and angry." She laughed. Then she sat up and faced him. "You're unhappy. I'm unhappy. But we're both used to living here in our separate worlds. Now and then doing something together with Millie and Lyn." She shrugged. "Might as well keep on this way. Inertia of the customary. That ought to be one of Newton's laws."

David stood. Her tone sounded so different, more like the quirky, wry humor he remembered from their early years. "Good. Shall I continue to sleep in the Crow's Nest, or return to our bedroom?"

"Either way." She yawned. "Although I haven't missed your snoring."

"Okay. I'll stay put." He touched her lightly on her arm. "For now."

Again he sat back down. "Another thing, I got a call from the director of Winslow Farms saying we're behind on our payments. I thought you made the last one, earlier this month." He waited, but Nell didn't react.

"She really laid the guilt on me. Said Jody's making progress. 'We'd hate to turn her out for lack of funds,' she said. 'She might regress and think her parents don't love her enough to see this through.'"

"I'm pinched this month and still trying to recoup from the robbery. Can you send them a check, David? Even a partial payment will probably work. Or maybe get a loan?"

David agreed to send what he could the next day. His chest tightened. At least he and Nell were talking, even though he had to swallow anger and anxiety. They had agreed to alternate months.

On Wednesday at the staff meeting, David told the assembled that he'd spoken too soon, that he and Nell were working things out to stay together. He asked Deborah and the office staff to make sure anyone they might have mentioned the separation to would learn that, on the contrary, he and Nell were not heading for divorce. He added to himself, *at least for the present.* They nodded agreement. Deborah asked if there was anything she could do to help. He urged her to correct the news flying around the Presbyterian Retirement Village and any other places where she might have mentioned it. Then he explained the plans for the Hugo clean-up.

Thursday, the men departed the church parking lot in six pick-ups, David riding with Skip Milner. His son, Casey, brought a friend, Max Sumter, in another truck. The others included men who'd remained on the periphery of Harmony Church's activities for years. With the exception of helping to build a Habitat house. David enjoyed the camaraderie all three days. At night over beers, the men complained about sore muscles, but they did so with pride and satisfaction. Skip, Casey, and Max were the only ones who normally spent their work days wielding hammers, saws, crow bars, screw drivers and nail guns. The others—salesmen, small business owners, and real estate agents—took up the tools with the eagerness of young boys given a chance at last to exhaust themselves in all-out physical effort. They reveled in being freed from phones and desks, including David.

The task of moving debris into large piles was accomplished by bulldozers and front loaders. The men from Harmony Presbyterian teamed up with some Methodists and Baptists from Columbia to work to restore a neighborhood in the small town. David, Skip, Casey, and Max spent most of Friday on one house smashed by an oak tree. Their chain saws whined and vibrated for hours, removing most of the branches. They convinced one of the heavy equipment drivers to pull the enormous trunk off the house. Only when the tree had been totally removed, could they begin to work on the splintered rafters. By Saturday, they'd covered the house with tarps and plywood as a temporary fix.

Casey and Max promised the woman who lived there that they would stay until they had the house completely repaired. When David asked how they could afford to be off work for a week, Casey told him neither of them had construction jobs at present and they would crash with friends in Charleston.

The rest of the group returned to Goodwin Saturday evening. They reconvened the following Thursday for another three days. And again the third week. The more intensely David worked with the men on the clean-up, the more energized he felt. He came home totally spent, but keyed up and practiced his sermon up in the Crow's Nest until after midnight, slept a few hours to wake up refreshed early on the Sabbath.

After three weeks in a row, the Harmony Church work crew agreed they had to tend to their regular jobs but would get together again in early December for another run at rebuilding in the low country. David proposed they meet for breakfast on Thursday mornings, as many as could. An almost casual invitation, really an afterthought, created a new group that would prove to be a life saver in more ways than one. Easy-going and gregarious, Skip Milner took over the leadership of the breakfast group.

David pondered the building experience and the restoration in him of what his grandmother used to call gumption. "Where's your gumption?" she'd ask him and Drew when they cowered from facing down bullies at elementary school. He felt God had led the Harmony crew in the Charleston area, and restored his soul in the process. He thanked God for leading him and the others to put their faith into action.

The San Francisco earthquake struck on Tuesday, October 17 at 5:04 p.m. local time. The media quickly forgot about Hugo in favor of the most recent disaster. The large bridge over the bay cracking, spilling cars and trucks, the sudden interruption of warm-up practice for the World Series between the Oakland Athletics and the San Francisco Giants—all much more dramatic than the depressingly slow clean-up on the coast of South Carolina.

So many upheavals in the natural world and in the political in 1989. David thought about the Exxon *Valdez* oil spill back in March, about Tiananmen Square massacre in China, the rumblings toward freedom in East Germany and the communist world, and now these natural disasters— all shaking up the world Americans knew and counted on. In his personal life too, upheaval and turmoil in his marriage. And Jody—gradually better, so the therapist said. Maybe they'd be able to bring her home before the year ended. They had become accustomed to a family of four and would need to integrate their firstborn back into the mix. He thought of Jody's mood swings, creating emotional trauma all around her. As much as he loved her, he had to admit he'd become used to thinking fondly of her—at a distance. And he knew it was time again to confront Deborah Baker. Yes, he needed gumption.

On Tuesday, October 24, David asked Judith to hold their calls and, before she could get away, he asked Deborah into his office. He gestured for her to sit on the sofa and he took the straight chair alongside. Deborah sat, spreading out her full gray skirt, her stockings swishing as she crossed her legs. She wore high heels of a burgundy red to match her blouse. She began to swing her foot, already impatient.

"Coffee or a Coke?" he offered in the most unhurried manner he could assume.

"No thanks. What's on your mind, Reverend Doctor?" She spoke rapidly as usual. "I've got to go to the Space for Hope this morning, you know."

"This won't take long. I think it's time for you to think about your future, Deborah."

"Meaning what?"

"Well, you've shown me and others that you have strong ideas of what should be emphasized with the youth and in the congregation generally. And, frankly, your emphasis is not what I would choose."

"You think I should not disagree with you, eh, Reverend Doc?"

"I believe you're showing signs that you may be ready to have your own church. Be a senior pastor and lead your own congregation. What about that?"

Deborah sat up straighter and fixed her eyes on him. She recrossed her legs and didn't say anything, but removed her nasal spray from her pocket and inhaled, coughed.

How was she processing what he'd said? Her face revealed nothing. "Right now, you have to deal with me, but if you had your own church, you'd have a freer hand to shape programs more to your liking, right?"

She cocked her head and eyed him at an angle. "I've been here at Harmony Church for one year this month. Isn't that too soon to be sending out my resume?"

"People move at different rates of speed. I'm just saying you ought to consider it."

"At the moment, I don't believe I've finished my work here at Harmony. The young people and some adults are turned on by what you call my emphasis. However, I still have more to accomplish." She stood up and smoothed her skirt. "But since you mentioned it, I'll think about what I might do and where I might be in the future.

"And, by the way, I've spoken to some of our members at the retirement home about you and Nell staying together. The ladies assured me that they're praying for you both." Deborah smiled at him, touching her nose. She opened the door. Right before she went out, she said, "You, too, David, might think about your future here. Just a thought." Her laughter rippled down the hall.

"That went well," he said to no one. Being around Deborah inevitably left him exhausted. Her nervous energy, something. He picked up the smooth black stone and put it to his forehead, his cheeks, and back to his forehead. It cooled his hot face. Her last jab got to him and she knew it. In the subtle chess game Deborah was playing, she'd made another move. He could only guess at what exactly she'd done.

He called Charlotte Ames and invited her to ride with him to the Village for a visit with their elderly members. She could help him accomplish some damage control.

That night he couldn't sleep for thinking about Deborah and how he wished he'd been more forthcoming. Instead he'd tried to appeal to her ambition. He'd been too indirect. As usual. Why couldn't he be blunt and just say—it's either you or me. I'm the senior pastor, so get your resume together and go. And yet there were more young people attending church than ever, and they were enthusiastic. When he finally slept, he dreamed.

In the dream, David was locked out of the church. He pulled on the large carved door handles. First the doors under the portico, then the ones on the parking lot side. He couldn't find his keys. No wonder. He wasn't wearing pants. He had on his old swimming trunks, the swimsuit his grandmother had brought him from Hawaii when he was sixteen. He saw his hairy legs and old flip flops. He went to the choir room window and threw pebbles against the window, but the choir didn't see him and kept on rehearsing. Then he ran around to the office wing and banged on the door until his fists ached. He looked around for something to use to pry open the door.

Under a shrub he saw something shiny. A large block of ice. He shoved the block of ice onto the sidewalk. Inside, a large silver-gray porpoise grinned out at him, full of confidence that David would free him. "I don't know what to do," he said aloud and woke up.

All his covers were off. A strong wind blew the shade back and forth. He got up and closed the window, went to the bathroom and returned to bed.

The dream continued unimpeded. He picked up a crowbar and chipped, banged, pried, hacked until the huge block of ice lay in chunks, puddling fast.

He turned back to the church door. He spoke to the porpoise, "I'll get you some water to swim in. Just a sec." When he turned back, the porpoise had changed into a slender naked boy, who laughed and waved. "See you. I'm outta here." The boy lifted his arms as if to fly, laughing as he ran down the street and away.

David woke up, his heart pounding hard. He slipped out of bed and grabbed his journal. He recorded what he could remember, puzzling over all the elements—locked out of the church, the block of ice with a porpoise captured inside, chipping it out with the crow bar, like the ones he'd used during the Hugo clean-up. The porpoise transformed into a boy who ran away. Was his subconscious telling him what the future held? Or describing his present state? Maybe both.

Porpoise. Purpose? Was his purpose locked up in a block of ice?

# 33

# Emily

E mily finished her afternoon class, American Lit of the Twenties. She straightened her office to prepare for David's arrival. She'd asked him to counsel one of her students Glenda Mae, who'd tearfully consulted her last week. Did she know a pastor who might help her without condemnation? So she'd described her own minister, David Archer. When she asked him, he readily agreed to listen to the girl but suggested that they meet in Emily's office. He had never seen her small faculty office, just temporarily hers, since she was a mere instructor hired on a year-to-year basis. She was assigned whatever office the English department could free up. Zoe Elderton took students to England for the fall, so Emily occupied hers for the semester. She felt fortunate to be on the first floor with a window and not far from the departmental secretary. Zoe's books filled most of the bookshelves, but Emily had found one shelf she could call her own. The drawers on the right of the desk had been emptied for her to use. She quickly stashed the load of ungraded essays just as David knocked on the door.

"Come in. You're early." She motioned him to the futon that doubled as a sofa. He pulled off his cap and jacket. She took and hung them on the peg on the back of the door. "I'm glad to see you. Especially early. We have time to talk before Glenda Mae is due."

"I hope I can stay awake to visit with you and of course listen to your student, but I feel like I'm about to fall on my face. I haven't slept well for two nights." He leaned back, his head against the wooden frame. With his eyes closed he said, "Sorry, Em. It's not your company."

"David, stretch out. I sometimes take a quick nap right where you are. Here, use this pillow. Sleep." She handed him her big soft pillow with the words "*Carpe Diem*" embroidered in red. "I have plenty of papers to grade."

David let out a deep sigh and muttered thanks. Emily turned her desk light on and the harsh fluorescent overhead off.

She sat at her desk, pulled out the stack of student essays, and looked at David's head lying against the pillow. His gray and black hair was thinning at the crown. One arm cushioning his head. She hoped the counseling would go well. She'd recommended David to the chaplain last week. The more David did this sort of work, the better chance he'd have of gaining a fresh perspective. Anything to get him away from the intricate machinations of church politics should help.

Emily marked one of the essays. Billy Hudgens had written on the green light in Fitzgerald's *The Great Gatsby*. She recalled David's story about his first love, a girl at Oxford who had been named Daisy after Gatsby's love. She spun the chair around and watched David sleep. His breath was long and deep. His navy sweater vest rose and fell in a smooth deep rhythm. Whatever would she do without David's friendship?

She thought of the discussions her women friends had had about men. Can men be friends without becoming lovers? She always stood up for friendship. Natalie and Madeleine would chuckle and chant, "Ain't she sweet? So innocent, so naïve?" Emily was certain, well, fairly certain, that she and David would remain friends, never become lovers. She looked at his lined face, the thin white scar on his cheek, deep folds beside his mouth, smile creases branching out from his eyes, with sunken darkness beneath that underscored his fatigue. His lips. She wanted to draw his face, especially his mouth, as he slept. They had at least ten minutes yet before she had to wake him.

Her breath caught as if she were doing something wicked. She quietly opened the top drawer and took out some typing paper. With her green grading pen, she began to line out his wide mouth, chin, and the strong jaw line. The faint line of his scar. She felt an odd stirring in her gut and recalled the first time she'd experienced it. In response to David that time too, but several lifetimes ago. Before her marriage, before her children were born when she'd been in grad school and returned to Little Rock and he'd been there too, seeing what was left of his family. She'd been quite young, but pretty old for feeling lust for the first time. If that wrenching inside could be named, she supposed it was lust. Now so many years later, she was accustomed to this knot of desire in response to particular men. Her way of dealing with it was to acknowledge the feeling and let it go, later maybe allow it to enter her art—even when the particular subject had nothing directly to do with sex. Now the rush of desire moved from her eyes to her belly to her pen as she drew David's sleeping face.

Then his eyes opened and he was looking at her without moving. For a long moment neither said anything. Emily held back the response that ordinarily popped right out. She was accustomed to deflecting any sexual overture. Something chirping and cheerful as a wren—that was her way. This time she told herself to wait. Just wait and see. A fluttering began under her ribs. She steadied her pen and continued to draw.

David's role with everyone, even dear friends, was that of listener, the one who waited and consoled, remained still, quiet. Now only his eyes moved over her face.

She felt those eyes as a caress. She felt as if she were tracing over the contours of his dark thick brows, his fine nose, over the thin scar on his cheek, his lips. Emily caught her breath.

She stopped drawing. If they kissed, all their years of modulated companionship would change forever. She knew this with absolute certainty. She wondered what he wanted. Regardless, she reverted to the old conditioning. Chirpy and cheerful distraction. "It's time, David," she managed, but her voice sounded deep and thick.

He sat up and held out his hand.

She gave him the drawing. "Been on the right side of my brain, I guess. Hope you don't mind?"

"Emily, may I keep it?" He stood close to her now. She breathed in his scent. Soap, pressed cotton, cedar.

"Yes, I want you to have it. Now, we've got to meet Glenda Mae at the secretary's desk."

He took her hand in both of his. "Thank you. For the nap. And for this." David bent and touched his lips to her hand.

"Off we go," she chirped. "I'll take my papers to grade down the hall while you talk to her in my office."

He smoothed his hair and straightened his clothes. "Fine," he said, still studying her face.

"You'll find Glenda Mae confused and depressed. I'm sure you'll be a good counselor for her." Emily's voice was back to normal, but her hand trembled as she switched on the overhead light and opened the door.

# 34

## Millie

‒‒‒※‒‒‒

Millie and Lyn were raking the side yard. It was cool and dry with wind that whipped up the top layer of their leaf pile from time to time. To Millie it looked like the back of a woman's head with a feathery coiffure caught up by the breeze. The woman's hair would be brown with reddish highlights. Not as auburn as Deborah's or as big. She hummed as she raked.

"Is this a punishment?" Lyn asked.

"No, silly. We have to do this to earn enough money for the ski trip."

"So it *is* punishment. I hate the idea of standing on those long slick planks speeding down icy snowy hills trying to balance and not break my leg. And I hate raking leaves." Lyn pulled her rake toward her with a meager supply of leaves. She made a path with them, gathering more and more as she neared the big pile. "It is fun to jump in them when we finish."

Millie frowned. Sometimes Lyn acted younger than eleven. "We've got too much to do to jump in them today."

"Well, as soon as we get a clear spot made in the yard that stupid oak sends down more. I think it's laughing at us."

A tiny bell jingled. They turned to see the black cat from next door stepping gingerly around a muddy patch in the yard. She walked over to the path of flagstones and headed their way but acted as if they didn't exist.

Millie watched to see what Lyn would do. She remembered how superstitious she'd been at her age, about nearly everything.

Lyn brushed her hair out of her face and stared. "Zulu, you are one snobby cat. Don't you ever say hi or boo or anything?"

Zulu crouched, her green eyes taking in the scene, tail twitching.

"Aren't you even a little bit afraid of bad luck?"

Her little sister shrugged. "What could be bad about a snobby cat? Except maybe for birds and chipmunks." Lyn leaned on her rake and watched Zulu.

"Never mind. Come on. We've got to get this yard finished before Mom comes back."

The wind picked up and the leaves twirled in a spiral. "Look, Mill, a mini-tornado. Cool."

The black cat walked right across their path. "Millie, what's wrong? You look pale."

"It's nothing." Millie started raking hard and fast. "Come on. Let's finish this. Help me dump this pile." She spread the blue plastic tarp and together they picked up the sides and carried the full tarp to the edge of the street. "One, two, three—dump!"

A boy on a bike wheeled into view. As he got close, Millie saw that it was Rivers Carlton. One super fine guy. She knew she looked awful. So, see it was bad luck, she thought. Why did he have to see her like this? Her baggy sweatshirt with the torn sleeve, her worst jeans, her hair a mess and absolutely no make-up.

"Whatcha' say, Millie? You guys working. Will wonders never cease?"

"Oh, hi, Rivers."

"This must be your little sister." He leaned his bike against the big oak tree.

"Hi. I'm Lyn. And we have to do this whole humongous yard. Want to help?"

Millie stepped on her foot, and mouthed, "NO."

Rivers took off his sweater. "Sure. Do you have another rake?"

"No," Lyn said. "But you can use mine while I go in and get us some Cokes." She skipped into the house.

He laughed and took Lyn's rake. "Smart girl, your sister." He raked with strong even sweeps and seemed to do twice as much as they'd done all afternoon.

"Say, Mill, would you go to a party the team's having next weekend? That's really why I came by. To ask you that."

Millie pushed back her hair. "You mean that? Go with you to a party?" She couldn't believe her good luck. "Yes. Yes, I would like that."

"One more thing. It's a Halloween party. Stupid I know, but I hope you don't mind dressing up in some kind of costume."

"That could be fun, I guess. What are you going to wear?"

"Don't know. Any ideas?"

"Maybe we could wrap each other in tape and go as mummies."

"Or Dracula and his girl friend."

"Or characters from the Addams Family."

"I like it. Let's see what we can find." Rivers swept his huge pile of leaves onto the tarp. She dropped her rake and picked up two corners. To-gether they walked the tarp of leaves to the street curb. "One, two, three, dump!" she said.

"Tell you what—I'll pick you up tomorrow after practice and we can look at Wilson's for something." He reached over and lifted a leaf from her hair.

"By the way, have you gotten the word what some of the guys in youth group are planning?" he asked.

Millie thought she saw worry cloud his features. And fine features they were. His eyes changed colors, sometimes almost green, other times brownish with flecks of gold. She called them to herself the color of the creek—creek water amber. "Uh, no. Haven't heard a thing. What?"

"Ace Murphy and Dunwoody Jackson have been harassing the new guy. Macon Collier's a freshman, moved here with his mom. They say he's a queer. Ace called me and said they're 'rallying the troops' whatever that means. Wants me to join them for some fun action."

"Nobody's called me. No surprise there. They know I'd tell Dad. Rivers, be careful. Ace has been a bully since forever. His sidekick's not much better."

"Don't worry, Mill. I'll be careful. Tell your sister that I'm sorry to miss the Coke, but I gotta' go."

"Thanks for the help, Rivers."

"No problem." He hopped on his bike and smiled. "See you tomorrow, Mill."

Millie watched him ride away, his white shirt and jeans moving in the smooth rhythm of his pedaling. She took her rake and danced around the yard. Rivers' blue sweater lay draped over the iron bench. She'd give it to him tomorrow. She held it to her nose and breathed in the smell of peppery boy sweat and something sharp like mint or sage.

# 35

# David

David had given out all the candy in mini-wrapped bits and then his own stash of regular sized Snickers. He'd had enough of the trick or treaters. Nell was conveniently out of town on a buying trip with Flora.

The girls were at Halloween parties, even though it was a school night and both had rides home. So he had to answer the door. Or did he? It was nine o'clock and carloads of kids had been working the neighborhood since seven. Now only teenagers would be coming by, and he had only two candy bars left. He turned off the lights.

The girls were due home around ten, and both swore they'd finished their homework. So now he might have a few precious moments of quiet to write. He turned off all the front lights and went up to his Crow's Nest study. Calvin padded upstairs behind him.

A quiet time—so rare these days. The church programs and committee meetings took so much thought and energy he had to force himself to do what he loved best—to study the scriptures and write his sermons. And he and Nell had received a letter from Jody. The first she'd written. He pulled it from his stack of papers and read it again.

*Dear Mother and Daddy,*

*My therapist Amy here at Winslow Farms has given me this assignment. To write you. She calls it a* **cleansing ritual.** *I call it Dump-the-shit-on-the-'rents. Sorry—Everyone here talks that way. OK. Whatever.*

*I'm supposed to start out on a "positive note." So here goes—*

*Thank you for letting Millie visit back at Easter. I think about her and our time together a lot. I hope you liked her hair. Also, I hope she's kept up the dye job. You may have to fly her up here for a re-do. (Just kidding.)*

*I'm doing OK. No more overdoses. So far. (Just kidding.)*

*Good teachers. Ask Millie. (My classes this fall give college credit.) I've become a potter and a painter. More about this later.*

*Now to the Dump part—This is hard to say to you. Please try to receive what I have to say. Even you, Dad—always at a distance, like God himself. Even you, Mom, preoccupied with who-knows-what.*

*The thing is this—No matter how hard I tried, I've always felt like a Big Disappointment to both of you.*

*Something's wrong with me.*

*The message that came early in my childhood is that I'm a bad person. After Millie and later Lyn came along, the message was reinforced. They could make you smile and laugh. They filled you with delight.*

*I made you frown. I could do better. How many times did you say to me, "You can do better than that." The Big Disappointment. That's me.*

*Then, to make matters worse, one night during 11th grade, I went to one of those stupid high school parties. You know the kind—*

*where the parents were out of town—and I lied and said I was spending the night with a friend. Anyway, this older guy, someone in college, a friend of a friend, gave me something he swore I'd love. Ecstasy. He was correct. I did love the experience—everything around me shimmered with beauty and peace. Ecstasy. Well named. I was taken out of my miserable self, and no hang over. Perfect bliss. At least for a little while. And several times. No, lots of times more. One small white pill, but kinda expensive. But later on, something was wrong—a bad batch or something. Then hallucinations. Scary.*

*Anyway, my life changed.*

*When I tried to tell you guys, no one at home understood. Or heard.*

*I had to get away from that crowd, not that I had any real friends there anyway.*

*My therapist has speculated that maybe I was too indirect. And that's why you didn't see or hear me. Could be.*

*Now you know why I had to go to St. Margaret's. That's not everything, but at least when you read this letter, if you do, you'll get a better picture of me—your Big Disappointment.*

*I hope my therapist is correct—that this will help you, and maybe me too.*

*Love,*

*Jody*

*P.S. You can let Millie read this letter. Not Lyn—she's too young.*

He needed to study it before he responded. Nell left it with him to answer.

Maybe tonight he could even devote some thought to the play about Joseph of Arimathea he'd sketched out. Mostly legend and myth.

Nothing really biblical, except the reference to his giving his own crypt for the burial of Jesus in Matthew, but he'd always been fascinated by him. Ever since Jim Gedding had told him that he'd researched him and would write a book some day. But all Jim's hard living as a journalist, smoking and drinking and never sleeping, had finally told on him. He'd dropped dead last winter.

David still grieved for him. Jim had been harsh in his judgments and pronouncements like the great prophets of old, always pushing David to urge the congregation to fight injustice and to do things that troubled the more staid members, like remembering prisoners.

David leaned back in his chair. Calvin pushed his muzzle onto his leg, brown eyes gazing at him with canine sensitivity. Sometimes David felt Jim's presence as if he were haunting him, pushing, nudging, nagging him in his best acerbic, curmudgeonly manner to more courage in the pulpit, more real action. As if Jim's raspy voice were in his ear, David heard *Why don't you ask those guys at Thursday Breakfast to consider the prisoners? Furnish transportation for the families? How 'bout it?* Thanks, Jim. Calvin settled with a sigh beside him, thumping his tail.

The phone rang and rang far away. He'd turned off his ringer in the study. It might be one of the girls. With some effort he hauled himself up and went for the phone.

"Dad? It's Jody." David woke up with a start.

"Jody. How wonderful to hear from you." He waited for her to say why she was calling out of the blue. At first, nothing.

"Is Mom there? Or Millie?"

"No, darling girl. Millie and Lyn are at parties all dressed up. Your mother is out of town with Flora for her business." He laughed feebly. "I guess you're stuck with me."

"Dad, can we talk about my letter? You did get it, didn't you?"

"Yes, yes. We both have read it. I haven't had a chance to answer it yet, but I want you to know that your candor means more to me than you can ever know."

"I'm trying to understand why you haven't had time. You're there for other people. Why can't you be there for me, too?" Her voice cracked and she coughed. "You may find it easy to expose your innards to others, but it's hard as the devil for me. Tell me what you think of me now. Do you hate me? Am I an even bigger disappointment than before? What?"

David took a deep breath, exasperation threatening to expose itself. "No, Jody, I don't hate you and you may not believe this, but you have never been a big disappointment for me."

"What? Just a little disappointment, huh?"

"Wait. Let's start again. Your letter pierced my heart. I want to apologize for being blind and deaf to what happened to you in eleventh grade. I don't know where my focus was at the time, but I should have been more aware of your need. Jody, I'm sorry."

"Well, what's done is done. Anyway, I am not a good person. You and Mom are right to be disappointed."

"Jody, let me ask you something. Have you heard of projection? It occurs to me that you are projecting onto me and your mother feelings you actually have about yourself."

"Oh, Dad, so now you're turning to psycho-babble. Just what I need— another expert on what's wrong with me. Give me a break."

"It seems to me that you may have a measure of a family character-istic I grew up with—in both my parents and in myself. It takes different forms, of course, but it comes down to the desire, the need, the compul-sion, to be perfect. Or to try to be perfect. An impossible expectation. Perfectionism can be a ruthless god—an idol, if you will. I also believe that there's a verse in the New Testament that has done a great deal of harm, especially in people like ourselves: 'Therefore, be ye also perfect even as thy heavenly father is perfect.'"

"Ha. Now you're quoting scripture at me."

"Darling girl, are you not hearing me at all? I'm saying what you've been chasing is not only impossible, but downright wrong. And the same for me. Perfectionism is the woeful ego at work. Always judging ourselves, never forgiving ourselves for being simply a fallible human being."

"Okay, Dad. Obviously, my letter must have hit a nerve. You obviously have given this a lot of thought."

"I guess I have, but I've never expressed any of it. In my mother, Mary Frances, she got tripped up by bipolar swings and spent an awful lot of time in bed when I was a teenager. Something I didn't understand then and basically ignored. In Dad, his expectations of what he believed he should do in his life and his ministry kept him trapped until finally he gave up. Quit. In myself, no doubt you could point out my failings explicitly. On the inside, I feel indecisive. Some call me passive. All I can say is that I'm trying to release the hold perfectionism has on me—with the help of a good therapist."

"My perfect father goes to a therapist?"

"Yes, your *imperfect*, hesitant, blind father gropes along, and she does help me, to some degree."

"Dad, my therapist Amy is good, but she sure makes me do a lot of work. What kind of therapy does yours use?"

"Not sure. Madeleine Crispin's her name. She's given me some breathing exercises that help me relax. She gives me assignments, some of which I follow through on. I tell her dreams sometimes."

"She may be using a combination. Like cognitive therapy and other things I've forgotten the names of."

"I'll ask her on my next visit. Jody, are you feeling healthier now?"

"Maybe. Amy seems to think I'm in pretty good shape. By the way, I'll be coming home in December. Coy Ames has asked me to be one of her bridesmaids. How 'bout that?"

"That's great, Jody. This news makes me very, very happy. Millie and Lyn and your mother will be beside themselves. Will you be able to move home? Or is it to be a long visit?"

"We'll have to see closer to the time. Definitely for the holidays. Coy had planned to be married at Kiawah, but changed her mind. So it'll be at church."

"That's another piece of good news, since Preston asked me to officiate, and Christmas is a crazy time for me to take off for Kiawah. Thanks. They haven't thought to tell me."

"Guess I'll see you in a month and a half. Tell Mom and the sibs. Prepare them to receive the inmate from the funny farm."

"Jody, I'm so glad you'll be home for Christmas. I love you."

"I love you, too, Dad." David heard something of the Jody he used to know.

# 36

# Emily

※

Emily was about to make her first trip to Little Rock since Ted's stroke. After Hugo, Tom moved into another apartment in Charleston, with his stereo and captain's chest saved, but everything else had to be resupplied. With fall term well underway, he had to focus on his college studies and not worry about his father. Tim would stay with Natalie and Preston while she was away. Ted's day nurse Alexander moved into the house and assured her that he could supervise Ted's care and make sure the physical therapist worked with him every day. When her brother phoned that their mother's condition had deteriorated and she should come soon, Emily made final arrangements to fly the next day, trusting she'd done all she could to take care of Ted.

He couldn't move much at all, but with his left hand and a small blackboard, he made his wishes known. Ted had always been a large man, but since the stroke, he'd swollen from an aging football athlete to a grotesque parody of an obese buddha. She had to work to see the old Ted within his current body.

Emily peeled and cut up two red pears. The long slippery white fruit was one of his favorites. She also washed a bunch of grapes, thinking again about the night in the hospital back in August when he curled into a fetal position, rasping a message to her and the boys. She had bent close to his mouth to hear, "I'm dying, right? I die soon." Her heart caught at his words. She refused to answer his question. Instead she'd said, "Ted, would you like a grape?" He'd mumbled his assent. She'd placed a green grape in between his pink lips and watched him chew and chew, a remembering expression on his face. The skin on his face had a polished look. His eyes—so blank since his stroke—took on a tiny bit of expression. "More?"

"Yes, please," he'd answered. On his side he received and chewed and swallowed the small cool grapes. "Thank you," he'd whispered and then slept.

Now Emily wiped her tears away with a dish towel and carried the grapes and slivers of pear to Ted on his favorite plate, one Tim had painted at camp years ago.

Ted was more or less sitting up in the hospital bed.

Alexander met her at the door. He was a big man with a dark chocolate complexion, his head bald and shiny. He had a wide mouth that wore his usual warm smile. "Now, Ms. Parks, don't you worry about one single thing. Mr. P and me'll be fine. Won't we, Mr. P?"

"I know that, Alexander. But it's hard to leave. Let me feed this to Ted and I'll call if I need you."

"Sure thing. I'll be in the breakfast room working the daily jumble."

When Emily approached the bed, Ted glared at her and turned his head away.

"Ted, dear, I'll be leaving for the airport in a few minutes. I brought you some pear slices. May I help you with them?" She was trying too hard and she knew it. She still had not mastered the balancing act of no-nonsense professional assistance and treating his invalid state with pity and worse—condescension.

He muttered something she couldn't quite catch.

"What, dear?"

"Nothing." He beat his left fist on the railing.

"Ted, you know I have to go. Mother's dying. I've got to see her one more time. You'll be fine. You're so much stronger than just two days ago. You're getting better every day."

"No. No. No." He turned his face away.

Emily picked up the plate and went to the other side of the bed, sat down and attempted to feed Ted a bite. He opened his mouth and accepted the pear. She ate a sliver. "Don't you love the grainy sweetness? Just a little tartness. So smooth."

She put down the dish, wiped her hands on the towel and smoothed his floppy mass of what had once been golden hair now mostly gray. "Ted, you said you wanted me to go."

"No. Nothing I can . . ."

"I'll hand you the chalkboard. Write what you're trying to say."

He struggled to sit up straighter, but listed to starboard.

She called Alexander. Immediately he stood beside her and straightened Ted again to an upright position.

"You two old football players get along great. Thanks."

On the chalk board Ted scratched out with his left hand, "Now you are Ulysses. I am Penelope. Please don't wait ten years to come back to me."

She kissed his face, his mouth complete with pear juice. "Ted, you old warrior, you're still my Ulysses. I will return in one week." She kissed his honey-brown eyes, one by one, hoping to wipe away the fear she saw there.

Tim bounded in, dropped his book bag, and raced into the bathroom. Emily wondered if anyone in high school used the restrooms there. The kids used to joke back and forth about developing a ten-hour bladder to make it until they got home. When he emerged, she met him in the hall beside her suitcase. "Tim, I'm counting on you to let me know how your dad does in my absence. Your grandmother may not make it this time, but I'll call you with an update."

"Be safe, Mom. We'll be okay. Alexander says I can act as his intern. Maybe I can learn some things and get a job at the hospital next summer." His dark hair flopped over his forehead the way Ted's used to do when she first met him. Tim would probably top out at 6'2" or 3," taller than both his dad and brother. Gangly was the word for Tim. He surprised her now by hugging her in a full embrace, closer and longer than she would ever have expected from a sixteen-year-old. Tears sprang to her eyes, which she did not want him to see. Just as she separated from him, she heard Natalie's horn out front.

Tim reached for her suitcase and carried it out.

"One more thing, Tim," said Emily. "Would you call the church and tell David about my mother and that I'll be in Arkansas for the week? Please give him Uncle Don's number. And ask if Deborah can lead the discussion class next Sunday."

"Will do. Bye, Mom."

# 37

# David

avid felt overwhelmed. His mother Mary Frances Archer had not
only given him the job of executor, but she'd left him, as she said
in her last letter, all her letters and papers. As her only heir remaining,
he had received her meager savings two years ago. He had this one
precious week away from South Carolina in Little Rock to sort out her
things, and he was the only one to do it.

The realtor had called to say his mother's unit had sold at last. He
needed to empty it immediately. The closing would be in two weeks,
so regardless of all he needed to tend to at church, he had abruptly
departed, leaving Deborah to preach and his clerk of session in charge
of calling him in case of emergency. Judith, too, promised to keep him
informed.

Mary Frances had returned to Little Rock and lived in the retirement village in what she called her favorite town of all those that his
father had served in his ministry. She must have packed and repacked
this ridiculous number of files every place she'd ever lived from her girl-
hood through fifty-two years of married life to her years of widowhood,
her last few years spent in the Presbyterian Home, Ivy Cottage.

After his brother died, none of the family had been able to talk together the way they once had—or the way he remembered when he and Drew were children. Even as teenagers, conversation around the table at night had been vigorous, unsparing, on all manner of subjects. His dad Claude had insisted they hone their arguments with reason, not just hot feelings, whether on politics, religion, or strategies on the basketball court. His mother used to put in her opinion as she served up the pot roast or creamed spinach, always standing with the hot dish beside the table, as if she had no right to speak while she ate, but only while she was serving. At least that was his memory. Faulty as memory could be. Later, his father had grown increasingly morose and taciturn. His mother, the vivacious, seemed to shrink into herself, a subdued yet still lovely shell of her former self, the essence hidden from view, only a shiny brittle exterior of a once colorful insect. Rather like the time when she'd been sick with depression when he was young.

His eyes stung with the memory of his beloved brother. David had been off on his Rhodes scholarship when Drew shot himself. The old guilt chafed at him for not being present when his father faced the firestorm of racial hatred in Little Rock back in the late fifties. Drew, certainly the more sensitive of the two of them, had chosen to work in an auto mechanics shop the summer between the school years, the time the governor had rallied his forces, and closed down all the Little Rock high schools. Drew loved to work on cars, yes, but he should never have been in that spot at that time. The harassment proved relentless. And it didn't help that he too had been laid low by clinical depression. Work with his hands was supposed to have been therapy. David had not been there for his brother or his father or his mother.

He slammed his hands against the dusty file cabinet. Over and over until both hands throbbed with red-hot pain. "Forgive, forgive, forgive me." He let the tears flow. Then he grew angry at himself for weeping. No amount of grieving could restore Drew or his father or his mother, or the early family joy imprinted in his memory. Nostalgia colored the tableau of his early childhood like old black and white photographs tinted with oil paints.

Three days in Little Rock and he hadn't finished going through his mother's stuff. He'd met with the lawyer and the realtor, both friends of his mother in her church. Mary Frances Langtree Archer had also owned a rental property across town near their old church, and of course all the cottage furnishings, clothing, and papers. The legal paperwork had been completed months ago, but David had put it all aside. He'd convinced himself he'd been too busy to focus on his mother's estate. The physical act of sorting through her things had helped him feel and acknowledge the loss of his mother. And the business-like contact with her legal and financial counselors had helped him sort out not just her affairs, but some of his own. He asked the realtor to work on selling the rental property as soon as possible. The sale of his mother's cottage would bring blessed relief from the money he and Nell owed Winslow Farms and possibly clear up other credit card debts. Gratitude. Now he felt gratitude. If he had to, he could lug her papers home to Goodwin.

He piled his dirty clothes into a duffle bag and headed to the laundry-mat near the Western Hills Presbyterian Church. He fed quarters into the first relatively clean and empty machine, poured in detergent. He walked around outside while the wash cycle churned. He strolled over to the church he remembered from his youth. Preacher Dick they'd called the minister, a man who led many vespers at Ferncliff Church Camp. He recalled how he'd wrap one arm across his chest while he exhorted the campers gesturing with the other arm. No one seemed to be around the play yard. He walked around to the office door and found the door unlocked. The wall had a trophy case with years of cheap basketball trophies. A further wall had portraits of former pastors. He located the one he'd known as a teenager.

"May I help you, sir?" A tall, exceedingly thin woman, who wore a clerical collar above a dark blue suit, stood beside him. David introduced himself and why he'd wandered over.

"A colleague from South Carolina! This is a major treat for me on a draggy sort of day. I'm Beth Wafferton, the pastor here. Please, come in and let me fix you up with a Coke or some coffee. Choose your poison."

He followed her into a makeshift all-purpose room. They sat at a long table. A ping pong table was set up at one end of the room, and an accordion door could close off a section of the room, so a class could meet at the kitchen end, another at the other side. Concrete walls painted a neutral beige with windows that cranked open at even intervals gave some light into the basement room. The sanctuary must have been built up the hill and above these ground-level rooms.

Beth was single, had been in the ministry ten years and serving Western Hills just two. David at first assumed his usual role of listening. As she talked, he couldn't help wishing she was his associate, not Deborah. He told stories about Preacher Dick and his leading the young people into seeking what God was calling them to do with their lives. David told her how inspired he'd been at fourteen by this man of God. He wished her well and returned to the laundrymat.

He waited for his clothes to dry and jotted ideas in his notebook. He wrote, *My true calling—what is it now? Must return to my beginnings. The source. Energy, spirit, remember Ferncliff. I can almost smell the sawdust in the rustic meeting house, the damp woods near the cabins, the lake with four mountains surrounding camp, whiff of bacon frying in the kitchen near the boys' cabins. Rowing on the lake with my first crush, a girl with long braids and braces on her teeth. Vespers by the lake with the song leader belting out songs of praise. Nostalgia NOT what I need now. So what is it? What to do, Lord, with this challenge in my path. What, O God of love and mercy, should I do to keep our church a place of healing and abundant life doing what we can for your glory in places of need in our city?*

He waited, doodling around the page.

An answer closer than hand or feet came to him. Not a voice, but as clear as a voice:

*Fear not. Do what you do best. Be strong in your strength.*

The dryer buzzed. His clothes were ready. He closed his notebook and finished the laundry, drove back to his mother's cottage.

The phone was ringing as he entered. It was his secretary Judith to tell him that Emily Parks was in Little Rock also. She gave him the telephone number where Emily could be reached and the news that her mother was at death's door. That knowledge shook him. He called Donald Garland, Emily's brother, and soon talked to her. She sounded frail and shaky. "My mother's in ICU at St. Vincent's. She's not going to make it this time."

# 38

## Charlotte

When Charlotte and Natalie arrived at the Knitters' Circle, the leader and two other women were talking in soft tones and stopped when they saw them approach. The only thing Charlotte heard was "She's got at least 147 people on her side." Then an array of false smiles.

Jerry Ann, the leader, spoke up. "Charlotte, Natalie, come into the circle. We were just discussing some—uh—plans for later." She picked up her needlework.

Charlotte hadn't been to the knitting group for several months. Jerry Ann now was crocheting a baby hat of yellow and white yarn. As the others gathered, she saw that everyone had moved on to new projects, except for her. Well, she'd been busy. She pulled out the scarf and began counting rows to see where she was in the pattern. The yarn was a soft wool, teal-colored, and would be perfect for winter. She'd give it to Natalie or maybe to Hannah or her granddaughter. For Christmas. As slow as she knitted, probably not until the Christmas a year from now. Again, she let the gossip flow around her and decided she'd do best to keep quiet and pick up anything that might help David and the church.

The young blonde with the braid down her back—Charlotte remembered her name was Valerie—flounced into her chair, whipped out her knitting, and began talking. "You'll never believe what Deborah shared with me. She was practically weeping when she told me. Y'all, someone's been spreading a vicious rumor about her, our Deborah." She paused, so everyone leaned forward and waited. "A cruel, vicious, heartless rumor."

Jerry Ann jumped in. "What, Valerie? Don't keep us in suspense."

"Yeah," Natalie said, "What in the world?"

"Deborah said that someone in our church is telling people that she uses cocaine."

When she heard that, Charlotte dropped five stitches off her needle and kept her head down.

"That's ridiculous," one woman said. Everyone murmured agreement.

"When Deborah told me, she broke down and cried. Said she does have a chronic condition, a lung problem. She said that causes her to have to take a prescription drug. And she has to use nasal spray. Nothing illegal. And she actually sobbed on my shoulder."

"I can't stand to think that anyone would say such a thing about Deborah Baker."

"She cried? I've never seen her show strong emotions, except from the pulpit when she gets passionate about her causes," Natalie said.

"Did she tell you who was spreading that poison?"

"No. I pushed, but all she said was that we need to squash the rumor." She looked around the circle and nodded at each woman. "That's why I'm telling you. We can't have her made a victim."

The women agreed. Charlotte knew she hadn't said anything to anyone and felt sure Emily hadn't either. The only place it could have come from was Deborah herself. Hmm.

"Does anyone have any other news?" Jerry Ann asked.

"Well, our preacher has gone to Little Rock to clean out his mother's house, so Judith says."

"I thought she died several years ago. Why now?"

"Guess we must keep him too busy here." They all chuckled.

"His mother's place sold, so he had to clear it out," Natalie said.

"Emily Parks is out there in Arkansas too. Her mother's near death," Jerry Ann said.

"That's interesting. Two of ours in Little Rock. That's off the beaten path."

"So Deborah will be preaching while David's gone, right? She's on a campaign."

"More power to her. I hope more in the congregation will see things her way. How homosexuality is a sin and those people had better mend their ways and repent."

"Oh, Jerry Ann, don't you recognize that gays are made that way. By God," Natalie said.

The young Valerie said, "Hey, y'all, let's not get in a fight. The knitting group is supposed to be peaceful and a chance to relax with each other."

"Okay." Jerry Ann looked Natalie in the eye. "We'll give it a rest. But Deborah's right, you know."

Natalie held her tongue. Charlotte smiled at her daughter-in-law. Needles clicked for a while in the quiet. Then the woman with white hair said, "So Emily Parks and David are in the same city, way across the Mississippi. Hmmm."

Natalie said, "He'll probably have a part in the memorial service when the time comes."

Charlotte wished Natalie hadn't said anything more.

# 39

# David

David was alarmed when he saw Emily's face. Always fair-skinned,
she looked paler than ever, drained of all color. Even her light blue
eyes looked silver-white. Her voice shook when she said her mother had
hemorrhaged, yet she'd called no one in the retirement home. Now the
oxygen mask covered Charlie May's nose and mouth as she lay flat on her
back. Emily's brother, Don, and sister, Julie, stood on either side of the
bed. As Emily and David approached, they stepped aside. Only two family
members could be in ICU at a time.

Emily introduced David. Don spoke up, grasped David's hand. "I
remember your father well. He was one strong man. It's a pleasure to
meet you."

Her sister shook his hand and said, "Emily has nothing but great
things to say about you. Thank you for being here."

David thanked them. As they left, he wondered what Emily might
have said. Emily held her mother's hand. There was an IV attached. Her
arms were restrained and her hands looked swollen. Charlie May's face
had a yellowish tinge. She seemed feverish. A feeble breeze wafted from
an oscillating fan set up at the foot of the bed.

Emily asked the nurse if they would adjust her mother's position so that she was lying more on her side. The way she preferred to sleep.

After she was shifted, Charlie May let out a deep sigh as if now she could relax.

"I'm here, Mother. Don and Julie and I are all with you. This is David, my friend."

Her mother's eyes, light blue like Emily's, roamed helplessly, then fixed on Emily's face. A watery gaze. Then a wild look before she shut her eyes. "I think she focused on me for a minute."

Emily and David joined the others in the waiting room. Don took the initiative. "David," he said, "Would you pray with us?" They all stood in a circle and held hands.

In a way he was taken by surprise. Emily had told him that his brother and sister were not especially religious. But David complied as best he could. First silently he asked God to help him forget his own concerns and use him as a conduit of his grace. Then he prayed that the family around Charlie May might know in their hearts that all of them were surrounded and infused by God's ever present love and mercy. Perspiration prickled his underarms.

Julie said she had to get home to her children, and Don needed to go back to work. They agreed to meet the next morning since there was nothing they could do, except stay beside their mother as often as possible.

Emily sat on the sofa in the waiting room and David joined her. He picked up her hand. So white and slender and small. He held it to his lips. And then looked into her eyes. Her face took on its healthy pink color. He reminded himself he could not take her in his arms. Even if they'd been in a more private place, he could not acknowledge his heart's desire. Never would he be able to. She was dealing now with a dying mother. At home she was caring for an invalid husband. Once a formidable seemingly invincible man and his good friend, Ted Parks was trapped in a heavy body that refused to move at his bidding.

Emily shivered as if shaking off an involuntary impulse. She studied his face with an intensity he found unnerving. She stood so he stood up too. "I'm going back in to be with Mother. May I call you later, if, you know, anything happens?"

"You may call me any time. I'm staying there alone at Mother's cottage until I've emptied it. You will not bother anyone. So please call me. It doesn't matter what time."

She embraced him, thanked him, and quickly left before he could acknowledge to himself the electrical current that shot through his body.

David walked around the hospital grounds, past the line of Leyland cypress trees, across sidewalks beside the parking garage, and back toward the sloping lawn toward the mental health facility. He recalled his month practicum in pastoral counseling between his junior and senior years at seminary. In that very building before they upgraded and added to it. Patients deemed insane were his daily companions. Funny, original, bizarre, but hardly frightening as he had supposed. He recalled one occupational therapy hour when several newbies had come in. One attractive woman with a lisp and eyes that didn't quite work together sidled up to him and asked what he was in for. He'd smiled appreciatively for including him in their group, but he had to tell her he was the seminary student learning about mental health and illness. She'd laughed and guaranteed him that she and the others would be glad to teach him every little thing he needed to know.

He'd learned about boundaries that had become walls every bit as forbidding as the Berlin Wall, complete with barbed wire on top and broken glass throughout any possible escape routes. He'd found each person fascinating, even those locked away from others and themselves, and each one could occasionally be reached by touch. A hand on a shoulder, a handshake, a direct gaze where sometimes he felt almost dizzy at the stare that came back to him, as if the patient were sucking him into a vortex. He had to learn his own boundaries that summer. Also, he learned how droll human beings could be and grew quite fond of the patients.

As he circled back to the front of the hospital complex, he saw Emily heading toward a car. He called to her.

She turned, her tense shoulders dropping visibly. She was carrying two bundles. "She's almost gone. Mother's in a coma, or close to it. I so need to talk to her." Her voice caught. "Not sure what exactly I want to say, but it feels so unfinished."

"Here let me carry your stuff." David reached for the bundles. "Will you allow me to buy you some supper, unless of course you're eating with your brother's family or your sister."

"No, they've gone home already. Don let me use a car to come and go. I'll stay tonight probably at the hospital."

David matched his steps to hers and they climbed to the second level of the parking garage. As they reached the blue Ford Galaxy, they agreed he would follow her to the cafeteria.

They found a table in the back away from other diners. Emily talked about how she remembered Franke's as a child, their perfect custard pie, which she had now on her tray. He recalled how half their congregation had eaten at Franke's after Sunday services, so much so that finally his father had decreed they had to find another Sunday dinner place. He'd already greeted, squeezed hands, hugged lonely widows, smiled till his smile muscles ached.

"Where did you end up going?"

David laughed. "Mostly we went home to ham sandwiches, chips, and Jello salad and my mother's martyred sighs. Drew and I loved it. We could wear our jeans and relax."

They ate in silence for a few minutes.

Then Emily told about the last time she took her mother to the cafeteria. "She had one of her favorites—vegetable soup, corn bread, and pie. But all she did was stir the soup and break the cornbread into little pieces. She said she was sorry, but these days she couldn't keep anything on her stomach. Then she said an unusual thing for her. She looked up at me with tears in her eyes and said 'my children take good care of me.' Charlie

May has always been stubbornly determined not to depend on her adult children for anything. She never wanted to be a burden. She carried that to an extreme. She's usually as prickly as one of those wild flowers with minute thorns up and down the stems, the ones with tiny compound leaves that close up when you touch them. Touch-Me-Nots, we used to call them. My mother, the Touch-Me-Not."

"I remember seeing those. Little pouffy flowers like miniature mimosa blooms."

"Right. If Charlie May Garland were a wild plant, that's what she'd be."

"Okay, I'll ask you one. If Deborah Baker were a plant, what would she be?"

Emily didn't hesitate. "She'd be poison ivy."

"That's harsh. You really think she's poisonous?"

Emily studied his face with that tight intense concentration she had. He felt his face and neck flush.

"David, yes. I'm afraid for you and for Harmony Church. If she were an animal, I'd say a badger. No, some kind of creature that collects followers and commands larger and larger territory. Maybe a mountain gorilla, although much better looking."

David considered what to answer. Her blue eyes took on a fierce ready-for-battle intensity, then softened.

"Sorry. She's your associate. You may not feel that way. And it's uncharitable of me not to find some good in her. I know she had a terrible childhood, and I'm sorry about that."

"No need to apologize. We're far enough away from Goodwin where we ought to be able to say anything to one another we need to say."

"I've always felt we could do that anywhere, even at home in Goodwin."

"Yes. You're right."

David watched Emily cut a wobbly bite of custard pie away from the crust and eat only the custard with obvious pleasure. "Speaking of that freedom to say whatever we need to say to each other, let me ask your advice. What do you think I ought to do about Deborah, if anything?"

"The first thing that occurs to me is for you to keep on doing what you're doing, and let some of the rest of us confront the trouble she stirs up."

"Sounds good in theory, but right now she's managed to attract a lot of followers bent on splitting the congregation along political lines." He ate a bite of his chocolate cake. "Not long ago, I did hear a sort of answer to my prayer of what I should do. What bubbled up plain as could be were the words, 'Do what you do best. Be strong in your strength.'"

"Well? There's your answer."

"I need for you to tell me where you see my strength. To tell you the truth, I've somewhat lost my way. Something about Deborah leaves me confused."

"Me, too. David, your capacity to listen, to feel what we're feeling and express it clearly, to admit you don't know all the answers." Her eyes pierced him. He studied his chocolate cake. "And you do bring scripture that lends light to our dilemmas today. That, my friend, is a definite strength."

She waited until he looked up. "As our Buddhist friends might say, 'Don't be tossed away.'" Emily shrugged. "Keep giving us from the pulpit what is saving your life now, what the good news is for you."

"In other words, don't fall into the trap of arguing the issues she keeps bringing up?"

"That's what I think." Emily wiped her mouth, put down her napkin, and scooted out her chair. David took the hint. Supper and consultation were over. She had to go.

"Thank you, Emily. I know you have to get back to the hospital."

They walked to their cars. He stood beside the driver's side as Emily fastened her seat belt. She lowered the window.

"David, you asked me. I'll tell you again. Keep to the way you've been showing us from the pulpit and in your life how to live honestly. Just be yourself. Don't be tossed away."

"Thank you for that good word." He turned to go, then turned back.

"By the way, thank you again for teaching the class with Deborah, exploring the issues she deems so important. It couldn't be easy—since you see her as poison ivy."

"That class is where I've learned about her. I have to keep my guard up all the time. Not my style. I've only broken out with a rash three times so far."

"Really?"

"David, I'm kidding. But I do have to be wary. The class is pretty divided on the subjects, but so far they haven't been vicious to one another. Now, with you and me out of town, no telling what she'll do."

# 40

## Emily

꿈

Emily woke up from a deep sleep to the sun beating down. She was covered with sweat, sticky, uncomfortable. The dream returned in snatches. She had been riding a bicycle up a steep hill and had to carry a game she'd bought in her left hand. She'd bought it in a hurry and only after she'd started riding did she realize that the board game was not new. She felt cheated, but was too far from the store to take it back. She had to get home to her son by a certain time. She examined the box before she went up the next hill to determine how she could carry it without spilling the little men and dice. It was a Parcheesi game and two corners of the box were split. She put a big rubber band around the box and started up the hill. It was a hill in Little Rock, but it changed into a crowded block with obstacles and planters and teenage gangs hanging around with their bikes parked in inconvenient places. She sighed and took a deep breath, settled down astride the bike, allowing the feeling of the bike seat under her and between her legs to keep her grounded, present right where she was in this difficult place. She pulled harder on the bike to take her home through the obstacles. She smiled at the people now and then, determined to make it home with game box intact, home to her sick son.

Where was she? The bed was actually the big vinyl chair in the ICU waiting room. She sat up and stretched. The waiting room had fewer people than when she'd lain down. The clock on the wall said 3:30 p.m. Her sister would not be there until five, and Don even later.

Emily asked the nurse if she could go in to see Charlie May. "She's been quite restless this afternoon," the nurse said. "It would do her good to see you."

"She's awake then?"

"Well, not actually awake, but she may hear you and know that you're there."

Emily stepped into the curtained area of the large ICU and again felt the shock of seeing her mother basically tied down, with an oxygen mask covering her nose and mouth. Her body looked alien with tubes stretching out to feeder bottles, IVs, and catheter tube to the urine bag below the bed.

"Charlie May, it's me, Emily. I'm here with you. I want so much to know that you hear me. Squeeze my hand, if you can, please." Her swollen hand didn't move.

"I love you, Charlie May. You never thought you were a good mother. But despite what you think, I know you loved me. And Don and Julie." She thought to herself—*in your own way to the best of your ability.* "We are taking turns to be with you, because the hospital only allows one or two visitors at a time for just a few minutes." Emily ran her fingernail gently along her mother's fingers and around her hand. "You've never liked to be touched very much, but I wish I could hold you and rock you the way you used to rock Julie when she was a baby. And probably me too and Don but I was too young to remember." There was so much more she'd like to say, but she couldn't bring the words out past the knot in her throat. After watching her mother's face and the struggle she had breathing, Emily glanced at her watch and bent to kiss her mother's cheek. Her cheek, soft as a kitten's ear, felt feverish and damp. "I love you," Emily said. Her mother let out a breath, a low moan coasting out on the exhale.

"Good-bye for now," Emily whispered and squeezed her hand, careful not to disturb the attached pulse taker on her index finger. Her mother's eyelids fluttered but her eyes remained closed.

Emily left the ICU waiting room determined to find fresh air and maybe a soothing meal. She pictured a baked potato with butter, melted cheese or sour cream on top. As she walked through the lobby of the hospital toward the cafeteria, David met her by the door.

"You're here." She leaned quite literally against him. "Sorry. I'm a little shaky. Not sure I'll see her alive again."

David walked with his arm around her. All she wanted to do was keep walking just like that, in step, under his protective warm shoulder, his body matching hers. She allowed herself to feel what she was feeling. If he knew her the way she knew herself, he would stay away from her. If he knew how she'd betrayed Ted, David would be repulsed utterly. She worried that Deborah would one day tell him about her abortion. Then there would be questions of why. She gave an involuntary shudder, which David immediately responded to.

"You're trembling. Come on, let's get out of here." David had turned her toward him but still held her arms, to keep her from collapsing. "Please, Emily, let me take care of you. We'll go somewhere safe where you can sleep and eat, talk or not talk. Whatever you need."

"David, there's nothing I'd like better than that, but I have to be here when Julie and Don get off work."

"Don't worry. I'll have you back by then. Sit down here by the fountain. What would you like to eat?"

While David bought her a baked potato with everything on it and a Coke, Emily considered what to do. She felt like saying to him, forget the baked potato. Take me to bed with you. She could picture lying in his arms, caressing his body, being caressed.

He walked toward her carrying a large bag of food and drinks. His thick hair flopped on his forehead and his face wore an open hopeful expression.

*Oh dear,* she thought. *If we go off the hospital grounds, I won't be able to resist. He might, but I won't.* "David, thank you. Why don't we eat at one of the tables out in the atrium? That way, I'll be here for sure when Julie and Don return. Anyway, I think it's beginning to storm outside, judging from all the wet people coming in."

He stopped and his face lost its luminous expression. "If that's what you want."

"It's not what I want, but it's best. For now."

"You're probably right." He led the way to a table away from the traffic in the atrium. They ate without talking. He ate fried chicken and licked his fingers after each piece.

"You're enjoying that like Tim or Tom would." She laughed. "And this baked potato is giving me comfort, but mostly sitting here with you is what is actually giving me comfort."

"That's all to the good, I suppose. Though I have to say, if you'd allowed me to, I would have taken you to my mother's place for a rest in her guest room." He didn't say more, but his eyes caressed her face as he spoke.

Emily met his eyes although she was afraid her desire was too apparent. "You know," she said, "when awareness of death is close at hand, the urge to merge intensifies." She didn't want him to think she was making fun of the tension between them, but she had to do something to lighten the moment.

"You've got that right." He smiled at her and straightened his back. "Hmm, the urge to merge. So true." He wiped his mouth and hands with the towelette the cafeteria had furnished with the chicken. "Are you ready to go back upstairs now?"

As they walked toward the elevators, he said, "You know, Emily, that's one of the many reasons I cherish you. You name what's going on."

The elevator opened. "I'll leave you now. Call me at Mother's if anything changes, or if you want me to come to you." He would not return unless she called him. The closing elevator door felt like a rending, leaving most of herself on the other side.

# 41

## David

While David waited for the Salvation Army truck to arrive to pick up most of his mother's furniture and clothing, he sat at her walnut desk with paper and pen. He needed to talk with his old friend and colleague, Jonathan Savant. He wrote a long letter recalling how they used to talk every Sunday night when they held pastorates in the same town and then explained his present situation. He told him about the pleasant years at Harmony Church and how things had now changed, recalling that Jonathan had warned him: "There's a snake in every garden." He closed by saying that he'd like to meet Jonathan in the Dallas airport on his way back home to Goodwin next week. He'd call Jonathan after he had a chance to read the letter.

David rose from his mother's desk and stretched his arms over his head. The scent of lavender wafted toward him making the hairs on the back of his neck perk up. Was it his mother's presence?

He had not dreamed of her or his dad after their deaths. Now and then he felt close to his father, especially when he added to the quotation notebook Claude had used for sermons.

The whiff of lavender brought back his mother. The way she studied his face in silence and then pronounced judgment on what he'd been worrying over. She could slice through his tangled thoughts with a few words. "Son, you ruminate like a bovine. Stop thinking. Just act. Trust yourself to find the way as you go."

She used to say that a lot when he was a teenager. "Thanks, Mom," he said aloud. Her words had been buried for years. Like he'd buried most of their family life after Drew's death. Could lavender bringing back these words from his mother be one of the mysterious ways the Lord answered his unspoken prayer? He'd like to think so.

David sealed the envelope, addressed it, and searched for a stamp. He'd walk to the Heights Post Office. The phone rang just as he was locking up. He ran back in. Emily's voice quavered. "They said she's expired." Emily half-laughed, half-sobbed. "Expired, like a subscription."

"I'll be right there. Are Don and Julie with you?"

"Yes, we're all here. I said you would help us plan the service. Will you?"

"We'll talk about all that when I see you." He'd mail the letter on the way. He called Salvation Army to postpone the pick-up.

From the moment David entered the ICU Waiting Room, he could tell by the looks Emily's brother and sister gave him and each other that they suspected he and Emily were having an affair. They never said a word, but he'd seen that expression before. He thought ruefully to himself, *If only.* No, he yearned for much more than an affair.

He set about to dispel their assumptions by playing up his role of minister to help them plan the memorial service for Charlie May. The group gathered in a small consultation room near the ICU—Don and his wife, Julie and her husband, and Emily. The young doctor asked them if they'd like to see their mother. Donald said he would not. Julie followed suit. Emily said she needed to see her and turned instinctively toward David. He asked if she would like for him to go with her and she nodded. That's when the look again passed between Don and Julie.

Emily held his arm tightly as they stood beside the bed. No monitors were beeping. Charlie May no longer had the hard plastic mask over her nose and mouth. The nurses had cleaned their patient and combed her hair, placed her hands at rest, no longer restrained or hooked up to IVs.

"Her suffering is over," the doctor said quietly.

"Yes. I needed to see her without the paraphernalia. She looks so— her skin's so yellow. My mother who so loved birds of all kinds. In death she looks like a yellow wax bird." Emily's voice caught and she leaned into David.

He put his arm around her. "Would you like to sit for a few minutes?"

"No, I need to go. Thank you, Doctor."

Don outlined the plan for the schedule and service. Together they listed who would make calls. David offered to call the Goodwin friends for Emily. Emily and Julie worked on the obituary notice. Don said that Charlie May's pastor at Western Hills Church would lead the service, but he asked David to read the scriptures, whatever verses he thought best.

David made his exit after assuring them he'd make the calls from his mother's house and would speak to the pastor, whom he'd met, and they would coordinate the service.

He walked up the hill from the hospital to the parking lot at a fast clip.

He'd go for a long hard walk. A sharp wind cut through him, which he welcomed. Maybe it would relieve the tension building up inside. One of the calls would have to be to Nell. Maybe she'd join the others who would probably drive over to support Emily.

As it turned out, only Natalie and Preston drove from Goodwin to Little Rock, bringing Tom and Tim with them. Emily and Ted's daughter, Meredith, flew in from Boston with her boy friend Joel. The service was held on Saturday, November 11, with a reception afterwards in the fellowship hall that had been named for Emily's father, Emerson Garland, after his death years ago. Charlie May's bridge group attended and spoke warmly to

David afterward, and asked about Ted. David particularly enjoyed meeting some of Emily's old friends from her high school days.

While Natalie talked with Emily and her friends, Preston pulled David aside. "I'm not exactly sure what's going on, but the division within our Harmony congregation is worse. People know we're close friends, so I don't hear much directly, but Mother told me the nominating committee had outvoted her on everyone she put forward. Except one, Skip Milner. You need to get home and mind the store." David assured him he would be flying home to Goodwin on Monday afternoon.

At the Dallas/Fort Worth airport, David and Jonathan Savant met for lunch at a restaurant called Monkey Bar. All the televisions mounted above the counters showed different sports events, but one displayed different dramatic pictures—with the words muted—of East Germans celebrating the Fall of the Berlin Wall. People danced, partied, hammered out pieces of the concrete wall while uniformed guards stood by watching, a few joining in the gleeful destruction. David gestured to the TV, "What do you know? A revolution without bloodshed."

Jonathan agreed and added, "One journalist reported that a GDR official said, 'The only choice was to open up the pressure cooker, or watch it explode.'" Jonathan gripped David's hand, then embraced him in a bear hug.

"Thanks, old friend, for contacting me. I've missed those Sunday evenings too. No one here quite measures up. At least no one I've found yet who's willing to leave his pride at the door. You and I, we could always admit our failings. And call each other on what we saw."

David knew he'd done the right thing to write Jonathan. Relief poured around inside him, as if a pool that had been plugged up with dried leaves, now swirled free. His friend, always thin, seemed gaunt, his hawk nose more pointed. His hair, no longer dark, had receded slightly and was at least half gray. His brown eyes wore the same crinkly amused look.

They traded news of their families as they ate their burgers, and then talked about the rising tide of reactionary conservatism in their denomination, and at Harmony church in particular. David expressed his concern about the subtle moves Deborah had made. "She works insidiously, I'm afraid, using strategically placed whispers and innuendos. Maybe even outright lies."

Jonathan listened and now and then compared what he heard with situations he knew. Then he said, "You know, David, at a certain point, you may have to recognize that it's a lose/lose situation."

"Has it come to that?"

"Only you can know that. If you think it's close to impossible to pull the church back from the brink, you should plan your exit strategy."

"I want what's best for Harmony Church." He brought his fist down hard on the counter. "Damn it. I don't want to lose my church. Or have the church lose its distinctiveness as one of the few that honors honest inquiry and is at least on the moderate side of liberal."

"At this point, what would be best?"

"The best—" David thought for a moment before answering. "The best would be for her to resign." He shuffled his feet back and forth, watched the TV screen replaying the crowd of East Berliners swaying with candles and singing. "So, somehow I have to get her to agree."

"Do you have anything you can use against her?" He laughed. "To be brutally frank."

"Not much. However, a few friends may be able to help. You know, help persuade her."

"In other words, they may know something. As my old college roommate used to say, 'Use your friends, you made them.'"

David thanked Jonathan and promised to keep him up-to-date. They promised each other they'd keep in touch, and then laughed and admitted they'd do the best they could, given the circumstances.

# 42

## Charlotte

By the Monday before Thanksgiving, the renovations on Charlotte's house were complete. Everyone who worked on the house attended Charlotte's party—Houston and his crew, Charlotte's neighbors, and Natalie and Preston, of course. David and Nell with Millie and Lyn. Emily Parks, her son Tim. Julian Denyar and his musician grandson Wyman. Charlotte's new tenant and new members of Harmony church—a widow and teen aged son, Macon Collier. Deborah Baker with some of the senior highs plus her avid follower Myra. Charlotte's oldest friends, Margaret and Alice, drove over from the Presbyterian Village.

The big white tent in the backyard sheltered the barbecue, slaw, rolls, shrimp, potato salad, cakes, beer, wine, Cokes, hot cider, and lemonade with enough tables and chairs to accommodate most of the crowd. Blessedly, it was a warmish night for Thanksgiving, so people floated in and out of the open doors, sat on the back steps, and danced on the flagstones near the musicians. Music floated, bounced, and sometimes boomed through the house, yard, under the sycamore trees, and around the corner. Gaines Street hadn't seen this much life in the oldest part of Goodwin since before the crash of '29, except for the modest hoopla at the end of WWII. No one called the cops. Everyone in a three-block radius came—out of curiosity and for some non-turkey food. Most stayed late until Charlotte thought her eighty-one-year-old feet and legs would give out.

One guest she'd asked on the spur of the moment at their last official meeting was Irv Monk Wolfe, her private investigator, who looked unusually scruffy and wore ill-fitting clothes that he must have bought at Goodwill. Irv sidled up to her in the living room as she poured more cider into the punch bowl.

"Now, Ms Ames, ma'am. I sure appreciate your party. Yes, ma'am. I've met some folks you told me about, and I think this contact will give me some new clients. But I have to be moving on."

"Thank you, Mr. Wolfe, for coming. For helping me initiate new life in this old place. It's my hope that this house can be a microcosm of what our world should be—an international and interracial peaceful community."

"Good luck with that. I'm too much of a cynic to believe in such, but good luck with that." He beat his hat against his leg, repositioned the crease at the top and replaced it, sprigs of black and silver hair sticking out over his ears and the back of his neck. "If you need my services again, please call me, ma'am."

As she turned back to the guests, she saw David's wife, Nell, beside the ficus tree. Elegantly attired as always, Nell stood tall and straight in a fitted, teal knit two-piece dress, belted with a camel-colored leather belt. She looked to Charlotte like a large buxom bird of prey, watchful, aloof, alone. Charlotte went to her.

"Nell, this gives me the opportunity to speak to you about Lyn and her flute lessons."

"What? You're probably tired of trying to get music out of her."

"On the contrary, Lyn is one of my favorite students. She's training her mouth and her breathing. And she practices."

That comment brought a small smile to Nell's lips. Her gray eyes remained somber. "Nell, how are you doing? David's told me that your business is going well."

"Did he also tell you that we're not separated, after all?"

"Yes, as a matter of fact. I hope you're both okay with that decision."

"Well, for now we do agree it's the best thing. You know, for the girls, at least." Nell touched her dark hair, still perfectly in place.

Charlotte could tell Nell wished to change the subject, but for the life of her she couldn't think of what to talk about. In the momentary silence, the guitarists outside began the folksong from the sixties, "Where Have All the Flowers Gone?" and soon the remaining crowd was singing in unison. Charlotte put her arm around Nell. "Let's join the group, shall we?" Nell seemed to lean on her as they made their way to the back porch and into the yard. Charlotte loved her pastor and always sympathized with his point of view. This night for probably the first time, she felt Nell's vulnerability. Her heart went out to this woman who'd kept herself apart from Harmony Church people. It might be her pride, like some people said. Nell's family had been in the social elite of Atlanta at one time. Or maybe when she signed on to be David Archer's wife, she'd had no idea what the role of minister's wife entailed. Charlotte gave her a motherly squeeze and they sat on the stone bench by the fence.

Julian Denyar's grandson Wyman played the portable keyboard and now was striking up Bob Dylan's "Forever Young." The guys on guitar joined in. Wyman sang. Soon the crowd sang, too. Charlotte spoke into Nell's ear, "Oh, I love that song. And sometimes—like tonight—I believe it's true. Even for me."

Nell pressed her arm and said, "Me too." She turned toward Charlotte and said with surprising intensity, "May I tell you something? Stefan, one of my young colleagues in the antique business, introduced me to his uncle in Charleston. An importer and appraiser who works in New York and Charleston. He's maybe sixty and quite prestigious in the field." Her voice sounded breathy like a young girl's. She spoke in a conspiratorial undertone. Charlotte strained to hear her. "He wants me—uh, to join forces with him. You know, to go into business, and maybe something more." Nell giggled.

Charlotte could hardly believe her ears. Nell talking so much and so personally.

She muttered, "I hope it works out for you." Then she said, "You know, Nell, I'd like for you to come with Natalie and me to the next Knitting Circle. They all would do well to know you better and vice versa. How about it?"

Nell said, "Call me."

Across the flagstones, Charlotte saw Deborah lean into Julian Denyar and say something that brought a vigorous nod and laugh. Charlotte remembered that she must report to David what she'd learned while he was in Little Rock. Deborah, as temporary moderator, got the Session to vote to bring in a speaker for the Marriage and Family Values Symposium. Deborah had received special funding for it from one of Harmony's richest members, who would serve as chair of the symposium. At the meeting everyone assented without questioning her enough about the contents of the message. What few questions Charlotte raised, Deborah's disciple Myra Owens disparaged. No doubt, David already knew of the Session decision, but he had not discussed it with her. She wondered where David was at the moment, probably circulating among the neighbors and Charlotte's new tenants, making everyone feel welcome. Now and then, he should tend to Nell, make her feel comfortable. She surprised herself feeling critical.

The high school boys knotted up on one side of the yard, under the old rose arbor. Charlotte recognized a few like Rivers Carlton and Ace Murphy and his sidekick. A few others. One boy sat by himself on the back steps near the workshop. It was her new tenant's son. A gentle fellow who played the violin. Rivers left the group and went to Millie's side. The two sat down beside the new guy. Charlotte nodded her approval.

Later, she called Hannah and woke her up to tell about the party she'd avoided attending. She described who came and the music, every-thing she could say in a dash before her daughter hung up.

"You're sure the neighbors thought it was okay, Mother? Sounds like a liberal interracial shindig to me."

Charlotte heard the tease and the annoyance in Hannah's tone. "So what? We're on the brink of the final decade of the twentieth century. Surely, Goodwin, South Carolina, has progressed past the prejudiced fifties by now. Anyway, I wanted every single person who worked on my house to be present. And they were. And they seemed to enjoy it and everyone else did too."

"Thank you, Mother, for filling me in on your hoedown, but I've got to hang up. My work begins exceedingly early tomorrow. As no doubt you know, Friday after Thanksgiving is our biggest handbag sale day." And the phone went dead.

Charlotte recognized the little stab inside when she had to separate from her daughter either by phone or in person. Again she faced the truth. She needed contact with Hannah, but Hannah could take it or leave it.

Charlotte picked up the trash bag beside the back door and headed out to the garbage can. She hadn't finished her story. It upset her that Hannah couldn't wait to get off the phone. Resentment simmered in the back of her mind. What had she done so wrong in raising her daughter? She and Fred had lavished their love and attention on her and on Preston, yet she knew in her heart of hearts she would not be welcome to make her final home with either of them and their families. Her daughter-in-law Natalie would be more likely to invite her to live with them than Preston would. It simply wouldn't occur to him. Hannah would scoff at such a notion. Charlotte hauled the big trash can to the pick-up place by the curb. She stood a moment to catch her breath and rest her hip.

The moon, almost full, shone brightly through the tree limbs of her beloved sycamore trees. The balls hung from the bare limbs like tiny dark ornaments. She breathed in the cold crisp air. "Dear God, thank you for letting me rebuild my house. Thank you for the people who came to celebrate with me, bringing their joyful hearts, music, and laughter." She stretched her arms over her head toward the luminous white light above and the tree branches entangling the night.

Yes, she'd been correct to transform her old house. Now she'd have people of different ages and backgrounds living in close proximity. They would all take care of each other. She liked the idea of helping this transitional neighborhood become a true community, beginning within her own house. She walked around back and checked the yard. The tent was ready to be picked up the next day.

# 43

# Emily

The art of losing Elizabeth Bishop called "One Art." Emily read and reread the poem at her desk. She'd taught it in her comp and lit classes at Freestone U any number of times, but this reading seemed to slide a boning knife between her ribs. After the last week of her mother's life, she returned to her invalid husband. Ted seemed more immobile and taciturn than when she left. Her students had made little progress on their research papers, as if her absence entitled them to work on calculus and their fraternity or sorority duties and procrastinate on English. Tom had returned to Charleston and college classes, and Tim was back to his high school routine. Both seemed okay. The boys could mask their feelings well, having practiced this art every time they were near their father since his stroke.

Emily had written copiously in the red cloth-covered journal—every feeling and moment of her mother's last days. She'd written too with abandon about David and what he meant to her, how he'd been right beside her at the hospital and later at the church. The tension of longing between them grew with every contact. Whoever said that death, the awareness of mortality, is the most powerful aphrodisiac had definitely been correct.

Also being out of their usual lives worked a terrible spell. Yet they had not given in to what to Emily was becoming more and more obvious. The current between them had been palpable.

She wrote it all down in the red journal. And now her journal had disappeared. Had she lost it in Little Rock? Surely not. Charlie May's death had left her discombobulated, weak, and fluttery inside, as if she were hungry, chronically hypoglycemic. Yet any time she ate, she threw up. Her mother's death made Emily literally sick. Losing the journal was like losing her mother twice—all the details she'd written to hold the memory and try to make sense of it all. Losing the journal left Emily more vulnerable, exposed, sick.

She couldn't have left the journal at her brother's house or her sister's. No, she'd written in it on the way home. So it had to be somewhere in Goodwin. Ted, confined to his hospital bed in the den, could not have found it. Alexander, the perfect nurse and helper for Ted, was thoroughly professional and too genteel to pry.

Where? Emily searched her Freestone University office—the book shelves, under piles of ungraded essays and quizzes, through every desk drawer. She walked to the library where she might have left it and asked, embarrassed at how much it meant to her. The reference librarian gave her a quizzical look but asked all her assistants. The answer all around was *No*. No one had seen the red cloth-covered journal the size and weight of a square children's book.

She had to let it go and grade papers. After marking the essays from her morning class, Emily stretched and stood by the window. Maybe, if she could remember the last time she wrote in the journal, she'd remember where she left it.

Who had come to see her after she got back to Goodwin? Natalie and Preston came and brought supper the first night back. They'd eaten in the den beside Ted. Who else?

Charlotte Ames and her best friends Alice Sharp and Margaret Temple brought food for the freezer from their church circle. And Deborah

Baker dropped in with Myra Owens to bring Home Communion to Ted. Could Deborah have picked up the red journal? Or Myra, her devoted follower?

Emily felt her temperature rise. The journal contained just enough private information to be dangerous fodder for someone as conniving as Deborah. A frightening thought. Deborah might be an ordained minister, but Emily couldn't trust her. She saw with absolute clarity that she considered Deborah an enemy, a person out to undermine everything she held dear. For someone who had blithely felt free of hard feelings toward anyone until she met Deborah, Emily saw that Deborah caused an instinctive animosity to rise inside like a piercing fire alarm. She thought again about the veiled threat Deborah issued at the Space for Hope if Emily should dare to reveal what she'd discovered in the rest room stall. Charlotte had told her about the "false rumor" Deborah said was circulating. She'd effectively cut off anything they could use against her. If Deborah had taken the journal, no telling what damage she could and likely would do to Emily, and David, too. And it had to have been a deliberate act.

Now Emily had to figure how to get the journal back.

After the American lit class and her office hours, she checked on Ted with Alexander. Sleeping peacefully. The physical therapist had worked with him for an hour without much progress. Emily told him she'd be after five getting home.

She drove to the church. The secretary said Deborah would be in later. Emily told her she'd left something in Deborah's office and would just go pick it up. Before Judith could protest, Emily walked down the hall to the door marked with Deborah's name and a cartoon caricature of the Old Testament Deborah, dressed in a toga with lots of leg showing, her strong right arm holding aloft a shining sword while she stood triumphantly over her hapless victim.

Emily knocked, then turned the knob. The room was dark and emitted a mixture of scents—something pungent, slightly floral. With the overhead fluorescent on, Emily quickly looked in the book shelves. Gaining nerve, she moved to the desk. The top right drawer would not open. The other drawers held papers, books, and miscellaneous office supplies. She looked for a key to the locked drawer, but found nothing. Just as she walked to the sofa, Deborah entered, not at all surprised to see her.

"So you left something in my office, did you?"

"I've lost my red-cloth covered journal and thought maybe you found it." Emily hoped she wasn't blushing.

Myra Owens clipped into the room, a big plastic smile on her face. "Emily, hello. Judith said you were here. What a nice surprise."

"Emily came looking for a lost journal." Deborah sat in her swivel desk chair.

"Sit. Both of you, sit down. Let's talk."

Emily sat on the edge of the straight chair by the door. Myra sank into the cushiony sofa, dropped her shoes on the floor, and drew her legs under her. It was obvious that Myra spent a lot of time relaxing on Deborah's sofa.

"So, Emily, why would you think I might have found your precious notebook?" Deborah said, glancing at Myra and smiled. Myra let a tiny giggle escape.

"Myra, do you know something about my journal? It was a hardback, with a cloth cover in Chinese red, square, about the size of a children's book." She looked from one to the other. "Remember when you two brought communion to Ted right after I got back from Mother's funeral? I thought maybe in gathering up your things afterward, you might have picked it up. Accidentally. Of course." Emily heard the desperate tone in her own voice. She figured Deborah heard it too.

"It contains what? Something incriminating, perhaps? Something you would just as soon no one else see?" Deborah rocked the desk chair back, studied the ceiling tile.

"Of course. It's my private journal. My mother just died and I wrote out details about the last few days of her life. My feelings." She choked back a sob.

Myra sat up and patted her arm. "Now, now. We know how hard it is to lose your mom—even if you didn't get along well—especially then, I guess. Now it's too late to fix the relationship."

Emily studied Myra's intent round face. How would she know that she and Charlie May didn't get along? Was this a guess based on Myra's own life? Or had she and Deborah read the journal?

Deborah set her chair down with a thud and swung around to face Emily.

"Oh, did we tell you that Myra and I visited Nell yesterday? Not at home. At her place of business." Deborah placed her hands together, stretching her fingers to meet like a tent, the long red nails flashing with emphasis. "We had a good talk."

"We took her lunch," Myra added. "It was our second visit with her."

Had Deborah changed the subject to get her to think about something besides her mother? Or was this a subtle threat that they had read the parts about her feelings for David and took it upon themselves to inform his wife? Her face felt hotter. Better not react. "And how was Nell? Busy as ever, with all that jewelry, I imagine."

"While David was out in Arkansas—with you—Nell joined forces with me in the campaign against abortion and the gay lifestyle. In fact, she gave me a sizable contribution to a special fund I'm creating."

Now on the edge of the sofa, Myra chimed in. "It was not hard at all to convince her. She said we were the first people in David's church—that's the way she put it—to come to see her or show any interest." Myra laughed and nodded toward Deborah, who in a quiet voice said, "David's church, hmm. We'll see."

"That's our Deborah. Such a force for good. And so persuasive."

"So were you fighting the good fight yesterday?" Emily wondered how much they would reveal.

"No. Yesterday was strictly personal. A pastoral call, you might say," Deborah said. "You're such a good friend to David. You might give him a warning. Trouble is heading his way." She stood up. "From more than one direction. And soon."

If Emily were to draw Deborah in a cartoon right that moment it would have shown her rubbing her hands and smacking her lips. Emily stood and faced her. "What about my journal?"

Deborah smiled and took a key from the pocket of her skirt, unlocked the drawer of her desk. "Could this be the one you lost?" She placed the Chinese red square book in Emily's hands.

"Oh, Deborah, thank you." She held it to her chest. "Losing it was like losing my mother twice." She decided not to mention David. The less said the better.

"You know, Emily, you should be careful what you write." She slipped the key back into her pocket. "You can never tell where something like this might end up. Or how many copies might be floating around."

"I'm just relieved to have it back." She nodded to both women and made her escape. She heard them laughing as she walked down the hall.

By the time Emily reached her car, her hand trembled so much she could hardly put the key in the lock. She waited for the fluttery feeling to subside. She had to reach David. In the effort to clarify her emotions for herself, she had endangered him.

# 44

## Charlotte

The week after Thanksgiving, Lyn Archer arrived for her flute lesson out of breath. Charlotte calmed her with a cup of hot chocolate. She blew on the steaming mug, stirred the marshmallow around with her spoon, but stayed flushed, her eyes frantic. Charlotte sat opposite at the table and waited.

"Mrs. Ames, I'm scared. You remember you asked me to keep my eyes peeled—whatever that means. Anyway, you asked me to do some detective work a while back?" She brushed her hair back, tucked a long strand behind her ear.

"Well? Have you discovered something?"

"Maybe. I think so." Lyn studied her hot chocolate and held the mug to her lips. "Whew, still too hot." She stared hard at Charlotte, then looked around her, as if she suspected someone might jump out of a closet. "Mrs. Ames, I'm worried something or someone might be planning to hurt you."

"Probably not, dear. But what have you heard?"

"This doesn't make much sense I know, but I overheard a conversation between my sister Millie and her friend Rivers. They were on the phone and talking about what the Senior High young people are planning to do. When Millie said your name, I snuck into Dad's office upstairs and listened in on the extension. By the time I got on the phone, I'd missed two pretty important things. Like when and what they're planning. Millie was real upset. She said she refused to participate. Rivers said, 'I'm with you, but they're going to do it, even if half the group chickens out.' Then he said something about gays, but I didn't catch what that had to do with anything. When they started talking mushy with each other, I hung up."

"Lyn, dear, I don't think you have anything to fret about. I appreciate your keeping your commitment to spy for me. Now we must turn our attention to music."

"What if you're in danger?"

"The church's youth group may protest under Deborah Baker's urging, but I do not believe they'd do anything to harm me. Deborah knows that I oppose her on certain issues, but I'm too insignificant for them to initiate any action involving me. So finish your cocoa and wash your hands, so we can begin your lesson." She wouldn't put anything past Deborah, but she refused to give it a second thought.

Before retiring that evening, the last day of November 1989, Charlotte walked out into the big front hall, thinking about the olden days when she and Fred used to park the large wicker baby carriage there in the corner by the door. How proud they'd been over their two children. They'd take walks around the block. Fred held Hannah's hand and Charlotte pushed Preston in the buggy. Sometimes Hannah was allowed to reach high to the handle and help push her little brother. Now the dark hall felt cool and drafty with smells drifting in from the three new kitchens. Soy and pickled vegetable odor with grilled fish from Seigi Yano's apartment upstairs. Yano-san would be in Goodwin for at least a year as a loaned executive to a joint manufacturing venture. Across the hall from Yano, Houston and Rising Fawn's supper sent the fragrance of steak and sauteed onions wafting down, making her mouth water. Houston and Rising Fawn were basking in their new place. Both acted as gracious hosts to the other tenants. From the kitchen downstairs, across from her, the odors of yeast bread and barbecued pork intermingled with all the others. The new people from church, Sally Collier and her son, Macon, seemed happy to find the apartment. Charlotte was pleased to have a musician close at hand. Macon, in the ninth grade, practiced his violin every day after school. Charlotte breathed in the mixture of scents with satisfaction.

In her kitchen, she warmed up leftover chicken casserole and brewed some decaf, doctored it with cream and sprinkled cinnamon on top. The warmth and taste brought back the days long ago when she was pregnant with Preston. Fred had to be away for long periods. The coffee with cream and cinnamon became her comfort, easing her anxiety and loneliness. She used to sing a nursery rhyme to baby Hannah, actually more to herself: "Crosspatch, lift the latch. Sit by the fire and spin. Take a cup and drink it up, and call your neighbor in." She gripped the mug in both her hands. Well, now she'd called her neighbors in.

Charlotte woke up to loud knocks on her door. The clock light glowed 1:30 a.m.

Sally Collier stood at the door in her bathrobe. Frantic. "I heard his screams. He was supposed to be home two hours ago. Went out with some guys from Youth Group." She sobbed. "I thought it would be safe. Help me."

Charlotte pulled her inside and embraced her. "Sally, what's happened?"

"We've got to hurry. Call 9-1-1." Sally pulled away and ran out to the porch. Charlotte followed, throwing on her coat. Horrified, she stared at a blazing torch. Her heart pounded, her breath came in short gasps. Guys in dark clothes and ski masks encircled one of her young sycamore trees. She saw a boy in a white shirt tied to the tree. Macon Collier.

Houston and Rising Fawn appeared beside her. "We've called the law," Houston said.

"What are you doing?" she yelled. "How dare you?" She ran out into her front yard.

Sally dashed to her son. "We're here." She fumbled with the ropes. Houston quietly moved her hands and began untying the cords.

Suddenly the flame of the torch leaped into the smallest sycamore, catching the branches and the few remaining leaves and balls. The boys in ski masks jumped apart and ran this way and that. That's when she heard voices from the two who stood still: "Guess we got that fag and the old bitch, too, didn't we?" and "This oughta show 'em." One threw down the torch in the gutter and called, "We better get gone, fast." They ran to a car up the block.

Sally walked with her arm around Macon back to the porch and into their apartment. Neighbors from across the street came out on their porches. Houston and Rising Fawn stood on either side of Charlotte, holding her up. "We called 9-1-1. Don't worry," Houston said.

By the time the fire engines and the police arrived, the boys had disappeared. Her neighbor Mr. Saunders said, "There's a boy on the ground over here."

Charlotte went to investigate. "It's Rivers Carlton. Rivers, I can't believe you are one of the thugs."

Rivers gave no response. Mr. Saunders stooped beside him and felt his head. "I think they attacked him. Young man, are you able to talk?" Rivers moaned. "We need EMS."

Charlotte whispered to Fawn, "I think my heart's acting up. Will you get help, please?" The two walked back to the porch. Charlotte sank down onto the glider and watched Houston run over to the policeman before she lost consciousness.

# 45

## David

On the morning of Friday, December 1, 1989, David visited Charlotte's room in Cardiac Care. Emily Parks sat beside the bed where Charlotte held court, describing what she called the Night of Terror. Emily said she'd heard Charlotte's story three times since she arrived to visit, as one person or another from the church had dropped by. "With every telling, the story is, shall we say, enhanced. David, you'll never know what to believe."

"She's up to her old tricks, eh?" He leaned over Charlotte and kissed her lightly on her soft cheek. Then he allowed himself to speak to Emily. "Good morning, Emily. How's Ted?" He stood beside her chair facing the bed.

"About the same. Not really any improvement." She turned her attention back to Charlotte. "Charlotte thinks some of our church's young people might have been among the people who tied Macon Collier to a tree in her yard. And likewise burned up a tree."

"Yes, well. From the myriad phone calls to the church this morning, I'd say you may be correct, Charlotte. Parents are hot. Some afraid that you'll press charges. Others calling to assure me and anyone else who'll listen

326

that their son or daughter did not participate, would never do anything so hateful. The matter will be resolved soon." He pulled the rolling chair from the corner and sat. "Charlotte, I'm concerned about you. What does the doctor say?"

"Thank you, dear David. Whatever the episode was, it's over now. Just a ticker trick called atrial fib."

"Charlotte, that's nothing to make light of," Emily said. "After what you've been through, I hope you can truly rest. By the way, David, what has Deborah said about last night?"

"She hasn't been in today. Called and told Judith she'll be away until early Sunday."

"Convenient. This way, you get to take all the crap." Emily's blue eyes blazed.

"How did you learn about Charlotte's Night of Terror?" David asked.

"Natalie called me early as she was leaving for class, asked me to look in. She knew I don't have to teach today."

Charlotte stirred. "May I ask you to do me a favor? Some weeks ago, a letter turned up in the old mantle. I never read it. Been too busy. But lying here, I keep thinking about it." She reached into the drawer of the nightstand and produced her keys. "How about retrieving it for me?" She handed the house key to Emily.

"I'll be glad to, but where should I look?"

Charlotte laughed. "Wish I could tell you exactly. It's either in the top drawer of the nightstand by my bed, where I stashed it originally. But seems like I moved it. You could try the cedar closet off the sleeping porch. If it's there, it would be in the old family Bible. The letter looked ancient, at least from the envelope." She pulled the sheet up under her chin. "I recall taking some items up there not too long ago."

"Charlotte, where is the sleeping porch?"

"Oh, my dear, it's up the stairs on what you might call the mezzanine. The door stays closed, but it's not locked. The cedar closet is on the right. Everywhere else you'll find windows."

"I like a treasure hunt, and I'll bring you back the secret document." Emily stood.

David stood also. "Charlotte, I'll go too and check on the Men of the Church group. The guys have organized themselves to take care of your damaged tree. Take out the ruined one and replant. Everyone feels bad that this happened."

Emily said, "David, if you'll ride with me, I need to discuss something with you."

Charlotte thanked them for coming to see her and wished Emily luck in finding the letter. She reached into the drawer beside her. "Wait. David, your horoscope today might prove apropos. 'You'll find your world more harmonious today with the alignment of your guardian moon and the nearest planets. Pay close attention to a loved one.' And, Emily, you're Pisces, I believe. Yours is 'You are fearless in facing the uncertainty ahead, trusting yourself to forces, like the mighty sea, that are greater than you.' There you are." She waved, leaned back on her pillows, and closed her eyes.

David looked into Emily's face. They laughed and called out their good-byes.

In the car, David watched Emily's face as she drove through traffic toward Gaines Street. Her face seemed to move through a spectrum of hues from white to a deep blush as she told him the story of losing her red journal and retrieving it from Deborah Baker in the presence of her ally Myra Owens.

She parked the Camry up the block from Charlotte's house and turned off the motor. "David, I haven't told you the worst. Besides writing about my mother's last days, I confess I also wrote out some other feelings." She looked at him, locked eyes with him. "About you. How drawn to you I am, how I want to be with you." She looked down at her hands still holding the steering wheel. "How much I love you. How impossible it all is."

David reached for her right hand, uncurled her fingers from the steering wheel. Holding her gaze, he kissed her small hand, each finger, the palm. "If you only knew how much I—" His voice sounded thick to him, shaky. He stopped.

Before he could say anything else, Emily blurted out how worried she was that her journal could ruin him, that Deborah could and probably would use the journal against both of them, as if they'd acted on these feelings.

"Come on, Emily. Let's go find that letter for Charlotte and not let Deborah's shenanigans get to us. You've got the journal back in your possession, right? She may be just trying to frighten you away from whatever you have on her."

"That is the way her mind works, I suppose. She's correct—I am scared."

They walked on the sidewalk to Charlotte's front yard. Four men were working on the sycamore trees. David spoke to them while Emily went into the house and up the hall stairs to what Charlotte called the mezzanine.

When he got there, she'd opened the cedar closet. He stood in the doorway of the sleeping porch, breathing in a starchy smell mixed with dust and something faintly lavender. A white iron double bed dominated the room with a white counterpane and white curtains at the windows that covered one side of the room and the rear wall behind the bed. He closed the door, moved to the windows, looked out at the Saunders' house next door. Behind the curtains were old rolled-up shades. He systematically pulled them down one-by-one at all the windows, careful not to let the old crackly shades tear, all the time talking in a low voice, to himself, "Stop ruminating. Just act." The sunlight now spread its muted glow across the bed, the wood floor, and on Emily in the doorway of the large walk-in closet.

He went to the door of the sleeping porch and snapped the cast-iron clasp into the locked position. Only then did he walk to Emily, holding out his hand. She stepped down, her hand in his as if he were leading her onto a dance floor. The fragrance of cedar wafted out as she pulled the closet door shut. Without words, they embraced and kissed. Frantic at first, then blissfully searching and slow. He registered how her slender body was narrow and firm compared with Nell's. She surprised him at how fast she unzipped her boots and shed her clothes while he fumbled to undo his belt, drop his pants and take off his stubborn long black socks. He lifted her easily in his arms and carried her to the bed. The squeaks and groans of the old bed made them giggle, but still they didn't speak. Every time a thought threatened to take him out of the moment, he took a deep breath, absorbing Emily's scent, sharp as rosemary, smooth as French vanilla.

Later, cradling her under his right arm, he caressed her arm and dozed. Emily propped herself up on her elbow. "Until today, I'd never noticed the scars on your left hand. All that rough skin on the tops of your fingers and the distorted fingernail. What happened?"

"It's from long ago." He found it difficult to return to the past, away from the here and now. He opened his eyes and gazed at Emily, her flushed face, shining eyes. "As a young child, I reached up to the ironing board and the hot iron landed on my hand. I don't remember anything about it, but the burns left their marks. A warning of what happens when I put my hands where they don't belong."

"Does that precept apply today?"

"On the contrary. We belong together." He sat up and started putting on his clothes. "There are certainly plenty of obstacles ahead to keep us apart."

Emily dressed and slipped into her boots. "Yes, well. One thing more. I've argued that friendships between men and women can exist without sex. Now I don't know."

"I believe it is possible. But with us, Emily, it's different—you and me—there's something inevitable. Like the horoscope Charlotte gave you today—or was it a hundred years ago?—a force stronger than we are has us in its grip. Not theologically sound, I suppose. But God knows how much and how long I have loved you."

"Speaking of Charlotte, weren't we here to find something? Oh yes, a letter."

Emily stretched. She opened the closet door and pulled the cord hanging from a single light bulb. On a cedar chest, under a stack of old magazines was a large black family Bible. She turned the gilt-edged pages one by one.

"Look and see if there's a pocket at the back. Maybe it's there."

"Sure enough, here's an old letter with fancy cursive the way they used to write. I hope it's the one she wanted." The envelope had sepia writing and smudges of red clay. She put it in her bag.

David smoothed the bed up and raised the shades one by one. He checked the room to make sure they hadn't left anything. He lifted the latch. "Back into the world." He leaned down and kissed Emily one last time. "For whatever lies ahead."

"Afraid so. Lies. The operative word." She walked ahead of him down the stairs.

"Does that comment mean you have regrets?"

"Not at the moment, David. My feelings for you haven't changed and will not because of today. How about you?"

"How can I regret the fulfillment of my dreams? You have my love whole and entire. The challenge now will be to work out how we can be together fair and clear and open to the world."

"Good luck with that." Emily's voice had taken on a hard edge. He decided to let it go for now.

# 46

# Emily

When Emily entered the hospital room, Charlotte was propped up reading the newspaper. Her white hair looked freshly shampooed, with her characteristic combs in place to give it a wavy up-do. She glanced over half-glasses.

"You must have found it. There's a decided glow in your lovely face, Emily."

Emily held up the letter. "We found this in the back pocket of the family Bible. Hope it's the one you're looking for." She hoped, too, that the glow Charlotte mentioned would wear off by the time she returned home.

Charlotte reached into the drawer beside the bed and pulled out a slender letter opener. Of course, she'd use a silver letter opener. Emily laughed. "Did you actually bring that from home when you packed for the emergency run to the hospital?"

"Oh no, my dear. Preston graciously brought everything on my list. Or rather Natalie did." She studied the contents. "My goodness, there's a letter within a letter here. Look. Someone has added a note on lined paper and inserted it into this old one." She read silently. "I believe the sepia ink writing comes from my great aunt, Molly Daimon. Judging by the words I can

332

decipher. Something about relieving my mother's burden of indebtedness. I had heard about that from Mother years ago, that Aunt Molly paid off her house mortgage." She unfolded the notebook paper, read, and gasped.

"What is it? Are you all right?"

Charlotte handed her the note. Fred Ames had written to "My dear wife or anyone who finds this after we both are gone." Emily scanned the first paragraph. "I have failed you, dear Charlotte, and myself." She read on.

"As you can see," Charlotte said, "if I had found this letter earlier, I wouldn't have had to hire the private investigator." Her eyes were dry, her tone acerbic.

Emily read to the end where he begs forgiveness for his addiction to gambling. Then he adds, "One thing more. I made the terrible mistake of confessing my gambling habit to the young minister I helped bring to Harmony, believing I did so in confidence. As far as I know she kept the confidence, but I have paid dearly for her silence. In just three months I paid out $27,000 to her out of my retirement fund. She didn't call it blackmail and neither did I—because the money was supposed to go for a special mission. Now I suspect the special mission was herself. I have to write this down, or I can't live with myself." Emily stood up and put her coat on. "Charlotte, we must get this note to David ASAP."

"Why, oh why, did Fred have to hide the letter? Why didn't he just tell me?"

Her eyes watered. She sniffed and wiped her nose with a tissue.

"Charlotte, may I take this to David? It's important to substantiate the damage Deborah has done."

"Don't you think it's strange and ironic that Fred so carefully hid his letter inside Aunt Molly's? Hers told of paying off indebtedness, while he confesses to what has led to our indebtedness."

"Yes. Maybe the placement stresses his sense of failing you." Emily took her free hand. "I'm so sorry you're having to suffer this. May I show the note to David?"

"Please do, my dear. You may make a copy and then return it to me."

꙳

It would be late afternoon before Emily could see David. She had to tend to Ted after the therapist finished and before the home health nurse arrived. Tim had promised to cook supper, his most recent agreement for sharing responsibilities at home. That meant spaghetti or hot dogs. Emily took a stack of student essays to grade while she sat with Ted. His leonine head and now massive body filled her with a confusing mixture of revulsion and compassion. She kissed his forehead. "The therapy tired you, didn't it?"

He grunted a low "Yes. Always." He turned his head away from her. His eyes remained closed.

She switched on a tape of his favorite music—John Denver, Harry Belafonte, and some from the early eighties. Not Christmas yet. The attempt to put on Christmas tunes made him furious. She figured his frustration boiled over at the thought that he'd been incapacitated since August. Now it was already December with little improvement.

She'd call his secretary and see if she could come over with some of his case work. Angie could help him. Emily started the grading, reading rapidly through the top five essays, then doubling back to read slowly and mark them. Ted slept, snoring.

Emily's mind returned to the sleeping porch and David.

At 4:30, she left for the church with the letter. David met her in the office and immediately copied the document, returning the original to her. Judith spoke to her and went on with her typing. David asked Judith to hold his calls, that he and Emily would be in a short meeting. He led her into his study.

As soon as the door closed, David kissed her, a deep, inquiring kiss, which she answered with complete abandon, then pulled away. "Let's talk about what we're going to do," she said. She felt fidgety. Making out in the pastor's study was surreal, dangerous. Wrong.

He smoothed back his thick hair and straightened his clothes. "All right. What do you suggest?" He moved to behind his desk. "I've had a hard time concentrating. But I may have made some key decisions. What about you?"

Emily sat in the straight chair opposite the expanse of walnut desk between them. She leaned toward him. "If this were a movie or TV show, my husband would be conveniently murdered, or would die a well-timed death of natural causes. Real life, unfortunately, is more like a Chekhov story where the lovers must work out their prosaic, morally ambiguous lives as they go forward. Or maybe like Edith Wharton's *Ethan Frome*, where we're stuck with living out complicated consequences of our actions. I hope without bitterness. Without hurting those we committed ourselves to love long ago." She stood and paced, sat back down. "You asked. That's what's been going through my mind. Especially today, sitting next to my inert, angry, invalid husband, whom I cannot and will not leave."

"I hear what you're saying. I respect that." He rubbed his face as if he were scrubbing muddy water away. "Okay. Maybe we'd better discuss what to do with the letter Fred wrote. And anything else that might be brought to bear on Deborah's maneuvers." He ran his right index finger over the scarred fingers.

"I'm not sure you know this, David. At the Space for Hope in June, I found a white powder she dropped in the restroom. I think she was refilling her nasal spray with it. Charlotte and I had the powder tested by that P.I. she hired. It was cocaine. He told us that field test can't be used in court since he wasn't law enforcement."

"So you do have something on her."

"Yes, but she plays an insidious game, and has threatened to reveal something about me to Ted. Namely, that I had an abortion back in January. Plus, she no doubt has copied my journal that implies an affair with you."

"You had an abortion?" He reached across for her hand. His large hand warmed hers. "I remember how sick you were that rainy day when I got you and Natalie to meet me at Dix. That was the time?"

She nodded. If David knew all there was to know about her, he would never want to be with her. She wasn't worthy of him.

"I'm sure you had a good reason." He waited. "How has that affected you?"

"The main thing is that I had to do it, but I have grieved. So I guess I'd say that abortion should be the woman's choice, as I've always believed. Still, the aftereffects are powerful. The choice shouldn't be made casually. Enough of this. I've got to go, so let me make a suggestion."

"Certainly."

"I think there are several issues that the Session should look at, or at least the personnel committee. The letter from Fred is the closest we've got to hard evidence of Deborah's misbehavior. The cocaine use is close to hearsay. Plus, she's spread the word around that drug use is all a vicious rumor, propagated by her enemies. We'll have to have more. Mostly, I think that burning a torch and beating up a boy because the kids think he's gay in Charlotte Ames's front yard is most egregious. It's an outrageous example of Deborah's leading the young people down the wrong path. Even if she didn't instigate it, she influenced them."

"So many parents and teens have called the church about the incident. You're right that this may be the one issue to convince Deborah to drop her so-called Soldiers for Christ Movement."

"Could it be enough to get her to move out of here?"

"She'll deny that she organized it."

"What shall we do about her innuendos about us? My journal's incriminating."

"For now, nothing. She has nothing without admitting that she took your journal and copied it. That wouldn't look good, so she'll not publicize it."

"Just use it as a veiled threat. Okay. The less said the better." She rose from the chair. "David, I don't know that we can ever be together. Let me say—I will feast on the memory for a long time." She knew she'd better get out of there. She couldn't trust herself not to touch his face, his scarred hand. She left before he moved from behind his desk.

# 47

## David

Jody arrived home by train at 5:00 a.m. on Thursday, December 14. David and Millie drove across Goodwin in the dark, deserted streets. He let Millie have the wheel. She'd been practicing in parking lots on Saturdays. This was her maiden trip on downtown streets. He reassured her from time to time with quiet instructions thrown in as tactfully as he could manage. When she parked in the gravel lot near the station, she let out a "Whew." He felt the same relief but kept it to himself.

Jody looked older, taller, more self-contained than ever. Millie jumped up and down and ran to hug her sister. David waited until Jody glanced his way and then he opened his arms. She didn't exactly fly into his embrace, so he walked to her and hugged her slightly resistant body. He thought, *a lot like Nell.* "Jody, precious Jody. I'm so glad to have you home." Then he began gathering her luggage. "You must have brought everything."

"No. I left a remnant. To save my spot. Just in case." She linked arms with Millie and they climbed in the back seat. "Dad, you can chauffeur us. Millipede and I have a lot to catch up on." He drove home to the music of their chatter and laughter. *Thank you, God, for bringing her safely home again,* he prayed.

Later, after an early breakfast David walked to work. It was a frigid day with pockets of crunchable ice on the edges of the street. He remembered walking to school as a boy, in galoshes. He'd delighted in smashing thin patches of ice, splashing through muddy water up to his ankles. Back then his hat had ear flaps. He could have used something like that now. His ears ached with the cold under his cap. Periodically, he closed his gloved hands over his ears to warm them. Had he become deaf and blind to who his congregation actually was, misjudging his people and their desire to grow in the faith? He'd acted on the belief that they wanted to become God's adult children, no longer fed on archaic literalistic language. So many professionals—engineers, scientists, lawyers, and physicians—joined Harmony expressly because they liked a thinking faith. They liked what he preached and often had said so. Would they stand by him? Now perhaps more members than he realized preferred Deborah's approach and how she'd stirred the young people to campaign for what the surrounding political and social environment preferred, the ultra-conservative view. What David considered reactionary, unthinking, and unacceptable.

It was only two miles to the church. The winter wind cut through his rather thin trousers. Although he shivered, he welcomed the cold outdoors—harsh, natural, indifferent. The way of Nature, blessedly not personal. Personal confrontation and indictment would come soon enough at the afternoon meeting at the church.

When he arrived, David went first to the dark sanctuary. He sat in a pew beside the I Ams of Christ window, the jewel-like chiseled glass sprinkling the adjacent pews and floor and himself with red, blue, turquoise, purple, and yellow reflections. The Advent wreath with its stately purple, pink, and white candles stood on a slender pedestal in the nave, close to the pulpit. The majestic walnut cross loomed above the communion table, its center open orb calling his attention to Christ for all the earth.

As he had every day, morning and night, since he and Emily made love on the funny old bed in Charlotte's sleeping porch, David prayed, confessing his sin, admitting his guilt, asking for divine forgiveness. This day he also thanked God again for bringing Jody through her turmoil and restoring her to the family and to good health, hoping that indeed she was in good mental health, even if she still maintained a rather arch attitude toward everyone in the family, except Millie. Images of Emily's sweet body flashed through his mind. He also thanked God for bringing Emily into the world and into his life. He prayed for guidance. He waited in silence.

Two Psalms came to mind. Verses from Psalm 139 about God being present from before birth throughout life and even "If I make my bed in Sheol, you are there." And then Psalm 51. King David's confession and plea for cleansing became David Archer's own.

Preston Ames dropped in later to report that he had taken his mother back to her house. "She's back in her high heel Ferragamos, raring to go. And the new sycamore is in and she found the planting and the pruning of the others quite acceptable. The new men's group did a good thing."

David suggested they go somewhere for lunch before the meeting at 2:00.

Preston drove them to the small Thai restaurant not far from the church. They had the place to themselves. When Preston asked him how he was bearing up, David surprised himself by opening up about Emily. "I hope this comes under doctor-patient confidentiality, Pres." Preston reassured him that he would not say a word not even to Natalie. "If Emily tells Nat, that's up to her. She'll have to hear it from her."

They ate their curried chicken, vegetable and cashew dish with sticky rice. David liked the blue and white china, especially the round rice bowl with the opening for the blue and white serving spoon. He looked up to find Preston laughing at him. "What? So far I haven't found anything funny in this situation."

"Forgive me, but it amuses me to think that suddenly you, of all people, need forgiveness. David, you're in the Grace Business, and now you have to apply it to yourself. Ho, ho, ho. I love it."

David flushed. He felt sweat under his arms. "I guess you're right. So far I haven't made much progress in that direction, though I've tried."

"Welcome to the club, brother. The human club. It's high time."

"One thing is certain. I've had to take a hard look at some of my unexamined beliefs. Inside myself I believed I was righteous. We're taught 'The righteous shall live by faith.' Well, I must have interpreted that to mean good. If I lived by faith, then I'd be good. Maybe not perfect, but certainly good, morally good." He sipped his hot tea.

"How about right? Do you usually consider yourself always right?"

"That too." David regarded his friend. "Pretty humbling experience—this kind of guilt. One thing that keeps coming back to me is Jesus writing in the dust at the feet of the woman taken in adultery, after he's said, 'He who is without sin, cast the first stone.'"

"I've always liked that too. No one stones her, and Christ doesn't condemn her. He tells her to go and sin no more."

"Yes. Not sinning again can be difficult. The truth is I would like to be married to Emily someday. And that confession reveals a few more broken commandments." He finished off his chicken and rice.

"While we're talking about adultery and such. Although I denied it when you asked me back in the summer, I'll tell you now. Yes, Deborah seduced me. I yielded. I yielded to her wiles freely. She's a bad girl. And I enjoyed her—right there in my examining room."

"I suppose you couldn't own up to it while I was so filled with self-righteousness. Unintended, I assure you, but your revelation at this moment is instructive as well."

They finished off the rice and tea, paid and left for the church. David silently thanked God for Preston, his friendship, his truth telling.


Four men and one woman from the presbytery's Committee on Ministry were already seated in the conference room when David arrived. Not a single one of them would meet his eyes as he greeted them, shook their hands and took his place at the head of the table. He'd asked that at least two of his elders meet with them, but they had not arrived. It was five minutes until two. The man to his right rustled papers and cleared his throat. David thought he must be the chairman, a man unfamiliar to him. Maybe he should have been more active in presbytery matters. Then he'd know more of the ministers and laymen from the smaller churches surrounding Goodwin. Church politics had never appealed to David. Too late for such regrets now. He smiled at the visitors in turn and waited.

Judith came to the door. "Sorry to interrupt, but Judge Knapp is tied up in court and won't be able to attend. Dr. Preston Ames said he'll be right over. Also, Mrs. Mildred O'Bryant can't get out of her driveway. Iced in, she says." Her face registered her distress.

David thanked her. "Will you call Payton West? He retired last month. Maybe he's free this afternoon. And, Judith, would you bring us some coffee?" She agreed and quietly closed the door.

No one had much to say after a few pleasantries about the weather. The woman expressed how glad she was that they hadn't lost power over night. David thought, *But power has been lost.*

Judith returned with coffee, cream, sugar and artificial sweeteners, mugs and spoons on a tray along with Christmas cookies. David thanked her with what he hoped was his usual good cheer. The atmosphere lightened up considerably as they occupied themselves with the hot coffee and cookies.

"While we wait, why don't we introduce ourselves?" David said, gesturing toward the man to his right. "As you know, I'm Claude David Archer, pastor here at Harmony Presbyterian for the past seven years."

The others said their names and what church they served in the presbytery. The chairman said, "Reverend Troy Garland from Six Mile, been there for close to fifteen years." David wondered if Emily might be a distant relative. Her maiden name was Garland. He knew her Aunt Helen had lived in South Carolina in some small town, but Garland was her father's name of course, not Helen's. He'd better stay focused.

"Mary Beth Watkins from Gaffney, an elder," she said. The others spoke up: Reverend Benjamin A. Macatee, Honea Path church; Vann VonBerke, an elder from Gruel; Reverend Moses Trinidad, from Fair

Play. David thanked them for coming and said he knew they'd be fair and open-minded. "At least I hope you will be."

Preston opened the door, walked over to David and shook his hand, nodded to the others around the table. In an undertone to David, "You know, I've got your back."

Mary Beth Watkins spoke warmly to Preston. "He's my eye doctor. Saved my little Sara's eyes after a bad accident. Sit here, Dr. Ames, beside me, your forever grateful patient's mother."

David breathed easier. This might not be so bad after all.

Then Payton West entered. A fairly new member who moved to Goodwin after his wife died to be near his daughter's family, West had been a successful investment banker and saw his role in the church as overseeing the ways and means of spending money. A kindred soul to Julian Denyar, the treasurer. David hoped suggesting him hadn't been a bad idea. The expression on West's face made him look like he'd been called in to untangle an inferior employee's incompetent maneuvers. His thick neck above a tight collar and broad shoulders, slim waist and strong arms gave him the appearance of an aging body-builder. His set jowl to his oblong bald head radiated bluster and disgust. David shook his hand, which felt clammy, and introduced him around the circle. He gestured to the seat beside him.

"You do have a knack for names, Dr. Archer," the chairman said. "I'll give you that." The Reverend Troy Garland stacked the papers in front of him and called the meeting to order. Troy Garland, a tall, slender man in his forties carried himself with his head pitched forward followed by his shoulders rounded as if to protect his concave mid-section. Dressed in a black suit with a black sweater vest, he reminded David of a ravenous turkey vulture. The man had a difficult assignment on this day, and David hoped that he could be objective and not be swayed by the fact David's church had been alive and growing for the past seven years while Troy's church struggled on with ever decreasing numbers.

"Gentlemen and Mrs. Watkins, we are called together for the unpleasant job of assessing accusations that have been made against Dr.

David Archer by members of the Session of Harmony Church. And further, we must determine what action, if any, we would recommend to the full Committee on Ministry as well as to the Session of Harmony Church. Thank you all for taking on this responsibility." At this point, Troy passed out a memo to everyone.

David had not seen the memo until now. The treasurer and the entire Finance Committee had signed it. He was accused of absconding with the entire Pastoral Care Fund, money entrusted to the pastor for special needs within the congregation.

David almost laughed out loud. How could that be? The fund was money he as senior pastor could disburse discreetly as needed to members of the church who faced dire financial need. He knew for a fact that he had not touched any of that money for the past two years, not since Belle Thatcher's husband ran off with their children's swim coach and left Belle with nothing. The memo said absolutely nothing about differences over theology or social issues, or all the turmoil that Deborah had stirred up the past few months. David caught Preston's eye. Was he wavering in his support? Was he as surprised as David? He could read nothing in his friend's face. A blank. He looked around the table and thought he saw a hardened attitude in most faces, as if the mere mention of missing money condemned him in their eyes.

The chairman read the memo aloud, then paused, waiting. No one said anything.

"Okay, Dr. Archer, what do you have to say to this matter?" Troy Garland's eyes twinkled as if he admired someone who could pull off such a heist, at least for a while.

"This accusation states that $20,000 has disappeared. How do you account for the missing funds?"

"Sir, I cannot answer that. As far as I knew, until five minutes ago, the entire fund was intact." David spoke directly to West, "I have not used any of the Pastoral Care Fund since 1987, and that amount has been replaced. Could this be a bookkeeping error?"

"Ridiculous. The Finance Committee has been over the books and invite this committee to examine them as well." Payton West's head glowed a deeper crimson. "My question is, if you did not use up the funds, why were you not aware of who did? As senior minister, you should know what's going on in your organization. That's been my experience in business, at any rate."

The chairman thanked Payton West for his comments and asked for others to ask questions or make comments. The minister from Fair Play wiped cookie crumbs from his mouth and suggested that perhaps David Archer might consider hiring an attorney, that the situation "borders on the criminal." Vann Von Berne from Gruel cautioned a sensible response. "Surely, a church like Harmony would not let that much moolah just vanish into thin air." He paused, nodding at each person on the committee by turn, and added, "It is obvious to me that this is a shocking surprise to Reverend Archer. I think we should give him ample time to investigate on his own." The minister from Honea Path muttered, "Or escape to Costa Rica or the Grand Caymans." Then the elder from Gruel turned on him, "Nonsense. Let's give the man the benefit of the doubt." This went on for a while and finally Chairman Troy called them back to order. David looked at Preston, hoping he'd speak in his defense, willing him to offer something to help.

But it was Mary Beth Watkins who attempted a defense. "Dr. Archer, perhaps you gave out some of the special fund to people in need and you've just forgotten. I know how things, even important things, can just slip your mind when so much else in your life is troubling." She referred, no doubt, to Jody's illness, or maybe the trouble with Nell. Women had a way of keeping track of misery. She smiled at him. He tried to smile back.

Preston straightened in his seat. "Mr. Chairman, I've known David Archer for all seven years he's been here. I was on the pulpit committee that called him. He is a man of utmost integrity. I would trust my life with him." Preston spoke in a quiet tone, and with conviction. David silently thanked him for speaking up.

David lifted his hand, as if in school, and Troy Garland acknowledged him. "I would like to say that this allegation is a complete surprise to me." He turned toward Payton West and said, "You're correct, sir, I should have kept up with exactly what the financial situation was in our church instead of delegating so much to others. Since I knew that I had not used anything from the Pastoral Care Fund, I did not focus on that line item in recent financial reports. I concentrated more on pledges received and the ongoing programs and missions of Harmony church." David paused, took a sip of cold coffee. "I'd like the opportunity to ferret out exactly what has happened and schedule another meeting to report what I find to you."

Before the chairman could suggest that such a motion be made, Moses Trinidad from Fair Play said, "I move that this committee admonish Dr. David Archer for the loss of $20,000 unaccounted for, as reported in said memorandum from the Harmony session. I further move that the committee recommend that Dr. Archer seek another position and take an immediate leave of absence, pending investigation of the missing funds."

Troy Garland asked and got a second to the motion from Macatee of Honea Path. Mary Beth Watkins amended the motion that David Archer be allowed to remain through January and then take a leave of absence. "In the spirit of Christmas, don't you know." And Vann Von Berke seconded the amendment. Mrs. Watkins held up her hand, and said, "Remember we must vote on the amendment first."

The discussion that followed left David's head spinning. He found it impossible to believe that he could be falsely accused and then, before he could get to the bottom of what happened, be forced out of his church. The last word was spoken by his own elder, Payton West, who posed the question, "How can you as a committee ignore the report of the Harmony finance committee and the church's treasurer?"

The committee voted for the amendment and then voted on the motion. That vote ended in a tie, which the chairman broke by voting for the amendment. Mary Beth Watkins and Vann Von Berke, both the laymen, voted against the motion. The chairman stated that this decision would have to go to the full Committee on Ministry before it would become the official recommendation for action, but he advised David to begin the process of leaving Harmony Church. "Assuming the motion passes the full committee next month, you will soon be relieved of your position. And, David, I suggest you hire a good attorney."

Preston was the last person to leave the room and asked if he wanted him to stay and David said no, that he needed to think about what happened. They agreed to meet after work at The Mug.

David sat alone in the conference room. Deborah Baker must have been at the root of what happened. He didn't know exactly how she'd done it, but he meant to find out. His friend Jonathan was right when he'd warned, "There's a snake in every garden."

He laid his head on the cool walnut conference table and tried to pray. No words came. No answer either. Nothing. He let the reality of what had just transpired enter his consciousness. The faces of the people, their accusations cloaked in customary Presbyterian decorum. Would it have been different if Mildred O'Bryant had been there, not iced in? Instead of Payton West? Probably not. There seemed to be an inevitability to the outcome. Still, he had to find out where the money had gone, who was behind this and how to clear his name.

Judith walked in. "Oh, I'm sorry to interrupt your thoughts, Dr. Archer. Just want to retrieve the coffee things." She gave him her worried look.

"It's fine, Judith. Go right ahead. I appreciate your bringing something to break the ice, so to speak." He pulled himself up and straightened his suit jacket. "I'll be in my study working on my sermon."

At his desk, he jotted a list. He had only four weeks to preach before the motion would go before the full COM. Sermon ideas that had been kicking around in his notebook came to mind. The words of the chairman, Troy Garland came to mind. He needed a lawyer. The best lawyer he knew was Ted Parks, now felled by the devastating stroke. Still, Emily had said that Ted could communicate in a limited way. It would be difficult seeing

Emily again. Now he needed Ted's help. How ironic. David took a deep breath and called.

"Oh, David," she said. "Hi. Funny you should call. You read my mind, as you have a way of doing. Ted is terribly restless and wants to see you."

"Tell him I want to see him as well. Tell him I need his legal help. I'll be at your house in ten minutes."

He grabbed his notebook and his coat. Then he remembered that he'd walked to the church and would have to go get his car. It would take longer. He asked Judith to phone them back and say it would be more like thirty minutes and walked out into the cold weather.

The meeting with Ted took the utmost in patience. For both of them. David explained all that had transpired at the COM subcommittee meeting, the accusation, and the time limit of one month until the issue would be brought to the full Committee on Ministry. Ted showed no expression, but Emily reminded him that he could not show affect. He seemed to be listening and following, but his responses were sluggish. Basically, David needed to know what he should do and what options were open to him. At Ted's request, Emily stayed in the room. Ted's speech was halting and seemed to take all his energy. Emily handed him his small board and marker and suggested he write out what he needed to say. Using his left hand, he listed what David should do. "First, you have to get help. Call Preston to line up the treasurer for an interview and a look at the books by my CPA."

To Emily, he said, "Call friends. Have them over here tomorrow." Ted tried to straighten up. David and Emily got on either side and lifted his upper body. Ted turned his head toward David and in a hoarse whisper said, "We'll do this. We'll find out who's responsible. And. Clear. Your. Name." He reached across with his good hand and caught David's forearm. "Thank you. Thank you for thinking I can help you. Or anyone any more."

David assured him that he was the best.

Emily walked him to the door. "You know, David, he's right. You've given him quite a boost by asking for his help. Thank you. I'll call some people right away."

He found it hard to leave the doorway. "Didn't Charlotte Ames hire a private eye not long ago? Maybe we could get him to investigate what happened to the money."

"I'll ask her to bring him tomorrow. David, this is all terrible. It's unfair. And I'm convinced that Deborah is behind it. Is that too awful to say?"

David held her gaze. It took all his strength not to take her in his arms. Instead he took her hands in his. "First, we'll investigate. Then we'll see what to do and who is responsible. I share your suspicions. But she would have had to forge the checks."

He left before either of them could do or say anything else.

# 48

## David

Friday, David arrived at the church early. After time in the dark sanctuary, he went immediately to his desk. He kept the checkbook for the Pastoral Care account in a locked drawer. The bank statements with canceled checks were there too. Because he hadn't needed to use it in so long, he'd let the bank statements come in and hardly looked at them, simply chunked them into the drawer. Now he studied the statements from the last six months. Checks for several hundred dollars at a time showed his signature, paid to the order of an elderly member of the church. He didn't know her well, but remembered that Esther Piermont, a widow, suffered from dementia and lived in a care facility. Deborah called on her. He looked back at his checkbook and found no recording of these checks. Thumbing through the blank checks, he counted eight missing. Not in any order but scattered through the book.

David called Ted and told him what he'd found so far. Emily got on the phone and said that Preston was to meet the CPA at lunch and that Charlotte had talked to Irv Wolfe, who would get right to work. The rehearsal for Coy and Brad's wedding would be at 4:00. David suggested that they all meet in his study between the rehearsal and the dinner. Emily said she'd notify everyone.

David went deeper into the bank statements, studying the canceled checks from 1987 and the records of deposits to replace the money used to help Belle Thatcher. Then he advanced to disbursements after Deborah Baker came on staff and studied the signatures on the checks, pulling out a magnifying glass. He supposed his signature would be easy to copy. He wrote his name on a pad five different times and then compared the writing with the canceled checks. An expert would be needed to prove the difference, although he knew his writing slanted more to the right than to the left as the signatures on the checks did. He'd ask the private investigator about this.

He turned his attention to his sermon. For the third Sunday of Advent, he was slated to preach on "The Miraculous in the Midst of the Mundane." He practiced reading aloud what he'd written. His heart wasn't in it. Too many conflicting feelings bombarded his mind—shock, anger, puzzlement, disgust with himself for being too trusting of Deborah, and the undercurrent of turmoil over Emily.

He paced. He went back to his script. The words drew him in. The miraculous it seemed to him was that God could and would make His Presence known in the mundane life of ordinary people. Joseph, deciding to put Mary aside quietly (rather than divorcing his pregnant betrothed and having her stoned, according to the Jewish law in the first century), listened to the message from his dream, believing that God was speaking to him through it. Mary herself accepting the amazing announcement from the angel. The shepherds and the wise men from the East. He put his hands on the cool window glass and gazed out at the bare trees and cloudy sky and prayed, "*O God, help me, your sinful servant, see and believe the way Joseph and Mary did that you continue to be present and reveal yourself—if we have eyes to see and a heart that trusts. I need help trusting that you will see me through this trouble, that you will work for the good of all the people involved for this segment of your Church.*"

Now he had to find Deborah. She had managed to vacate the premises for a week of "educational leave" after Macon had been bullied and tied to the sycamore tree. She'd also managed to avoid him since her return. Judith located her at the Space for Hope and David asked her to return to the church by 2:00.

At exactly 2:00 p.m. Deborah breezed into the church office. Judith showed her into his study. Deborah waved her away. "Thank you, my dear Judith."

Judith mumbled something that sounded to David like, "I'm not your dear."

He laughed. Deborah laughed. "Well, come in," he said. "Tell me what you've done to rectify the situation with the young people and Macon Collier and Charlotte Ames."

"That's one situation you don't need to trouble your head over, Reverend Doc."

She perched on the arm of the sofa. Deborah wore a dark blue suit and dark hose with matching dark blue heels. She crossed her legs and dangled one shoe on her toes. "At the meeting with the Senior Highs, I told them I believed the demonstration went too far. We met yesterday afternoon to write a letter to Macon and one to Charlotte, expressing regret that such a thing happened."

"So the group is taking responsibility for the bullying and the burned tree?"

"Not exactly. The group is writing to apologize for whoever the people were under those ski masks, admitting nothing. A gesture of good will, you might say."

"Has anyone told you who took part?"

"The nature of that kind of demonstration is that it's anonymous, so we'll never know for sure, will we?" She stood, replaced her shoe. "It's my understanding that the police questioned Macon, but he said he couldn't identify the boys."

David added, "We know Rivers Carlton wasn't involved since the gang knocked him out for trying to stop them. Or that's the report Charlotte received. He didn't identify them either."

Deborah walked to the door. "Not surprising. No one likes a snitch. I encouraged all the young people to help Mrs. Ames in the yard or wherever. That ought to placate the parents who were needlessly upset, and maybe keep Charlotte from suing over her precious trees."

"Deborah, Charlotte Ames has no intention of suing. I'm not sure what Macon's mother might do. She's understandably very upset. While you were away, I spent the better part of two days with Mrs. Collier and Macon. The main point is that Charlotte and I and many of the parents and youth are alarmed that such hatred and prejudice were demonstrated. It's time for your Movement to cease."

"No problem. We're wrapping that up anyway. It's served its purpose." She posed in the doorway for a minute. "Well, I'm off to call on the sick and the infirm."

David restrained himself. It was hard to believe how cavalier she sounded. He wasn't ready to confront her about the money. "Deborah, I expect you to attend the next staff meeting."

"Yes, sir. I'll be there." She saluted and sashayed out.

Next David went into the inner office where the financial secretary worked and closed the door. He explained the situation to Maria, who blanched, and told him she had no idea that's what Julian Denyar and the finance committee had been up to when they'd asked for all the details of the account David had charge of. She reminded him that she had no responsibility for the Pastoral Care account and had left all those records entirely up to him.

"No one's blaming you, Maria. I'm simply trying to ascertain how the funds disappeared when I have not touched them." He studied her face. A delicate row of sweat beads appeared along her hairline. "I'm hoping you can tell me if anyone else has accessed the account."

"No, sir. Not to my knowledge."

She scratched her head. "One day Myra Owen came in with Deborah to ask about the designated fund for the Family Values symposium. She and I spent some time figuring on that. It's the one Payton West contributed to. He said he preferred to give to that because of Deborah than give to the annual budget."

David suppressed a groan. "If much of that goes on, we'll not make our budget. We need our wealthy contributors to keep faith with the total program of the church."

"Yes, sir. Anyway, while I worked with Myra, Deborah left. I assumed to go to her office, but she might have—you know—gone into your study, or something."

"Thank you, Maria. Please keep me informed of anything you learn or remember that might help." David patted her gently on her broad shoulder.

The group of friends and the private investigator gathered in David's study. Preston was all business and took over as unofficial chairman. Natalie, as mother of the bride, was antsy, fretting that they might be late for the rehearsal dinner at the club. David urged her to go ahead, that he'd drive Preston over when they finished. Natalie left. Charlotte introduced Irv Wolfe to them, in case they'd not met him at her party. Irv asked about where the checkbook was kept. When David showed him the locked drawer, Irv went right to work with his fingerprint powder and brush. Everyone watched with fascination as he pressed sticky tape on the impressions. He asked if he might take David's fingerprints, "so as to rule out yours from this collection." David chuckled and complied.

Preston reported on the lunch with Ted's CPA, Robert Humphrey. He wasn't a member of Harmony church and that could be a decided advantage, for objectivity. Emily took notes, hardly looking up from her notebook. David opened the drawer and let Irv dust for prints on the checkbook. "By the way," Irv said, "You don't keep your key in a secure place. Anyone could find it in two minutes, max."

"I guess I trusted everyone. Didn't really think about it." David pointed out that the missing funds were not included on the Session's finance report until the current month. "I looked back over the past three months, and nothing showed up. Someone waited to pull this stunt all at once."

The CPA, Preston said, would be talking to the bank. Irv Wolfe said he had ways to track down whether the old lady received any more of the money. They all agreed to meet on Monday the 18th at Ted and Emily's. David thanked everyone. "I need all the help I can get."

# 49

## Millie

Millie hardly believed her good fortune. Jody asked her into her room to help her dress for the wedding. Jody's bridesmaid dress hung from the molding above the closet door. A teal taffeta with a sweetheart neckline and pouffy sleeves, the fitted bodice came to a vee at the waist with a full swishy skirt. She had pumps that were dyed teal to match the dress. Millie watched her dress, handing her things when she asked.

"I want you to see something, Millipede." Jody stretched her bare arms out for Millie's inspection. "See, I haven't cut myself for three months and nine days. Not once."

"Oh, Jody. That's great. You know I never told anyone."

"I know. I trust you."

"What about the sleeves on the dress?"

"Coy gave us all a choice. Short pouffy sleeves or long sleeves with the pouf near the shoulders, like her dress. I chose long. Just in case. So no scars would show." She stood before the long mirror in her bra and pantyhose. "Now, hand me the dress and help me into it without messing up my hair."

Millie lifted the dress over her sister's head and stepped back. "You look beautiful."

"Something else I want to tell you." Jody stopped and turned from the mirror to Millie. "Any time I think I have to cut or I'll burst, your face comes to mind, with those hurt-child blue eyes." She looked back at herself in the mirror. "You don't know it, Millipede, but you helped save me. Or as therapist Amy would say, you helped me save myself." She walked over to her book bag, her taffeta swishing. "I brought you something. It's for Christmas, but I want you to have it now." She handed Millie the collected poems of Gerard Manley Hopkins. "Your man, Hopkins. He's not half bad. He knew some rough times himself."

Millie hugged her sister. "Thank you, Jody. How's your teacher, Mr. Strayer?"

Jody tried to step into her shoes but couldn't manage it. She sat in the chair and stuck out her foot. Millie knelt and put each dyed heel on. "I feel like a shoe salesman."

"I'd never willingly buy these things. They kill my feet. And they're basically hideous. Mr. Strayer actually got me reading some way-out stuff by this scientist-priest whose work was suppressed by the catholic church during his lifetime. Pierre Teilhard de Chardin, a French guy who went to China as an archeologist. You'd love his ideas of the 'Cosmic Christ.' He believed that God in Christ is himself evolving as God continues the awesome creation of the universe."

"Wow. You sound like the philosopher now."

"Well, I don't understand half of what I read. Mr. Strayer explains it some."

"Jody, sit at your dressing table and I'll put on the piece for your hair. It's lovely."

"Coy wanted to have real flowers in the little coronets, but these are life-like enough and won't fall apart." Jody turned this way and that, satisfied.

"Dearly beloved, we are gathered together in His name to unite this man and this woman in holy matrimony," David intoned. Millie watched him with pride. Every Sunday she heard him, but somehow on this occasion, her dad looked taller, more erect and surer of himself than usual. Rivers sat beside her. That also filled her with happiness. Lyn on her other side, then her mother. She glanced down the row. Surprisingly, Deborah Baker sat on the other side of her mom with her arm around her shoulder as if to give comfort or protection.

Millie punched Lyn and gestured toward them. "What's that about?" she whispered.

Lyn whispered back, "Deborah must have gotten to her."

"Shh-h, girls." Nell frowned, her eyebrows high.

As the ceremony ended, Coy and Brad beamed as they walked up the aisle, followed by the attendants paired up. Jody smiled at Millie as she and her partner walked in step to the vestibule.

The wedding reception at the Goodwin Country Club provided a chance for rumors to fly around, table to table, at the buffet tables, and on the dance floor after the bride and groom danced with each other and then with their parents. Millie and Rivers danced. She didn't know the contents of the gossip, but she could tell something was up. As she and Rivers waltzed near a table, the people stopped talking and watched as they circled away.

"Am I paranoid, or are people talking about us?" Rivers spoke into her hair over her ear. She liked the feeling of his lips so close.

"Probably not so much about us. Maybe about Dad. And Mom. See over there, Mom's sitting on the sidelines with Deborah beside her."

"Yeah, so?"

"Well, my parents separated during the fall. Dad stayed at home, though. He started sleeping in his study on the third floor—the attic really. They'll probably divorce some day. I don't know. It makes me sad."

Rivers twirled her around and dipped, as the music stopped. He walked her out to the enclosed porch. "Please don't be sad. I'm going to get us some lemonade. Sit here. Don't move." He loped through the double doors.

She stretched her legs out. Her feet hurt. She eased the high heels off and wiggled her toes covered by sheer blue hose. Her dress was an electric blue taffeta with a fitted bodice and full skirt, an echo of the bridal outfits. Her mother had lent her an evening bag, small and silvery. Millie had put in her lipstick, a Tampax, and a tissue. Now she explored the contents. A small satin pocket held a card from The Sanctuary at Kiawah. Nell must have used it when she and her dad spent Labor Day weekend there. A phone number was written on the back in an angular hand she didn't recognize. She remembered hearing her dad say he wished Nell were a happier person. So did Millie—wish her mother were happier. She'd worked hard to please her, to make good grades, to interpret Jody's outbursts to their mother, to make peace. Jody was right to call her the Peacemaker in the family. She recalled how her father once had said to her—"You're in the beatitudes—'Blessed are the peacemakers, for they shall be called children of God.'" That comment alone had created a place for her to be. She hoped Jody was finding her own special place now.

Rivers returned empty-handed. "Come on, Mill. Let's dance. They're playing some good music now."

"My lemonade?" She struggled into her heels and stood.

"Oh, sorry. Guess I forgot. Deborah needed me. Let's get out there."

Millie saw that a new music group had started playing. Wyman Denyar and the Hardhats. They played "I'm Your Boogie Man" and after that "Play That Funky Music, White Boy." Millie and Rivers danced until they were both sweating, singing, and laughing.

"Love this old seventies music, don't you?" Rivers yelled.

When they finally sat down again, she asked him what Deborah had wanted.

Rivers didn't answer directly. He looked away from her into the middle distance. Not a good sign, she thought.

"What is it, Rivers? What's wrong?"

"She spoke to me confidentially. So I don't know what I can say."

"Come on, Rivers. What's on her mind?"

"It's not good. You'll be mad." He pulled out a handkerchief and wiped his face. "Come on, back to the porch." He held her hand. His hand felt different and sort of clammy.

"Okay, spill it." She looked directly into his eyes, such an unusual shade of light brown. Dreamy eyes. Creek-water green/brown.

He looked away and then back to her. "Millie, she implied that your father, our highly esteemed minister (as she put it), may have gotten someone pregnant. And she had an abortion early in the year."

"That is insane. Not my father. He'd never do that. I don't believe it."

"She told me, in confidence, that she knows for a fact that Emily Parks went to the abortion clinic in January. Deborah went with her."

"Sure, they went to the clinic and so did another member of the church and good friend—Natalie Ames, the mother of the bride. They protested the protesters. It was on TV news."

"Deborah Baker protested the anti-abortionists? Really? That must have been before I joined the group."

"Yep. Then she saw the light, so she said." Millie paced around the porch. Christmas lights in the shape of hot peppers flashed on and off around the expanse of windows. "Why would she spread such a malicious rumor? With no basis in fact. Emily and Ted Parks have been friends with my parents forever."

"Do you think that could have been what people were yakking about when we saw them stop talking?"

"Dunno. What else did she want?"

"Not much. She asked me to dance with your big sister. Deborah said that Jody could use a friend, since she just returned from what she called the mental facility."

"So did you?"

"Did I what?"

"Dance with Jody?

"Sure. That's what took so long. She's pretty just like Deborah pointed out, but she didn't have much to say." He walked along with Millie. "Let's cut out of here."

They walked out the side door of the porch into the cold night. "There's Orion's belt. I always look for it on a clear night." He put his arm around her and pointed to the stars.

"Deborah also said something else I know you won't appreciate, and I thought was totally uncalled for and not true."

"Okay. Out with it." Millie faced him. She liked how tall he was, the tallest boy she'd ever dated. Really, just the second guy she'd ever dated.

"When she urged me to dance with Jody, Deborah said something about you not being any more sophisticated than your naïve father and that if you didn't dye your hair, you'd be rather plain, didn't I think so. I said you're not plain at all, and I walked away. That's when I danced with Jody. One dance."

"She's trying to hurt me for some reason. What is that all about?"

"Whatever she intended, it backfired with me. Come here, you." He led her to the evergreen trees and kissed her. A long perfect kiss. In that moment, all the rotten stuff she'd heard dissolved out into the cold night air, up to Orion's belt and away.

# 50

## David

When David arrived at Emily and Ted's house, he saw by the cars that Preston and Natalie, Charlotte, and Irv Wolfe had already come. Tim met him at the door.

"Out for Christmas, are you, Tim?"

"Yes, sir. Come in. Everyone's in the den. Alexander and I moved Dad in there."

David followed Tim down the hall. The aroma of hot cider drifted toward him. Multi-colored Christmas lights shone from the corner of the den. Emily had a fire going in the fireplace. "Everything looks festive. Too bad this isn't a holiday party."

"Yes, sir. My dad wants me to tell you and everyone what I told him last night. So I hope it's okay for me to be in the meeting."

"No problem. Please join us." David admired the tall, thin young man. He had his mother's dark hair and fair skin. His older brother Tom looked more like Ted with golden bushy hair, tawny complexion, and large build. "Is your brother back from college yet?"

"He's supposed to be here, but stayed in Charleston to work another week at the hotel. He's a part-time bellhop. Needs the tips, I guess." He gestured to the empty straight chair near the fireplace.

Emily hopped up from a hassock and greeted him. "Good morning, David. How about some hot cider?" She moved to the table and ladled out a steaming cupful, added a cinnamon stick, and handed it to him.

He thanked her, searching her eyes. She'd dropped an invisible veil between them since he'd consulted Ted for legal advice. The distance might be justified, but he felt shut out. He accepted the cup and walked around speaking to each person, stopping at Ted's side. "Thank you, friend. I hope you're feeling up to this." He took Ted's good left hand in his.

Ted nodded and spoke. "I've asked Preston to moderate."

Preston took over the meeting, calling first on Irv Wolfe. The P.I. reported that there were other fingerprints on the drawer and the checkbook, and that those belonged to Deborah Baker. "At least, that's her name now." He then went on to say that the checks supposedly for the widow with Alzheimer's had been endorsed in a shaky hand, but that "only the first one in the sum of $258 had in fact been given to the widow in question." Her companion at the time remembered the visit with Deborah and identified her from the photo, said she was "utterly charming," but there had been no other visits.

Preston thanked him and asked Tim to report what he told Ted. Tim cleared his throat and said, "This may not be anything important, but at one of our Senior High meetings, Deborah got to showing off. She had us each write our names three times on a piece of paper and pass them to her. Then she showed us how she could copy any and all of them perfectly. And, by God, she did it. I still have mine somewhere."

Emily laughed. "Don't try to dig it out of the junk in your room. You'd be at it for a month, I imagine."

Natalie stood and walked to Tim. "This could be crucial. If you can find that piece of paper, we might be able to use it to show the COM sub-committee. Maybe you should go look, even if it takes a while."

"Will do." Tim waited for his father's dismissal. Ted nodded. Tim left to hunt.

"Forgery, drug use, blackmail, stealing—this is juicy stuff." Irv turned toward Charlotte. "I never expected so much good stuff from a church. Presbyterian, especially."

"Believe me, we didn't either," David said. "Now, what shall we do?" He looked around the circle. "All of you are dear friends. I depend on your good judgment."

"Deborah doesn't have to know, does she?" Charlotte said, "that what evidence we have can't be used in court. We could meet with her and imply that she's in major trouble. Legal trouble." She turned toward Irv. "By the way, how did you obtain Deborah's fingerprints?"

Irv shrugged. "Simple. They're on record. Seems she trades in her name for another one the way some people buy new cars. She's had at least three entirely different names over her scant thirty-three years." He crossed his leg over his knee and thumped the side of his boot. "Must be hiding something."

Emily looked up from her notepad. "A lot of people in the congregation are crazy about Deborah. They'll rebel if she's asked to leave."

Preston stood by the fireplace. "That may be true, Emily. We're here to clear David's name. If that means bringing charges against Deborah to the Session and then presbytery's COM, so be it."

David listened to all of them, one by one, studying their faces as if he were seeing them again after long absence. How fortunate to have friends who would stand by him no matter what. He knew what he had to do. He leaned forward. "Thank you. Here's what I think. I must meet with Deborah and work out a plan that will be best for Harmony church, for everyone concerned."

Ted struggled to speak. "David. Take. Someone. With. You. My CPA. Preston. Witness."

David knew that ordinarily he should take his attorney with him. Deborah might have someone with her, too. Julian Denyar and Myra Owen, probably. Preston had met with Robert Humphrey, but the CPA wouldn't have the figures from the bank exec until later in the week. David wanted to see if he could work things out with Deborah before Christmas, but it might not be possible.

Emily said, "David, what if Ted sends a letter to the head of the COM sub-committee as your legal counsel? I'll type it for him. He could state who's working on tracking down the missing $20,000 and when such a report will be ready for their consideration. It will show due diligence and the fact that Robert's not a member of the church and can be objective."

"That sounds good to me," David said. Still he felt strongly that he had to talk to Deborah. And he hadn't confronted Nell with the news from the COM either.

The group disbanded close to 11:00 a.m. and David headed to the church.

David paced his office and then came to a decision. He filled out the Personal Information Forms to seek a new position, just in case. Then he called Jonathan Savant and asked him to be a reference. He phoned Preston who also agreed to be a reference. The forms went into the mail to the General Assembly headquarters that afternoon. At 2:00 p.m. he went to Deborah's office.

"To what do I owe this visit, Reverend Doc?" Deborah's voice possessed a nervous edge.

"I'd like to talk to you candidly before a committee meets with you, Deborah."

"That sounds forbidding. Come in. Sit down."

David closed the door and stood beside her desk. Deborah remained standing also. He told her about the fingerprints on his checkbook and commented on the timing of the treasurer's report about the missing funds.

"Don't you remember urging me to help the less fortunate in our congregation?" Deborah lifted her big eyes, blinking back tears. "All I did was save you a little time and effort. After all, you and Nell were going through so much stress. With Jody. And your marriage."

"Deborah, save all that for a more sympathetic audience. I'm on to you. Now, thanks to you, my ministry is on the line."

"How can you think so ill of me? You're the master of always seeing things from the other person's perspective. How about my perspective?"

"Deborah, I have a difficult time doing that with you. What is your view?"

"My view? Well, let's see. I think I have the support of many important people in Harmony church. They have money and they prefer what I'm advocating."

"Here's my view. Your efforts are causing disharmony in the church we've been commissioned to serve. And I do believe I understand something of your mindset. So let me outline for you some of the charges that may very well be brought against you." David ran through the list Irv Wolfe had named so blithely.

Deborah's face paled and tightened. She sat down at her desk. For just a moment she seemed to be stymied. But only for a moment. She straightened her back. "And what about you and your precious paramour? I doubt you want that getting out."

"You are a worthy adversary, Deborah. I'll grant you that. Here's what we're going to do." He proceeded to outline a plan of action, then waited for her agreement.

"I'll let you know," she said.

"Good enough," he said and walked out. He walked outside into the cold December weather, breathing deeply. Ready for whatever the future might hold.

At home that evening, he found Nell in her dressing room, applying make-up. She saw him in the mirror and turned away, reaching for her robe. "I'm going out. You can have the house to yourself," she said, her voice hard.

"Nell, I need to talk to you before you leave."

"I have nothing to say to you. And I already know everything you're going to say. Your lovely associate, Deborah Baker, has kept me informed, since she correctly deduced that you were not doing so." She dropped her eyelash curler in the drawer and slammed the drawer shut. "By the way, you were correct. Back in the fall. We should separate. You have desecrated our marriage with one of our friends. Little Emily in Little Rock. What in the world does Ted think of that? If he doesn't know yet, he soon will."

"Nell, please. Listen. I'm sorry. But we did not do anything in Little Rock. You must be referring to Emily's journal, which simply expressed feelings, not actions. Deborah got hold of it and drew her own conclusions. Erroneously." He knelt down beside her. "It is true that more recently I did cross the line. And I do confess that I love Emily Parks. But we will not be together again. We have both sworn it."

"How gullible do you think I am? As gullible as you, perhaps? That's what Deborah thinks—that you are hopelessly naïve, a permanent innocent, easily preyed upon. In short, a fool." She spit out the words, as if to rid herself of something foul.

"Dear Nell, please." David looked around the dressing room. The brief feeling of release he'd known after meeting with Deborah had evaporated. On the wall beside her magnifying mirror was a photograph of Lyn playing the flute. Next, a picture showed Millie and Jody playing with Calvin. There was no picture of him. She'd eliminated him.

"Please excuse me, so I can finish dressing." She got up and stood at the door waiting.

"Okay, Nell. This fool is leaving." David took one more glance at her. "You look pretty, Nell. Have a good time." He left.

# 51

## David

Early Sunday on the last day of 1989, David Archer drove to Harmony Presbyterian Church with all three daughters. The streets were treacherous with the possibility of black ice. When they entered the building, David directed the girls to his study where they would wait until Sunday school time. He went into the sanctuary to sit for a while. The organist practiced and the women arranging the poinsettias carried on without disturbing him.

David contemplated the I Am window. At the apex, an open door with chiseled glass Chi Rho and a cross in the center. The door was wide and open. "I am the Way, the Truth, and the Life." That was the scripture the designer had in mind, but the verse that came to David's mind was from Revelation. He looked up the reference in the pew Bible he vaguely remembered: *"I know your works. Look, I have set before you an open door, which no one is able to shut. I know that you have but little power, and yet you have kept my word and have not denied my name."* He reread the verse and stared at the door with Christ filling the opening. A thrill ran through his body. He sought confirmation. His answer had come. He thanked God and left the sanctuary, confident in his decision. Now he had to meet the Session.

The elders gathered for the routine brief Session meeting after Sunday school and right before the worship service, usually to receive and approve new members or children to be baptized, to hear news of members who were in the hospital or had died. On this the last day of 1989, David told the assembled that he had something he wanted them to approve and then it would be taken to the congregation for a vote after the two weeks' waiting period required in the Book of Church Order. The elders regarded each other with questioning looks, but no one had heard anything in advance.

"After much prayer and thought, I have come to the realization that it is time for my tenure with you to come to an end. Therefore, I ask you to approve the severing of our relationship, contingent upon the agreement of the congregation, and approval by the Presbytery. Likewise, what I ask for myself and my pastorate here at Harmony, I also request on behalf of our associate pastor, Deborah Baker, who has already moved away, as of yesterday. She has drafted a letter which I will give to the Clerk of Session and ask your approval of her request as well as mine." David saw the stunned expressions around the table.

The table buzzed with questions and statements of appreciation for David. And some, among them Myra Owen, cried. Myra said, between sobs, "How could she move away? She didn't say a word to me. I thought we were close."

Charlotte asked David, "Where are you going? Where has Deborah gone?"

He said, "First of all, I'm not sure where Deborah is at the moment. She has expressed the desire to return to grad school for more education, particularly in the field of psychology. And someone in the congregation has made substantial scholarship money available for her to do that." He let the anonymous gift to Deborah soak in before he answered about himself.

Julian Denyar harrumphed. "I have a feeling she'll land on her feet. Some prophet, leaving the field of battle without a word to anyone. And you, sir. I have to say, once you were exonerated by the COM from the financial problem, you've conducted yourself in a most responsible manner. As far as I can tell, the only notation on the report of the COM sub-committee will be a mild reprimand for not properly supervising the disbursement of the discretionary funds entrusted to you."

David smiled at the picture of a prophet on a battlefield. He thanked Julian and explained that he had sent out his Personal Information Form and would be looking for a call. "In the meantime, I hope we can all pull together for the good of our church." Then he called for a motion and a second, and the session voted to accept his and Deborah's requests. He said that he would serve as moderator and pastor until the congregational vote was taken.

His final sermon of the year had been in the works for weeks. With the most recent developments, however, what he had to say had grown more urgent. David looked out at his congregation with such a strong mixture of love and regret, he was afraid for a minute he'd choke up. He took a deep breath and let the anticipation for a new life fill him. Charlotte Ames sat in her usual pew, dabbing her eyes, and nodding her encouragement. Emily sat between Tom and Tim. He smiled at them and at Preston and Natalie. Their son was home from boarding school, his head bent over a sketchpad. Judge Knapp yawned. Millie and Lyn had placed Jody between them and somehow persuaded her to sit down close. David caught Julian's eye and nodded. Julian touched his forehead in a salute.

"This year in the Chinese calendar has been 'the year of the snake,'" David began. "The snake, or serpent as it's called in the book of Genesis, has long been for the Judeo-Christian culture a symbol of temptation, evil, of turbulence, exile from the Garden. Anyone who has kept up with the news of the world will affirm that 1989 has been a year of upheaval, disturbance, and drastic change. Natural disasters and those which were man-made have plagued us.

"In March, the Exxon *Valdez* oil spill caused massive pollution in Alaskan wilderness and a long, expensive clean up. In June, what had been a largely peaceful student demonstration in China became a violent massacre by the Chinese government. Tiananmen Square conjures pictures of ruthless violence by the military against their own people. In September we experienced Hurricane Hugo and its costly aftermath, followed soon by the destruction of the San Francisco earthquake.

"While all that devastation continued, other drastic changes have transformed the world for good, for freedom. Just last month, the wall separating East from West Germany was breached. Remember when President Reagan called for the communist regime to 'tear down this wall.' Every day now more of the wall is being hacked away. Some of you have actually chiseled a portion and brought back a piece for me. More and more people of Europe can move around freely. Communist power so feared for decades is waning. The regimes in Romania, Czechoslovakia, Poland are rocked by change toward freedom from tyranny."

He bowed his head. "Yes, the year of the snake is marked by turbulent change."

With a deep breath, he glanced at his friends in the congregation. "Closer to home, we have experienced the year of the snake. Many of you have felt the sting and shock of sudden change. A diagnosis of terminal illness, loss of job, a death in the family. Certainly, my family and I have felt the tremors of change. This year, 1989, altered my perceptions, shook me out of complacency, blindness to the needs of loved ones. Transformed me. I have witnessed how prayerful, faithful people can help one another. During the Hugo disaster, our people along with many from all over South Carolina and other states helped restore homes and property. I have personally felt your loving support during Jody's illness. We are thankful to have her restored and home. Of course, off she'll go again soon to college, but for the moment she's here with us.

"The year of the snake can be seen as dreadful and troubling, certainly disruptive of our usual life. Even senselessly cruel. We make mistakes that affect cherished relationships. Sins of omission and commission cut and wound others.

"But the year of the snake can also be seen as transformative. Change produces opportunity. Our associate minister, Deborah Baker, shook up our way of seeing current issues. Certainly, my way of looking at the issues was shaken and I reexamined my principal stands, and reaffirmed them. Now she has left us to seek further education. While I found her disconcerting in some ways, I value the challenges she offered me. I believe God brings people to us who can teach us something we need to learn.

"An important lesson I needed to learn is that a disruptive year, as this one has been for me, has the power to break me open to receive the new. The snake in other cultures is a symbol of new life. Just as the snake sheds its skin to make way for growth, so I hope this year will prove to be one of new growth for each of us. The writer of Ephesians urges us to 'grow up into the fullness of knowledge of Jesus Christ.' Let us all pray for growth into the people God intends us to become—part of God's new creation. Thanks be to God. Amen."

As David spoke to people after the service, he could tell that word of his plans and the session's action had already spread. Handshakes were firmer, hugs longer, and the words of gratitude seemed to be spoken with genuine feeling. Nothing perfunctory, not to him.

He didn't have to wait long for a personal backlash. Jody stood in line and when she got to him, she hugged him and spoke ferociously in his ear, "Why did you have to talk about me in your sermon? Don't you want me ever to come back?"

"Darling girl, I had to say something. Of course I want you here with me in church."

He walked to the coat rack and helped her on with her coat. She flipped up the hood.

"Dad, you know what? Your sermon made me think. I still don't know why bad things happen, but you didn't really address that, did you?"

"No, I suppose not. The question of why remains one of life's great mysteries."

⚡

# Epilogue

## Ozark Retreat Center
## Petit Jean Mountain, Arkansas

On a fine day in the middle of May, 1992, David's office phone rang. A man who identified himself as the head of a large psychological clinic in Tucson—Dr. Douglas Elford—said that David had been listed as a reference for one Vivian Monroe.

"Who?" The hair on the back of David's neck prickled.

"Viv says she worked with you at a church in South Carolina as associate minister."

"Viv?"

"Yes, Viv. Vivian Deborah Baker Monroe is her full name."

"Oh, Deborah." He laughed. How like her to change her name yet again. "I knew her as Deborah Baker. Just to make sure we're talking about the same person, tell me about her."

"Vivian has reddish blonde hair. She's, shall we say, comfortable with her sexuality. Very personable. Charming. She's shown innovative, yet effective, ways of dealing with patients. She's finished a month's practicum with us here and we're looking to hire a new therapist. Now that she's completed her degree as an MSW, we think we'd like to hire her."

David took in a deep breath. What chutzpah for her to list him as a reference. He would say what he could as honestly as possible without ruining her chances at a new life. After all, he'd needed a fresh start and thanks to Jonathan Savant's going to bat for him, David had received a call to become Executive Director of the new retreat center in his home state.

"Yes. The woman you describe whom I knew as Deborah did return to school for a masters in psychology or social work. She served as associate pastor at Harmony Presbyterian Church in Goodwin, South Carolina, for a little over a year. Her responsibilities included youth work, congregational care, local missions, occasional preaching, and assistance in worship." He hoped to leave it at that.

"How would you qualify her effectiveness, Dr. Archer?"

"I can say that many people responded positively to her personality and approach. She and I had diametrically opposed ways of looking at social issues, and soon it became apparent that we should each seek new avenues for our ministries. That's the time she entered your field of endeavor, I believe."

"You sound somewhat guarded in your response, sir. Is there any-thing else I should know? All the committee members are quite high on her. She's smart and personable and frankly has charmed us all."

"You've named her strong points exactly. The only thing I can add— First, remember that she and I ended up as adversaries, so you must take that into consideration should I cast aspersion on Deborah...uh, Vivian. Just a cautionary note—power and money are exceedingly important to her. And she may have lifelong scars from some childhood trauma that may have affected her capacity to feel emotions as other people do."

"Thank you, sir, for that. I guess we all are among the walking wounded."

"You're correct there, Dr. Elford. Let me add a word of warning. She seemed to lack any, well, scruples. Especially when money or power were involved. I wish you and your colleagues good luck in your dealings with Vivian Deborah Baker Monroe. Also, she had a cocaine habit that came to light toward the end of her time with us. So you do need to be aware." He wondered if Monroe was a newly acquired married name, but did not ask.

"I appreciate your words, sir. But she is one charming, personable young woman."

David got the feeling it didn't much matter what he'd said. The man had made up his mind.

In August, 1992, Ted Parks suffered another stroke. Soon thereafter he contracted pneumonia and died in September. Emily called and David flew to Goodwin. The current minister at Harmony church had not known Ted well and seemed to welcome David's help with his old friend's memorial service.

The next January, a rare snow on Petit Jean Mountain created sparkling winter days for the retreat center. Emily visited and they made plans. On a weekend in early June 1993, between conferences and church retreats, their best friends all came, even though it proved awkward and downright difficult for some. Natalie, who would serve as matron of honor, flew into Little Rock from L.A. where her one-woman show of door paintings had opened, appropriately called "Open and Shut." Preston drove his mother Charlotte's van from South Carolina. The new van was especially equipped to take her wheelchair. A recent hip replacement couldn't stop her. The two of them met Natalie's plane.

Madeleine Crispin closed her office for the week announcing she would be on vacation in Arkansas, much to her receptionist's amazement. "Arkansas? After Costa Rica, Paris, and Rome. Laos, Thailand, Bali, and Bhutan?" Dale flew with Madeleine from Goodwin and shared a rental car from Little Rock to Petit Jean. Meredith and Joel flew in from Boston.

Julian Denyar drove over in his new Cadillac. He parked it facing out, so he could leave as early as possible. He nodded curtly to the familiar faces and shook David's hand without speaking.

When David accepted the call for this new work, Nell announced immediately that she would never go again to the sticks of Arkansas with him. She would take the girls to a decent-sized city, namely, Charlotte, but she'd let them finish the year in Goodwin. She left him in charge of selling their house while she set up her business in North Carolina and "tested" her relationship with Stefan's uncle. After their divorce, Nell had nothing at all to do with David.

David stood at the podium in the open-air chapel beside Jonathan Savant who would officiate. Beside him stood Jody, Millie, and Lyn holding bouquets of daisies and fragrant lilies. They were all dressed in shiny deep green dresses and looked beautiful. Natalie in a full-length dress of forest green proceeded toward them with long strides matched by a wide smile. Julian's grandson played the piano in the corner with Rivers Carlton on guitar.

David looked at those gathered for the ceremony. *Dearly beloved*, indeed. His retreat center staff had decorated the open air chapel, and they all stood at the back smiling, then turned as Emily walked toward him, with Tim and Tom on either side of her. She carried a bouquet of daisies, yellow roses, and some kind of exotic orchid in the center. She wore a dress he'd never seen, mint green and flowing. A breeze lifted her dark hair but did not disturb the coronet of flowers and vines wound around the crown of her head. The long loose sleeves rippled and her long skirt swayed as she glided up the aisle.

He took in a deep breath of pure joy. *At last, at last.* He inhaled her beauty, exhaled the awe trembling inside him. The wind picked up. Pages of the pulpit Bible fluttered. David placed one hand on the Bible, without taking his eyes off Emily as she came near.

The End

# Acknowledgments

꜀꜀꜀

Because this novel has been in the works for so many years, there are far more people I'd like to name than I have room to mention. However, I'd be amiss if I didn't say that Natalie Goldberg's seminal book, *Writing Down the Bones: Freeing the Writer Within*, woke me up to a process that I've used in teaching and writing ever since, long before this novel began. Later, at her workshops and silent retreats, I learned and grew. Thank you, Natalie. Also, I'm grateful to Presbyterian ministers, who, from my childhood on, have helped to instill in me a love for and knowledge of the Bible and a lifelong devotion to serving the church of Jesus Christ.

To readers of manuscript drafts, I thank especially Brenda W. Bruce, who listened with her sensitive ear to the early chapters read aloud; Lydia Dishman, first and last reader and editor; Keller Cushing Freeman, editor, provider of space and advice; Virginia Postrel, who offered incisive critique and suggestions; Jo Ann Walker, who read and encouraged me at just the right moment; Lud Weaver, minister and adviser on matters of church polity. I appreciate their taking time from their busy lives to focus on this endeavor. All mistakes and lapses in judgment are mine, not theirs.

I wish to thank my various writing companions over the years: Linda Robertson, for Wednesdays spent with our computers and her dog and cat; Eli Connaughton, for our meetings on Tuesday mornings at Coffee Underground to sip lattes and write; and fellow writers in my Writing-On-The-Spot Workshops.

Thanks are due to those whom I interviewed: Pete Peery, Vonnie Vance, Fred Carpenter, Carl Muller, Archie Scott. I'm grateful to the staffs of Coffee Underground and Panera's on Augusta Street.

I'm grateful to Emrys Foundation for providing encouragement to writers at all stages of development; to Mindy Friddle, teacher of the Writing Room Novel Workshop; to the foundation for awarding me a residency; to Carol Young and Brooks Gallagher for the use of their mountain house. I'm grateful to Metropolitan Arts Council and SC Arts Commission for an Individual Artist Grant. Thanks are due Jill Hendrix and Vally Sharpe for embarking on this publishing venture.

The Wildacres Retreat Center has provided innumerable opportunities for writing, revising, and sharing my work. I am grateful to the Blumenthal Foundation for creating and maintaining Wildacres, to Amy and Philip Blumenthal; to Mike House and Kathryn House for their generous hearts. For the Writers Workshop each summer, I'm grateful to Judi Hill and my teachers—Gail Galloway Adams, Luke Whisnant, Ron Rash, Susan Woodring, and the other Achers who, like me, return to the magic mountain every year.

And to my family, I'm eternally grateful for their love and encouragement. Virginia and Steve, Sam and Jamie, John and Amy, Bill and Karen—all heard rumors for years that a novel was underway. Now—surprise. It's here. Most of all, my appreciation and thanks go to my husband Sam who showed infinite patience and wholehearted understanding as he supported writing retreats for me to work in solitude, and nudged me gently toward completion. Thanks for believing without having read it and loving me through the long trek.

# About the Author

A seasoned workshop leader and editor, Sue Lile Inman, a native of Little Rock, Arkansas, and alumna of Agnes Scott College, has taught English at Clemson and Furman universities, and has published prose and poetry in regional magazines and literary journals. She leads Writing-on-the-Spot Workshops two semesters a year and teaches other writing classes from time to time.

A founding member of Emrys Foundation, she served as the *Emrys Journal*'s first editor and is a past president of the board. Her published books include poetry—*Voice Lessons* (1998) and *Miriam in the Wilderness* (2005)—and nonfiction—*Growing in Faith: A History of Westminster Presbyterian Church, 1947-2007*. Since 1963, Sue and her husband Sam have made their home in Greenville, South Carolina. They have four adult children and four grandchildren. *Year of the Snake: 1989* is her first novel.

CPSIA information can be obtained at www.ICGtesting.com
Printed in the USA
LVOW12s0833080615

441558LV00004B/6/P